BLUE FIRE

The wind gusted, buffeting Leah, and Cal caught her arm when she teetered. His touch shocked her, a shock that redoubled when he suddenly took her other arm and jerked her a step closer to him. She looked up in surprise into the blazing blue fire of his eyes.

"Espy was right about something else, too," he said.

"What?"

"About me wanting to kiss you," he murmured fiercely in the second before his lips closed over hers. The kiss was hot and demanding. Surrender was impossible . . . and unnecessary. She had only to stand there and let him have his way while the glorious sensations washed over her and triumph swelled within her. *Cal Stevens did want her!*

Too soon he tore his mouth from hers and lifted his head to look down at her.

"I broke my word," he said in a voice that told her he seldom did. "What are you going to do?"

Tension fairly vibrated through him as he waited for her reply. The same tension hummed through her, too, making everything so clear, she wondered how she could not have seen the answer before.

"Let me go, and I'll show you."

BLAZING TEXAS NIGHTS

VICTORIA THOMPSON

ZEBRA BOOKS
KENSINGTON PUBLISHING CORP.

With thanks to Dot Brown
whose suggestion that this idea
could be an historical
resulted in this book.

ZEBRA BOOKS

are published by

Kensington Publishing Corp.
475 Park Avenue South
New York, NY 10016

First printing: March, 1992

Printed in the United States of America

Prologue

Leah played in the only scrap of shade the late afternoon sun had left at the end of the long front porch. Tenderly, she wrapped her grimy rag doll in the piece of fabric she used for a blanket and cradled it lovingly to her ten-year-old bosom, crooning softly.

Her baby was a boy because Leah knew how important it was to have boy babies. Only boy babies could grow up to be men and carry on the family name. When Leah grew up, she would have lots of boy babies. Then Papa would be happy, and he wouldn't yell at Mama or make her cry anymore.

Then they'd *all* be happy, and Leah could forget what she had heard Papa say that night so long ago when they'd thought she was asleep. She could forget he'd said Leah might as well be buried out in the graveyard with all the other babies who had died because she was nothing but a useless girl. When she had a boy baby, Papa would know he was wrong about her. He'd love her then, and he wouldn't ever say that about the graveyard again.

Leah would take good care of her babies, too, just like she took good care of her dolly. She bent down to give her doll a kiss, but the sound of an approaching wagon distracted her. Company in the middle of the week? How strange. She squinted into the setting sun and identified the vehicle as a buggy with the hood up, concealing whoever was inside. Leah didn't recognize the buggy as belonging to anyone she knew. Laying her doll down as gently as if it had been a real babe, she scrambled up and hurried to the edge of the porch where she would have a better view of the visitors.

The cowhands had just returned to the ranch for supper, and they stopped their unsaddling to watch the arrival. Leah was thinking Mama would be upset to have company when Papa was away, then she noticed the horse tied behind the wagon was Papa's horse. When the buggy came closer, she saw the man driving it was Papa, back from his trip a few days early.

He had a woman with him, a plump Mexican whom Leah had never seen before. The woman held a large basket in her lap and stared blankly before her, as if she didn't know where she was or else she didn't care. Papa pulled the buggy to a halt in front of the porch steps and jerked the brake. He was yelling for his wife before he had the reins tied off.

"Martha! *Martha!* Get out here!"

Martha Harding came hesitantly out onto the porch, and Leah instinctively took a step toward her, as if she could somehow intervene to stop the hurt she knew was coming. She knew because Papa had the mean smile on his face that meant he was going to make Mama cry. Leah shivered and took hold of a support post to steady herself.

"Bradley," Martha said, automatically hunching her shoulders as if she expected a blow. "I wasn't looking for you for a few more days." Her voice sounded tired, and she looked tired. Her skin and her once-luxuriant hair were as faded as her well-washed calico dress. Only her eyes still held any spark of life, and now they were wary, wary and frightened by the malice she saw glittering on her husband's face.

"I brought you a present, Martha," he was saying. Bradley Harding was a tall man who looked even taller next to his stoop-shouldered mate. "It's something you've been needing for a long time."

He turned back to the buggy, and for a moment Leah thought everything would be all right. The Mexican woman was the present, a maid to help with the housework because Mama wasn't well anymore.

But Papa was reaching into the basket the blank-faced woman held in her lap, and he pulled out a bundle of rags. At first Leah couldn't imagine what it could be, and then she heard a tiny mewling whimper. *A baby's cry.* Her apprehension evaporated, and she stared in wide-eyed fascination.

Papa thrust the bundle of rags into Mama's arms. "It's a son, Martha. This isn't the first time I've given you a son, but it'll by God be the last. *If* you can manage to keep this one alive."

Martha gazed down at the infant she held, her eyes glazed with shock and mortification. As if the baby sensed her less than favorable reaction, his whimper became a wail. Instinctively, she jiggled him, but the

7

motion alarmed him, and the wail swelled into a howl of terror.

"He cost me a hundred dollars," her husband was saying, shouting above the clamor. "I just wish to hell I'd known ten years ago I'd have to buy myself a son. I'd've done it then and saved myself from plowing a barren field."

Leah didn't understand what he meant, but she saw her mother flinch and heard the murmur of outrage from the men who had drawn nearer to hear what was being said. Martha looked up and saw them staring, witnesses to her humiliation. Her expression froze and she tried to square her shoulders in a semblance of dignity, but two tears slid down her cheeks, more terrible in their silence than a scream of agony would have been.

Leah ran to her, not really knowing what she would do, only certain her mother needed her. But when she reached Martha's side, she actually saw the baby for the first time, its tiny face red and squinched in distress, its small fists clenched as it cried out its fear.

It's a *baby,* she thought inanely. A real live *boy* baby, the kind Papa had been telling Mama she'd better give him or die trying. And he was so small. How could anything so small be alive? How could anything so small be so important? But she knew he was, knew he was the most important thing that had ever happened in her life. And he was beautiful, too, with his golden fuzz of hair and his fat, round cheeks.

"I'll hold him, Mama," she heard herself say, and her mother didn't even seem to notice when Leah took the child from her unresisting arms.

"Don't drop him," her father commanded, but

Leah wasn't going to drop him. The baby was heavier than her doll but lighter than she had expected, and he seemed perfectly made to fill her arms. She cradled him to her bosom, the way she'd practiced with her doll thousands of times, and crooned softly, rocking the baby as gently as she rocked her doll. The latest howl ceased abruptly, and the tiny eyes flew open in surprise. Those eyes were as blue as the Texas sky and, to Leah, they seemed even larger than the sky. Framed by tear-spiked lashes, they gazed at her intently, more intently than anyone had ever looked at her before, and Leah imagined this mere wisp of a human being knew more about her in that moment than anyone ever would again.

"Don't cry, baby," she murmured. "You're home now, and I'll take care of you." She could actually feel the tension draining out of the child, and the little fists relaxed as those enormous eyes continued to watch her.

Above them her parents were arguing. Papa shouted and Mama cried, but Leah barely heard. Lost in the baby's fascinated gaze, she wandered away, into the cool dimness of the ranch house. Sounds of the argument faded into insignificance, and they were alone, just the two of them. The baby grabbed the end of her flaxen pigtail in one determined fist and tried to stuff it in his mouth. The curling end slipped into his nose instead, and he sneezed in surprise, startling a laugh from a delighted Leah.

No wonder Papa wanted a baby so badly, she thought. Babies are wonderful creatures, so much better than dolls. She smiled down into the baby's cherubic face, and miracle of miracles, he smiled back, the sweetest smile she had ever seen in her short life.

Outside she could still hear her father's angry shouts and her mother's plaintive sobbing, but she knew they didn't matter anymore. Nothing mattered except the small, soft bundle in her arms. Mama might not be happy to have him, but Leah was. Leah knew how to take care of him, too, and when Papa saw what a good job she did, he'd know she wasn't worthless at all.

"You're mine now, baby. Nothing they say or do can hurt us, and whatever happens, we'll always have each other, won't we?"

As if he understood, the baby smiled again and made a noise that sounded to Leah like, "Yes."

Chapter One

"Miss Leah! Where are you?"

Leah looked up from the column of figures she had been adding and shook her head in dismay. How many times had she asked her foreman not to yell like that in the house? On the other hand, old habits die hard, and Pete Quincy had been yelling in this house since Leah was a youngster. She couldn't really expect him to change now.

"Coming, Pete," she called back, carefully inserting her pen in its holder before wiping her hand on a rag she kept nearby for just such purposes. Then she removed her reading spectacles and put them back in their case. Rubbing the telltale red marks she knew the glasses made on the bridge of her nose, she rose from her chair, straightened her sensible black bombazine gown, and moved at a ladylike pace toward the front room in the massive ranch house.

In the seven years since her father's death, Leah had made many changes to the house, softening the harsh masculine furnishings he had preferred with crocheted doilies and needlepoint pillows, but the place still retained the practical simplicity necessary for a working ranch. In the cavernous front room which had defied all her attempts to achieve coziness, Leah found Pete Quincy and a strange man.

The stranger had removed his Stetson, a courtesy she did not often receive on a ranch populated mainly by men who had known her all her life. He was a large man, several inches over six feet, she guessed, broad of shoulder and narrow of hip. He wore faded Levis and a dark blue work shirt with a blue silk bandana at his throat. He'd made some effort at brushing away the trail dust, but she could see he'd ridden quite a ways to get here.

Perhaps he'd ridden out of necessity, too, she conjectured, studying the rugged face. It was a face unused to smiling, and it wasn't smiling now. Eyes the color of a stormy sky stared at her above his hawklike nose, and his thin lips were pressed into an implacable line. His lean cheeks were shadowed with a hint of a beard that would be as relentlessly black as the hair he had finger-combed into some semblance of order after removing his hat. He looked like a man who'd spent at least a little time on the wrong side of the law.

Beside him, and nearly a head shorter than he and almost a hundred pounds lighter, stood her foreman. Pete frowned sourly through his grizzled beard, and his faded brown eyes squinched in disapproval. He cocked a thumb at the stranger. "I told him we wasn't hiring, but he said he wanted to see you anyways. Said it was personal."

Many riders imagined they could overrule the foreman and finagle a job by charming the plain spinster who ran the Rocking Horse Ranch. They quickly learned otherwise. Leah smiled primly and folded her hands at her waist. "Mr. Quincy is correct. We aren't hiring."

The stranger glanced at Pete, a little impatiently, she thought. "And I told him, I'm not looking for a job. I've got some business with you, Miss Harding. Personal business."

Leah let her smile fade. "I can't imagine what business we could have, Mr. . . . ?"

"Stevens. Calhoun Stevens." He said the name as if he expected her to recognize it. She did, and she stiffened instinctively. Had she been involved in a range war, Cal Stevens would have been among the first men she would have tried to hire. But she wasn't involved in a range war.

"It's about your brother," he added.

Her brother? He could not have said anything more likely to capture her undivided attention. How would a man like Cal Stevens know innocent, seventeen-year-old Brad? She could think of no legitimate reason.

"Miss Leah?" Pete asked solicitously. Her shock must have shown on her face. Indeed, if as much blood had rushed from her head as she suspected, she must have paled noticeably.

"It's all right," she said tightly. "Will you leave us alone, please, Pete?"

"I don't know, Miss—"

"Please," Leah insisted. Whatever Mr. Stevens had to tell her about Brad, she didn't think she wanted Pete or anyone else to hear it.

Pete scowled at Stevens, then at Leah, then back at Stevens again, as if debating whether he should obey

13

her wishes or follow his own instincts. After a long moment he shook his head in disgust. "I'll be right out front if you need anything," he growled, as if he were warning Stevens.

The tall stranger didn't smile, but he must have found the very idea of *Pete* warning *him* singularly amusing. She waited until her foreman's footsteps had receded down the porch steps outside.

Leah pressed her folded hands against the churning in her stomach. "What has my brother done, Mr. Stevens?"

He seemed genuinely surprised. "Nothing that I know of, Miss Harding."

Her relief was fleeting. "Then why have you come here?" she demanded, wondering if the mention of Bradley had been just a ploy to get her alone so he could change her mind about the job.

"I . . ." Strangely, he seemed at a loss for words, and for a second the toughness that appeared to be such a natural part of him faltered just slightly. But he quickly regained his composure. "I've been trying to think of an easy way to say this, but there just ain't one."

Increasingly apprehensive, Leah managed a disgruntled glare. "Perhaps if you just say it out and get it over with, Mr. Stevens. I have work to do."

"All right, here it is, straight out. I'm your brother's father."

The words made no sense to her. How could he be Bradley's father? Bradley's father—and her father—was Bradley Harding, Sr., the man who'd raised them both, who'd given Brad his own name, who'd . . .

Except that Bradley Harding *wasn't* Brad's father at

14

all, not his real one at least. As if it had happened yesterday, Leah remembered the day he'd brought the baby home, the son he'd always wanted, the son his wife's ailing body could not produce.

Leah had fallen in love that day, and her love had bound Brad to her more closely than blood ties ever could. Because he cried whenever her mother held him, Leah had become his mother. The simpleminded Mexican wet nurse her father had brought home fed him, but Leah cared for him in every other way. After her mother's death before Brad was two, Leah had dedicated her life to him, and now, seventeen years later, he seemed more like her son than her brother.

And she had no intention of letting some no-account stranger come along to claim him at this late date.

Because her knees felt alarmingly weak, she said, "Perhaps we'd better sit down, Mr. Stevens."

Cal Stevens waited until the woman had sat down in one of the wingbacked chairs beside the fireplace. He'd seldom been in a lady's parlor, and he'd never been invited to sit in one. Still holding his hat, he took the matching chair, seating himself cautiously as if half-afraid the chair might collapse under his weight. It didn't. Feeling awkward, he hung the hat over the arm of the chair and clasped his hands together, acutely aware that they were trembling slightly.

Cal had been in many dangerous situations in his eventful life, but he'd never faced an adversary he feared more than he feared Miss Leah Harding. She sat rigidly straight, the way he'd seen proper ladies sit, her back not touching the chair. Her hands lay in her lap, but he noticed they were clenched just as tightly as his. Not a good sign. It was all right for him to respect her as a worthy adversary, but if *she* feared *him,* he would never get what he wanted from her.

"I assume you have a story to tell me, Mr. Stevens," she said. Her voice had lost some of that arrogance she'd had when she thought him a man looking for work, but she was still a long way from friendly.

"I do," he said, "and I'm not much of a storyteller, so I hope you'll be patient."

She smiled a little at that, although the smile held no mirth. "You needn't worry about your abilities. You have selected a topic guaranteed to hold my interest."

She was prettier than he'd expected, he noticed irrelevantly, especially when she smiled. She didn't look twenty-seven, either, the age he knew her to be. He'd made it his business to learn everything he could about the Harding family in the past month, especially about the woman who, since the death of her parents, served as his son's guardian.

She didn't seem to know she was pretty, though, or at least she didn't care. Her light brown hair was scraped back into an uncompromising spinsterish bun, and the dress she had on would have looked just right on his grandmother. His grandmother had been dead for twenty years.

"Well," he began, wishing he had more experience putting his thoughts into words, "I reckon it's best to start in the beginning. I grew up down near San Antone. We had a dirt farm there and raised a few head of cattle before the war, but I was kind of a wild kid, and I didn't want to push a plow for the rest of my life."

She nodded as if she could readily believe this. Encouraged, he went on.

"When I turned seventeen, the war was going on, and I decided I wanted to be a soldier. I signed up for Hood's Texas Brigade."

He hesitated, uncertain how to phrase what came next. If he had never sat in a room like this, he'd most certainly never spoken of begetting a bastard child to a woman like Leah Harding.

"Forgive me if I urge you to skip over your battle-field experiences, Mr. Stevens," she said sharply.

"There's no need. It happened before I left home. There was this girl, Amy Weeks. We'd been keeping company and . . ." Oh, hell, he thought and just said it. "I sowed my wild oats with her before I left. She was your brother's mother."

Miss Harding stiffened even more, and Cal cursed himself for being so crude, although he couldn't imagine what other words he might have used.

"And so," Miss Harding said, her voice as stiff as her spine, "may I know what has inspired you after nearly eighteen years to finally lay claim to him?"

"I didn't know about him 'til now." Cal felt the familiar anger boiling up and checked it, knowing he would gain no ground with Miss Harding if he took his frustration out on her. "I never went home again after the war except to visit now and then. By the time I got back the first time, Amy was long gone. Your pa gave her some money for the boy, I guess, and she took off someplace. Nobody ever saw her again."

"How convenient," she murmured, but Cal ignored the provocation.

17

"My folks knew the boy was mine, but they decided not to tell me. They figured he was better off with a family someplace, and I sure as he . . . I mean, I didn't have any way of taking care of a baby even if I'd wanted to, which I probably wouldn't have, not then anyways.

"But a couple months ago, I got word my ma was dying. She wanted to see me, and I figured I'd disappointed her too many times already, so I went. She told me then. She said she couldn't face her Maker with that lie on her conscience. She even remembered the name of the man who'd taken the boy, Bradley Harding."

"And now you've decided you *do* want a child, and you've come to take him off my hands, is that it, Mr. Stevens?"

She was every bit as angry as he had been when he'd discovered someone had stolen his son, and he supposed she had a lot more right to be. "No, Miss Harding, I know it's too late for that. I just want to meet him. I want to see what kind of man he's become, to see if he needs anything—"

"He most certainly does not need anything, as I'm sure you know perfectly well." Leah couldn't remember ever being so furious, not when Mama had made Brad cry, not when Papa had cursed him for being clumsy or failing to do some task to his satisfaction. But then, neither one of *them* had ever threatened to take Brad away from her, either.

With difficulty, Leah controlled her temper, knowing instinctively she'd need all her wits about her in dealing with Calhoun Stevens. "Mr. Stevens, you will forgive my skepticism, but it does seem odd to have you suddenly appear on my doorstep to claim a child who just happens to be quite wealthy — "

"I told you, I just found out about him," Stevens insisted. His sun-darkened face had turned a dull red beneath his tan.

"Who happens to be quite wealthy," she repeated, thinking bitterly that the wealth was a direct result of her hard work in the seven years since her father's death had left her in control of the ranch and Brad's destiny. "And I suppose the fact that he happens to be the sole owner of the Rocking Horse Ranch didn't influence your need to see him in the slightest."

Once again he seemed surprised. *"Sole* owner? What do you mean?"

Leah could have bitten off her tongue. What had possessed her to reveal this piece of information? But of course she'd assumed he knew, assumed the knowledge had motivated him to come here in the first place, perhaps even motivated the concoction of this whole fairy tale. "I think you know perfectly well what I mean," she bluffed.

His dark brows lowered in contemplation. "Are you saying your father left this place to the boy alone? To a bastard kid he *bought,* for God's sake, instead of to you, his own flesh and blood?"

The humiliation of it still burned, and Leah felt her cheeks growing hot under Stevens's amazed scrutiny. "It's common knowledge. I assumed you knew." And now she was certain he had known. What else could have inspired a man like Cal Stevens to take a fatherly interest in a child he hadn't known existed?

If he was even Brad's father at all. Perhaps he'd simply heard the story of Bradley Harding's obsession

19

with having a son and his final act of revenge against his only living offspring for having been born female. Perhaps Stevens had seen a way of claiming a portion of the boy's wealth and a life of ease for himself.

And now that she noticed, dark, brooding Stevens bore absolutely no resemblance to Brad with his golden blond hair and his almost feminine beauty. How could Stevens possibly expect her to believe his wild tale? "Mr. Stevens, I'm sorry, but . . ."

Her voice trailed off when she heard the sound of a running horse out in the ranch yard followed by Brad's shout of greeting to Pete who must still be standing guard outside.

No! she thought and was on her feet in an instant, as if she could somehow stop Brad from being there before she could get rid of Stevens.

She glanced over and saw Stevens had risen, too. His height and obvious strength seemed ominous. "Is that him?" he asked, and she thought he actually looked apprehensive.

She wanted to lie but knew it would be futile. "Yes," she said, more than apprehensive herself. She couldn't let them meet, couldn't let Stevens tell Brad his wild story. A man like this would seem romantic to a seventeen-year-old boy who had never really gotten along with his own father, and the thought of being sought out and claimed after all these years . . .

"I don't want him to know who I am," Stevens said, surprising her.

"No, of course not," she quickly agreed. She would have to think up a plausible explanation for his presence here, but before she could, she heard Brad's footsteps on the porch. He hadn't even taken the time to put his horse away. She'd told him a hundred times he shouldn't take advantage of his position here to shirk such minor responsibilities. . . .

He burst in the door like a blond tornado. *"Leah!"* he shouted before he saw her standing there. "Oh, sorry. I've gotta talk to you right away. I—" He saw Stevens and stopped in midsentence, his cheeks flushing with embarrassment. "Didn't know you had company." The statement held a silent question.

"Brad, this is . . . ah . . . a friend of mine, Calhoun Stevens," she managed, feeling suddenly breathless.

Brad instantly forgot whatever crisis had brought him tearing back to the ranch, and she saw his young face lighten with recognition. Just as she had feared, he was inordinately glad to meet a "known man."

"Mr. Stevens, it's a pleasure," Brad exclaimed, hurrying across the large room to offer his hand.

Stevens hesitated an instant before taking it, and Leah watched him as if he were a rattlesnake her brother was picking up by the tail. His chiseled features remained rigid, as if he were holding his emotions very tightly in check, and he didn't speak. Leah wondered if he did not know what to say or if he didn't trust his voice. Or perhaps he simply wanted her to *think* he didn't trust his voice.

To her surprise Leah noticed Brad was almost as tall as Stevens—he'd grown so much this last year—and they were similar in build, too, or would be when maturity filled out Brad's lanky form.

Shaking off that traitorous thought, she heard Brad saying, "I heard how you followed them greaser rustlers right across the border even when the army turned back. That took guts." The boy was smiling

21

broadly, his cornflower blue eyes literally shining.

Stevens dropped Brad's hand with apparent reluctance, and his lips curled slightly. "Some folks thought it took stupidity."

"They weren't cattlemen, then," Brad asserted, smiling broadly. "If there was more men like you who're willing to chase them damn greasers back to their hidey-holes, they wouldn't dare show their faces up here, and we'd lose a sight less cattle."

Stevens's lean cheeks quivered for a moment, and before Leah could imagine what was coming, the face she'd decided rarely smiled did so with alarming brilliance. For a long moment during which Leah neither breathed nor blinked, Brad and the stranger smiled at each other with identical smiles. In that moment, the differences between them—blond hair and black, youth and experience—vanished, and the striking resemblance stunned her.

She was still in shock when Brad said, "Well, then, what brings you here to . . . ?" He glanced at Leah as if just recalling what she had said when she'd introduced them. "You're a friend of Leah's?"

Plainly, he could hardly credit such a notion, and he turned back to Stevens for verification. Now was the moment she had been dreading, the opportunity for Stevens to refute her claim and stake his own, but he merely looked to her and waited, content to follow her lead.

"Yes," she heard herself saying, praying her voice didn't sound as artificially cheerful as she thought it did. "Mr. Stevens and I met . . . uh . . ." Her mind was racing. "Last winter," she decided, "when I was in Dallas."

Stevens nodded once, silently approving her lie, but Brad took it to mean agreement. "And now you've come here to . . . ?" His gaze darted between them speculatively. Obviously, he sensed the tension between them and completely misinterpreted it. His dazzling smile blazed again, this time in triumph. "By God, Mr. Stevens, I'd about given up hope Leah'd *ever* find a man to suit her. And she never said a word about you, either! That's a woman for you, I guess."

He was shaking Stevens's hand again while Leah gaped at them in horror. Good heavens, what was she going to do? She couldn't tell Brad the truth, but how could she allow him to think Stevens had followed her home to *court* her?

"Where are you staying?" Brad asked him when he'd finished pumping his hand.

Once again Stevens glanced at Leah for a cue, and she saw he was as nonplused as she by this turn of events. Her opinion of him rose slightly, and it rose even more when he said, "I don't know that I *am* staying. I just got here, and your sister and I haven't really had a chance to talk yet."

Brad's grin had turned mischievous, and Leah felt dread, knowing that grin always meant trouble. "There's no sense in you going to town or anything. We've got plenty of room in the bunkhouse since we let the extra hands go for the winter. You can stay right here . . . where you'll be close to Leah," he added provocatively. "I'll go tell Pete."

He was out the door before Leah could stop him. She turned helplessly to Stevens who was staring after the boy intently. He kept staring even when Brad had disappeared from sight. They could hear him talking excitedly to Pete, and Stevens held himself perfectly still, not even breathing, as if compelled to hear Brad's voice for as long as he could. The voices faded when Brad and Pete began to walk away.

Only when they could no longer hear them did Stevens turn back to her. The expression of wonderment on his face took her breath. "He looks just like Amy."

Leah didn't dare tell him Brad resembled him, too.

"He's a fine boy, Miss Harding," he continued solemnly. "You've done a good job."

The compliment was as welcome as it was unexpected. Who had ever acknowledged her role in raising Brad? And how could he have known about it? But his sensitivity only frightened her more, proving as it did that he was more than he seemed, and consequently more dangerous even than she had feared.

"I don't suppose you'll be going on your way now that you've seen him," she said.

Instantly, the wonderment faded, and he was once again the cold-eyed gunslinger. His hands closed into fists and for a second she knew real fear, but he was only trying to control his own emotions. "Look, Miss Harding, I can understand why you don't want me near your brother."

"Your fatherly instincts at work, no doubt," she snapped.

He flinched slightly, but he refused to back down. "You could call it that, I guess, and that's the reason I don't want him hurt any more than you do. You've got to believe me, Miss Harding. I don't want to take him away from you."

"What *do* you want then?"

He closed his eyes and drew a breath, as if he were seeking the answer from someplace deep within himself. When he opened his eyes again, they looked so much like Brad's, she could hardly bear it. "You know who I am, Miss Harding. You know the kind of life I've led, and it doesn't look to change any from here on out. I'm already thirty-five years old, and there's not much chance that I'll ever meet some nice woman, settle down, and raise a family." He gestured toward the door through which Brad had gone. "That boy is the only family I'll ever have. I just want to know him."

She hated him then, because she could feel his pain too clearly. She had also forfeited the opportunity for a home and a family of her own, but she had done so because she *had* Brad. He was *her* child, too, the only one *she* would ever have, the only one she had ever wanted.

Vaguely, she realized she was beginning to accept his story about being Brad's father, and she called herself a fool. He was waiting for her to say something, perhaps for her to give her permission for him to steal her brother from her.

"You'll understand that I'm still skeptical of your story," she said. "Would you mind if I checked it out?"

He shrugged. "I figured you'd want to. You've got every right, and you don't have to put me up in the meantime. I can find a place in town."

Instinct told her to send him away, but even if she refused to allow him to stay at the ranch, she knew Brad would relish nothing more than sneaking off to see a notorious gunslinger. Better to keep him here where she could watch them both.

"You're welcome here, Mr. Stevens, at least for the time being."

Her invitation, ungracious as it was, surprised him. "I can work for my keep."

"We'll worry about that later. For now I'll settle for your promise not to tell Brad exactly why you're here."

This amused him. "You'd rather he think I'm courting you?"

Leah didn't know which was worse, the sheer embarrassment of it or knowing that a man like Cal Stevens would never ordinarily look twice at a woman as plain as she, much less court her. "If necessary," she said, hating the heat she felt in her cheeks.

"Well, then, I reckon I'll go get settled in." He picked up his hat from where it still hung on the arm of the chair and settled it on his head. When he turned back to her, all trace of amusement was gone from his face. "I'm much obliged to you, Miss Harding. I won't forget what you've done."

Leah didn't think she'd ever forget it either. She only hoped she wouldn't regret it.

Cal was still marveling at his luck when he stepped out onto the porch. He hadn't even expected Leah Harding to believe his crazy story, much less put him up on her own ranch. Or rather, the boy's ranch. Now that was a curious thing he'd have to look into.

The boy was loping back across the yard to the house, and Cal stopped in his tracks to admire him. Who would have ever thought Cal Stevens could make something so wonderful? The boy was grinning from ear to ear. Plainly, the idea of a notorious gunfighter courting his sister delighted him. Cal only wished Miss Harding found the idea equally amusing. Dealing with her would be like picking cactus barehanded: he'd have to be almighty careful. He only wished he had the slightest idea of how to begin.

"Pete'll get you all set up in the bunkhouse," the boy reported, grinning his heart-stopping grin. "You'll come up to the house for supper, won't you?"

Cal wondered what Miss Harding would think of this invitation, but he decided she'd asked for it by not correcting the boy's mistake about their relationship when she had the chance. "Sure, I'd be proud to."

The boy shook his head in amazement. "My sister and Cal Stevens. I reckon I know now why she waited so long. Couldn't no man around here hold a candle."

Ordinarily, praise like this made Cal uncomfortable—probably because it was usually insincere—but he found himself reveling in the admiration of his own son. This wasn't exactly why he'd sought the boy out, but it would do for starters, and he could certainly use it to his advantage. "Things are a little touchy between me and your sister just now. I'd appreciate any help you can give me with her."

"Sure," he said eagerly. "I'd be glad to put in a good word for you—"

"No," Cal inserted quickly. "I mean, if you'd try to make things easier between us, less awkward." There was no sense in having the boy think the two of them wanted to be alone, especially when Cal's main purpose in being here was to get to know his son.

"Oh, yeah." The boy nodded vigorously. God, he

looked exactly like Amy except he was even better-looking than she had been. The girls wouldn't stand a chance. Cal resisted an urge to reach out and touch him.

"And don't worry, I know just how to get on Leah's good side," the boy assured him. "We'll have you two hitched in no time."

He punched Cal playfully in the arm as he moved past him on his way back into the house. Once again, Cal watched him go, waiting until Brad had closed the door behind him before moving on toward the bunkhouse with a resigned sigh. The Harding's foreman waited there for him, and the old man looked none-too-pleased about his new guest. Cal supposed he had more than one person to win over if he wanted to remain with his son.

Leah had been shamelessly eavesdropping on the conversation between Brad and Stevens, but they'd been speaking too softly for her to make out what was said. From the way Brad was smiling when he came in, however, Leah was certain Stevens hadn't yet revealed his secret.

Brad removed his hat and tossed it carelessly onto one of the empty pegs beside the door. His blue eyes shone with suppressed excitement, and Leah's heart dropped. She would have her work cut out for her in keeping him from idolizing the infamous Mr. Stevens even if he never found out the man claimed to have sired him.

Leah tried to match his cheerful smile and, determined to divert any discussion of their mysterious visitor, said, "And what brought you racing home in the middle of the afternoon, sweetheart?"

Brad's smile vanished, and his eyes widened. "Oh, jeez, how could I have forgotten?" he muttered. "Oh, jeez."

He had actually paled. "Brad, what is it?" She hurried to his side and took his arm. "Is something wrong with the cattle? One of the men? What is it?"

Brad was shaking his head as he allowed Leah to lead him to the sofa. When they were both seated, he hazarded a glance at her and again murmured, "Oh, jeez."

He looked so distressed, she wanted to hug him to her and smooth the golden hair back from his troubled brow as she'd done when he was a child. But Brad had put her on notice several years ago that he would no longer tolerate such feminine ministrations. Instead, she lay a comforting hand on his arm. "Brad, what is it? Don't worry about upsetting me. You know —"

"I ain't worried about that," he assured her, running his own fingers through the gold of his hair. "It's just . . . I know you'll be mad and hurt and . . . but shoot, Leah, I'm a grown man now."

Of course she knew better, and what that had to do with anything, she had no idea, but she said, "Of course you are, dear, so you shouldn't be afraid to tell me whatever it is you have to tell me."

He drew a deep breath and let it out in a long sigh, still refusing to meet her eye. Then he said, "I'm getting married."

Since this was so far from what she had expected to hear, Leah needed a few seconds to comprehend it. "Married?" she echoed stupidly.

"Yeah, married," Brad confirmed, his confidence growing now that he had broached the subject and encountered no hysterical outcries. He looked Leah straight in the eye. "Me and Espy. We want to get married."

"Espy Wilkes?" Leah asked incredulously. She'd known Brad had been over to see the girl a few times, but she'd had no idea things between them were serious. Nor did she understand what might have inspired a seventeen-year-old boy to contemplate marriage, particularly to Espy Wilkes. The girl couldn't be more than fifteen, and although her red hair made her rather striking in appearance, she was still nothing more than poor white trash. Her father had squatted on land nobody wanted, and everybody knew he and his brood of motherless children lived off the cows he stole one and two at a time from his more prosperous neighbors. Still, she would have to go carefully with Brad if she was to make him see what a foolish idea this was. "This is . . . sudden, isn't it?"

"Not so sudden," he insisted stubbornly. "We been seeing each other pretty regular all summer."

"You have?" she asked in surprise.

He looked guiltily away. "I knew you wouldn't like it, so I didn't tell you." Then he lifted his chin in the defiant gesture she knew so well. "But I'm a grown man. I don't need your permission to call on a girl."

"Of course you don't," she agreed reasonably, holding her anger at bay. Later there would be plenty of time to rant at him for playing right into Espy Wilkes's hands, and Leah had no doubt this marriage business was all the girl's idea. Nobody could blame

30

her for wanting to get away from the squalid life she must lead in that one-room shack with her drunken father and four younger siblings, but Leah had no intention of seeing Brad taken in by her. "It's just that you're such a *young* grown man. I'm surprised you're so anxious to take on the responsibilities of marriage. You're awfully good-looking, Brad. You'll have your pick of girls, girls even prettier than Espy, and . . ."

Brad had stiffened beside her, and his profile set stubbornly. "I don't want any other girls. She's all I want."

"But Brad, she's young, too, even younger than you, and certainly too young to consider marriage. I'm sure I'd have no objection to your becoming engaged if this is so important to you, and after a year or so, if you both still feel the same, *then* we can discuss marriage."

"We can't wait a year!" Brad insisted. His cheeks had reddened, and he still refused to meet her eye.

"I know it seems like a long time," she explained, still forcing herself to be patient, "but if it's true love, it will only grow stronger, and — "

"We can't wait, I tell you!" he exclaimed, jumping up from the sofa to tower over her. "We can't wait at all! Don't you understand? Espy's gonna have a baby!"

Leah covered her mouth to hold back the cry of protest. *No!* this couldn't be happening, couldn't be *true!* Brad wouldn't . . . He *couldn't* . . . Not with Espy Wilkes, of all people!

But of course he could. He was, after all, a man, for all she'd tried to deny it. And he would if a girl let him, and Leah had no doubt Espy Wilkes would let

31

him if she thought it would get her a wedding ring. But Leah couldn't allow Brad to throw his life away on a girl like that. What in heaven's name was she going to do?

For the first time in seven years, Leah wished her father were alive. Bradley Harding wouldn't let some conniving little chippy ruin his son. He'd restrain Brad by force, if necessary, something Leah could never do alone. She would have to rely on her wits.

She lowered her hand from where it still covered her mouth and tried to steady her voice. "Brad, I'm terribly disappointed in you."

He was blushing furiously now, obviously ashamed but defiant, too. "I couldn't help it, Leah. It . . . it just happened, and Espy, she cried something awful after the first time, but — "

"The *first* time! You mean this happened more than once?" Leah couldn't believe Brad would let himself be duped like this.

"We're in love, Leah. I didn't think you could understand about how a man and woman feel, but now . . ." He gestured toward the bunkhouse where Cal Stevens was, and Leah felt the color coming to her own cheeks. "You know how it is when two people just have to be together. We'd've gotten married someday anyhow, sooner or later. Now it'll just be sooner, is all, and I'm glad," he added defiantly. "I don't like the idea of her living in that shack, waiting on the old man and those kids like she was some kind of slave. I want her here, where I can take care of her."

Leah stared at him in open-mouthed horror. What in heaven's name could she say to him? And should she say anything at all? If the girl really was with child and Brad really was the father, she didn't know what she could do besides allow them to marry. She knew it was her soft, woman's heart clouding her judgment. If only she were a man . . .

The frustrated lament of twenty-seven years echoed in her head, and before she could stop herself, she thought of Cal Stevens. *Cal Stevens* would never let some conniving little chippy ruin his son, either. *If* he was really Brad's father, of course, and *if* he really cared about the boy.

But even if he didn't, even if he was only interested in benefiting from Brad's inheritance, he wouldn't want to share Brad with a wife. Like her father, he'd never let sentiment influence him, and consulting him would at least be a good test of his true feelings for Brad.

When Leah didn't reply, Brad started pacing restlessly. "We've got to get married soon, before folks can tell," he was saying.

"Everyone will know when the baby is born anyway," she pointed out reasonably.

"But we don't want to wait. I thought we could get the preacher here tomorrow and—"

"Tomorrow! Brad, we can't possibly do anything so quickly. I must meet with Mr. Wilkes and . . . Don't you at least want Espy to have a nice dress?" she added in desperation.

This swayed him, but only for a moment. "Don't think you can talk me out of this, Leah. You don't have to give your blessing, you know. We can run away."

They most certainly could, and Leah didn't relish the thought of going after the fleeing couple. "A few days won't make any difference," she argued, "and you don't want to give people any more to gossip about than they'll already have. Surely, Espy won't object to having a decent wedding to remember."

"Well, maybe you're right," he allowed grudgingly, "but don't think I'm going to change my mind, Leah. We're getting married whether you like it or not."

"Where are you going?" she demanded when he headed for the front door.

"To see Espy. She's pretty upset 'cause she figured you wouldn't like us getting married. I want to tell her everything's gonna be all right."

He slammed out, and Leah made no move to stop him. Dear Lord, what was she going to do? He was only seventeen, just a baby himself, and to take on the responsibility of a family, too.

Seventeen, the same age Cal Stevens claimed he'd been when he sired Brad. Blood will certainly tell, she thought without amusement.

Cal had taken great pains with his appearance as he prepared for supper. He wore a new shirt and his least-worn pair of Levis, and he'd carefully oiled and combed his hair. He'd leave his hat behind tonight so as not to mess it up. Anybody would've thought he was going to meet a lover instead of a seventeen-year-old boy, but Cal was as nervous as he'd ever been in his life.

For the first time in that life, he really cared what someone thought of him, and not just the boy, either. Winning the boy would be easy—it was a battle half-won already, although Cal would have preferred the boy liked him for himself and not because of his overblown reputation. Winning the sister would be the trick because without her approval, he'd be out on his ear. The least he could do was look respectable, he told himself, tucking his shirttail in a little tighter as he made his way across the ranch yard to the house.

The front door stood open to the evening breeze, and Cal knocked on the frame. "Hello, the house," he called, giving the traditional greeting.

Twilight had dimmed the room, and he didn't see Miss Harding until she stood up. Her black dress blended into the shadows, but her pale face stood out in stark contrast.

"What's wrong?" he asked, instantly alarmed by her expression.

She scowled at him. "What are you doing here?"

The question took him aback, but he said, "I came for supper. The boy invited me. If you don't want me—"

She waved away the protest. "I didn't mean to be rude. I just didn't realize it was so late." She looked around as if just noticing the room had grown dark, and she moved to the table where a lamp stood. Efficiently, she struck a match and lighted the wick. Cal noticed how the light painted streaks of gold in her light brown hair. She made a pretty picture if you overlooked the drab dress. Cal found himself wondering what might be concealed beneath its ill-fitting folds and hastily chased the thought away.

"Where's the boy?" he asked to fill the silence.

She whirled around on him in sudden fury. "His name is Brad," she snapped. "Can't you remember it?"

He remembered it only too well. How could he explain that he hated the thought of calling his son by another man's name? "That's not what I would have called him," he said.

Comprehension lightened her face, and he noticed her eyes seemed to have changed. In the daylight, they had been the color of fine-grained oak, but now they looked as dark as coffee. "I wonder if I'll ever cease to be amazed at your fatherly sensibilities, Mr. Stevens."

Her sarcasm irked him, but he didn't let it show. "Where is . . . Brad?" he forced himself to say.

"He's out . . . visiting. I don't suppose we can expect him for supper, which is just as well since you and I have some important matters to discuss."

Cal had been expecting this, only not quite so soon. "I told you to check my story if you want—"

"And I will, have no fear." She was moving back to the chair she'd occupied this afternoon, and she motioned him to the other one. When they were seated, she folded her hands and smiled strangely. "I think congratulations are in order, Mr. Stevens. It seems you are going to become a grandfather."

The words made no sense to him, and his confusion must have shown because she said, "If you remember, Brad had something to tell me when he came bursting in here this afternoon. After you left, he finally got around to mentioning his urgent need to marry a certain young lady who is a neighbor of ours."

"Good God," Cal murmured when the truth had dawned.

"Precisely," she agreed. "If he really is your son, it seems he has inherited at least one of your less desirable characteristics. Isn't there a saying about

36

the apple not falling far from the tree?"

Cal might have been angry at her if he wasn't already furious at the boy. He jumped up and began to pace, unable to sit still another moment. "Who's the girl? What's she like?"

"Not exactly the girl I'd choose to be Brad's wife. Her mother is dead. Her father runs a three-cow outfit and calls himself a rancher, although others call him a rustler, among other things. The girl, Espy is her name, takes care of the house, such as it is, and her four brothers and sisters. I don't imagine she's turned sixteen yet."

"So naturally she sees this place and pictures herself in it as Brad's wife," Cal said, furious in a way he'd never been before. "There might not even be a baby at all. Have you thought of that?"

"It's probably too much to hope for."

"Maybe not. He's just a kid. He might not even know how to . . ." Cal caught himself, suddenly remembering to whom he was speaking.

She was staring intently at her folded hands, but she said, "I believe that may also be wishful thinking."

"I don't reckon you asked him about it."

"Not . . . precisely, no."

Of course she hadn't. Instinct demanded that Cal take a hand here, but he was painfully aware he had no rights at all, and he certainly shouldn't risk offending Miss Harding by meddling in her affairs. Still . . . "I can talk to him, if you like. I mean, I can ask him things you can't, and there's no sense in getting in a lather about this if she thinks she's in trouble just because he kissed her or something."

He practically held his breath, waiting for her answer. It was a long time in coming, which told him how difficult it was for her to give. "I would appreciate that, Mr. Stevens." Then she looked up, and in spite of her obvious embarrassment, he could see she was still determined. "And if you find it's possible, then what?"

"Then we find out about the girl," he said, continuing to pace. "First of all, is there a baby at all, and if there is, if she's been involved with any other men."

"She's only fifteen!" Leah protested.

Cal couldn't believe she was so naive, but he didn't press the issue. "Then we find out if she can be bought off. Maybe the old man put her up to it just to get some money out of you."

When he glanced at her again, her shocked expression stopped him in his tracks. "Is that what you would have done if Brad's mother had come to you eighteen years ago?" she asked coldly.

Cal felt the weight of her contempt and knew he probably deserved it. "I don't know what I would've done, Miss Harding. I'd like to think I would've done the right thing, whatever that is, but I also hope my folks would've at least tried to stop me from doing something stupid that would ruin my life. That's what I want to do for my son, and I figure that's what you want, too."

She looked away, staring off into space as if she were giving serious consideration to his reply before passing judgment on him. When her gaze returned to him, she said, "Of course Brad's future is my first consideration, but there's a baby to consider, too. I couldn't let Brad's child grow up in squalor the way the Wilkes children are."

"Then you can take the kid yourself," he said impatiently. "It wouldn't be the first time you've raised some other woman's bastard, would it?"

He instantly regretted his harshness when he saw her stricken expression. "Look, I didn't mean . . ." he began but she cut him off.

"No, you're right, of course," she said, quickly regaining her composure. "There are other alternatives. They're both too young for marriage anyway, much less for the responsibility of a family."

"What are you going to do?"

She sighed, and he noticed a lot of the stiffness had gone out of her so that now she looked almost weary. "I suppose the first step is to see her father."

Cal couldn't stand the thought of her facing the old man alone, but once again he realized his impotence. "If you don't mind, I'd like to go with you," he ventured.

She bristled instantly. "I don't need a man to protect me or to handle things or to—"

"I can see that!" he snapped. "I don't want to 'handle' anything, anyway. God knows, I'd probably make a mess of it, and you'd be a fool to trust me, but it can't hurt to let the old man know you've got somebody backing your play, Miss Harding."

He'd surprised her, and he thought she seemed pleased by the surprise. "And what do you think my 'play' should be, Mr. Stevens?" she asked after a few moments.

Since she really seemed to want to know, he told her. "Well, you can't let him see you care about the baby because he'll take advantage of it." Cal was pacing again. He thought better when he moved. "And be sure to let him know right off you don't approve of the marriage and plan to fight it. Maybe that'll scare him. A man like that might cut his losses and take what he can get." He glanced at Miss Harding and caught a strange expression on her face. "What is it?"

She shook her head as if to clear it and smiled mirthlessly. "I just realized, watching you pace. Brad does the same thing when he's upset."

Cal had only a moment to absorb this observation when someone said, "Supper is ready, señorita."

He looked up to see a stout Mexican woman in the doorway of the hall that he assumed led back into the depths of the house. She looked at him blandly, as if finding a strange man in the parlor were a common occurrence.

"Thank you, Juanita," Leah said absently.

"I should set another place?" the woman asked.

"No, I don't think Mr. Brad will be here for supper. Mr. Stevens can just take his place."

Cal found the prospect of sitting down at table alone with Leah Harding slightly unnerving. "If you'd rather be alone, I can eat with the men," he offered.

"And have them wondering who you are and why you're here? Certainly not." She rose from her chair and started toward the hallway down which the Mexican woman had already disappeared. "Right this way."

She led him to a cavernous room almost filled with an enormous table that could have easily seated twenty people. Two places were laid opposite each other at one end. When they were seated, the Mexican woman came out of what he supposed was the kitchen and began to serve.

"Juanita, this is Mr. Stevens. He'll be visiting us for a while."

Juanita looked at Cal again, still without any apparent interest, then resumed her serving. When she had finished, she disappeared back into the kitchen.

"Juanita was Brad's wet nurse," Miss Harding explained. "She's a little slow, but she's not as stupid as she seems, so don't underestimate her."

Cal had no intention of underestimating anyone he had met at the Rocking Horse Ranch.

Following Western custom, they ate in silence. The fare was simple—beans and fatback and cornbread—but the elegance of the surroundings lent an air of unreality to the meal. Had Cal ever imagined dining with a lady like Leah Harding in such surroundings? Not that he could remember.

In the flickering lamplight, he could almost imagine he belonged here, sitting across from his woman as they ate their evening meal together at the end of a long day. Once again he noticed the golden highlights in her hair and the way her skin looked like satin. Honey-colored hair and honey-colored eyes. Cal couldn't help wondering if her mouth tasted like honey, too.

If she really had been his woman, after dinner they would sit by the fire together. She would sew or do whatever women did while he told her what he'd done all day. Then they would go into their bedroom, alone, and close the door, and she'd take off the dress that hid what she really was, and she'd come to his bed, sliding between the sheets wearing only a thin nightdress or maybe nothing at all, and he'd hold her to him and kiss her honeyed mouth and . . .

Cal caught himself and looked up guiltily, but Miss Harding was eating calmly, oblivious to his wicked fantasies. Heat from his daydream burned in his loins, and the visions he'd conjured would probably haunt his dreams tonight, but there was no harm done so long as he didn't give Miss Harding even the slightest hint of how heartily he was lusting after her.

Maybe if things were different . . . But no, he had to admit that even if he weren't here to claim her brother as his son, Leah Harding would never look twice at a man like Cal Stevens. His attraction to her was something he could never reveal, not only because Miss Harding wouldn't appreciate it but because she'd run him off with a shotgun if she knew about it. The thought made him smile, and he lowered his head so she wouldn't see.

When they were finished eating, Juanita brought them huge slabs of apple pie and more coffee. Cal wasn't certain if it was really the best pie he had ever tasted or if the fantasy had completely engulfed him.

"You probably want to smoke," Miss Harding said when they had both finished their pie and coffee. "I don't permit smoking in the house."

"I'll go outside," Cal said, thinking he'd better escape soon or God only knew what he might start imagining.

"I expect Brad will be home soon. You'll speak to him about . . . what we discussed when he comes in?"

Cal nodded grimly as they rose from their chairs. "He might not take too kindly to a stranger meddling in his affairs though. In fact," he added, "I'm still surprised you'd allow it."

"I'd allow it," Miss Harding said as they walked back toward the parlor, "because I need all the help I can get under the present circumstances, and as for Brad, I'm afraid he'd be only too happy to have you meddle in his affairs." Cal thought he heard regret in her voice. "His father . . . my father, that is, never knew how to talk to him. Papa was never quite satisfied with anything Brad ever did, and their encounters usually left Brad in tears when he was small and in open rebellion when he got too old to cry. Any man who is kind to him will have his undying devotion."

"I wasn't exactly planning on being kind," Cal protested.

Miss Harding smiled knowingly. "But you will be. I saw the way you looked at Brad this afternoon, Mr. Stevens, and the way you reacted when I told you about his problem this evening. As easily as you might kill when necessary, you'll never be other than kind to your son."

She was right, but . . . "You sound awful sure."

"Sure of what? That you'd be kind?"

"No, that he's my son. You haven't even had time to check my story."

"And I will, never fear, but I know what I'll find when I do." She sighed, and he thought he detected a hint of despair. "A man like you would never risk making a fool of himself unless the stakes were very high. At first I thought you might be after Brad's money, but I don't think you'd risk your pride for mere money, Mr. Stevens. I may be wrong, it wouldn't be the first time, but I think you'd only risk your pride for the one thing your skill with a gun can't get you."

"And what's that, Miss Harding?"

She smiled her unhappy smile. "Love, Mr. Stevens. Love."

Chapter Two

"That's the craziest thing I ever heard, Miss Leah!" Pete Quincy insisted when she'd finished telling him about Cal Stevens's claim to be Brad's father. She had summoned him after Stevens left, and they were sitting in the small room she used as an office. "You don't believe it, do you? I mean, a man like him might say anything. I heared he's killed forty men!"

"You know how reputations tend to become exaggerated," Leah scolded. "The true number is probably closer to four, if he's killed any at all."

"Humph." Pete frowned his disapproval. "Don't make no nevermind. A man like that can't be trusted nohow, and here you've gone and took him in under your own roof. If your pa was alive, he'd—"

"Turn over in his grave, I know," Leah said, having learned that confusing Pete was the best way to win an argument with him. "Besides, I'm not taking Mr. Stevens's word for anything. I've already told him I plan to check out his story."

"How you gonna do that?"

"The question is, how are *you* going to do it," Leah

told him sweetly. "I felt certain you wouldn't trust anyone else with this job."

"Dang right," Pete assured her.

"You'll need some details, and Mr. Stevens should have no objection to supplying them. He said he grew up near San Antonio, but you'll have to ask him the name of the town. I imagine his family's name is the same as his, and he said the girl was named Amy Weeks."

Pete was shaking his head. "Won't make no difference what I find, though, will it? You already made up your mind about this fellow."

"I am . . . almost certain he's telling the truth, yes," she admitted.

"Never thought I'd see the day when you'd take in a killer," he muttered.

"Is that really what's bothering you about him?"

Pete wagged his head again. "No, there's more, and I think you know what it is. He's an awful lot like your pa."

Leah stiffened, an instinctive reaction even after seven years of freedom from her father's tyranny, and she forced herself to relax. "I thought so, too, at first, Pete. They are a lot alike in many ways."

"Yeah, mean and ornery and don't care who they hurt," Pete growled, but Leah shook her head.

"I'm sure Mr. Stevens can be a very dangerous man, but you haven't seen him when he's with Brad or when he's talking about him."

"He's just putting on a show for you, Miss Leah. A man like that —"

"I'd think after all these years you would have learned to trust my judgment," she said sharply. "Do

46

you think I'm likely to be taken in by a man like my father?"

"He ran your life for twenty years," Pete reminded her. "Old habits are hard to break."

Leah fought her rising fury. "And when he died, I vowed no man would ever have control over me again, and I plan to keep that vow. The other difference between my father and Cal Stevens is in the way he treats me."

"And how's that?" Pete's expression told her he thought he already knew that Stevens had charmed her.

"He treats me with respect, as if I were his equal." And that, she knew, was probably the main reason she was finally willing to accept his story.

Pete was muttering. "If your pa was alive—"

"But he isn't alive, Pete, and as much as I hate to admit it, I need a man who can talk some sense to Brad. If nothing else, Mr. Stevens is, without doubt, the one person he is most likely to listen to on any subject."

Pete's eyes narrowed suspiciously. "What subject you figure the boy needs talking to about?"

Leah had been dreading this revelation since it illustrated too clearly Brad's lack of proper male guidance. "It seems young Bradley has gotten Miss Espy Wilkes in trouble and is dead set on marrying her."

"Christ Almighty!" Pete exclaimed. "Oh, I'm sorry, Miss Leah, but *Espy Wilkes,* for God's sake! She ain't much more'n a baby herownself!"

"Apparently, she's old enough for all sorts of mischief. In any case, I must do everything I can to prevent such a marriage if at all possible."

"And you figure Stevens is the fellow to help you?"

"As I said, he seems most likely to get Brad to listen to reason on the subject."

Pete grunted his grudging agreement. "If you've got him on your side, he's the most likely to scare the be-jeepers out of Homer Wilkes, too. I reckon you'd already planned to take him along with you when you go to see the old sidewinder."

Although she hadn't actually admitted it to the man himself, she certainly had. "Yes, and Mr. Stevens has even suggested several alternative solutions to the problem."

"Such as?"

"Paying off the girl and her father."

Pete shook his head doubtfully. "Wilkes'd be a fool if he took money when he could marry his daughter off and have the whole ranch, too."

"*He* wouldn't have anything even if they did get married!" Leah cried in outrage.

Pete only smiled wisely. "You got a lot to learn about families, little lady. Yourn was mighty stand-offish, but these crackers, they stick together closer'n stink on sh . . . Well, you know. All's they got is each other, and what one gets, he shares with the rest."

"I'd never allow them here!" Leah informed him.

Pete gave her a pitying look. "It ain't your ranch, Miss Leah."

The reminder stung, and for the first time Leah began to realize just exactly what her father's revenge against her might cost. "You'd better go see Mr. Stevens, Pete," she said, forcing the words through a constricted throat. "You'll want to leave first thing in the morning."

"Jeez, Mr. Stevens, how dumb do you think I am?" Brad complained, thoroughly affronted. The two were sitting on the corral fence in the moonlight, the perfect spot for a sensitive father/son chat, Cal had thought, since it was too dark for the boy to see how uncomfortable he was in this novel situation.

"I'm sorry, but the first thing us old folks think when a girl accuses a boy of getting her in a family way is that maybe she's got some funny ideas about exactly how babies are made."

"Well, I know how even if Espy didn't, at least not until we did it. And she's gonna have a baby all right, just in case you think she lied just to trap me. She's been puking up her breakfast every morning and her stomach's getting big. The reason she told me was because her pa had figured it out and she couldn't keep it a secret no more. He was mad as blazes, too. Blacked her eye and everything, that son of a bitch," Brad added angrily.

Cal thought he could understand the black eye even if he didn't approve of beating women. A man as worthless as Mr. Wilkes appeared to be wouldn't be much on expressing his disapproval verbally. A sound smack was probably the only way he knew to inform his daughter she had displeased him with her wanton behavior.

"You're still mighty young to be settling down with one woman," Cal ventured. After Leah Harding's rebuke this evening, he couldn't help thinking he should actually be counseling Brad about facing his responsibilities like a man, the way he hoped he would have faced his if he'd known about Brad eighteen years ago. Still, if the Wilkes family was as bad as Leah had said . . .

"Maybe I am a little young," Brad allowed, shifting uneasily on the fence, "but it can't be helped."

"Maybe it can," Cal offered, snatching at the uncertainty he heard in the boy's voice. Maybe Brad wanted to be talked out of it. "There's no law says you've got to marry the girl, not if you don't want to. The rest of your life is a long time to spend with a woman you don't love."

"But I do love her!" Brad protested.

"Love and lust ain't the same thing, boy. Lately it seems like you've been thinking with your talley-wacker instead of your brain. If you was to pick the woman you wanted to spend the rest of your life with, would it be a girl like Espy?"

"That ain't fair, Mr. Stevens!"

"Life ain't fair. That girl said yes when she should've said no, so she's as much to blame as you."

"But I can't just leave her. It's my baby, too!"

"Nobody said you had to leave her," Cal insisted. Even though the words fairly stuck in his throat, he had to keep his promise to Leah Harding. "You can take care of her without marrying her. Hell, I'll bet your sister would even take the baby to raise if it came to that."

He felt Brad's surprise and knew he'd gone too far. "Why'd she want somebody else's baby if you two're gonna get married? She'll have babies of her own."

Cal silently cursed himself. This father business was even trickier than he'd feared. "She hasn't exactly agreed to marry me yet," he tried.

50

"Oh, she will. It's not like she gets a lot of offers or anything, and when me and Espy get married . . . Oh, hell, Mr. Stevens, the stuff you said about Espy is true, but she's my girl and it's my baby. A man just can't run out on something like that, can he?"

Cal felt the question like a blow, and he was afraid his answer would tie the boy forever to the wrong woman. For the first time since he had laid eyes on his son, he was glad he didn't have the right to tell him what to do. "It's not my place to say. Just think over what I've said. We'll be paying the Wilkeses a little visit in the morning to talk things over."

"Are you going along?" Brad asked hopefully.

Miss Harding hadn't actually agreed to let him go along, but she was going to need the support whether she wanted it or not. "Yeah, I reckon I am."

Brad sighed with what sounded like relief. "I sure am glad to hear it. Leah can be mighty unreasonable sometimes."

Cal was certain of it.

Leah had waited up for Brad, but he had outlasted her, and she had finally given up and retired. At least Mr. Stevens had spoken with him. She'd seen them together out by the corral. She doubted he'd accomplished any more than she had, but if nothing else Brad knew he had two adults to deal with now.

The next morning, as Leah dressed, she considered the coming confrontation with the Wilkes family and found herself relieved to know Stevens was going to accompany them. She realized the knowledge should have annoyed her, and she certainly should have resented his interference. Leah had spent most of her life resenting male domination and resisting it whenever she could. Why she seemed to appreciate Cal Stevens's presence instead, she had no idea, but she managed to convince herself it was simply a result of this completely unique situation.

Leah had already dressed in her usual black and was putting the pins in her usual bun when she caught her reflection in the mirror. Not normally one to primp, Leah never spent much time considering her appearance, but looking at herself now was like looking at a stranger. Good heavens, she looked like an old woman!

First of all, her dress was ghastly. Why hadn't she noticed how poorly it fit and the way the black material had begun to wear? The sleeves were practically green in spots, and she would have to turn the collar soon if she intended to get much more use out of it. It wasn't at all the thing to impress Homer Wilkes.

Leah went to the cabinet that held her modest wardrobe and examined the pair of equally black and equally worn garments hanging there. How could she possibly have put these dresses on day after day without seeing how dowdy they were? And without *caring* how dowdy they were? She glanced down at the dress she wore and tried to imagine the impression she must make in it. What on earth had Mr. Stevens thought yesterday when confronted with such a scarecrow of a woman?

The thought shocked her. When was the last time she'd so much as considered what a man thought of her appearance? And why in heaven's name should she consider it now? Laying her hands on her burning cheeks, she tried to tell herself she was only concerned because of the importance of the occasion. A woman always felt more confident when she knew she looked her best, and Leah would need every shred of confidence she could muster for her meeting with Wilkes. That was it, she decided, and that was *all*.

She forced herself not to examine her reasons any more closely as she opened the trunk where, upon her father's death, she had stored away her girlish clothes when she went into what she had expected would be permanent mourning. The styles would be seven years old, but style wasn't particularly important on the Texas plains, and the Wilkeses weren't likely to know the difference anyway.

The colors of the gowns that lay inside, carefully folded and delicately scented from the sachets she had packed with them, seemed startling to eyes so long accustomed to drabness. Something pink and frilly lay on top, stirring memories of the moonlight dance at which a handsome young man had begged for her hand in marriage.

Leah quickly pushed it and the memories aside, digging through the soft layers until she found something not quite so bright. The honey brown color instantly caught her eye, and she pulled the garment from deep inside the chest. Oh, yes, she remembered this dress well. With its cheerful pink flowers against the brown background that matched her eyes, it had always been one of her favorites. She held it up, trying to judge whether it would still fit. Molding the fabric over her body, she realized fit would not be a problem. If anything, she was actually thinner than she had been seven years ago.

A dried up old maid, she thought bitterly, thinking how well the title fit her now. Well, she could have married. Mead Garland had begged her, hadn't he? And for a while she had seen him as her savior, the white knight who would take her from her father's house and finally relieve her of the burden of trying to please a parent who could never be pleased by a child who'd had the effrontery to be born female.

But her father's death had saved her instead, making marriage to Mead Garland unnecessary. Quite suddenly, she'd had everything she could possibly want, the ranch all to herself to run the way she saw fit and Brad to raise without her father's cruel interference. She hadn't needed a husband at all, and she'd given Mead Garland his freedom. He hadn't been particularly happy to have it, but at least they had remained friends.

A dried up old maid should be happy to have all the friends she could get, Leah told herself, absently smoothing the wrinkled fabric. The flowers blurred momentarily until she blinked away the uncharacteristic tears. Tears? What on earth was wrong with her? She must be more upset about this business with Brad than she'd thought.

"Juanita!" she called, hurrying out of the bedroom, the dress over her arm. "Heat up the iron!"

Cal sat on the front porch, smoking his first cigarette of the day while he watched his son pacing back and forth while they waited for his sister to appear. Leah had remarked on how he and the boy shared that trait of restlessness, and he'd certainly have to stop thinking of her as 'Leah' before he slipped and called her that to her pretty face.

Brad was a fine boy, Cal decided as he watched his son, even if he *had* listened to his tallywacker instead of his brain and gotten himself into a world of trouble. Like father, like son, Cal thought, taking a perverse pleasure even in this less-than-desirable evidence of his paternity. He even relished helping the boy with his problems, as if he had some right to. If he proved helpful, maybe Leah . . . no, Miss Harding, he corrected himself, would let him stay on for a while at least so he could get to know the boy better. Then, someday, if things worked out, he might even be able to tell the boy who he was and claim him for his own.

Lost in his own thoughts, Cal didn't notice they were no longer alone until Brad abruptly stopped pacing and said, "Jeez, Leah, what'd you do to yourself?"

At the mention of her name, Cal jumped to his feet and turned to find her standing in the doorway. God, what *had* she done to herself? If he'd thought her pretty last night, this morning she was *beautiful*. The black dress was gone, and the one she was wearing today left no doubt about her feminine charms. The bodice swelled enticingly and tapered to a tiny waist he imagined he could span with his hands, then swelled again with a hint of nicely rounded hips beneath the drape of her skirt.

Her hair was different, too, curled around her face, and Cal found himself longing to touch those wisps to see if they felt as soft as they looked, and then to let his fingers graze the sides of her face to see if *she* was as soft as she looked. Color bloomed in her cheeks, and Cal knew she must be embarrassed by the way they were both gawking like they'd never seen a woman before. He ought to say something, and he would in just a minute, as soon as he thought of something and got his tongue unhinged.

Watching the two men watching her, seeing their amazement, Leah was mortified. She felt the heat in her cheeks, prayed she wasn't really blushing, and resisted the urge to touch her hair self-consciously. When was the last time she had blushed? Not for many years, but since Cal Stevens had intruded into her neatly ordered life, she'd started doing it almost hourly.

"Good morning," she forced herself to say, refusing to acknowledge Brad and Stevens's surprise at her appearance. "Are you ready to go?"

For a moment neither of them replied. They were still staring, and Leah began to regret her impulse to use the curling iron this morning. Her mirror had shown her a pleasing effect and Juanita had blandly confirmed that opinion, but now Leah was beginning to doubt her own judgment.

Or maybe it was the hat she'd chosen to wear instead of the plain poke bonnet she usually chose. Perhaps the broad-brimmed straw adorned with pink flowers to match her dress was too youthful for a spinster. Maybe she looked like a fool. Maybe . . .

"You look real nice, Miss Harding," Cal Stevens said, his blue eyes shining, a perfect match for Brad's in the morning light.

The compliment sounded awkward on his lips, as if he weren't accustomed to offering flattery, and she supposed he wasn't. She wasn't used to receiving it, either, so her "Thank you" sounded equally awkward.

A few more seconds of silence ticked by, then Cal poked Brad with his elbow, and the boy jumped. "Oh, yeah! I mean, you do look nice, Leah. You look *pretty!*"

She knew it wasn't true, of course. No amount of primping and curling could ever make her pretty, and the amazement in his voice rankled a bit. "If you're trying to get on my good side, you'd do better to behave yourself this morning when we see the Wilkeses."

"I'm not a kid, Leah," he complained.

"I believed you've proven that," Leah chided, and Brad had the grace to flush. "If you want to be treated like a man, however, you will have to conduct yourself in a mature, responsible manner."

He looked to Stevens as if for interpretation.

"She expects you to keep your mouth shut and your temper under control," he obliged.

Brad started to protest, but Stevens didn't give him a chance.

"Brad'll go with you in the buggy. You never said one way or the other last night, but if you don't mind, I'd like to ride along."

"I'm sure we would both appreciate your company, Mr. Stevens," Leah replied, wishing Pete could have heard the exchange. Bradley Harding, Sr. had never asked anyone's permission in his life. But Pete would probably say it was another trick to win her over, and Leah really had no proof it was not.

Feeling suddenly depressed, she started across the porch. Stevens caught up with her and took her elbow as she started down the steps. It had been years since anyone had thought to help her down the steps, and his firm grip startled her. She looked up in surprise.

He seemed as surprised as she, as if he too felt the shock wave passing through her body. Embarrassed, she looked quickly away and concentrated on descending the porch steps without tripping over her own feet, but she didn't need to look at his face to see it clearly. As if that one instant had burned his image in her brain, Leah recalled every detail of his expression. The blue-black shadow of beard on freshly shaved cheeks, and the slight tilt of his finely chiseled mouth. The pale tracery of squint lines beside his eyes, smoothed out by his wide-eyed surprise, and the crystal clarity of those eyes which were even more like Brad's than Brad's own.

The hint of bay rum which he had used after his shave did not disguise his own musky scent, a scent so disturbingly compelling that Leah found herself holding her breath to protect herself from it.

When they reached the buggy, Leah allowed Stevens to assist her into it. Only when he finally released her arm did Leah expel the breath she had been holding in a long sigh that sounded suspiciously like a sigh of relief. Embarrassed all over again, she glanced up to see if Stevens had noticed, but he was watching Brad's reluctant approach. When Stevens's gaze touched her again, he looked as if he wanted to say something to her, but Brad was already close enough to overhear.

Instead he simply looked at her, and in his eyes Leah saw her own doubts and apprehensions reflected. He was, she realized with a start, as concerned about this morning's work as she. Instinctively responding to the bond between them, she lay a gloved hand on his arm, and this time she saw the shock wave go through *him*. Just as instinctively, he covered her fingers with his other hand, and Leah felt the touch like a brand burning through the fabric of her glove. Her mouth dropped open in surprise, but before either of them could react further, the buggy dipped with Brad's weight when he climbed in the other side.

Instantly, they jerked apart as if they had been caught doing something indecent. Leah felt her cheeks burning yet again, and she didn't dare even glance at Mr. Stevens as he moved away toward his horse. Sitting stiffly, afraid Brad could sense her embarrassment, she stared straight ahead, waiting for the boy to slap the horse into motion. When he didn't, she allowed herself to turn toward him expectantly.

He looked chagrined but defiant, an expression he'd worn often in his short life. "Leah, I'm mighty sorry to put you through this. I know I've shamed you, and you've got every right to be mad. There's nothing I can do to make it up to you, but at least . . ." His gaze darted to where Stevens now sat his horse, waiting for them to start off, then back to her again. ". . . at least you've got somebody of your own now, so you don't have to worry about being alone."

He didn't wait for a reply before starting the horse, which was just as well because Leah was much too stunned to make one. *She didn't have to worry about being alone?* What on earth did he mean by that?

Pete's warning came echoing back: "It ain't your ranch, Miss Leah." Did Brad imagine she would simply leave when he took a wife? And where did he imagine she would go? Brad and the Rocking Horse Ranch had been her entire life. Without them, she had nothing. And no one. Suddenly and for the first time in seven years, she felt the maddening frustration of being female. As her father had often said so contemptuously, a woman truly was a helpless, fragile creature, dependent her entire life on the kindness and largess of men, first her father, then her husband.

Leah had always thought she'd successfully bypassed the curse of other females by her unique role in Brad's life, but now she saw that role quickly coming to an end. For the first time ever, she began to doubt her decision to remain unwed. As burdensome as a husband could be, he would have offered a source of security. Instead, she now found herself at the mercy of a seventeen-year-old boy who resented her power over him and, quite possibly, of his fifteen-year-old bride who would have every reason to want to rid herself of Leah's influence in their lives.

Like most trips in which the destination is undesired, this one seemed unusually brief. Before Leah had even gotten her emotions back under control, she caught sight of the Wilkes homestead. The ramshackle buildings huddled together at the edge of a trickle of water too feeble to even be called a creek. A corral held several horses whose brands Leah guessed would be suspect, and two small, ragged children played in the dirt in front of the house.

At the sight of the buggy and the accompanying rider, the children bolted into the house. In a few moments, Homer Wilkes appeared on the doorstep. As usual, he looked as if he'd slept in the faded jeans and shirt that hung on his raw-boned frame. His graying brown hair dangled in untidy hanks around his shoulders, an enormous, untrimmed mustache drooped on either side of his mouth, and his chin carried several days worth of stubble. Although Leah supposed he wasn't much older than Cal Stevens, he looked ancient, probably as a result of having spent every spare nickel he'd ever earned on whiskey. Although Wilkes wasn't carrying a rifle, his stance indicated he was on the prod. As the buggy approached the house, Leah saw his weathered face was twisted into a forbidding scowl. Apparently he was more than ready to do battle with the formidable Miss Harding.

Brad drew the buggy to a halt in front of the rickety steps leading up to the front door. " 'Morning, Mr. Wilkes," Brad called with strained enthusiasm. "I've brought Leah. She wants to talk to you."

"She'd better, you worthless pup," Wilkes spat. His rheumy glare shifted to include Stevens who sat his horse somewhat apart, hands folded on the pommel, his face carefully expressionless. "Who's that?"

"That's Cal Stevens," Brad offered quickly. "Mr. Stevens, this here's Mr. Wilkes."

Cal nodded and Wilkes stiffened noticeably. Although he didn't take his eyes off Stevens, he spoke to Brad. "There's no call to hire a gunfighter. This here's a family matter."

"Mr. Stevens doesn't work for me," Leah said before Brad could speak. "He's here as a friend of the family."

Reluctantly, Wilkes turned his gaze back to the couple in the buggy. Plainly, he did not believe her.

"It's true," Brad assured him. "Mr. Stevens and Leah are —"

"— friends," Leah supplied before Brad could make matters more awkward than they already were. "And as a friend, he offered to accompany us here today to settle this unfortunate business."

Wilkes grunted, although he seemed far from pleased at the prospect.

When Wilkes made no offer, Leah said, "We have a lot to discuss. Perhaps you will invite us in."

He grunted again, made an exaggerated gesture of welcome, then disappeared into the house. Leah swallowed her seething annoyance at the man's rudeness and reminded herself he had no reason to welcome the family of the man who had seduced his daughter. From his point of view, they were the villains of this piece, and if Leah hadn't suspected Wilkes himself had had some part in all this, she would have felt a whole lot guiltier.

Brad helped her out of the buggy, and Stevens met them at the stoop. Feeling loath to enter the dingy hovel, Leah glanced at Stevens and once again saw empathy shining in his eyes. As if sensing her need, he took her arm, and his strength seemed to radiate through his touch. Lifting her chin, she strode resolutely into the house.

The interior dimness stopped her for a moment, and as her eyes adjusted, she saw exactly what must have inspired Brad's desire to rescue poor Espy. The cramped room held two tumbled beds built into the corners on either side of the crude mud-and-stick fireplace. A rickety homemade table covered with the remains of breakfast and surrounded by assorted stools occupied the rest of the space in the room. The place stank of unwashed bodies, spoiled food, and whiskey, but the worst part was the human inhabitants.

The children they had seen in the yard now crouched, doglike, on one of the beds with a third, slightly older girl. All three of them had the same red hair as their older sister, hanging down in ratty tangles around their thin shoulders. Huge eyes stared at her out of three grubby faces.

"You younguns, git out," their father commanded gruffly, and the three scattered like quail, darting through and around the three visitors still standing just inside the door to disappear outside.

Startled, Leah looked up to see Espy rising from where she had been sitting in a rocking chair in the corner to her left. The girl was even smaller than Leah remembered, thin to the point of emaciation, but her thinness only accentuated her natural beauty. The red hair had been carefully combed, its masses of natural curls tamed with a rawhide clasp, and eyes as green as grass stared out of the delicate face. Espy took a step forward, hugging herself as if she were in need of comfort, and when the light from the doorway struck her fully, Leah saw the bruise beneath one of those enormous eyes.

She cried out involuntarily in protest and turned furiously to Wilkes. "You've been *beating* her!"

Wilkes glared right back. "Just gave her a smack or two. Maybe if you'd beat your boy now and then, he wouldn't go around attacking innocent young girls."

"Pa!" Espy cried, and Brad took a step toward him before Leah grabbed his arm, but it was Cal Stevens who changed Wilkes's attitude with only a suggestion.

"Maybe you'd like to ask Miss Harding to sit down."

The cold steel in his voice sent shivers up Leah's spine, and it must have had a similar effect on Wilkes because he said, "Have a seat, Miss Harding," with only a hint of sarcasm.

Leah pulled one of the stools closer, testing it with her hand first to make sure it rested securely on the uneven dirt floor before trusting her full weight to it. When she was seated, she motioned for Brad to take another of the stools. He straddled it reluctantly, glancing suspiciously from Espy to Wilkes and back again, as if expecting the father to strike the daughter again at any moment. Stevens remained standing, legs spread and arms crossed, amazingly formidable in his silence.

Wilkes watched him for a long minute until apparently satisfied he wasn't going to do anything untoward. Then he took a seat across the table from Leah and Brad and crossed his own arms belligerently.

Leah waited for him to speak, but she soon realized everyone was watching her, expecting her to speak first. Never having faced such a situation, Leah couldn't imagine what they expected her to say, then she realized it really made no difference. "Brad tells me," she began uneasily, "there's going to be a baby."

"Damn right," Wilkes snapped, reaching out to grab Espy who hovered as far from the table as she could get in the tiny room but who was still within arm's length of her father. He jerked her forward, stumbling, until she caught the table edge. "Look at that!" Wilkes commanded, pointing at the swell beneath her stained apron.

The girl spread her hands protectively over her abdomen but nothing could conceal her condition. Leah had been too startled by the blackened eye to notice it before. Because of the girl's slenderness, her pregnancy was even more pronounced than it might have been. Inanely, Leah realized Pete would have said she looked like a string with a knot tied in it.

Leah looked up and caught the girl's gaze, at once terrified and defiant. She was little more than a child, but life had hurt her in ways Leah couldn't begin to imagine.

"I brought my girl up right," Wilkes was saying. "It was your boy what ruined her, and now he's gotta do right by her."

The girl started to struggle, trying to wrench free of her father's grip, but he refused to let her go.

"Pa, you're hurting me!" she cried, tears blurring her emerald eyes, but tears didn't move Homer Wilkes.

"I'll hurt you, all right, you little bitch!"

He raised his free hand to strike her. Brad was already halfway across the table when Stevens's voice stopped them all.

"Wilkes!"

Every head jerked around, and Leah shivered at the coldness she saw in his eyes.

"Let her go, Wilkes." For a heartbeat, no one moved. Leah couldn't even breathe, then slowly, Wilkes's raised hand lowered and at last he released the girl. She scurried away, rubbing her bruised arm, her gaze darting between Cal Stevens and her father with the wariness of a wounded animal.

Brad went to her and wrapped his arms around her,

but she stood stiffly in his embrace, her tormented gaze locked on Wilkes. Seeing Brad and the girl together like this only made Leah more painfully aware of what children they were. Not innocent children, but certainly helpless enough to require all the assistance she could give them, and she could give them a lot.

Mentally, Leah reviewed the questions Cal Stevens had raised. The girl was obviously pregnant, and Leah couldn't believe a child so young had been with more than one man. No, this was Brad's baby and Brad's responsibility. Leah couldn't even consider leaving the child to grow up in this hovel under the influence of this monster, not even if she provided financial assistance, not any more than she could consider taking the child from his natural mother. That left her with only one option, an option she had no intention of stretching to benefit Homer Wilkes.

Leah turned to Wilkes, only then realizing that she had at some point risen from her seat and now stood looking across the table at her adversary. "Mr. Wilkes," she said sharply.

The man jumped and reluctantly looked from Stevens whom he had been watching the same way Espy had been watching him.

"Mr. Wilkes, you must understand my position. I have plans for my brother, and those plans do not include marriage to a girl like your daughter."

"Leah!" Brad cried, but Leah ignored him.

"What's wrong with my daughter!" Wilkes snarled, planting both palms on the unsteady table and leaning closer to her.

Leah resisted the urge to recoil at the smell of him

66

and stood her ground. "For one thing, she's carrying a bastard child."

"It's your boy's bastard!"

"Leah!" Brad's voice held pain and outrage, and Leah wanted to scream at him to be quiet before he ruined everything, but once again Cal Stevens came to her rescue.

"Let your sister handle this, boy."

Brad's outrage was palpable, but mercifully, he held his peace. Leah hurried on. "Of course, if Brad is responsible, I am more than willing to provide for the child. We can't allow it to grow up in . . ." Leah glanced around in disgust. ". . . in poverty."

Wilkes stiffened in feigned outrage. "If you think you can buy your brother out of this, you're dead wrong, missy. That's the trouble with you Hardings, you think your money can get you out of everything, but it won't work this time. Your boy's going to do the right thing by my girl."

"But Mr. Wilkes, I would be more than generous," she argued. "You'd never have to worry about money again, at least until the child reached adulthood. Think of it, Mr. Wilkes, twenty years of living off the Hardings."

She saw the glitter of greed, but as she'd hoped, he was too cunning to snap at the second best offer when he still had hope of the best. "I don't want your damn money," he insisted righteously. "Nothing can buy back my daughter's good name."

"And that's all you're concerned about, your daughter's welfare?"

"You're damn right, and he's going to marry her if I have to hold a gun to his head to do it!"

"My apologies, Mr. Wilkes," Leah replied, just as falsely repentant as he had been falsely outraged. "I'm afraid I misjudged you. You're absolutely right, Brad *should* do the right thing and marry your daughter, which is, of course, what he wanted to do all along. I know you hate to give up your child, especially when she's been such a help to you, and I might have been tempted to offer you a little something to ease the pain of your loss, but now that I know your opinion of Harding money, I wouldn't dream of insulting you again."

Leah smiled at Wilkes's gaping surprise. A long moment of silence followed, broken finally by Espy's scornful laugh. "She snookered you, Pa!"

Wilkes's mouth closed with a snap, but before he could collect his wits, Leah turned to where the girl still stood in Brad's protective embrace. Espy sobered at once.

"I explained to Brad that it will take a few days to get the preacher out to perform the ceremony," Leah said, looking the girl over from head to toe. The dress she wore had been washed nearly colorless, and beneath the tattered hem, she was barefoot. "Perhaps we can use the time in having a trousseau made for you."

The girl glanced at Brad for an interpretation, but he just shrugged his shoulders.

"Some new clothes," Leah explained patiently. She might hate the thought of marrying her brother to a girl from this place, but at least she could provide her with some decent clothes to stand up in.

"My girl don't need no charity!" Wilkes protested, but everyone ignored him.

Espy's eyes lighted. "Yeah, that'd be all right." She

squared her narrow shoulders with a pathetic attempt at dignity. "I could use some new duds. You hear that, Pa? I won't never have to go barefoot again, neither!"

"You little whore!" her father shouted. "You think they don't know why you done this? You think she loves you, boy? She don't love nobody but herself. The whole time she was spreading her legs for you, she was thinking about that big house and whatall your money could buy her!"

Leah was terribly afraid he was right, but she wouldn't give him the satisfaction of letting him know it. "Brad," she said as if Wilkes hadn't spoken, "we should probably take Espy into town this morning so the dressmaker can get started. We can't have everything ready before the wedding, but at least she'll have a nice gown for the ceremony."

"And shoes," Espy said. "I'll need new shoes, too."

"Certainly." The word almost stuck in her throat, but Leah managed to conceal her disdain when she turned back to Wilkes. "We'll let you know when the ceremony is to take place. I'm sure you and your other children will want to attend." She glanced at Stevens, surprised to see an expression of frank admiration on his face. He quickly schooled his features into blankness again, however, allowing Leah to recall what she had intended to say next. "Mr. Stevens and I will wait outside while you get ready, Espy."

Leah swept out of the cabin, not stopping until she reached the side of the buggy. Stevens was right behind her. They stood there a few minutes while Leah drew deep breaths of the clean air to flush the memory of that squalid house. How could people live like that?

"You did good, Miss Harding," Stevens said at last.

Leah started at the compliment, her second in a single day and the only two she could remember in many years. Things had certainly changed since Cal Stevens had turned her world upside down. She only wondered if she deserved this particular compliment. Her help had doomed her brother to a lifetime with a girl who quite likely had used his youthful lust just to win herself a nice home and pretty clothes.

As if reading her thoughts, he said, "At least you fixed it so the old man can't ask for money for himself."

She looked up at him. "But that wasn't what you advised me to do. You wanted me to pay them off and be rid of them."

"That was before I saw this place," he said grimly, glancing around at the broken-down buildings and the corner of the barn where the three youngest Wilkes children skulked. They'd been joined by the fifth sibling, a gangly boy of about thirteen who scowled back at them. "You couldn't've left her here, not with the old man, knowing what he'd do to her and the baby, too."

His sanction made the decision a little easier to bear, and Leah savored the novelty of having a man approve of her actions. "I appreciate the help you gave me in there."

His lips twitched into a self-mocking grin, so like the one she'd seen on Brad's face a thousand times that her heart ached. "Sometimes it's handy to have a hired gun on your side."

She returned his smile, wondering why she hadn't noticed until now how handsome he was. "I don't think I ever knew just *how* handy one could be. I should have met you years ago."

His grin faded, and Leah instantly regretted her words, knowing he must be thinking of all the years of Brad's life he'd missed. "Then maybe you won't mind if I stick around at least until the wedding."

"Of course not," she assured him. She hadn't really given any thought to his leaving at all. How long would he stay once Brad was married and settled? And how would Brad react when he learned this mysterious man was his real father? Ordinarily, she would have predicted Brad would want to keep him around, but the novelty of a new bride might overshadow a father he no longer needed. She could almost have pitied Mr. Stevens if his situation hadn't mirrored her own so closely.

"We're ready," Brad called as he and Espy came out the door. Espy had removed her apron and found a pair of cracked shoes that looked as old as she. She'd thrown a threadbare shawl around her shoulders and slapped a limp straw hat over her fiery curls, but in contrast to her pathetic apparel, she looked radiant. Leah supposed she had good reason to be.

Leah climbed into the buggy and Espy crawled in beside her to sit between her and Brad. They were crowded and might have been more so if Espy hadn't molded herself so closely to Brad's side.

"You really gave it to Pa in there, Miss Harding," Espy said, covering her mouth to stifle a giggle. All the wariness she had exhibited before her father had vanished. She didn't even look back to see him standing in the doorway of the cabin, glowering at their departure. "He was gonna ask you for money *and* make Brad marry me, too, or at least that's what he claimed. 'Course, it's just as well, 'cause he would've just drunk it up and made everybody miserable like he always does. He was sure scared of that Stevens fellow. Who is he, anyways? I never saw him around here before." Leah felt a moment of panic about how to reply to this question, but Espy didn't wait for a reply. "How long do you think until we can get the preacher here, Brad? I don't mind waiting, though, 'cause I do need a new dress and I'd rather wait and do things right, 'cause a girl only gets married once. What color dress do you think I ought to get? I've always been partial to red, but . . ."

She chattered on happily, asking more questions without waiting for replies. It was the excitement that made her so silly, Leah told herself, and tried not to notice Brad's besotted grin or the way the girl kept letting her hand drop to stroke his thigh. Instead she concentrated on the small mound of the girl's stomach and the baby whom she was saving from a life of misery.

When they arrived in town, Leah instructed Stevens to keep Brad occupied while she took the girl straight to the dressmaker.

Nancy Otto was surprised to see them—Leah hadn't ordered a dress in years and Espy Wilkes had never ordered one in her life—but she recovered quickly. When Leah informed her that Espy and Brad would be marrying in a few short days, Nancy comprehended the situation at once.

Within minutes, she had the girl stripped to her

chemise and was taking measurements, pretending not to be shocked by the obvious evidence of her promiscuity.

"I want something red with lots of ruffles," Espy announced, "and maybe some feathers around the neck and . . ."

Nancy and Leah exchanged horrified looks over her head, but Nancy smiled sweetly when Espy had finished her list of outrageous requirements. "Red? With your hair? Oh, honey, that would be ghastly, but I've got some forest green silk that will just be heavenly with your eyes."

"Silk?" Espy echoed, all other thoughts wiped from her mind.

"India silk," Nancy confirmed.

"I don't want nothing from no filthy redskins," Espy insisted.

Leah rolled her eyes, but Nancy's smile never wavered. "No, dear, it's from India. That's a country far away, like China."

"Where's China?"

"On the other side of the ocean," Nancy said and hurried off before the girl could ask another question. As she had suspected, the sight of the silk removed all objections.

Nancy deftly persuaded the girl to settle for a sensible wrapper style dress instead of a more elaborate, fitted gown that she wouldn't be able to wear in a month or two. Then she proceeded to veto all Espy's ideas for hideous decoration until she had an ensemble that wouldn't embarrass Leah.

As Espy was slipping back into her own dress, Leah thanked Nancy for her help. "I'll take her over to the mercantile and outfit her with underwear and accessories. How long will it take for you to finish the dress?"

Nancy glanced at the girl's growing figure. "Under the circumstances, I'll have it ready in four days. Will that be soon enough?"

"I'm sure. We have to find the minister since he's out riding the circuit and get him back here, so that should be about right."

Nancy's professional gaze was taking in Leah's refurbished finery. "And what about you, Leah? Don't you need something new for the wedding, too?"

Once again Leah experienced the unusual sensation of self-consciousness over her appearance. What on earth was happening to her? "I . . . I've decided to come out of mourning," she said by way of explanation for her sudden change.

"Then you most certainly need something new. Don't you think so, Espy?"

The girl paused in the act of slipping on her shoes to consider. "Don't see why not." She smiled ingenuously. "It'll make you feel young again, Miss Harding."

Nancy pretended not to notice Leah's mortification. "I can hire someone to help me with the sewing so I'll have both dresses done on time," she said, already helping Leah off with her dress. Before Leah could reconsider, she had been measured and was examining various swatches of fabric.

"Lavender would be very flattering and properly demur for a woman of your advanced years," Nancy said with a twinkle. Leah smiled in spite of herself.

"Lavender would be perfect," she agreed, holding

74

the swatch next to the pattern she had chosen and trying to imagine how she would look in the finished dress. Anything would be an improvement over what she'd been wearing, of course, and she indulged in a small fantasy about appearing in the gown and seeing the look of approval in Cal Stevens's startlingly blue eyes . . .

Good heavens! What on earth had inspired such vanity? She felt herself blushing and turned quickly away from Nancy's questioning stare. "We'd better hurry, Espy. The gentlemen will be wondering what has become of us."

Within minutes they were out on the street again. Espy seemed blissfully unaware of Leah's lapse and chattered happily about the things she'd be buying in the general store.

Leah hurriedly made the necessary purchases, concerned that Brad and Mr. Stevens might return at any moment and catch them selecting ladies' undergarments. Espy took her time over the shoes, however, so Leah was unoccupied when Mead Garland entered the store.

"Leah, what a nice surprise," he said, greeting her with a dazzling smile.

She hadn't encountered her former beau in several weeks and then only at church on the monthly Sunday when the preacher was in town. She was equally pleased to see him and gave him her hand. "Mead, you're looking well."

Indeed he was, well and prosperous, as the only attorney in town had every right to. His suit had obviously been tailor-made and showed off his gold watch chain to perfection. Until she'd met Cal Stevens, she had always thought Mead a tall man, but now he seemed shorter somehow. She noticed he was thickening a little around the waist, too, and his brown hair had thinned a bit, although at thirty he was still far from middle-aged. He was also still as charming as ever, and just as free with his compliments, too.

"And you, my dear Leah, are looking much better than well. Do I dare hope you have emerged from mourning permanently?"

"I believe I have," she declared recklessly, thinking she could never bring herself to don black again.

Mead's chocolate brown eyes were dancing with delight. "Perhaps you'll even allow me to call on you again and renew my offer of marriage?" he teased.

"Don't make a fool of yourself, Mead Garland," she scolded. "If you aren't careful, I might accept and then where would you be?"

"Married to the most beautiful woman in Texas," he declared gallantly. "I've never recovered from the disappointment of losing you, you know."

"I can tell you've been wasting away," she replied just as outrageously.

He laughed, patting his slight paunch. "No one trusts a skinny lawyer, Leah. I have to look lazy for professional reasons."

"Of course," Leah agreed. It felt good to laugh and tease, even with Mead.

Or especially with Mead, a tiny voice warned her. You may soon regret not having married him when you had the chance if that little tart throws you out of your home.

"Miss Harding, what do you think of these?" Espy called from across the store, holding up a high-button shoe of butter yellow for her inspection.

"I'm afraid it would clash with your gown," Leah replied, her high spirits evaporating. "Why don't you get brown?"

"Brown is so boring," Espy complained. "I know, I'll get both!"

Of course, Leah thought.

"Who is that?" Mead inquired in a startled whisper.

"Espy Wilkes," Leah replied, also in a whisper.

"Wilkes?"

"Homer Wilkes's daughter."

Recognition dawned and was quickly followed by surprise. Mead was much too well-bred to ask what on earth Leah was doing advising the girl on her purchases, but the question burned in his eyes. Leah could think of no reason not to answer it either, since soon the whole county would know anyway.

"Espy and Brad are going to be married soon. Very soon."

"Brad? Your Brad?" he asked in astonishment.

Leah nodded resignedly.

"But he's just a boy! Leah what are you thinking of to allow this?"

Leah drew a deep breath and let it out in a sigh. "I'm not 'allowing' anything, Mead. If Brad doesn't marry her soon, her father will be after him with a shotgun."

"A shot . . .?" Mead's eyes grew large. "My God," he murmured.

"Exactly."

"Oh, Leah, I'm so sorry. You must be beside yourself."

Before Leah could answer, Espy was beside her,

showing her the two pairs of shoes she had selected. "Wait'll my sisters see these. They'll pure-dee die of jealousy." She noticed Mead looking slightly shocked. "Who's he?"

Leah refused to be as rude as the girl. "This is Mr. Mead Garland, Espy. Mr. Garland, this is Miss Espy Wilkes."

Mead sketched a small bow while Espy considered him gravely. "Pleased to meet you, Miss Wilkes."

"You're that lawyer fellow, ain't you?" she asked.

"Indeed," he replied, refusing to be nonplussed. "May I congratulate you on your coming nuptials?"

"You could if I knew what they were," Espy replied with a sly smile that Leah realized with a start was supposed to be flirtatious.

"Your wedding," Leah explained, not the least amused, although Mead appeared to be.

"Oh, yeah, thanks," she said smugly, batting her eyes. "Me and Brad are getting hitched just any day now. Maybe you'll come to the wedding."

Mead gave Leah a questioning look. She hadn't really planned to invite anyone except the immediate family to the ceremony, but having an old friend by her side for the ordeal would be comforting. "The wedding will be private, but we would be pleased if you would join us. *I* would be pleased," she added, in case he thought she was only being polite.

"In that case, I would be honored. When is the happy day?"

"We don't know yet, but we'll send you word as soon as we do," Leah said. From the corner of her eye, she saw someone entering the store, and Espy started waving.

"We're over here, Brad!" she called.

Brad and Cal Stevens were striding down the aisle toward them—good heavens! They even walked alike!—and Brad was grinning broadly. "I see you've met Espy, Mr. Garland. Did Leah tell you we're getting married?"

"She certainly did. May I wish you happiness?"

"You sure may," Brad said, clasping Mead's hand and pumping it enthusiastically. Leah didn't know if she could keep up the pretense much longer and was just going to suggest they should be going when she noticed Mead and Stevens eyeing each other warily.

"Oh, I'm sorry. Mead, this is Cal Stevens. Mr. Stevens, Mead Garland. Mr. Garland is our attorney and an old friend of the family."

Mead obviously recognized Stevens's name. Stevens didn't offer to shake hands, and strangely, neither did Mead. The two merely nodded in instant, mutual distrust. Leah was just thinking how odd that was when Brad said, "Yeah, Mr. Garland's an old friend all right, and you and him have got something in common, Cal. Mr. Garland was engaged to Leah once a long time ago, and Cal's engaged to Leah now."

Chapter Three

Leah couldn't be sure who was more surprised in the awful moment that followed. Naturally, Espy was the first to find her tongue.

"Ain't that something? Brad, you never said a word! No wonder he come with you this morning. Maybe we oughta have a double wedding!"

"We aren't . . . *officially* engaged," Leah managed, giving Brad a look that would have killed him on the spot if he'd been paying any attention. She didn't dare look at Cal Stevens.

"Then I'll reserve my congratulations," Mead said, ever the gentleman, although she could sense how stunned he was by the announcement. "How strange I've never seen you around before, Stevens."

Leah winced, wondering what on earth Stevens would say, but he didn't say anything until she finally looked at him. Once again he was waiting for her lead! "Uh, Mr. Stevens and I met in Dallas, last winter," she said, hoping that was the same story she'd given Brad. "He's just . . . visiting for a while."

"I see," Mead said, although he obviously didn't.

Plainly, he did not understand how Leah had gotten involved with a notorious gunfighter, but he was too polite to inquire, at least in front of other people.

"Brad, why don't you take Espy to the counter so she can have her purchases wrapped?" Leah said, hoping to break up this uncomfortable group and hasten their departure before Brad could make any more unfortunate explanations.

"Oh, Brad, wait'll you see whatall I got," Espy chirped, clasping his arm to draw him away. " 'Course some of the things you can't see until after we're married." Leah tried not to wince at the girl's coy giggle.

To Leah's surprise, Stevens said, "I reckon you've got some things to talk about. I'll get the buggy and bring it around," and left her alone to sort things out with Mead.

Would she ever get used to a man who didn't have to run every show? She was still speechless with amazement at his consideration when Mead said, "Leah?"

"Oh, Mead, I'm sorry. You must be terribly confused, and I wish I could enlighten you, but the story is entirely too complicated to explain here." Especially with Brad within earshot, she thought.

"And I have no intention of meddling in your affairs, Leah, but as an old friend and also as your attorney, I believe I have a right to be concerned for your welfare. I don't know how long you've known this Stevens, but I hope you're aware that—"

"I'm aware of everything," Leah assured him hastily, watching Brad and Espy out of the corner of her eye to see if they were listening. "Rest assured, you need not be concerned. I have no intention of marrying Cal Stevens or anyone else."

He seemed relieved, but he was still confused. "Then why did Brad—?"

"I told you, it's too complicated. I'll explain the whole thing later." She gave him what she hoped was a reassuring smile.

"Leah, if there's a problem or you're in some kind of trouble—"

"No, nothing like that." Leah patted his arm. "Now walk me outside." He obliged, although he was still puzzled and extremely curious. As they passed the young couple at the counter, Leah urged them to hurry along.

"You know I'm more than willing to help," Mead said when they were outside on the wooden sidewalk. "I can't imagine a situation I couldn't handle for you, Leah, and whatever it is, you can't possibly need to hire a gunfighter to solve it."

"I haven't hired Mr. Stevens." Leah should have appreciated Mead's concern, but when she recalled the confidence Stevens had shown for her ability to clean up her own messes, she couldn't help feeling annoyed by Mead's attempted interference. Instinctively, she searched the street for the buggy and felt amazingly comforted at the sight of Cal Stevens driving it up to the store.

His Stetson shaded his eyes so she couldn't read his expression, but his mouth was set in a grim line. Evidently, he didn't appreciate Mead's interference any more than she did. The thought made her smile, even as Mead frowned at Stevens's approach.

Mead didn't speak again, probably because he didn't want to speak in front of Stevens, then Brad and Espy came out. When Stevens climbed out of the buggy, they climbed in. Before Leah joined them, she turned back to Mead.

"It was very nice to see you, Mead. Don't forget about the wedding. I'll send you word as soon as we've set the date."

"I'm looking forward to it," he replied, but without much enthusiasm. His dark eyes still held questions Leah couldn't begin to answer, and she wondered if he would wait until the wedding before confronting her with them.

Her annoyance grew. What gave Mead Garland the right to question her in the first place? How strange that she had never noticed how overbearing he could be.

On the way home, Leah found herself glancing repeatedly at the tall figure riding beside the buggy, and several times she caught Stevens's eye as he glanced back. Each time they both quickly looked away, but Leah felt the impact of his gaze long afterwards and wondered why. Surely, she was above being charmed by a man simply because he was good-looking and treated her with a little consideration.

But if she wasn't charmed, why had he suddenly assumed such an important place in her life?

Brad and Espy decided to drop Leah off at the ranch so Brad could take Espy home and spend the afternoon with her. Since Leah was grateful not to have to face the Wilkes ranch or Homer Wilkes again so soon, she readily agreed. She stood in the yard and stared after the buggy as it disappeared in a cloud of dust, wondering after listening to Espy babble inanely

83

all the way home if she had done the right thing after all.

"Did you get things straightened out with your friend?" Cal Stevens asked, startling her. She hadn't realized he had approached her. He was still holding his horse by its reins.

"My friend?"

"The lawyer."

"Oh, Mead." Leah looked up at Stevens, surprised at just exactly how tall he was and at how small and delicate she felt next to him. "I didn't feel I could go into the whole story, so I just told him we weren't really going to be married."

Now Stevens was surprised. "And he was satisfied with that?"

"He has no right to be dissatisfied," Leah snapped. "He's just a friend of the family."

"Brad said you were engaged." The news did not seem to please him.

"That was seven years ago. It's over and done."

"Did he ever marry?"

What did that have to do with anything? "No."

He humphed, as if that proved something. Good heavens, did he imagine Mead was still carrying a torch for her after all this time?

"Many men never marry out here, Mr. Stevens, because of the shortage of women. You never did."

"I never had a chance to, which is why I can't figure out why this Garland fellow would've let you go."

Leah wasn't sure whether she had been complimented or not. The possibility that she had been disturbed her. "He didn't let me go. I was the one who broke the engagement. When my father died, Brad was my responsibility, and I didn't think it would be fair to burden a husband with it."

Stevens considered this. "Any man worth his salt would've welcomed a burden like that."

"Maybe you're judging other men by your own unusual situation, Mr. Stevens. At the moment you want your son, so you can't imagine anyone else thinking he might be a burden."

"Did Garland think he was?"

Leah looked away, uncomfortable under Stevens's penetrating gaze. "I . . . I didn't ask him."

"You didn't ask him?" he echoed in amazement. "You mean you just broke it off without finding out?"

Now Leah truly was annoyed. "I can't see where this is any of your business, Mr. Stevens."

"And he let you go without a fight?" he continued, as if she hadn't spoken.

"What kind of a fight could a gentleman put up when a lady has broken their engagement?" she demanded tartly.

"A big one if he's got any gumption at all. Hell, I'd . . ."

"You'd what?" she asked when he hesitated.

"Nothing." She couldn't be sure, but she thought he'd gone a dull red beneath his tan, as well he should. Who did he think he was, questioning her like that? "You're right, it's none of my business. Look, since I'll be around for a few more days at least, why don't you put me to work? With Quincy gone, you're shorthanded and—"

"All right," Leah said, a little disconcerted by the abrupt change of subject but glad for it just the same.

"What?"

"I said, all right." Leah thought it would be a good idea to keep him as busy as possible during his stay here. Since Brad would be absorbed with his bride, the two of them would therefore have little chance to get close. "You can ride out with one of the other men tomorrow to get the lay of the land."

He nodded. Leah thought their conversation was over, but he made no move to leave, and she found she didn't particularly want him to, either. It was just the prospect of going into that big, empty house knowing Brad was off with a silly girl, she told herself.

"Was there something else?" she prodded.

"I don't reckon you'll want me for supper unless the boy's here."

The thought of sitting in the huge dining room all alone made her shudder, but of course Stevens wouldn't be interested in coming to the house except to see Brad. She shouldn't have expected anything else, so why did she feel so disappointed? "There's no sense in keeping up the pretense unless Brad is here," she agreed stiffly.

He nodded again, his sky blue eyes not quite meeting hers. "Let me know if you need anything," he said and started away, leading his horse toward the corral.

Watching his long-legged stride—so like Brad's, she wanted to cry—she resisted the urge to call him back. Hugging herself against the sudden chill of loneliness, she forced herself to turn toward the empty house. She was actually beginning to look forward to the wedding. At least when Brad was married, he'd be home again.

Then the only thing Leah would have to worry

about was whether he would allow her to continue living here, too.

The days until the wedding passed in a blur of activity during which time Leah saw little of either Cal Stevens or her brother. Although she doubted Espy Wilkes would know the difference, Leah's pride demanded she have the place spotless for Brad's wife, so she and Juanita scrubbed the house from top to bottom.

In the process, Leah discovered Brad's old cradle. She and Juanita washed the years of grime off it and lovingly oiled and polished the fine wood until it glowed. Brad was delighted when he discovered it in the corner of his bedroom on one of his brief visits home.

"Espy's gonna love it," he predicted.

"I haven't changed the curtains in here or anything," Leah explained. "I suppose Espy will want to make her own decisions about colors."

Brad shrugged. "This'll probably be good enough for her," he predicted, looking around at the utilitarian muslin hanging in the windows. "She ain't used to much, you know."

Remembering Espy's requests for her wedding dress, Leah had an idea that in spite of her modest background, Espy had some plans of her own that extended far beyond muslin. She wouldn't be at all surprised if the new Mrs. Harding's first trip to town resulted in something like red velvet.

The wedding had been set for Saturday. Since the newlyweds wouldn't be taking a honeymoon, at least the men would be away from the ranch for the night, giving them as much privacy as possible. The prospect of spending the weekend alone with the lovers had Leah wishing she had someplace to go, too.

The Wilkes family arrived bright and early on Saturday morning. Espy had taken some effort to make the younger children presentable, although she could do nothing to provide them with clothes other than the flour sack garments she had made for them herself. At least they were clean, even though Leah didn't hold out much hope they would remain so for long when she saw the way they scampered out of the wagon and ran off to explore the outbuildings. Their father hardly seemed to notice. He was more interested in taking stock of those buildings, as if he were trying to figure out what the place might be worth. Leah ignored him.

"You look very nice, Espy," Leah told her when Espy too had climbed out of the wagon.

Instead of returning the compliment — Leah was feeling very elegant in her new lavender gown — Espy looked down at her own green silk dress. "It ain't very fancy," she said in disgust. "I told her I wanted some feathers. I don't know why I couldn't have feathers if I wanted them."

"But the lace is lovely," Leah said, holding her pleasant smile with difficulty. "I have a cameo that would look perfect with it, too. It belonged to my mother."

Espy didn't seem to notice Leah hadn't said "Brad's mother," but Leah caught herself and wondered at the way she had already stopped thinking of her parents as Brad's parents.

"I don't suppose you've got any diamonds," Espy said, unimpressed. "I think I'd like to have me some diamonds."

Just how rich did she think Brad was? "I'm sorry, no diamonds."

Espy shrugged and glanced around. "Where's Brad anyways?"

"He's in the bunkhouse, getting ready. It's bad luck for the groom to see the bride before the wedding, and we thought you'd be more comfortable in the house. You can use his room, which will be your room, too, after you're married. Come on, I'll show you." With a singular lack of enthusiasm, Espy followed Leah into the house, leaving her father and her siblings to fend for themselves.

Leah might have expected the girl to be awed by the enormity of the Harding home, but she would have been wrong. Espy looked around with a critical eye, as if she owned the place and were passing judgment on how the present tenants had been caring for it.

"You could sure have a party in here," she remarked as they made their way through the large front room.

"I thought we'd have the ceremony in front of the fireplace," Leah said.

Espy nodded absently, apparently not even noticing the tulle Leah and Juanita had draped across the mantle or the brass candlesticks they'd polished to a mirror finish.

Resignedly, Leah led the girl down the hall to Brad's bedroom, which was, Leah suddenly realized, right next to her own and which would give the newlyweds precious little privacy. Thinking she would probably be able to hear every sweet nothing the lovebirds whispered to each other, Leah began to seriously doubt the wisdom of her decision to let them marry in the first place. Keep thinking about the baby, she told herself as she ushered Espy into Brad's bedroom.

"I'll have Juanita bring you some hot water so you can wash up. The minister is in the bunkhouse with the men, but I'll send someone to fetch him so you can speak to him."

"Why would I want to speak to the preacher?" Espy asked, pausing in her tour of the room.

"I . . . I thought you might have some questions about the ceremony or something," Leah offered.

"No, so don't send him in here. I don't fancy talking to no Bible thumper if I don't have to. He'd probably just tell me I'm a sinner or something."

Leah thought she might be right. "Is there anything else you need?"

Espy was checking the drawers and had found the ones Leah had emptied for her. "You might have somebody bring my clothes in from the wagon. I can get unpacked while I'm waiting."

The prospect seemed to delight her, and she actually rubbed her hands together in anticipation.

Etiquette demanded that Leah stay with the girl, but then etiquette also imagined that a young bride would have fears to allay and nervousness to overcome. Since Espy exhibited none of those emotions, Leah felt justified in leaving her to her exploration of her new home. "I'll have your clothes brought in, then I'll see if I can find the cameo I promised you," she said and made her escape.

Leah had just gone outside and instructed one of the cowboys to carry Espy's bundle of clothing into the house when she heard a rider approaching. Squinting into the distance, she recognized Pete Quincy. With a start, she realized she'd all but forgotten about sending him on his quest.

Apprehensively, she glanced at the bunkhouse where Stevens would be keeping Brad company while they waited for the wedding. She had an impulse to summon Stevens so he could be here to meet Pete and hear the verdict in person, and she called herself a fool. What was wrong with her? She'd sent Pete out to check up on the man, and common sense demanded she hear the report in private. Pete might be going to tell her he was a complete fraud, so why did she have this overwhelming desire to have Stevens by her side when she heard his report?

She would have thought her disturbing interest in the man would have faded by now. She'd hardly seen him since he'd been helping out around the ranch during the day. There had also been no need to foster the fiction that she and Stevens were "friends" since Brad had spent virtually every waking moment at the Wilkes place, so she hadn't seen him in the evenings, either. Some distant part of her mind recalled the adage about absence making the heart grow fonder, but she dismissed it as Pete rode into the yard.

"What in blazes is going on?" he demanded the moment he was within earshot. She followed his gaze to the children swinging from the corral poles and sighed.

"You're just in time, Pete. We're having a wedding."

"Brad and the Wilkes girl?" Pete asked as he walked his horse over to where she stood on the porch steps and swung wearily down from the saddle. From the trail dirt and the shadows under his eyes, she suspected he'd ridden straight back from San Antonio without stopping.

"Oh, Pete," she said in dismay, "you didn't have to wear yourself out."

"I figured you'd want to hear all about him as quick as you could." He glanced around as if expecting to see Stevens standing in her shadow. "Where is he?"

"In the bunkhouse holding the groom's hand." Leah felt a headache coming on. "Please tell me you've got good news for me."

Pete grunted. "Don't know what you'd consider good news. Do you want it right here on the doorstep?"

Leah motioned for one of the cowboys who were loitering around the yard to take Pete's horse. "Let's go to my office."

Pete grunted again when he saw the draping over the fireplace — at least he'd noticed! — and followed her into the small room off the parlor. She closed the door and pointed to a chair.

Sitting down with a weary sigh, Pete scratched his beard and looked at Leah through narrowed eyes. "It's your dress," he concluded. "I thought you looked different. You've did something to your hair, too."

Leah couldn't keep from touching her curls self-consciously and resisted the urge to ask Pete if he thought she looked all right. He might very well tell her she didn't, and then what would she do? "I couldn't see Brad married in black, now could I?" she defended herself, then got to the point. "So what did you find out about Stevens."

Pete shook his head. "About what you told me, or

what he told you, I expect. He's got a sister still living in town, and the girl's folks are there, too. They all told me the same thing. Stevens got the girl in a family way, then went to war without ever knowing. The girl's folks are still mad about the whole thing. Seems she took the money your pa gave her and run off to New Orleans or someplace. They never heared a word from her again and figure she's dead or something, and it's all Stevens's fault."

"How could it be his fault if he didn't know anything about it?" Leah asked, slightly outraged.

Pete's bushy eyebrows went up a notch. "If he hadn't planted the seed, there wouldn't've been no trouble in the first place," he reminded her, making her flush. "Seems like you've gone over to his side all of a sudden, too."

"I'm not on anyone's 'side,'" she protested, but even she could tell she was protesting too much. "If he's Brad's father, and it appears he is, then he's family, in a way, and he's certainly made himself useful around here. You should have seen the way he handled Wilkes."

"*He* handled him?" Pete echoed smugly. "I thought he wasn't like your pa."

"He's not," Leah told him just as smugly. "He merely intimidated the man while I took care of the situation."

Pete glanced toward the window through which they could see the Wilkes children swarming over the yard. "Looks like you took care of things right and proper."

Yes, Leah was definitely getting a headache. "Pete, I couldn't let Brad's child grow up with those people."

"So you've took them under your own roof."

"Just the girl!" she said in exasperation.

"And what about Stevens?"

"What about him?"

"What's he gonna do?"

Once again Leah was surprised to discover she had no idea but that she certainly hadn't given a moment's thought to his leaving. Thinking of it now depressed her. "If he's Brad's father—"

"Just 'cause he tumbled some girl in a hayloft don't make him Brad's father," Pete said, nearly as exasperated as she. "Not his real father, leastways. A man can't just show up one day and claim a kid as his own after other folks have done all the crying and praying and slaving to make sure he turns out right."

He was right, of course. "Which is probably why Mr. Stevens hasn't allowed me to even mention the subject to Brad. He doesn't want to claim Brad, he just wants to get to know him."

Pete made a rude noise. "Looks like he's took you in good and proper. I always thought you had better sense, but looks like you're turning into a silly female after all."

Leah refused to be baited into an argument that would only prove Pete's charge. "Perhaps you should reserve your judgment until you've had a chance to get to know Mr. Stevens yourself. And now, I've got a wedding to attend, Pete, and so do you."

Pete groaned as he pulled himself out of his chair. "Just give me a few minutes to get cleaned up."

"We'll wait until you're ready." Leah suddenly remembered she had a cameo broach to find and hurried off.

By the time she had located it and presented it to Espy, who still wanted diamonds, Mead Garland had arrived. He burst into the house with all the cheerful good will she could have wanted in a wedding guest, and her spirits instantly lifted.

"Leah, you look magnificent," he declared, holding her at arm's length so he could get the full effect. "I do believe you're prettier now than when I proposed to you seven years ago."

Leah knew blatant flattery when she heard it, but she was gratified nevertheless and found herself wondering what Mr. Stevens would think of her appearance. Hastily pushing the thought aside, she asked, "Have you been to the bunkhouse?"

"Oh, yes, and the groom is getting restless, I can tell you. I wouldn't recommend delaying much longer."

"Well, then, would you be so kind as to summon the gentlemen and the Wilkes family, and I'll prepare the bride."

Espy was pouty with boredom by the time Leah got to her, and they needed no announcement to tell them the rest of the party had arrived. The Wilkes children were shrieking with excitement, and Leah winced at the sound of something heavy crashing to the floor. She was halfway out the door to intervene when an authoritative shout from the front room stopped her.

The voice was familiar, although she'd never heard it raised in anger before, and the silence that followed made her smile. Perhaps Cal Stevens had more claim to fatherly instincts than he thought.

"Sounds like you've got yourself quite a man, Miss Harding," Espy said slyly. "I've never known them younguns to quit for nobody."

Leah wanted to groan, but she forced herself to smile. "I'll go out and make sure everyone is in their proper places. Give me a minute, then make your entrance."

Espy's pout had vanished, and a smug grin replaced it. "I know what to do," she said with more confidence than a fifteen-year-old girl had any right to claim.

With a sigh, Leah left the room and made her way down the hall. She found her guests standing as still as statues, even the children who were huddled together as if expecting a collective blow and watching Stevens warily. Brad and the Reverend Mr. Virgil Underwood, a cheerful young man with bad skin and wearing an ill-fitting suit, stood beside the fireplace.

Leah wanted to cry out in protest when she saw how young Brad looked in his Sunday suit with his golden hair slicked back and his cheeks—still baby smooth—unnaturally pale. She offered him a wavering smile which he tried to return.

Tears prickled in her eyes, and instinctively, her gaze sought the one person here who might share her distress. She found him instantly. He stood just behind Brad, as if prepared to support his son physically as well as emotionally, and looking surprisingly natural in his brand new broadcloth suit. His deep blue eyes held the same anguish as her own.

Vaguely, she saw that the wedding guests had lined up to either side of the fireplace, with the Wilkes family on the bride's side, Cal Stevens and Mead Garland on the groom's—although they were being careful not to stand too close to each other—and the cowboys mingling in the middle. Placing a hand over the knot of apprehension in her stomach, Leah moved across the room and took her place between Stevens and Garland.

Mead smiled encouragingly to her as she passed, but she barely saw him because she was so intensely aware of Stevens. As she had once before, she felt herself drawing strength from his presence. She needed that strength a moment later when Espy appeared in the doorway.

The girl paused, striking a pose as she visibly savored the novelty of having everyone's undivided attention. Then she moved with surprising grace across the expanse of floor and into the center of the group to stand beside Brad.

Although Leah would have thought it impossible, the boy had paled even more, but his eyes were shining as he gazed appreciatively on his bride. The girl did look beautiful, Leah had to admit, although she found Espy's self-satisfied air a little off-putting.

"Dearly beloved," the minister intoned, and began the ceremony.

Strong fingers touched Leah's elbow, and startled, she looked up at Cal Stevens. His sun-darkened face was full of concern, and Leah once again felt the sting of tears. Blinking, she tried to smile reassuringly but found herself reaching for her handkerchief instead. She'd sworn she wouldn't weep like a silly female, but knowing Brad was being forced into adulthood long before he was ready and actually seeing the smug little chit who'd connived to get him there smirking up into his face was more than she could bear.

Dabbing frantically at the tears before they could fall, she heard Brad promising haltingly to love and to cherish Espy for as long as they both shall live. A very long time for one so painfully young, she thought, and the fingers still holding her elbow squeezed reassuringly.

She swallowed a sob as Espy returned Brad's pledge, her voice almost shrill with complacency. While Brad placed the ring on her finger, Leah fought for her composure and regained it just as the minister pronounced them man and wife.

Self-consciously, Brad bent to kiss his bride, and Espy threw her arms around his neck with an exaggerated enthusiasm that staggered him.

The children laughed outright while some of the cowboys coughed suspiciously, but no one on the groom's side found the display amusing. Only when Brad came up from the kiss, flushing and grinning, could Leah even force herself to smile.

"Come on, gents, time to kiss the bride," Brad announced, and the cowboys swarmed up without hesitation.

"When do we eat?" one of the younger children was whining. "Espy said we'd eat!"

No one paid him any mind. When the cowboys had each claimed the bride's favors with her hearty participation, Homer Wilkes took his turn, pumping Brad's hand and kissing his daughter's cheek as if he had thoroughly approved the match from the beginning.

"Looks like you've done all right for yourself, girl," he praised her, although Leah noticed he was looking over Espy's shoulder at the brass candlestick when he said it. Probably wondering if it was made of gold, Leah thought acidly.

"Ain't you gonna kiss the bride?" Espy called to the

two men who still flanked Leah. The girl was flushed, too, but whether from pleasure or whisker burn from the enthusiastic cowboys, Leah had no idea.

When neither of the men beside her moved, Leah went forward, feeling the loss of Stevens's touch as she went, although he followed close behind her. Brad was still grinning, and she tried to mimic his apparent joy although she still wanted to weep. For once he didn't object when she slipped her arms around him for a hug that she needed even if he didn't, and for once he hugged her back. She kissed his beardless cheek and whispered, "I love you," before she pulled away again. She hadn't said it in so many years, and although Brad said nothing in return, she saw the sentiment returned in his shining eyes.

Then he turned to Cal Stevens and shook his offered hand. Stevens murmured congratulations, and Brad slapped him on the shoulder. "Now Leah needs somebody else to take care of her, and I reckon I know who's up for the job."

Mortified, Leah quickly turned to Espy whose satisfied smirk set her teeth on edge. "Espy, welcome to the family," Leah said as graciously as she could manage and kissed the girl's cheek.

"Yeah, we're sisters now, so I reckon I can call you Leah, can't I?" Espy said.

"Certainly," Leah said, trying desperately to warm to the girl who was now Brad's wife. "I hope you'll be happy here."

"Can't figure why I wouldn't," Espy replied, but her attention had already shifted to Cal Stevens.

He was offering to shake her hand. Espy clasped it but used it to pull him close, then wrapped her other arm around his neck and pulled his face to hers. This kiss was loud, and Stevens looked as annoyed as Leah felt over the outrageous display. He pulled away and murmured something unintelligible.

Fortunately, Mead Garland had the presence of mind to step in. "May I offer my congratulations, Mrs. Harding?" he asked, bending down to peck the girl on the cheek before she could wrestle him down for anything more enthusiastic.

"Mrs. Harding," she echoed. "Now don't that sound fine? Pa, I think you'd better call me 'Mrs. Harding' from now on."

Her father snorted in derision, and the children laughed again, although Leah noticed the little one was still whining about food.

"I believe our dinner is ready, if you'll all come into the dining room," Leah said. Taking the bride and groom by the arm, she led the way and quickly got everyone seated.

The meal was an ordeal for Leah who could hardly manage to eat a bite of the food she and Juanita had spent days preparing. Everyone else seemed to enjoy it, although Leah found herself sitting too far from Cal Stevens to judge the genuineness of his smile. At least she had Mead Garland at her elbow making pleasant conversation to distract her. He even got up and made a toast to the bride and groom at the appropriate moment.

After the meal was finally over, the guests went outside so the men could smoke. Espy and Brad sat on the porch, holding court, while Leah strolled restlessly up and down, longing for the guests to leave so she could retire to her room with a cold rag on her forehead.

She was at the far end of the porch when Homer Wilkes intercepted her.

"Well, now, looks like we're family whether we like it or not," he said with a feral smile that revealed yellowed teeth.

Leah didn't bother to return the smile. "So it would seem."

He glanced around. "Always figured me and mine deserved something better. Ain't fair the way some folks got everything and others got nothing."

"Everything the Hardings have, we've worked for, Mr. Wilkes," Leah said, holding her temper with difficulty. She wanted to order the man off her property, but since his daughter had just married her brother, that would hardly have been appropriate.

"And what're *you* gonna do now that your brother don't need you to work for him no more?" he asked slyly.

"What do you mean?" Leah asked, feeling the first prickle of alarm.

"I mean a growed man with a wife and family don't need his sister to play nursemaid to him anymore. Seems like he wouldn't *want* her around neither."

Leah opened her mouth to reply, but before she could utter a word, a presence loomed at her elbow, and Cal Stevens said, "Miss Harding, is anything wrong?"

He hopped nimbly up onto the porch beside her, his height comfortingly imposing. Wilkes stiffened, but he refused to back down.

"I can't see where Brad needs no hired gun, neither," he said.

"I told you, Mr. Stevens is a friend of the family," Leah said, her voice tight with fury.

Stevens was keeping his own emotions well hidden, but his eyes were cold. "Did you have some business with Miss Harding?"

Wilkes silently debated his answer before admitting, "No, I reckon I'm finished,"

"Then you'd best see to your children." He nodded toward where two of them were rolling in the dust nearby in what was apparently a life and death struggle.

"Hey!" Wilkes shouted, jumping off the porch.

The instant he was gone, Stevens turned to her. "Are you all right?"

"I would be if I could just murder something," Leah replied through lips stiff with fury.

Stevens smiled the glorious smile that always took Leah's breath. "Something named Wilkes, maybe?" he suggested.

Suddenly, the anger drained out of her, and Leah felt herself smiling back at him, but before she could reply, Mead Garland was with them.

"What's the matter?" he demanded. "What was Wilkes saying to you?"

The memory still galled her. "He was remarking that Brad no longer needs a sister to take care of him."

Mead glanced at Stevens, as if waiting for him to say or do something. When he didn't, Mead said, "That's nonsense, Leah. You shouldn't let the man disturb you."

"It's not true either, is it?" Stevens said. She and Mead looked at him in surprise. "I mean, she's the boy's legal guardian until he's twenty-one, isn't she?"

Of course, Leah hadn't thought of that! Brad would still need her, and . . . But Mead was shaking his head and frowning gravely.

"Ordinarily, yes, but when a man marries, he's considered legally an adult, no matter what his age."

Leah's heart sank as she began to consider what this might mean to her. Brad now owned the Rocking Horse Ranch outright and could do with it what he pleased, and he had a wife who seemed unlikely to appreciate the presence of his spinster sister.

"So the boy owns the ranch outright now?" Stevens was saying.

Mead glanced at Leah, obviously uncomfortable discussing the family's private business with a stranger, but she nodded her consent.

"Yes," he said, though still reluctant.

"Does Wilkes know this?" Stevens asked.

"I have no idea," Mead said. They both looked at Leah, and she thought she saw sympathy in their gazes. All three of them were beginning to understand the real ramifications of this wedding.

"And who gets the ranch if something happens to the boy?" Stevens asked after a moment.

Leah was startled that such a thing would have occurred to him, but Mead didn't seem disturbed at all by the question, only displeased at the answer he was giving.

"His heirs will get it . . . his wife and children."

Stevens's expression hardened, although Leah could not have said what emotion he was concealing behind his hooded eyes, and she was too preoccupied with her own to worry about it. She had been right when she'd felt like a helpless female at the mercy of her male relatives, and Brad was already making noises about not needing her anymore. Of course, he still thought Stevens was romantically interested in her, but perhaps that was just a convenience that fell in with his own plans to be rid of her. Well, this was still her home, and no one had the right to . . .

"Miss Leah?" Pete called from the yard.

Grateful for the distraction, Leah turned to him.

"Me and the boys'll be heading for town now if you don't need us for anything else." Saturday night in town was a time-honored tradition.

"No, go ahead, and have a good time," she called back, fighting to recover her hostess smile. If the men were leaving, she could safely run the Wilkes family off, too. She turned back to Stevens and Garland. "If you'll excuse me, gentlemen, I must see to my other guests."

She hurried off, not wanting to see the pity in their eyes. Wilkes was skulking near the porch steps, watching her suspiciously. "I'm sure you'll want to take some of the leftovers from the wedding supper with you, Mr. Wilkes. There's more than we could possibly eat before it spoils. I'll have Juanita wrap it up if you'll bring your wagon around to the kitchen."

He obviously wasn't ready to leave just yet, but Leah had given him no choice. Casting her a dark look, he turned away and headed for the barn where he'd left his vehicle. Within a half-hour, the Wilkes family and the minister were on their way, and Mead Garland was saying his good-byes to the newlyweds.

"I'm always at your disposal, Brad," Leah heard him say and wondered if he would continue to be so charming to her now that she was no longer legally in charge of the ranch.

As if to answer her unspoken question, he came to her and took both her hands. "I hope you'll call on me if you need anything, Leah," he said softly, for her ears alone. "The boy will need a lot of guidance. Regardless of what the law says, he still needs you."

"I hope he realizes that," she said with false brightness.

"If he doesn't, I'll remind him," Mead said gallantly. He was turning to go when he caught sight of Stevens standing nearby. "Leah, you never did explain who that man is and what he's doing here."

"I will, later, but it's not something you need concern yourself with."

He smiled. "You'll forgive me for my impertinence, but everything about you concerns me, my dear. I can't help remembering you might have been my wife, and you must know I still care what happens to you."

Once again Leah was reminded that if she had married Mead Garland she wouldn't now be worried about where she was going to live. The injustice of being female weighed on her, making it impossible for her to return his smile. "Thank you for your concern, Mead, but you mustn't worry. I'm sure I'll be fine."

He either believed her or wanted to be convinced. He took his leave, and she stayed on the porch to watch him out of sight when the newlyweds went back in the house. She was not alone for long.

"Miss Harding?"

She looked into Cal Stevens's face. From where she stood on the second step, he was a few inches shorter than she, although her momentary height advantage couldn't dispel the aura of power emanating from him or allow Leah to feel completely at ease in his presence. He was watching her, apparently as wary as she. Didn't he realize her power was gone, that she no longer had any authority over him?

"Quincy told me what he found out," he said, his deep voice stirring a chord within her which she resolutely ignored.

She nodded, hugging herself against sudden chill, and managed a small smile. "Congratulations, Mr. Stevens, it's a boy."

He didn't return her smile. "I'd like your permission to stay on for a while."

Yes, she thought, she wasn't ready for him to leave just yet, but . . . "You must realize you no longer need my permission, Mr. Stevens," she said, trying to keep the bitterness from her voice.

"The boy may own the ranch outright now, but you're still the only one with the right to say how much he can know about me."

His deference was only a small balm to her wounded pride and this time she couldn't keep from sounding bitter. "And I can now have no objections to your telling him everything."

Stevens frowned. "I don't think I want to tell him just yet. It's a pretty hard thing to hear, and he's already got a lot on his mind just now. What do you think?"

Leah was struck with the irony of having the notorious Cal Stevens, a man whose mere name struck terror in the hearts of grown men, seeking advice from Leah Harding. She *really* wished Pete Quincy were here to hear this, and her father, too. "I'm afraid I must agree with you. We have no idea if he'll be angry or happy at the news, but in either case, he'll be upset, and at the moment you're right, he really has enough to think about. Perhaps in a week or two . . ."

He was nodding, and his rugged features had relaxed in relief. "You're right, thanks."

They stood there for a moment, their conversation over but neither of them making a move to leave. Leah didn't know what held *him,* but she told herself *she* was only loath to go into the house and intrude on Brad and Espy. "I want to thank you for helping today," she said to fill the silence. "I appreciate the support you gave Brad, and I'm sure he does, too."

He grinned, and Leah realized she had been waiting to see him smile again. "He needed it, too. I was afraid we were going to lose him there for a while. I reckon he finally realized what he was getting into, and it scared the he . . . heck out of him."

"It scares the heck out of me, too," Leah admitted ruefully. "I just wish I thought she loved him."

"They're young. Maybe they'll grow into it."

Leah wondered if he really believed that, but she appreciated his attempt at comfort. "At least Brad cares for her. I don't suppose I can blame him. She is a pretty little thing when she's cleaned up."

"Not as pretty as . . ." he began but caught himself.

"As pretty as what?" she asked, wondering why he suddenly looked so disconcerted.

He shifted his weight and glanced away for a moment, as if silently debating the wisdom of answering her question. When he looked back, his expression was almost comically determined. "As pretty as you," he said almost belligerently.

It wasn't the most gracious compliment she'd ever received, but she felt herself blushing like a schoolgirl. "Me?" she echoed faintly.

"Yeah," he said gruffly, as if he were arguing with her, which told her better than anything else how unaccustomed he was to being charming. "You must know you looked more like a bride today than she did."

"Why, thank you," she murmured, self-consciously smoothing the collar of her dress and wondering why this awkwardly given flattery should mean so much more to her than Mead Garland's lavish praises. The heat from her blush was spreading to the strangest places.

They stared at each other across the inches separating them, and Leah began to imagine the warmth was radiating from his body. The eyes that were so often cold now burned like the blue heart of a flame, and for a moment Leah couldn't seem to get her breath.

How long they stood like that, staring at each other, Leah could not have said, but just when she began to think she might never breathe again, he shook his head slightly, as if waking from a dream, and said, "Well."

The spell was broken, and once again Leah felt the heat in her face. Instinctively, she retreated to the next step, and just as instinctively, Stevens moved back a pace. The new distance between them helped, and Leah found she could breathe once more, although she pressed a hand to her bosom to keep herself from panting. "Are you . . . are you going into town, too?" she asked inanely to cover her unease.

"No, I thought I'd stay around, in case you needed

anything."

"Good! I mean, thank you," she quickly corrected herself. What on earth was the matter with her? One silly compliment and she'd turned as witless as Espy. "We . . . we won't be having a formal supper tonight, so if you get hungry, just go to the kitchen and ask Juanita for something."

"Thanks," he said, but still he made no move to leave, and she wondered if he, too, had experienced that strange moment of . . . well, whatever had passed between them.

"I . . . I guess I'd better go in," she said, wondering what she would do if he asked her not to.

But of course he didn't. He didn't say anything at all, so she turned and started up the steps. She'd reached the top when he said, "Miss Harding?"

Her heart did a strange little jump in her chest, and she turned back, but he only said, "Thanks for letting me stay."

"You're quite welcome, Mr. Stevens," she said as primly as she could manage. "I only hope you've made the right decision by coming here in the first place."

"I hope so, too, Miss Harding. I hope so, too."

Having no answer, Leah fled into the house.

There she encountered Brad and Espy who were sitting on the sofa looking as if they'd just had a disagreement of some kind. Leah didn't want to know about it. She smiled perfunctorily. "I want to give the two of you as much privacy as possible, so I'll retire to my room now, and I'll tell Juanita to bring me my supper on a tray. The two of you can have the rest of the house to yourself."

Brad grinned. "Oh, I reckon we'll be going to bed, too, pretty soon."

Espy frowned, as a well-bred young lady should, and Leah flushed as any frustrated old maid would.

Frustrated? Now where had that come from? she wondered as she hurried to her room. She closed the door behind her and leaned her aching head against the smooth wood. After a moment, she realized she was listening for sounds of the newlyweds heading for their marriage bed and jerked herself upright. What on earth was wrong with her? In all her twenty-seven years, she'd never given more than a passing thought to the things that went on between husbands and wives, not even when she'd been engaged to Mead Garland.

Of course, those things had never been going on right under her nose, nor had they involved the boy she'd raised as a son. That was it, she decided, forcing herself to go over to the overstuffed chair that sat beside her wood stove and pick up the book she'd left lying there the night before. But when she'd finished two pages and suddenly realized she had no idea what she'd read because she'd been listening for the sound of footsteps in the hall, she rubbed her eyes and uttered an unladylike curse. It was going to be a long night.

Cal strolled slowly around the ranch house, being careful of his footing in the darkness. It wouldn't do to fall and have the occupants of the house hear and know he'd been skulking around in the night. Not that it was especially late, nor was he engaged in anything nefarious. No, he was just restless and being near the house seemed the most natural way to soothe that restlessness.

He supposed his unease had something to do with wedding nights. The whole concept conjured all sorts of visions bound to disturb a single man lying alone in his narrow bed, which was why he'd avoided that bed. Cal would have thought himself immune to such things, since he certainly didn't lust after the scrawny little chit his son had married today.

No, Cal's fantasies involved the woman he'd said looked more like a bride today than the bride herself, and she had, too. God, every time he saw Leah Harding, she got better-looking. It was enough to drive a man stark, staring mad. Or worse. She didn't help things by being nice to him, either. This evening when she'd thanked him, he'd needed every ounce of self-control he possessed to keep from taking her in his arms and . . .

But there was no sense in finishing the thought. If he ever did take her in his arms, he'd never get any further than that. She didn't have feelings for him, at least not the kind he had for her, and if she tolerated having him around, it was only for the boy's sake and because she needed him just now. Sometimes he wondered what might have happened if Brad hadn't gotten himself in trouble just when he did. Leah Harding probably would have sent Cal packing without ever letting him even get a look at the boy. Finding his son was all Cal had ever wanted out of this trip, and he should be grateful he'd accomplished so much and not torture himself thinking about crazy things like what life might be like if Leah Harding felt the same way about him as he felt about her.

Cal hurried around the corner of the house and tried not to wonder which window was Leah's.

Why hadn't she tried to go to sleep? Leah wondered when, at last, she heard Brad and Espy going into their bedroom. If she was asleep, she wouldn't be tempted to listen, wouldn't be *able* to listen.

She glanced at the untouched supper tray Juanita had brought her about an hour ago. She could carry it back to the kitchen and sit with Juanita for a while. But how long should she stay away? Returning too early would be worse than not going at all, and Leah had no idea how long would be long enough. Her ignorance on this particular subject was disturbing, especially when she realized Brad and Espy were already quite experienced.

Leah waited, trying not to listen while at the same time trying to judge just how soundproof the walls were. After a few moments, she relaxed when she found that all she could hear from the other room was the faintest murmur of voices. This wouldn't be so bad. She didn't suppose people talked when they made love, so she would have nothing at all to hear. Yes, everything would be just fine.

Relieved, Leah went to her dressing table and began to remove the pins from her hair. She should have done this long ago, she thought as the weight of her hair spilled free and she began to brush it the requisite one hundred strokes. If she had, she would be ready to snuggle down into her feather mattress which would muffle even the faintest noises from the room next door.

Then, suddenly, the noises from next door were no longer faint.

"Stop it, Brad!" Espy shouted.

"But we're married now. I've got a right—"

"You don't have the right to paw me if I don't want you to! Leave me alone!"

"You never minded before!"

"That was before!"

"Oh, I get it!" Brad yelled, his young voice hoarse with outrage. "Your pa was right! You just wanted to get me to marry you, and now that I have, you're—"

"That ain't true! He don't know what he's talking about. I'm just tired, is all, what with the baby and everything. Women get tired easy when they're in a family way."

"How do you know?" he challenged.

"My ma used to tell me. God knows, she was that way enough before she died."

"What does it matter if you're tired?" Brad demanded. "You don't have to do nothing but lay there."

Appalled, Leah wanted to cover her ears, but even that wouldn't block out the angry shouting.

"Leave me alone! If you really loved me, you won't be so mean to me!" Espy had burst into tears, and as disturbing as the sound was, Leah was inordinately glad to hear it. Brad wouldn't keep shouting at a weeping woman. She'd raised him to be sensitive and caring, and sure enough, the level of the voices dropped until she could no longer hear them.

Breathing a prayer of thanks, Leah raised her brush again. She'd done another twenty strokes when she heard, "And I'm sick to death of *'Leah this'* and *'Leah that.'* If she's so smart, why didn't she never catch herself a husband? Answer me that!"

Leah dropped the brush and jumped to her feet, although she had no idea what she was going to do now that she was up. She knew in the next moment.

Brad was murmuring something soothing, but Espy was having none of it. "How long's she gonna stay here, anyways?" Espy was screeching. "You don't need her no more 'cause you've got a wife now, and I hate the way she looks at me like I'm a piece of cow shit somebody dropped in her parlor."

There was more, but Leah didn't hear it, didn't allow herself to hear it. Grabbing her shawl from where it hung by the door, she fled, fairly running through the darkened house to the front room, then out the front door into the velvet silence of the night.

The voices were gone now. She was too far away to hear them, and she stood on the porch, gasping for breath. Oh, God, what have I done? What have I done? It seemed her soft-hearted decision to allow them to marry was going to end up hurting all those she had most wanted to help: Brad and the baby and, yes, even herself. This girl had shattered the comfortable world she had so carefully created for Brad and flung them all into a maelstrom of conflict.

The sob welled up in her throat, and tears scalded her eyes. What was she going to do? She had never felt so alone in her entire life, not even in those awful days before Brad had come into her life when nobody loved her. At least then she'd had hope that someday she wouldn't be alone anymore, that someday someone would care for her, but now she knew no one ever would. She didn't even have Brad anymore.

"Miss Leah?" The voice startled her, and she wanted to run from it because she couldn't let anyone see her like this, but then he was there, looming over her in the darkness, huge and strong and compelling.

"Miss Leah?" he said again when she didn't answer, "What's wrong?" Before she could tell him, he touched her. Just the lightest touch, his hands on her shoulders, gentle and caring and so tender she couldn't bear it another moment, and the tears poured out of her. In the next instant she was in his arms, weeping against Cal Stevens's broad chest.

Chapter Four

Cal knew he must be dreaming, but if he was, it was by far the most vivid dream he'd had yet. Leah Harding was in his arms, soft and sweet and clinging, her glorious hair a gossamer curtain down her back. Ever so carefully, he enfolded her, afraid she might evaporate in his grasp, but she was only too real, too enticing. He spread his hands on her back, marveling at how fragile she felt and how warm through the fabric of her dress.

Hardly daring to breathe, he savored her nearness, acutely aware of every place where he touched her and even more acutely aware of every place she touched him. Vaguely, he realized she was crying, although the thought of Leah Harding weeping was so difficult to conceive, he hardly trusted his own senses. What could have shattered her rigid composure, he couldn't imagine, so he simply held her, inhaling the tantalizing floral scent of her hair and tangling his fingers in the silken strands.

Oh, God, what sweet torment, and the torment became torture when her delicate little hands crept around to clutch at his waist. She was hugging him back! Desire knifed through him, weakening his knees and sending the blood roaring to his head. The night swirled around him, and he lay his cheek against her hair. Tentatively at first, he brushed his face against it.

How many times had he imagined what it would be like to wrap her hair around him, to trail it across his naked chest or see it spread out on a pillow beneath him? Suppressing a groan, he turned his face until his lips touched her temple. Her scent engulfed him, and he pulled her closer until he could feel the lushness of her breasts against his chest.

In another moment she would come to her senses and realize he had no right to hold her like this, but until then Cal would revel in her nearness and store up each and every memory for all the lonely nights ahead. Her skin beneath his lips was like warm satin, and he trailed his mouth down to the shell of her ear. This was, he decided, the closest he would ever get to heaven.

Leah emerged slowly from her fog of misery. Her anguish spent against Cal Stevens's broad chest, she felt drained and weak and immensely comforted. How long had it been since anyone had offered her solace? Too long, she thought, and she couldn't remember ever being held like this, as if she were something precious to be cherished. She felt his warm breath and the delicious scrape of whiskers against her cheek, and the sensation sent shivers down her spine.

Gradually, she became aware that her hands rested on his waist and of how firm his body felt through the fabric of his shirt. Firm and warm and agonizingly real, as real as the chest against which her tears were drying and her breasts were straining as if they would burst free of her bodice.

And someone's heart was pounding like a sledge-hammer until Leah could feel each beat reverberating through her, and she thought how odd it was she hadn't noticed her stays were so tight because now she could hardly breathe. But someone was breathing because she could hear the rasping sound against her ear, and it sent chills racing over her, but she wasn't cold because the chills were hot, and she was hot all over, especially where his lips were touching her face.

His lips shouldn't be touching her face, she thought vaguely. He shouldn't be touching her at all, but somehow that wasn't terribly important anymore, although she did wonder why he was kissing her ear, because he *was* kissing her ear, as difficult as that was to believe. She didn't want him to stop, but she did want to know why he was doing it, but when she lifted her face to ask him, his mouth closed over hers, silencing her question. It didn't matter, though, because she knew why then, and it was the same reason she was kissing him back.

His arms tightened around her, pulling her inexorably against the hardness of his body until her straining breasts flattened against his chest and the pounding of the heart — his or hers? seemed to shake her very soul. Instinctively, she wrapped her arms around his waist, clinging as if for her very life because she thought surely she was drowning in the surging swirl of emotion. She couldn't breathe, couldn't see, couldn't think. Only feeling remained, and she felt everything: the demand of his mouth, the solid strength of his body, and the raging fires of want. The kiss went on and on until even the darkness went black, and Leah began to sink into the foaming, racing tide of desire.

Then, suddenly, it was over. His mouth left hers, and for a moment they both stood gasping, their breaths mingling and their hands clinging. Leah had been right, she really was laced too tightly because she couldn't even draw a full breath, or perhaps that was because he still held her so closely. What on earth was he doing?

Before she could ask, his whole body went rigid. He murmured a horrified, "Oh, God!" and literally shoved her away. Startled, Leah stumbled and caught herself against the wall of the house. Then she gaped at him in mortified disbelief while she frantically tried to catch her breath. What in heaven's name had happened to her? She felt as if she had run a mile when she hadn't moved an inch.

He seemed to be having just as much trouble breathing as she. Only after what seemed an eternity could she speak again, and by then she had realized just how thoroughly he had insulted her; "Just what . . . do you think . . . you're doing?" she demanded, although the effect of her outrage was somewhat diluted by her breathless condition.

"Look, I didn't mean . . . That was a mistake . . ." he stammered, a little more in control of his lungs than she, but not much.

"It most certainly *was* a mistake!" she exclaimed, stiffening her spine in an attempt at dignity, although it was much too dark for him to see her clearly. She only wished she could see *him* clearly. Was he laughing at her? Oh, Lord, if he was . . . "How dare you take advantage of me like that!"

"I told you it was a mistake. It never would've happened if you hadn't been crying and—"

119

"I wasn't crying!" Leah lied, now totally humiliated. How could she have behaved so idiotically? "And how dare you suggest I was to blame for this . . . this *outrage?*"

Her demand seemed to take him off guard, but he recovered quickly. "Now wait just a minute, you were so crying, and you're at least a little to blame from the way you threw yourself at me—"

"*Threw* myself!" she cried, beyond outrage.

"Yeah, *threw* yourself," he confirmed mercilessly. "And I didn't notice you fighting any, either. In fact—"

"*Stop it!*" she shrieked and instantly covered her mouth in horror. What on earth had come over her? She was behaving like an hysterical female, the kind of woman she most detested.

But at least she had silenced his absurd accusations. Now he simply stood, arms akimbo, waiting. Briefly, she considered trying to escape, but he stood between her and the front door, and she doubted he'd stand idly by while she darted around him. Calling for Brad was out of the question, too. If he could hear her, he'd already be on his way, and he wasn't likely to appreciate her interrupting his wedding night to mediate a dispute about who had kissed whom in a moment of insanity.

"Mr. Stevens," she began in her most reasonable voice, although it was still slightly unsteady. She lay a hand over her clamoring heart and continued. "What . . . what just happened was most . . . regrettable, and—"

"Why *were* you crying?" he demanded suddenly. "And don't bother denying it again. My shirt's still wet from it."

Leah winced, glad the darkness hid her from his

probing gaze. "I suppose the tensions of the day finally caught up with me."

"And you expect me to believe you run outside and cry all over some man every time you have a bad day?"

"Certainly not!" she replied tartly, stung by his sarcasm. "I . . . I also overheard an argument between Brad and Espy."

"Overheard?" he asked suspiciously.

"I couldn't *help* overhearing," she hastened to explain. "His room is right beside mine, and they were . . . shouting."

"What were they shouting about that sent you out of the house like a bat out of —"

"None of your business!" she snapped. She had absolutely no intention of discussing the subject of that disagreement with Mr. Calhoun Stevens.

"I've got a right to know!"

"You have no right to anything around here, Mr. Stevens, and you'd do well to remember that!"

When she saw him stiffen again, Leah instantly regretted her harshness, but before she could say so, he said, "Does that mean you're not going to let me stay now?"

She shouldn't, she knew. He was a dangerous man, dangerous for the upheaval he could bring to Brad's life and for the upheaval he had already brought to hers and most certainly for what had just happened between them. They'd all be better off without him. She only wished she could forget how she had felt in his arms just moments ago so she could believe it. "Can you suggest any reason why I *should* let you stay?"

"Because you know I'm Brad's father, and because he

needs a man in his life right now, and I think you do, too."

"I!" she exclaimed, outraged all over again.

"Yes, because you can't tell him the things he needs to hear, but he'll listen to me."

"And how can I be sure I want him listening to you?" she demanded.

"You've sure changed your tune from this afternoon," he growled. "What happened to all that 'Thank you for your help, Mr. Stevens's stuff?"

He was right, of course. He had been of tremendous assistance to her. What might have happened if he hadn't gone with her to face Homer Wilkes, she didn't even want to imagine. "I will admit you've proven your worth so far, but I'm no longer certain I can trust you."

"Because of what just happened?"

Grateful for the darkness that hid her chagrin, Leah said, "Yes."

"All right, then, let's put our cards on the table, Miss Harding. I've been wanting to kiss you since the first day I rode in here, but you've never known it, and you never would've known it if you hadn't thrown yourself at me tonight. And don't bother denying it," he added when she would have. "We both know what happened, and you can't blame a man for forgetting himself when he's got a beautiful woman in his arms in the middle of the night, especially when she's forgetting herself, too."

Leah didn't know which part of this speech was the most astonishing. He'd wanted to kiss her from the day he'd ridden in here! He thought she was beautiful! But, she told herself sternly, none of that mattered. "I was very upset tonight."

"I figured as much," he allowed.

"It was . . . ungentlemanly of you to take advantage."

"Maybe you forgot, I was the one pushed you away."

Leah hadn't forgotten anything about that kiss. Her face burning in humiliation, she said, "Nevertheless, I couldn't possibly allow you to stay unless I have your assurance it will never happen again."

He considered her offer for a long moment. Finally, he said, "All I can promise is I won't be the one to start it."

"That will be quite sufficient," Leah said tartly. She certainly had no intention of "throwing herself" at him again, so she would be completely safe from now on.

"Then I can stay?"

Leah decided not to remind him it wasn't her decision to make. "Yes, you can stay."

If she had expected relief, she was disappointed. He seemed just as tense as ever, although she couldn't be perfectly sure without seeing his eyes. But of course, if she could see him, he would be able to see her, too, and since she had no idea how she must look at this moment, she couldn't allow that.

"It's very late," she said into the quivering silence.

"Are you sure you want to go back? They might still be fighting."

Once again he was right, although Leah had no intention of admitting it. "I'll sit up for a while. If you'll excuse me . . ."

She tried to go around him, but he didn't move out of the way, and she didn't dare try to push past him. "What were they fighting about that made you cry?"

Leah winced again. She couldn't very well explain to him they'd been quarreling about sex, nor could she admit Espy wanted to get rid of her. "It wasn't what they were arguing about so much as the fact that they were arguing at all on their wedding night," she hedged. "It made me doubt the wisdom of my decision to let them marry."

"You didn't have much choice. They'd've just run off."

She'd expected him to say he'd warned her to try to buy the girl off, and if she'd done what he'd said, none of this would've happened. That's what her father would have said, or a man like her father. "I suppose you're right," she said, wondering when he would stop surprising her. Or perhaps she was still slightly addled from his kiss. She shivered at the thought.

"You're getting cold," he observed, and she didn't correct him. "You'd better go in."

She also didn't remind him she'd been trying to do just that. Instead, she waited until he'd stepped aside, then swished by him as quickly as she could, holding her breath lest he reach out a hand and capture her again and pull her back into the warmth of his arms and . . .

But of course he did nothing of the kind. He'd promised, hadn't he? And Cal Stevens was a man of his word. Leah should have been relieved, but instead she remembered how wonderful it had been to have someone to share the pain, even for a moment. And to share other things, too.

She paused in the doorway, almost afraid he would call her back and wondering what she would do if he did. "Good night," she said.

"Good night." He would keep his word.

With a sigh, she closed the heavy door behind her.

Leah went to the kitchen and sat up far into the night, trying not to think about what had happened to her outside, until she was certain Brad and Espy were asleep. All was quiet when she finally crept back down the hallway to her room. She slept fitfully, haunted by dreams of men who kissed her then ran away before she could see their faces, but in spite of her restless night, she was up early the next morning. Gratefully, she left her bed for the distractions of the day which she hoped would keep her mind off the disturbing Mr. Stevens.

When the newlyweds made no appearance, Leah ate her breakfast alone and began to help Juanita with the morning chores. But only the indoor chores, since she wasn't yet ready to risk coming face-to-face with Cal Stevens in the light of day.

It was the Sabbath, but not the Sunday for the preacher to be in town on his circuit, so they would spend a leisurely day at home. By midmorning, Brad had stumbled out of his room to announce Espy was still sleeping soundly. He looked surly, not at all like a happy bridegroom, and Leah gave him a wide berth out of fear he would ask her for advice on how to handle his reluctant bride.

Leah was helping Juanita prepare Sunday dinner when she heard Brad shouting for Espy to get up because she had company. With a distinct sense of foreboding, Leah hastily removed her apron and headed for the parlor. There she found Homer Wilkes examining one of the brass candlesticks on the mantle.

"Mr. Wilkes," she said, startling him. "Is anything wrong?"

He showed her his yellowed teeth in what she supposed was an ingratiating grin. "Not a thing, Miss Harding, not a thing. But it is the Sabbath, so I thought I'd pay my oldest child a visit."

Oh, yes, on the day after her wedding and right at dinner time, too, Leah thought acidly. "You've brought your family?" she asked, wondering why she heard no din from the yard.

"Oh, no, them younguns is too wild for company." He grinned again. "I wanted a nice quiet visit with my girl."

I'll just bet, Leah thought, remembering Pete's warnings about how Wilkes would try to take advantage of his relationship to the Hardings. "You left the children to fend for themselves?" she asked in patent disapproval.

"They can cook just as good as I can," he replied, unconcerned. "Where's Espy, anyways?"

"Here I am," Espy said crossly, glowering at him from the hallway. To Leah's horror, she was still in her nightdress. At least she'd thrown the new robe Leah had purchased for her over it, although she hadn't bothered to tie it. "Who invited you here, anyways?"

"Now, Espy, is that any way to talk to your ol' pa?" Wilkes asked, unconcerned over her displeasure. Perhaps he was used to it.

"I'll talk to you anyway I want," Espy announced, tromping across the room to flounce down on the sofa. Her hair was loose and disheveled, but somehow the fiery mass of unruly curls was attractive. "You ain't in charge of me no more."

Good heavens, she's barefoot! Leah thought. And she didn't seem to care that her nightdress was practically transparent and that her robe gaped open scandalously.

Espy slumped back against the cushions and yawned expansively, stretching like a cat. Leah was just about to send her back to get some clothes on when the front door burst open to reveal Cal Stevens in all his intimidating glory.

Leah's breath caught in her chest, and her stomach did an abrupt little flip, but fortunately he hardly spared her a glance. He was looking at Wilkes, and he didn't look pleased. As if he had every right to, he came on in, closing the door behind him.

For a minute, no one spoke, then Brad finally said, " 'Morning, Cal."

" 'Morning," he replied, but he never took his eyes off Wilkes who suddenly seemed ill at ease.

"You got no call to come busting in here," Wilkes protested. "This here's a family visit."

"Why, Mr. Stevens is just about family," Espy piped in before Leah could think of a reply. "He's gonna marry Leah."

"Marry?" Wilkes echoed in fury. "How come you never said nothing about it, girl?"

Espy was unaffected by his anger. "Ain't that right, Mr. Stevens?" She giggled, then stretched her legs out in front of her and crossed her bare feet, exposing a scandalous amount of ankle and calf. She was looking at Cal, fairly simpering, while she waited to get his full attention. Good heavens! She was trying to entice him!

Fury flooded Leah, fury and outrage and another emotion so unfamiliar she couldn't even identify it. Then Cal looked at the girl, his sky blue gaze flicking over her and taking in every detail of her wanton pos-

127

ture and her lithe body faithfully outlined by the clinging folds of her gown.

"Espy!"

The girl jumped, and only when she looked at Leah did Leah realize she'd spoken aloud. "Go to your room and don't come back until you are properly dressed."

To Leah's dismay, the girl simply tossed her fiery mane. "I don't reckon I gotta listen to you either, do I, Brad?"

For the first time Leah looked at her brother and was gratified to see he was mortified by his wife's behavior. "Leah's right," he said, taking her by the arm and pulling her to her feet. "It ain't proper for you to be running around like this."

"I ain't running, I'm sitting!" she protested, jerking free from Brad's grasp.

"Then it ain't proper for you to be showing yourself to anybody but me," Brad insisted.

Espy glanced down at herself as if just realizing her scandalous state of undress. When she looked up again, she was simpering again. "Oh, my, I reckon I just didn't think. 'Course, Pa's seen me in my nightdress before, and I didn't know Mr. Stevens was gonna be here."

She actually batted her eyes at Cal! Leah's palms itched to slap the insolent grin off the girl's face, but her husband had the presence of mind to take matters into his own hands.

"Come on," he said, grabbing her arm again and jerking her into motion.

"You don't have to be so rough!" Espy protested as Brad dragged her along, but before she disappeared into the hall, she managed one last, soulful glance at

Cal. "Don't go away," she called, "I won't be gone long!"

Leah stared after her, aghast, not daring to look at Cal to see if he had appreciated the show put on for his benefit. And how could he not? He was a man, wasn't he?

"That girl, she's a pistol, all right," Wilkes declared into the silence. Without being invited, he slumped down into a chair and ran his grimy hands over the upholstered arms appreciatively.

"You got some business here?" Cal demanded.

Wilkes feigned surprise. "This is my daughter's house, ain't it? I come to visit her. You got any objections to that?"

Plainly he did, but instead of voicing them, he glanced at Leah, once again waiting for her lead. She felt his glance like a gentle blow to her heart that left her feeling slightly bruised and definitely moved. Somehow she managed to keep her outward composure, however, and didn't let herself think about how his mouth had felt on hers. Then she remembered why he was looking at her. He was waiting to know whether she wanted him to kick Wilkes out of her parlor. Would she ever get used to a man who consulted her before going off half-cocked?

She cleared her throat. "I'm sure we can have no objections to your visiting Espy so long as she and Brad have none." In view of Espy's reaction to her seeing her father, Leah felt reasonably certain the girl would soon put a stop to it.

Wilkes didn't seem the least bit concerned, not even when the echo of shouting drifted to them from the hallway. Leah jumped when she heard the bedroom door slam, but she was relieved to hear Brad's footsteps heading back toward the parlor. He stopped in the doorway, a little disconcerted to find three pairs of eyes staring at him expectantly.

"Espy's getting dressed," he announced unnecessarily.

"Just get up, did she?" Wilkes asked slyly. "You must've rode her hard last night, boy."

Leah swallowed her gasp of outrage. Was there no limit to what this man would do or say? Instinctively she glanced at Brad whose face had gone beet red.

"What'd you come here for, anyways?" he demanded.

"Like I was telling your sister, I just wanted to visit my girl in her new home, make sure she's getting along all right."

"And get yourself a free meal into the bargain," Brad snapped.

Wilkes widened his eyes in a parody of surprise. "Why, I ain't been invited to eat, Mr. Bradley, although anybody with any breeding would've done it long before now, with me being a relation and it being dinnertime and all."

"You're certainly welcome to join us, Mr. Wilkes," Leah said before Brad could escalate the discussion into an argument.

"Why, thank you kindly, Miss Leah," Wilkes said, affecting his ingratiating grin again.

Leah wanted to shudder at being addressed so familiarly, but she refused to give the man the satisfaction of seeing her disgust. Instead she would let him know he meant less than nothing to her. She moved to the sofa where Espy had sat and seated herself, folding her hands primly.

Only then did she trust herself to look at Cal who still stood poised like an avenging angel near the front door. "Why don't you sit down, Cal?" she asked, a little surprised to hear herself addressing him by his first name and even more surprised at how natural it felt.

He seemed a little startled at the invitation, but he quickly took the chair opposite Wilkes's, leaving Brad to join Leah on the sofa. Because Leah refused to exert herself for Homer Wilkes by making polite conversation, the four of them sat in strained silence for several minutes. At last Wilkes said, "Looks to be a mild winter. What do you think, Stevens?"

"Maybe," Cal replied unhelpfully.

Wilkes seemed undisturbed by the lack of encouragement and launched into a monologue on his opinions of what Brad and Leah should do to prepare the ranch for the coming winter.

Leah barely listened, acutely aware of the tension radiating from Brad and of Cal Stevens sitting so near. For a long time she resisted the urge to look at him, but finally the temptation overwhelmed her and she glanced up to find him watching her.

She quickly lowered her eyes, praying the heat she felt flashing over her would not translate itself into a blush. Why had she ever thought things between them would return to normal after what had happened last night? His kiss must have addled her brain even more than she'd feared.

Clutching her hands together, Leah stared steadfastly at the floor until she at last heard Espy strolling down the hall to join them. The girl wore her wedding dress again — naturally enough, Leah thought, considering it was the only decent garment she owned — and being the center of attention had brought the roses to her cheeks and a smile to her lips.

Or rather a smirk, Leah thought and scolded herself for being uncharitable. She rose to her feet. "I'll tell Juanita to set an extra place. You'll be joining us, too, won't you, Cal?"

Her gaze darted to him and lingered only long enough to catch his nod and to register the speculative amusement in his startlingly blue eyes. What did he have to be amused about? she wondered as she strode off toward the kitchen.

"So how do you like it without me, Pa?" she heard Espy asking. "Kinda lonely, ain't it?"

"Lonely? With all them kids?" Wilkes scoffed genially.

Leah quickened her pace so she wouldn't have to hear any more of the conversation. Espy no longer sounded displeased by her father's visit. In fact, she sounded delighted. So much for Leah's hope that the girl would discourage him from coming here.

The noon meal was a nightmare during which Leah forced herself to eat while Espy and her father traded witticisms and cackled at private jokes that no one else found particularly funny. Brad was clearly fuming, but Espy paid him no mind, and Cal Stevens seemed to be growing more amused by the moment. Leah wished she could find something amusing in the situation, but her last hope died when Wilkes addressed his next remark to her.

"And when're you and Stevens getting hitched?"

Dear God in heaven, how long would she do penance

for that deception? "I can't believe it is any of your business, Mr. Wilkes," she said as haughtily as she could manage under the circumstances.

"Well, like I said, I'm family now and naturally—"

"When the time comes, you'll hear about it," Cal said, his tone steely. The amusement had vanished from his eyes, she noticed, taking some pleasure in knowing he was at least as disconcerted by the question as she.

"I just hope you won't wait too long," Wilkes continued as if Cal hadn't spoken. "I mean, you can't expect Brad to keep his sister here forever, now can you?"

This time Leah's outrage fairly choked her, and Cal made an abrupt movement as if he wanted to launch himself across the table at Wilkes and was holding himself back with only the greatest effort. Brad was the only one able to speak.

"This is Leah's home, and she's welcome here as long as I'm here," he declared.

Wilkes's beady eyes narrowed, making him look even more like a weasel than he usually did. "It's Espy's home, too, boy. You considered what she thinks about all this?"

The question disconcerted Brad whose gaze darted uncertainly to his wife, then to Leah who knew only too well what Espy's opinion was.

Before Brad could reply, Espy spoke. "He knows what I think. I think it's time Leah had a place of her own. *Past* time, if you ask me," she sniffed, giving Leah a disparaging look that made her itch to slap her. "But there's no use in talking about it if Cal's gonna marry her, 'cause everything'll be took care of, won't it?"

Leah thought she might strangle on her mortification, and she looked to Brad to defend her, but it was Cal who said, "And what if she wants to stay here? Like she says, this *is* her home."

Wilkes snorted scornfully. "Is that why you decided to marry her? 'Cause you figured you could live here off her brother's place?"

Leah wanted to scream. This was like a bad dream, an unwelcome taste of nostalgia for what life had been like when her father was alive, when every meal had been a time of bickering and confrontation. After his death, she'd vowed she would never again allow unpleasantness of any kind to invade her home, and now here it was again only worse, far worse, than anything she had endured before.

With great effort she pushed herself up out of her chair. Clutching her hands together so no one would see how they were trembling, she said, "I don't believe this is suitable conversation for the dinner table. If you will excuse me."

She was halfway to the door when she heard a chair scrape. Who might have risen to follow her, she had no idea, but she didn't turn around to see. Without conscious thought, she headed for the parlor, realizing too late she should have gone to her room where no one would have dared disturb her, but she couldn't turn around now, not with someone behind her, someone with whom she probably didn't want to speak and — "

"Leah!"

She stopped dead at the sound of Cal's voice and, weak with relief, turned to face him.

"Come on," he said, taking her arm in his relentless grasp and conducting her on toward the parlor. Leah hated herself for feeling so grateful for his concern, but she leaned on his strength as he led her on, through the front room and out onto the porch.

The breeze felt good to her burning cheeks, and she inhaled deeply of the crisp, fall air, cleansed now of the scorching heat of summer but still comfortably warm. She hugged herself, holding in the rage that roiled within.

"For two cents, I'd ram his teeth right down his throat," Cal muttered. "You shouldn't let him rile you. He only says those things to get your goat."

For the first time that day, Leah allowed herself to look him full in the face. His dark eyes reflected her own fury, and she felt the tug of empathy. The tug was almost irresistible, so long had it been since she had had anyone to share her burdens, but with difficulty she managed to resist the urge to reach out to him. If she did, heaven only knew what might happen. He'd only promised not to start anything, and as she well knew, he was perfectly capable of finishing it.

"You mustn't do anything to him," she said. "That's what he wants, you know, to start trouble among us, and I won't have it. I've seen all the fighting and arguing I intend to see in my lifetime."

"You think the world's gonna stop fussing and fighting because you order it to?"

"The part of the world that lives in my house, yes," she replied, annoyed by the spark of renewed amusement she saw in his eyes.

"Like he said, it ain't your house." He spoke the words gently, but they stung nevertheless.

"How dare he — " She caught herself before she could reveal the depth of her outrage before him.

"How dare he what?" Cal prompted. "How dare he

135

remind you that Brad owns the ranch and you've got no claim to it? I'd figure that's the main thing he'd do. He's got a grudge against you, lady, for not giving him the money he figured he had coming for his girl."

"That doesn't give him the right to insult me in my own home!"

"Maybe not, but it ain't going to stop him, neither."

He was right, she knew, but that didn't make the words any easier to hear, nor did it solve anything.

Leah stared out into the ranch yard, vividly aware that she was responsible for the prosperity she saw there and equally as aware that she could lay no claim to it.

A few moments of silence ticked by, then he said, "Maybe you oughta tell Brad there's nothing between us. At least then he'd know you've got no place else to go so he'd put a stop to all this talk about sending you away."

Leah closed her eyes, fighting an overwhelming sense of weariness. "And if I tell him I never set eyes on you before you rode in here, how am I to explain your presence here? Are you ready to tell him you're his father?"

"No," he said so sharply she looked up at him again. This time his eyes were troubled, almost haunted, and this time it was she who felt empathy for his pain.

Compelled to touch him, she closed her hands into fists instead. "Oh, Cal, I'm sorry . . ."

"You've got nothing to be sorry about. You've done more for me than I had any right to expect, any right to even ask. It's not your fault things didn't work out exactly the way I planned."

"What exactly did you plan?"

His lips twitched into a mirthless grin. "I figured I'd

see the boy, tell him who I was, we'd shake hands and spend a few days together and then I'd ride on."

"Ride on!" she exclaimed in astonishment. "You were going to leave your son after you'd just found him?"

He looked away, up at the rippled clouds overhead in a way that told her how embarrassed he was to admit this to her. "Yeah, I . . . I didn't know it would be like this. I never expected to care so much about him . . . about what happens to him."

Leah covered her mouth to hold back a cry of anguish. It was dangerous to feel his pain, how dangerous she could only guess, but even more dangerous to let him know she felt it.

In any case, he seemed oblivious to her for the moment. "But that ain't your lookout." He squared his broad shoulders, and when he turned back to her, his eyes were guarded, concealing all emotion. "I'm just getting a little tired of seeing you embarrassed over me. It ain't right, and you shouldn't have to put up with it."

Oh dear! Leah's previous experience had left her ill prepared to deal with kindness, especially from such an unlikely source. Cal Stevens was like no other man she had ever encountered, a man of strength who never bullied and who wasn't too proud to defer to a woman, and now he was even being considerate of her feelings. If she didn't know better, she might think he cared about her, too.

The thought was so startling, for a moment she couldn't even think. *Could* he care about her, care about her as a woman and not just as Brad's sister? Well, he'd kissed her, hadn't he? And he'd kissed her the way a man kisses a woman, not the way a man would kiss somebody's sister.

But that was lust, her common sense argued. All men would take what they could get, and they didn't have to care for the woman.

But he thought she was beautiful. Surely that must mean something, since she wasn't really the least bit beautiful.

Or maybe he just knew what to say to turn a woman's head.

"Leah?"

She jumped, startled back to reality and his very real presence. "What?"

"You had a funny look on your face. Are you all right?"

She tried a reassuring smile. "Of course. Why shouldn't I be?" Stupid question, she cursed herself, and straightened her smile. "I mean, you don't have to worry about my delicate sensibilities. I can take care of myself. I'll have a little talk with Espy and explain to her that she needn't allow her father to visit her here if she doesn't want him to. I'm sure that will be the last we see of him."

"You don't know the Wilkeses very well then," he said, shaking his head. "Folks like that, they stick together because they don't have anything or anybody else, and if Wilkes thinks he might get something out of her or Brad, he'll stick like a blood tick on a hound dog."

Just what Pete had warned her about, she thought in dismay. "But she hates her father. You saw the way he treated her and—"

"Then she'll want him here so he can see how well off

138

she is now and so she can lord it over him that he can't lay a finger on her again. You saw how she acted this morning, showing off for him."

And showing off for you, too, Leah thought grimly.

She wondered if Cal had been enticed by it. She also couldn't stop herself from wondering if he had wanted to kiss *Espy* from the first moment he had seen *her* or if he thought *she* was beautiful, too. Mentally cringing from the prospect of asking such questions — and at what the answers might be — Leah decided she needed to get away from Cal Stevens, too, because he seemed just as capable as Homer Wilkes of inspiring uncharacteristic behavior in her. "I . . . I think I'd like to go to my room for a while."

"Good idea. The old man'll probably hang around for the rest of the day, so there's no sense in making yourself a sitting duck."

Leah nodded, unaccountably annoyed that he was so undisturbed at the prospect of losing her company. "What will you do?"

He shrugged, unconcerned. "Hang around and see what I can hear."

"What do you expect to hear?"

"I don't know. Maybe what the old man's plans are."

"What kind of plans could he have?"

"Something to do with getting his hands on the Harding money, you can be sure. Beyond that, who knows?"

Who, indeed, Leah thought as she headed back into the house, hurrying so she would make the privacy of her room before encountering the Wilkeses again. Part of her felt guilty for leaving Brad to deal with Homer alone, but another part of her recalled how eagerly he had wanted to marry Espy, and she decided he'd asked for this.

As she shut the door of her room behind her, Leah sighed with relief. Now all she had to do was fill the hours until Homer left.

One way, of course, would be to consider all of Cal Stevens's many sterling qualities. If she had judged him upon their first meeting as a heartless gunman incapable of tender feelings, she had been decidedly wrong. He still might be more interested in Brad's fortune than Brad himself, but Leah had absolutely no evidence to prove it. Quite the contrary, if he intended to cash in on Brad's wealth, he had passed up several excellent opportunities to reveal his identity and influence Brad over to his side. Instead, he chose to remain a virtual stranger to the boy whom he must long to claim as his own.

He even seemed reluctant to take advantage of the lie about his being her suitor. How odd that her impulsive fib had caused so many complications and given Espy just the excuse she needed to encourage Brad to get rid of his spinster sister. And Cal was even concerned about that.

Everything would be so simple if only she really was engaged to Cal Stevens.

The thought stunned her for a moment, just as she had been stunned a few minutes ago by the thought that Cal might really care for her. The whole thing was ridiculous, of course. She couldn't possibly consider marrying a man she'd only known for a week even if he did ask her, and he most certainly hadn't asked her. And where would they live? She had no money of her own, and Cal earned his living with his gun.

He had no place in his life for a wife or a family.

A family? Now where had that idea come from? Not that it was so farfetched. She was still young enough to have children if she chose to marry. But even if she chose to, she'd be a fool to choose a man like Cal Stevens. He simply couldn't provide for her.

The logic was flawless, but when Leah remembered his kisses, she could only wish the rest of her body were as easy to convince as her brain.

Several hours later, Juanita knocked on her door, then came in without waiting for her to reply. Leah had been reading, or trying to read instead of thinking about Cal Stevens, and she put the book aside. "What is it?"

"He is leaving."

"Cal?" she exclaimed, jumping from her chair in alarm.

"No," Juanita said in surprise, "Señor Wilkes."

"Oh." Of course. What had she been thinking? Juanita must think her an idiot, and from the look on her face, she did. While Leah had no desire to see Wilkes again, courtesy demanded that she bid her guest farewell.

She found him with Brad and Espy on the front porch. Cal stood in the yard. He'd brought Wilkes's horse around and now held it, waiting for him to come down.

"Well, there she is now," Wilkes said, far more pleased to see her than he had any right to be. "We was just saying it was a pity you got the headache and couldn't visit with us this afternoon."

"I hope you enjoyed your stay with us," she lied, glancing at Espy to see if the girl was still in high spirits after spending the afternoon with her father.

"*I* sure enjoyed it," Espy offered, and apparently she had. The roses still glowed in her cheeks and her eyes shone. "It's nice to have somebody around who don't look down on me."

Leah felt the jab but graciously ignored it. She had no intention of discussing this subject in front of Homer Wilkes.

"You come back now, Pa, anytime you want," Espy told him.

"Durn right I will. Like I said, this is your place now, just as much as Brad's, and I reckon you can have your own kinfolk in if you want to."

Brad put his arm around Espy's thin shoulders and tried to look masterful. "Espy can have anybody she wants to visit."

Leah was beginning to feel slightly ill, but she refused to betray her disgust.

"And there ain't nobody cares more about her than her ol' Pa," Wilkes assured him. "Life's an uncertain thing, boy, and you never know when a girl's gonna need her pa to take care of her again."

As she watched Wilkes go down the steps and mount his horse, Leah tried to make sense of his parting statement. What on earth could he have meant?

The instant Wilkes turned his horse, Espy lost interest in him. "I'm tired," she declared, sagging visibly. "I think I'll lay down for a while."

"Tired?" Brad echoed in astonishment, following her into the house. "You slept half the day. How can you be tired?"

"I'm in a delicate condition!" she whined.

Leah winced as the door slammed behind them. Dear Lord, what was she going to do?

"Did you hear what he said?" Cal demanded, and she looked up to find him looming over her.

Leah blinked in confusion. "He said she'd slept half the day and—"

"No, I mean Wilkes. Did you hear what he said about life being an uncertain thing?"

"Yes, I thought it was strange. What on earth did he mean?"

Cal's eyes had gone as cold as steel and just as hard. "Well, I can't say for sure, but my guess would be he's thinking about what would happen to him if his daughter became a rich widow."

"What!" Leah cried in horror. "You can't be serious! Even Wilkes wouldn't dream of—"

"People do a lot of strange things for money, Miss . . . Miss Harding."

His stumble over her name distracted her for a moment. "I don't think we need to stand on formalities, Cal, not when we're discussing my brother's life . . . your *son's* life. You can't believe Wilkes would . . ." She couldn't even bring herself to say the words.

"I don't know if he would or not, but I'm not willing to take the chance. Are you?"

"No! But what can we possibly do—"

"Take away his reason."

"How? We can't unmarry them!"

He grinned his mirthless grin, an expression Leah was beginning to recognize. "No need to. As things stand now, if anything happens to Brad, his wife inherits everything, right?"

"I assume so, but what — ?"

"Unless Brad has a will saying otherwise."

"But if he didn't leave the ranch to his wife and family than who — ?"

"You. It only makes sense," he continued when she would have protested. "He can make you the guardian for his children. He'd be sure that you'd always take care of them and Espy. Maybe he can even make that part of the will, I don't know. A lawyer could tell you, I guess. Anyway, the important thing is to make sure Espy doesn't stand to get everything if Brad dies. Then there's no reason for Wilkes to be interested in him dying."

"And he'd be safe! Oh, Cal, we need to talk to him right away!"

He caught her arm when she would have rushed into the house. "This probably ain't the best time to talk business with him. He and the girl're probably fighting again."

He was right as usual. "We shouldn't wait too much longer, though."

"No, and Leah . . ." He hesitated over her name, and she found she liked the sound of it on his lips.

"Yes?"

"Uh, maybe I'd better talk to him about it alone."

Anger burgeoned within her, and she shook free of his grasp in disgust. Just when she'd begun to trust him, he started acting just like her father, taking over and pushing her aside and . . .

"Now don't get your hackles up," he chided, easily reading her fury. "Think about it. You can't go to Brad and tell him you think he should make a will leaving everything to you instead of to his new bride."

She opened her mouth to protest, but the words died on her lips. Once again, he was right, and damn him, he knew it too, judging by the glitter of amusement in his blue eyes. He reached up, touched one long finger beneath her chin, and closed her mouth for her.

"That's better," he said with smile. "You stand around with that luscious mouth open, and God only knows who might come along and kiss it."

He was down the steps and across the yard, heading for the bunkhouse, before she could think of a reply, and even then words failed her. Why on earth would someone want to kiss her open mouth?

And why had the prospect turned her knees to jelly?

Chapter Five

When Cal asked Brad to go for a walk after supper that night, Leah sat up knitting until at last she heard Brad's returning footsteps. Espy had long since retired, claiming fatigue in spite of her late afternoon nap, so the house was quiet when Brad came in.

The sight of him caused Leah a stab of pain. He was no longer the carefree boy he'd been just days ago. Now his broad shoulders slumped and his beautiful face was haggard. When she considered the burdens he now bore, she thought it no wonder.

"Espy's gone on to bed," she told him, wondering if there would be another fight tonight or if Brad would let the girl sleep.

He grunted an acknowledgement, looking as if the news did not surprise him. So far marriage had been a singular disappointment to him, and Leah didn't hold out much hope that conditions would improve anytime soon.

"You and Cal were out there a long time," she observed when he made no effort to tell her about their conversation.

"Yeah," he said as he removed his jacket and hat and hung them on pegs by the door. "I was telling him he shouldn't let you get away."

"Get away?" she echoed uneasily.

"Yeah, I think you should marry him, Leah. He's a good man, and he thinks the world of you."

Leah's heart did a painful leap. "He does?" she asked in astonishment.

"Well, sure. I mean, he *must* love you. Why else would he come all this way just to see you and then hang around all this time?" Leah's heart dropped back just as painfully. Had she imagined Cal Stevens confessing his undying devotion? She must be losing her mind. "And why would he stick by you through this mess with me and . . . ?"

His voice trailed off, but Leah heard the bitterness in it. She ached for him, but she had to settle this misunderstanding about Cal once and for all.

"Marriage is an important step in a woman's life, as I'm sure you understand," she said gently. "I'm afraid I'm just not convinced Cal Stevens is the right man for me."

"Well, maybe you will be when I tell you what else he said to me," Brad said, coming over and sitting down beside her on the sofa.

Here it comes, Leah told herself. Try to act surprised.

"Cal thinks I should make a will and leave the ranch to you."

"Why on earth would he suggest such a thing?" Leah asked, hoping she sounded convincing.

Brad's young face twisted in disgust. "Well, he's wrong, I know he is, but . . . Well, he thinks I'd be safer if I did."

"Safe from what?"

Obviously Brad was loath to tell her Cal's suspicions. He looked away, up toward the ceiling, a habit he must have inherited from Cal who had done the same thing this afternoon. "Cal thinks it would be a good idea if I didn't give Mr. Wilkes any reason to make Espy a rich widow."

"Brad!" Leah cried, not needing to feign her shock. Hearing the words from Brad's on lips made the horror of it too real.

"I know, I told him it was crazy, but there's other reasons, too. I mean, Espy, she's pretty silly, and she wouldn't have no idea how to run this place even if she lived to be a hundred. She'll always need somebody to take care of her, and I'd rather it was you than her old man."

Caring for Espy Wilkes was the last task Leah wished to be assigned, but since the whole purpose of this will was to prevent anything from happening to Brad in the first place, that wasn't really a consideration.

She lay a hand on his arm. "I'm honored that you'd trust me to take care of your family, Brad. And I'm touched, too."

"Now don't go crying or anything," he warned in alarm, and Leah blinked obediently at the tears gathering in her eyes. "Cal says we can set everything down, nice and legal, so the old man can't get his hands on anything."

Leah tried to smile. "As much as I hate talking about such things, it *would* relieve my mind to know Homer Wilkes will never live in this house or control your children."

"That's what I think, too," Brad said. His youthful

148

determination made her want to hug him, but she restrained herself.

"You should probably discuss this with Espy, you know."

But Brad shook his head. "She'd just get mad. She doesn't know what's good for her."

"Still, you must explain to her what you intend to do." So she'll tell her father and you'll be safe, she wanted to add but managed to hold her tongue.

"I will, after it's done," he promised. "Cal thinks we should go to town tomorrow and see Mead Garland."

"I suppose we should. There's no use waiting, is there?" Leah would have gladly gone tonight, if she could.

"No, no use at all." Brad rose but made no move to walk away. Instead he glanced apprehensively toward the hallway that led to the bedrooms.

"She's probably asleep by now," Leah said, angry that Brad should be so reluctant to join his bride. "If you're quiet, I'm sure you won't disturb her."

"Yeah, you're probably right," he said, emboldened by her suggestion. Leah watched him stride away with new confidence and noted idly how much he resembled his father. He should know his father, too, she decided suddenly. It wasn't right for them to be so close and for Brad not to know. Besides, he needed something to cheer him up, and Leah suspected the news would be welcome indeed. She would talk to Cal about it the first chance she got.

Leah had suspected Espy would protest an early departure the next morning and would consequently

149

refuse to accompany them into town. The prospect of a trip to town — and the opportunity for shopping — was entirely too tempting, however, and a euphoric Espy cheerfully joined them for breakfast.

She chattered about what she planned to buy and did Leah think red velvet would be good for her bedroom drapes and would the dressmaker do them up or would they have to find someone else? Leah listened with only half an ear, nodding or shaking her head where appropriate. Obviously, Brad hadn't told her the true reason for their trip or she wouldn't have been so cheerful.

Since Leah couldn't abide the thought of sharing the buggy with Brad and Espy for the trip into town again, she had her mare saddled. For the occasion, she had dug her old riding habit out of the bottom of her trunk. Judging the deep plum color to be both sensible and properly demure, she felt no qualms about wearing it, especially when she noticed how well it still fit her.

Cal was waiting for them when they came outside, and if he was surprised to see that Leah planned to ride horseback, he gave no indication. Instead his gaze was knowing when it met hers, and she supposed he wouldn't have wanted to be cooped up with Espy either.

Then his gaze dropped, taking in her ensemble — or was it her figure? — with frank appreciation. For once the flush she felt was one of pleasure, knowing she looked good and had no need to be flustered by his attention.

"You're just full of surprises, ain't you, Miss Leah?" he asked with a grin.

"Whatever do you mean?" she replied, knowing she was being coy but somehow unable to resist the urge.

"I mean I never would've taken you for a rider."

"Why, Mr. Stevens, I'll have you know I've even ridden astride in my time."

"And what made you do a scandalous thing like that?"

The memory came in a flash, and instinctively she braced herself for the accompanying pain, but miraculously, it didn't come. "I . . . I did it to prove to my father I was as good as any man he had on the place." She smiled at her youthful foolishness and marveled that she no longer felt the terrible anguish it had caused her.

He shook his head in wonder. "Well, from where I'm standing you're better than any ten men."

"And she always was," Brad added, saving Leah from having to respond to this amazing compliment. Brad's wink had an "I told you so" quality to it, and she was sure Cal's flattery had only convinced Brad he had been right about Cal's feelings for her.

"Brad!" Espy whined. "Ain't you gonna help me into the buggy? I'm afraid I might fall. I'm in a delicate condition and . . ." Brad scurried off.

"We'd better be going," Leah said, having recovered from Cal's compliment, but to her dismay, Cal hurried to help her mount her mare.

He didn't lean down to offer her a boost, either. Instead, he clamped both his hands on her waist and lifted her effortlessly into the saddle. The move left her breathless, and she gazed down at him through widened eyes for a long moment before they both suddenly realized his hands still gripped her waist in a manner that was far too familiar.

Instantly, he released her and stepped back. She thought she saw the slightest trace of red crawling up his neck, although she couldn't be perfectly sure, couldn't really trust any of her senses at the moment because they all seemed to have gone crazy. The sun was suddenly brighter, making Cal's eyes as clear as polished crystal, and all she could smell was his clean, masculine scent that seemed to linger about her person. And all she could feel was his hands at her waist, holding her as he had held her in the darkness . . .

Oh, dear, she really *must* be going crazy! Hastily, she began to adjust her skirts and to find the one stirrup that she used when she rose sidesaddle.

"All set?" he asked when she had stopped fidgeting.

"Yes, thank you," she replied, pleased to hear her voice sounded normal and not the least bit breathless.

He swung up into his own saddle, and Leah watched shamelessly out of the corner of her eye, admiring the way he moved and the way he sat his horse and the way his strong thighs . . .

Oh, dear, oh, dear! She must stop this instantly! Kicking her mare, she started off, setting the pace, and Cal fell in beside her. Brad would bring the buggy up at a distance great enough to avoid their dust and far enough that Leah wouldn't have to hear Espy's incessant chatter.

They rode a ways in silence, enjoying the beauty of the day, the cloudless canopy of sky, and the wind rippling through the lush grass.

Cal was checking the landscape with the practiced eye of one who has stayed alive by being constantly alert, but he kept glancing over to make sure Leah Harding was still there, too. Sometimes he expected to wake up and find out she'd just been a dream and that he'd only imagined her perfection. God, she was beautiful. He couldn't see much of her face from beneath the brim of her flat crowned hat, but he knew exactly what she looked like, from the tilt of her cute little nose to the way her eyelashes curled up and turned blond on the ends.

And her body. Well, now, he knew all about that, too. The lush breasts lifted impudently by the corset she wore, just begging for a man's touch. The tiny waist he'd spanned when he lifted her into the saddle. Below that, he had to use his imagination some, but it wasn't hard. He could pretty much guess how much was padding and how much was woman beneath the draping of her skirts, and mostly she was woman. Even though she was the most ladylike female he'd ever known, he'd still been able to catch a glimpse of ankle every now and then, enough to know she was as pretty down there as she was every place else. Yeah, a regular little armful, as Cal had reason to know.

It sure was a good thing he wasn't the kind of man to settle down. If he had been, he couldn't think of anybody he'd rather settle with than Leah Harding. The prospect of waking up each morning with his arms full of her was almost enough to make a man stand in one place long enough to grow roots.

Realizing how dangerous his thoughts were becoming, Cal cast about for something to say to break the silence between them.

"Was he impressed?"

She looked at him in surprise, and her sweet mouth curved into a small smile. "Was who impressed?"

"Your pa, with your riding."

Her smile disappeared. "Oh, no, not really. Nothing I ever did impressed him."

"Why not?"

She tried to smile again, to pretend it didn't matter, but he could see it did, still, even after all these years. "Because I was a girl. He didn't have much use for females except to cook and clean and breed for him."

The color came to her face, and he knew she hadn't meant to say that to him, so he pretended not to notice the slip. "Weren't you jealous of Brad, then? I mean, the old man must've doted on him."

Her smile grew sad. "You would have expected him to, I guess, especially when he went to so much trouble to get himself a son, but Brad could never please him either. Brad was always too little to do the things Papa thought he should do. Then I would show him *I* could do them — things like riding and roping and branding and reading sign and, oh, a hundred things a boy has to learn on a ranch — and he would just get madder."

"Wasn't he proud that his flesh and blood was so smart?"

"Not if that flesh and blood was female. Sometimes when I think back, I think I made things worse by trying so hard."

"How could that have made things worse?"

"Because I was showing him what a wonderful boy I would have been if only I'd been a boy. It was like rubbing salt in an open wound."

"Especially because the boy he did have didn't measure up."

"Oh, he would have," Leah assured him hastily, as loyal to Brad as he would have expected. "Papa just expected too much. You can see for yourself how Brad turned out. He's a son any father would be proud of."

She'd touched a nerve, and Cal winced. So much

154

for his theory that talking was safer than thinking.

She saw the wince. "Oh, I'm sorry! I didn't think —"

"But you're right," Cal assured her. "His real father *is* proud of him. I only wish I could take some of the credit that he turned out so well."

"You can take some if you want. I mean, he is like you in many ways."

Cal felt a surge of pride. "What ways?"

"Mannerisms, the way he walks and carries himself. Sometimes the resemblance is . . . uncanny."

He hadn't even considered that the boy might be like him in ways other than hair and eye color. They both had blue eyes, but Brad's were more like Cal remembered Amy's being. But Leah thought they walked alike . . .

"I think it was the resemblance that finally convinced me," she was saying, "even more than Pete checking out your story."

Cal was grateful they were on horseback. If they'd been standing close, he might have thrown his arms around her in a rush of exuberance, and God only knew what kind of trouble such an impulse would cause. Yeah, it was a mighty good thing they were on horseback, or Miss Leah Harding might find out all the other things Cal Stevens had been dreaming about doing besides kissing her. Somehow he managed a sedate grin.

"And here I thought it was just my charm that had turned your head."

"My head isn't *that* easily turned," she chided playfully, making Cal want to reach over and snatch her right out of her saddle. God in heaven, if he wasn't careful he'd find himself in love with Leah Harding, and wouldn't that be a mess? He was already on notice because he'd dared kiss her in a moment of weakness. If she thought there was any more to it, she'd run him off in a flash.

But on the other hand, she didn't seem too upset about it right now. In fact, if he didn't know better, he might even think she was flirting with him. Wouldn't it be something if she fell for him, too? Of course, he knew it would never happen. A woman like Leah Harding had her pick of men, and she'd already turned down one with much better prospects than Cal Stevens would ever have. No, having Leah Harding was something Cal could only dream about, but dream about it he would.

Prudently, Cal turned their conversation to practical matters, like the condition of the grass they were observing and whether or not the clouds on the horizon would bring bad weather. By the time they reached town, Cal felt confident Leah had no idea what his private feelings for her were.

Leah led the way to the livery where she intended to leave their horses and the buggy. Brad and Espy had yet to arrive, and Leah hastened to dismount before Cal had the chance to offer her assistance. One such close encounter with him in a day was one too many.

By the time the buggy arrived, Leah had given the stable boy instructions, and soon the four of them were strolling down Main Street, Brad and Espy arm in arm with Leah and Cal walking behind.

"Leah, you ain't going with Brad to the lawyer's office, are you?" Espy inquired over her shoulder.

"Well, yes, as a matter of fact," Leah said, wondering what business Brad had claimed to have there.

"She's got to, Espy," Brad informed her. "Like I told you, we've got some legal stuff to clear up about the ranch and everything. She might have to sign something."

"I just don't want to go to Mrs. Otto's alone," Espy complained. "What if she don't remember who I am?"

"I'm sure she'll know who you are," Leah assured her, affected more than she wanted to show by the girl's uncertainty. Apparently, Espy Wilkes was used to being ignored. "And if she's forgotten, simply tell her you're Mrs. Brad Harding."

Espy brightened at once. "Oh, sure! Why didn't I think of that?" Without waiting for the others, she dropped Brad's arm and hurried off toward the mercantile, not even looking back.

Ignoring Brad's sigh, Leah forced herself to smile and took his arm in Espy's place. "Let's get this over with, shall we?"

Mead's office was the bottom floor of a narrow, two-story building at the far end of town. His living quarters were on the second floor so, as he had once explained to Leah, he was always available to clients. The front door tripped a bell when it opened, signaling Mead, who was working in an inner office, that he had visitors. At the sound of it, he hurried out. As usual, he was dapper in his conservative lawyer's suit.

"Brad, Leah, how good to see you," he exclaimed, grinning expansively as he shook Brad's hand. "And where's your lovely bride, young man?"

"Shopping," Brad said, politely returning Mead's smile, if not his enthusiasm. Leah noticed Mead hadn't mentioned Cal's presence.

"Is this a social visit, or do you have some legal business to discuss?" Mead inquired, still pointedly not looking at Cal.

"Legal business," Brad said, sobering instantly and glancing at Leah for guidance.

"Yes," she confirmed. "Now that Brad is married and full owner of the ranch, he feels he needs a will."

"Excellent idea, my boy," Mead said, slapping Brad on the shoulder with comradely warmth. "Come inside and we'll take care of everything."

He led the way to the inner office door, then stood aside so Leah and Brad could enter before him. With apparent casualness, he started to step in front of Cal, as if he couldn't believe he would dare follow the Hardings into his inner sanctum.

But of course Cal did intend to follow them in, and he and Mead collided. Mead stepped back instantly, apologizing, but his raised eyebrows spoke eloquently of his disapproval.

Leah quickly intervened. "Brad, you'd like Cal to sit in with us, wouldn't you?"

"What? Oh, sure. I mean, this was his idea anyways."

Although Mead's eyebrows couldn't go any higher, his face did turn a shade darker, but he stood aside again while Cal entered the room, then closed the door behind them.

"I'm surprised you didn't bring your wife with you, Brad. Not planning to cut her out of the will, are you?" Mead joked as he took his place behind his desk.

The others were taking seats in the straight chairs Mead provided for his clients, and they all froze guiltily. Leah managed a nervous laugh and forced herself to sit down. "Why, Mead, how perceptive you are."

He was obviously intrigued, and he settled more

comfortably in his chair, took up a pencil, and positioned a pad of paper in front of him. "Well, now," he said expectantly. "Perhaps you'll tell me exactly what you have in mind."

Leah glanced at Brad, and he nodded, silently giving her permission to start. Briefly, she explained their concerns about Brad's safety and Espy's inability to operate the ranch alone. She couldn't bring herself to name the intended heir though, so she turned to Brad.

"Mr. Garland, if anything happened to me, I'd want my family taken care of," he said. "That's why I think I ought to leave the ranch to Leah."

"To Leah," Mead echoed thoughtfully, nodding. He concealed any surprise he may have felt.

"Yeah," Brad confirmed, growing more confident in the face of Mead's obvious approval of the plan. "Cal said you could probably fix it so Leah would have to take care of Espy and . . . and any kids we have."

At the mention of Cal's name, Mead had glanced at him suspiciously, but he didn't allow himself to be distracted very long. He began scribbling on the tablet. "Yes, of course. There are several ways we can do this. I'll explain each of them and let you decide."

A half hour later, they had worked out the details, and Leah found herself named as guardian to Brad's yet-unborn children, a role she fully expected — and fervently prayed — she would never have to fill.

Mead took copious notes and asked countless questions, but at last he pronounced the arrangements finished. "I'll need a few days to draw up the actual will, perhaps even a week. How about if I send you word when it's finished?"

A week of worry seemed like a lifetime when Brad

wouldn't be safe until the will was signed. "We'd appreciate it if you'd get it done as quickly as possible," Leah said, hoping she didn't sound frantic.

"Of course, I'll make it my first priority." He smiled at her as he hadn't done in many years, not since she'd broken their engagement, and Leah was startled to realize he was looking at her the way a man looks at a woman he finds desirable.

Oblivious to the undercurrents, Brad rose to his feet. "If you don't need me no more, I reckon I'd better go find Espy before she spends me into the poorhouse."

Without waiting for a reply, he hurried out, leaving Leah and Cal to find their own way. Cal rose, too, and Leah realized he had not uttered a word during the entire process, a discipline her father could never have accomplished, and she found herself wondering what it would be like to live with a man so considerate.

"Leah, I appreciate your business," Mead was saying, "but why do we only see each other professionally?" He had risen, too, as if he couldn't stand letting Cal tower over him. Even still, Cal stood several inches taller, and Leah chided herself for making the comparison.

"We just saw you at the wedding," she reminded Mead, gathering her purse and standing to meet him as he came around the desk toward her. "That was surely a social occasion."

"But how long had it been since the *last* social occasion? I'm afraid I'm just not willing to wait until one of Brad's children gets married to see you again." He glanced at Cal as if trying to decide whether to discount his presence or not. Apparently, he decided to. "How about if I fetch you some evening for supper here in town? In fact, why don't you stay in town for the afternoon and we can make it tonight."

For some inexplicable reason, Leah felt herself blushing furiously and turning instinctively to see Cal Stevens's reaction. His rugged face was set in stone, his blue eyes cold and hard, and he didn't meet her eye when he said, "I'll wait outside for you, Miss Harding."

Miss Harding? Had something happened to make him revert to addressing her so formally or was he just doing so for Mead's benefit? Oddly, the answer to that question loomed far more important than her response to Mead's unexpected invitation.

Cal closed the door behind him with a decided slam, and Leah blushed again.

Mead frowned. "Honestly, Leah," he said in a whisper, as if he thought Cal might be listening at the keyhole. "Who *is* that man? You insist he isn't your fiancé, and then you permit him to sit in on what should have been a private, family discussion!"

Leah debated her reply for only a moment. "He's Brad's father."

The progress of Mead's expressions was easy to read: surprise, confusion, understanding. "Good God!" he exclaimed, then shook himself and assumed his lawyerly calm again. "How do you know? I mean, how can you be sure? You can't possibly—"

"He had a story, which turned out to be true when I sent Pete Quincy to check on it," Leah said, a little impatient with Mead's interrogation, "and of course there's the evidence of my own eyes."

Mead's expressive eyebrows drew together in consternation. "There is no physical resemblance, Leah. You can't deny that."

161

"Ah, but there is if you observe them together, Mead. Little things you might not notice, especially because their coloring is so different. But I did notice, and I believe his story."

"Oh, Leah," he murmured, still obviously skeptical. "And what was Brad's reaction to all this?"

"He doesn't know yet," she said firmly, "and Cal . . . Mr. Stevens isn't ready to tell him, so I must beg you to honor my wishes in keeping the secret for me."

"Of course!" Mead assured her, taking her gloved hands and squeezing them gently. "Leah, you must know I would do whatever you asked." He smiled. *"Whatever* you ask."

"I won't ask you to do anything very difficult," she assured him, amused by his fervency.

Abruptly his smile disappeared again. "But why have you told people this Stevens is your . . . your *suitor?"*

"To explain his presence here to Brad since we can't tell him the truth, and I'm afraid I must ask you to play along about that, too, at least for the time being."

"Leah!" he chided, then stopped when he saw her expression. "All right, but only because you have asked me. You see," he added, grinning with mock innocence, "I promised you anything, and I'm a man of my word."

She couldn't help smiling at his teasing, but she also felt a slight sense of relief when she said, "So, as flattered as I am by your invitation, I'm afraid I can't accept it."

"At least not yet," he corrected. "Stevens can't expect you to keep up this charade much longer, though. The very idea of people thinking you would marry a man like that—"

"Mead!" Leah exclaimed, more defensive than she should have been. "He's Brad's father."

"So he says."

"He is, and I won't hear anything against him."

"You're awfully protective of the man, Leah," Mead mused. "Are you sure he means nothing to you?"

"How could he?" she exclaimed, hoping she wasn't blushing yet again. Thank heaven Mead knew nothing about the kiss she had shared with Stevens or the silly fantasies she had been entertaining ever since. "You know how I feel about Brad, though, so you should have no trouble understanding why I . . ." Her voice trailed off when she realized she couldn't complete that sentence in any unrevealing way.

But she didn't need to explain to Mead. "Of course, my dear, but you're entirely too protective of the boy. He isn't a child any longer. He's married and soon to be a father, if my instincts do not deceive me. You should let him deal with Stevens himself, and if he takes my advice, he'll send the man packing."

"Mead! How can you say such a thing!"

"Because everyone knows the character of gunfighters," Mead insisted. "They sell themselves to the highest bidder with no regard to right or wrong, and they kill indiscriminately—"

"Cal would never do a thing like that!"

"*Cal?*" Mead echoed in surprise, and Leah resisted the urge to cover her mouth.

"Cal Stevens isn't that kind of man," she insisted instead.

Mead seemed awfully disturbed by her defense of Stevens, even more disturbed than she would have expected. "You believe him to be Brad's father so natu-

163

rally you cannot bring yourself to think badly of him, Leah. I wouldn't expect anything else from a lady as soft-hearted as I know you to be, but — "

"But nothing," Leah said. "I won't stand here and argue with you about Cal Stevens, especially when this is none of your business in the first place!"

"Leah!" he cried, visibly shocked. And hurt, Leah saw with dismay.

"I'm sorry, Mead, but you of all people should know how much I hate having anyone interfere in my business."

He smiled tolerantly, forgivingly, and a little sadly. "And I'm sorry, too. Sometimes I let myself forget that I have no right to be concerned about you, although I am, Leah, more than I can tell you."

Now it was her turn to be shocked. "Mead, you're very kind," she said lamely, hoping she had misunderstood.

"It's more than kindness," he said, disabusing her of that notion. "I've never stopped caring for you, Leah. Surely, you must have known, must have *sensed* my feelings for you have never changed."

Leah had had no inkling, and she didn't want to have one now. Her life was already too complicated. "I'm sorry, Mead. I . . ."

"I know, you can't think about it just now, and I can't blame you. The only person to blame is myself. Perhaps if I were a different sort of man, I would have come to you years ago and . . . I don't know, taken you by force or something." He grinned ruefully at his own absurdity. "But I'm not that sort of man and never will be. I'm the sort who could love you from afar for seven years while I waited until Brad didn't need you any-

164

more, hoping all the while that when that day finally came, you'd turn to me again."

Leah stared at him in utter astonishment. "I . . . I don't know what to say, Mead."

"You don't need to say anything, Leah. I can see I've hidden my feelings entirely too well. You'll need some time to absorb it and to adjust to your new situation. At least now I have the assurance of knowing your affections are not otherwise engaged, and I can dare hope . . ." He grinned again. "I suppose hoping is what I do best."

He looked so sweetly sad, Leah wanted to kiss his smoothly shaven cheek. Instead, she squeezed the fingers that still gripped hers. "You've given me a lot to think about," she said noncommittally.

"And to dream about, too, I hope. Oops, there I go again. Just remember I love you, Leah, and I always have. When you're ready, I'll be waiting."

He lifted her fingers to his lips and kissed them lightly. Leah was too stunned to resist, and when he released her hands, she stepped quickly away and took her leave, hardly knowing what she said or even if her farewell was coherent. By the time she reached the front door, she was fairly running, but she stopped dead when she emerged onto the sidewalk to find Cal Stevens leaning against the building, waiting for her. He straightened the instant she appeared.

His face was shadowed beneath the crown of his Stetson, but the anger radiating from him was like the heat from a roaring furnace. "And what's wrong with you?" she demanded more sharply than she had intended.

"Not a damn thing," he snarled, crossing his arms

belligerently. "You ready to go?"

She most certainly was not. "How dare you use that language with me!"

His jaw twitched, but his expression remained fixed. "Oh, excuse me, Miss Harding. I forgot myself, but then, I'm just a no-account gunslinger, and my manners ain't the best."

"You were listening!" she accused outraged, but when she saw the ripple of shock go through him, she knew she was wrong.

"I didn't have to listen," he said through clenched teeth. "I figured that's what he would've said about me, and I reckon I was right."

"Do you care so much what he thinks of you?" she asked in amazement.

"I don't give a damn what he thinks of me. Are you ready to go or not?"

"Then why are you so angry?" she demanded, ignoring his question.

His lips tightened until his mouth was a thin, pale slash in his sun-darkened face. After what seemed a long time, he asked very quietly, "Are you going home with us?"

"Why shouldn't I?" she asked in confusion.

Again he hesitated, as if weighing his words carefully. "I figured maybe . . . maybe you'd stay in town and have supper with him tonight."

Reaction hit her in a flood tide of emotions that swirled so rapidly, she could hardly tell one from the other: surprise, amazement, and revelation. But she must be wrong, she told herself. It was impossible! Cal Stevens wouldn't be *jealous* of Mead Garland. He *couldn't* be! That is, unless . . . But it was un-

166

thinkable. Cal Stevens wasn't in love with her.

Memories of their kiss teased at the edges of her mind, but she shook them off. That meant nothing. She'd thrown herself into his arms. Of course he'd kissed her. An impulse of the moment, an opportunity too tempting to resist, nothing more.

Then why was he so furious over the mere suspicion that she might take her supper with Mead Garland?

Folding her hands primly in front of her so he wouldn't see them trembling, she said, "I informed Mr. Garland that I wouldn't be able to accept his invitation to supper."

"Why not?"

Leah's first impulse was to tell him it was none of his business, but of course it was. He had made it his business, and she had let him. "Because . . ." Briefly, she considered telling him the truth, that she had no intention of encouraging Mead's attentions, particularly after that fervent declaration of love which she could not return. But no, she couldn't humiliate Mead like that. "Because Brad still thinks you and I are . . . courting. He would certainly wonder if I started seeing Mead, too."

"Oh. Sure." He didn't sound sure at all, and he still sounded furious. "You ready to go?"

She didn't think she was, but if they stood in front of Mead's office much longer, he might come out to see what was keeping them. "Yes, I need to go to the mercantile for a few things. Then I'll go to Mrs. Otto's to help Espy choose her new wardrobe."

He nodded, a stiff jerk of his head. "I'll be in the saloon when you want me." Before she could recover the use of her tongue, he was gone, striding purposefully down the street toward the batwing doors, leaving Leah to gape in his wake.

Of all the insolent, uncouth, ill-bred, ill-mannered . . . Words failed her in her rage. How dare he walk off and leave her standing in the street? How dare he make her think he cared whether or not she took supper with Mead Garland and then just stroll away as if it didn't matter a whit?

And how dare he make her think he was jealous and then leave before she could find out for sure!

Cal couldn't remember ever being so mad. The trouble was, he couldn't figure out if he was more mad at Leah or himself.

Not that he had any excuse for being mad at Leah. She hadn't done a damn thing except get herself invited to supper, and she hadn't even accepted. The problem was that Garland had invited her right in front of Cal, just like Cal was a servant or even a piece of furniture and his presence — and his opinion — didn't matter one goddamn bit.

In his more rational moments, Cal told himself it was a good thing Garland had treated him that way. It proved nobody knew how he felt about Leah. Cal just wished to hell she hadn't looked over to see what his reaction was. It was enough to make a man think she cared what he thought, even when he knew that was crazy. She didn't give a damn what Cal Stevens thought. She'd just been embarrassed.

Then he'd made a damn fool of himself out on the sidewalk, making her tell him the only reason she'd turned Garland down was so they could keep Brad from finding out the truth. What had he expected her to say, that she wouldn't dream of seeing another man because she was in love with Cal? Now he really was being a damn fool.

Cal spent the rest of the morning nursing a beer in the saloon until he felt reasonably sure he could face Leah again without any more attacks of insanity. Brad found him when they were ready to leave, and just as Cal had expected, Leah made no attempt to engage him in conversation on the ride home. Instead, she watched him warily out of the corner of her eye, as if she were afraid he might do something else untoward. He somehow managed not to.

When they got back to the ranch, Cal left immediately to join the men out on the range, as far away from Leah Harding as he could get.

Cal Stevens certainly didn't act like a man in love, Leah told herself over and over again during the next three days. If anything, he acted like he couldn't stand the sight of her, and he'd done his level best to avoid her company at every opportunity. So much for her plan to discuss revealing his identity to Brad.

And so much for her plan to cheer Brad up. Although Leah would have thought it impossible, things between the newlyweds had gone from bad to worse. Tonight was the worst of all, and Leah lay awake to the sound of their raised voices, a captive audience to the drama.

"I told you, I'm too tired!" Espy insisted shrilly, her words carrying easily through the wall.

"You're always too tired!" Brad snapped back.

"Leave me alone! Sometimes I think that's all you think about. That's the only reason you married me, isn't it? To get me in bed!"

"No," Brad snarled furiously, "I married you because you're gonna have a baby, and the reason you are is because you never minded spreading your legs for me *before* we was married!"

"What does that mean?" Espy demanded.

"That means I reckon I know why you liked it so much before. You wanted a soft life for yourself, so you decided to trap me into marriage!"

"I never trapped you into nothing!"

"Yes, you did, and we both know it. You just pretended you loved me before!"

"And you just pretended you loved me so you could get under my skirt! I hate you, Brad Harding! I wish you was dead!"

Leah's heart lurched to a stop, and she bolted upright in her bed, words of protest trembling on her lips, but Brad didn't need her help.

"You'd like that, wouldn't you?" Brad shouted. "Think you'd be a rich widow with all my money to spend without having to put up with me, but you're wrong! I've got a will now. That's what we was doing in town the other day. It leaves the ranch to Leah, so if I die, you don't get nothing!"

Espy's wail of anguish sent chills up Leah's spine. "That ain't fair!" she shrieked. "I'm your wife! And what about your baby?"

"You'll be took care of by Leah. It's in the will, all of it, so if you're thinking you'll be rich if you get rid of me, you've got another think coming!"

The sound of flesh striking flesh made Leah jump.

Brad's grunt of surprise became a howl of protest, and the sound of scuffling came clearly through the wall. Leah was out of bed, fumbling for her slippers and robe, ready to rush to break up the fight, when the sounds changed subtly. A coy giggle drifted to her, followed by a masculine whoop of triumph, then silence except for the creaking complaint of the bed ropes.

Her robe half on, Leah sank wearily back down onto her bed. Suddenly, she felt terribly alone, and reluctantly she recalled the comfort she had found in Cal Stevens's strong arms. What she wouldn't give for such comfort now, for someone to hold her and tell her everything would be fine even though she knew it wouldn't be.

At least Espy now knew about the will, and her father would know the next time he visited since Espy kept no secrets from him. Brad would be safe from that danger, but what could protect him from the life Leah foresaw for him with Espy as his wife? Curling up into a fetal position, Leah pulled the covers over her head in a futile attempt to drown out the sounds of coupling from the other room. Fistfights that ended in a burst of passion. Surely Brad deserved better than that.

Yet still Leah envied him. At least he finally got the passion, while Leah got only the echo. She hugged her pillow to her, calling herself a fool for even thinking about such things yet unable to stop.

How many years had she lain here alone without minding it, without even caring that there might be something else for her? She'd even turned down an opportunity to marry, and, she reminded herself, even now it wasn't too late. Hadn't Mead been hinting that very thing just a few days ago? *Someone* wanted her, had always wanted her, and she needn't lie alone if she didn't want to.

Unfortunately, when she remembered the tepid kisses she and Mead had shared during their brief engagement and compared them to the fire of Cal Stevens's, she knew she could never settle for anything less. Yes, better to be alone than to settle.

Then Brad moaned with pleasure, and silence fell, heavy in the darkness. An ache started, deep in her chest, and spread, seeping, until it filled her, an ache for the love she had never known and for the children she had never borne and for comfort she had never had. Leah cursed the fates. Why didn't Mead Garland make her feel the way Cal Stevens did?

And why didn't Cal Stevens feel about her the way Mead Garland did?

Morning brought no answers. As had become her habit, Espy slept until noon, stirring only when called to dinner at noon. Brad, however, was up at daylight looking far more content than Leah had seen him in days.

She had even begun to think things might begin to improve between the newlyweds until Brad came back from working that evening and tried to give his bride an exuberant kiss.

"Leave me alone! I've got the headache," she complained, pushing him roughly away. "Good Lord in heaven, is that all you ever think about?"

"You're my wife, Espy," Brad reminded her for what must have been the hundredth time. Leah fled to the kitchen where she could rattle pots and pans to drown out the sound of the argument.

She and Juanita were putting supper on the table when they heard Espy's squeal of delight. *"Pa! Now ain't this a surprise!"*

"No surprise to me," Juanita muttered darkly as she went to get another place setting.

Leah sighed and realized Espy wasn't the only one with a headache. Putting on her hostess smile, she went into the parlor to greet Homer Wilkes and ascertain whether or not he had brought the rest of his brood along.

He had not, and Leah found the two Wilkeses huddled on the sofa, Espy teary-eyed and confiding her grievances against her new husband, Homer nodding gravely. Brad looked on with barely concealed fury.

"Mr. Wilkes," she said without the slightest trace of welcome, "what brings you here?"

"Just come to see how you've been treating my girl," he said, his satisfied grin telling her things were every bit as bad as he had expected.

"Perhaps you aren't up to company just now, Espy," Leah suggested hopefully, but the girl shot her a mutinous glare.

"I'm always up to a visit from my kin," the girl informed her. "He's the only one around here who really cares about me."

Wilkes patted her shoulder reassuringly, but before anyone could reply to her outrageous statement, the front door swung open and Cal Stevens stepped in.

The sight of him struck Leah like an electrical charge, and she knew the others felt the same shock. Cal swept off his Stetson and nodded to the ladies. "Miss Harding, Mrs. Harding."

Leah opened her mouth to return his greeting, but Espy beat her to it, smiling brightly. "Why, 'evening, Cal. I been wondering when you was gonna join us for supper again. It's been an age. I figured you must've had a fuss with Leah over something." She glanced slyly at Leah, then back at Cal again, positively preening under his attention. "But just 'cause you're mad at her don't mean you can't come see the rest of the family."

"Espy, shut your mouth," Brad snapped, moving toward Cal and ignoring Espy's gasp of outrage. "You'll eat with us, won't you?" he asked, obviously grateful for Cal's support.

Cal glanced at Leah, silently telling her he was waiting for her invitation, and for some reason, Leah couldn't seem to breathe properly anymore. "Of course he will," she said, praying no one else could tell how very glad she was to have him in her house again. Lord, she'd actually *missed* him! "I'll tell Juanita to set another place."

She hurried out, drawing deep breaths so she wouldn't be panting when she spoke to Juanita and wondering why on earth she felt so happy when an evening in the company of Homer Wilkes loomed ahead.

Supper was as awful as she could have imagined with Espy determinedly flirting with Cal who just as determinedly pretended not to notice and Brad glaring and his father-in-law gloating. After supper, when the men had smoked on the porch and the women had cleaned off the table, they all retired to the parlor.

Leah couldn't imagine any group of people less suited to enjoying an evening of conversation together, and after Espy had held forth for twenty minutes describing all the new dresses Mrs. Otto was making for her, Leah was ready to scream.

Instinctively, she glanced at Cal, who was sitting in the wingchair opposite her own, only to find him watching her in return. The impact of his gaze held her, and she was unable to turn away even though she plainly felt the color rising in her cheeks. His expression was somber, as if he were considering something very carefully and weighing all the options before taking action.

After several labored heartbeats, he said, "Maybe you'd like to go for a walk, Miss Leah."

He'd spoken softly, for her ears alone, but his voice seemed to echo like thunder, and Leah was acutely aware that everyone else had heard the question, too, and was waiting to hear her reply. Refusing to acknowledge their sudden attention, Leah told herself she would have walked out with the devil himself to get away from this unpleasant situation. She managed a nonchalant smile. "I believe I'd enjoy a walk."

She rose from her chair and started for the door. "I hope you'll excuse us," she murmured as she passed the others.

"Kinda cold for a walk, ain't it?" Homer Wilkes remarked to no one in particular.

Following behind her, Cal hesitated a moment. Leah could practically feel his anger and sent him a warning glance over her shoulder. She needn't have worried. His rugged features were set in that implacable expression she was coming to recognize. He refused to be goaded.

Leah took her shawl from where it hung beside the front door and wrapped it around her shoulders.

"Can't figure why somebody'd go outside in the wind when they had a warm fire inside," Wilkes added provocatively.

"Why, Pa," Espy chided, "he can't kiss her in front of all of us, now can he?"

If Leah hadn't wanted to get away so desperately, she would have shaken Espy's teeth loose. Instead she pretended not to have heard and threw open the front door and left in a swish of skirts. Halfway across the porch she stopped, waiting for Cal to catch up and letting the crisp evening air cool the fire in her cheeks.

Cal closed the front door quietly, then came up beside her, his presence a palpable strength. She looked up and their gazes locked.

"Thank you . . ."

"I'm sorry . . ."

They spoke at once and stopped at once, grinning sheepishly at each other. "You first," he said.

"I was just going to thank you for rescuing me. I don't think I could have stood another minute of Espy's wardrobe descriptions."

"It was self-defense. I couldn't stand it either."

Behind them they heard Espy's voice raised shrilly. "I don't care if she does hear me!"

Cal stiffened and took Leah's arm. She surrendered gladly to his escort and allowed him to guide her down the steps and into the ranch yard where they could no longer hear the voices inside. A gust of wind teased at her skirt, and she wrapped the shawl more tightly around her.

"He was right about that, at least," Cal said wryly. "It *is* a might cold for a walk."

She smiled up at him. "Not for me. Last August I was

praying for an evening like this, so I'm going to enjoy it."

They strolled aimlessly, Leah following his lead as he moved toward the edge of the yard, away from the outbuildings and toward the far side of the house.

"You've been a stranger lately," she remarked as casually as she could.

He shrugged his broad shoulders, and Leah tried not to notice the latent power easily visible beneath the fabric of his shirt. "I don't like to intrude. The boy's got enough to worry about just now." That didn't explain why he'd been so angry at Leah or why he'd been avoiding *her,* but she let it pass.

"Has he . . . confided in you at all?" Leah ventured.

"About Espy?" She nodded. "Not really, but he's said enough. Sorta makes you wonder . . ." His voice trailed off, and he looked away, obviously uncomfortable.

"Wonder what?" she prodded.

Was he flushing? He didn't quite meet her eye. "How she got that baby in the first place."

No wonder he was flushing! Now Leah was, too, and she called herself an idiot for pressing the issue. Cal Stevens was the last person with whom she should be discussing Brad's sex life. "Uh, yes," she managed, unable to meet his eye now.

She stared off into the distance, absently admiring the way the setting sun had painted the sky with shades of orange and gold. Then she recalled the argument she had overheard last night. "He accused her of tricking him into marriage so she could have a soft life."

"Ain't hard to figure. She wouldn't be the first."

They walked on, around the side of the house, until

they could no longer even see the outbuildings and were likewise hidden from view from anyone who might venture out into the yard.

"I feel I should apologize for her behavior towards you," Leah said after a moment.

"What do you mean?" he asked. He seemed genuinely puzzled, and Leah forced herself not to notice how appealing he looked with the sun gilding his already bronzed skin.

"I mean the way she flirts with you. It's scandalous." The very thought made Leah furious, and she didn't allow herself to decide exactly why. When she looked up, she saw Cal studying her face intently and wondered what he saw in her expression. She tried to smooth it out as she had seen Cal do to hide his emotions, but she doubted she was as successful as he.

They had reached the rear corner of the house, the farthest from the rest of the ranch buildings, and they stopped. The wind gusted, buffeting Leah, and Cal caught her arm when she teetered. His touch shocked her, a shock that redoubled when he suddenly took her other arm and jerked her a step closer to him. She looked up in surprise into blazing blue eyes only inches from hers. He was no longer concealing his emotions, and the sheer intensity of his gaze held her helpless for a heartbeat that never came because her heart had lurched to a sudden and painful halt.

"Espy was right about something else, too," he said, his voice a hoarse whisper against the wind.

"What?" Leah whispered back. Her lungs weren't working either.

"About me wanting to kiss you."

Something turned over inside of her, and her jaw

dropped. This couldn't be happening!

"I warned you about opening your mouth," he murmured fiercely in the second before his lips closed over hers. The kiss was hot and wet and demanding, and Leah stood helpless, his hands pinning her arms to her sides while he plundered her mouth, claiming it for his own. Surrender was impossible . . . and unnecessary. She had only to stand there and let him have his way while the glorious sensations washed over her and triumph swelled within her. *Cal Stevens did want her!*

Too soon he tore his mouth from hers and lifted his head to look down at her. His eyes were blue fire and his breath came in ragged gasps that mingled with her own. Still he held her in a bruising grip, as if afraid she might struggle or even flee if he so much as relaxed his hold.

"I broke my word," he said. The anguish in his voice told her he seldom did.

"Yes," she breathed, acutely aware of the penalty she had imposed for it.

"What are you going to do?"

Tension fairly vibrated through him as he waited for her reply. The same tension hummed through her, too, making everything so clear, she wondered how she could not have seen the answer before.

"Let me go, and I'll show you."

Chapter Six

Knowing he'd ruined everything, knowing it was all over and he might never set eyes on her — Oh, God, or on his son — again, Cal slowly relaxed his grip on her arms, gradually gentling it into a caress until he wasn't even touching her anymore, then letting his hands fall limply to his sides.

She looked so beautiful he could hardly stand it, with her honey-colored eyes shining, her cheeks flushed, and her lips moist and rosy from his kiss. He stared, memorizing every detail for the long years ahead when he would be alone and . . .

She was moving. He braced himself for a slap, but she wasn't moving like that. She was lifting *both* arms, hesitantly, carefully, as if not quite sure, then she laid her hands on his shoulders, as lightly as a butterfly's touch. Dear God, what . . . ?

Frozen in disbelief, he watched as she came up on tiptoe, lifting her face until her lips were only a hair's breadth from his, until he could taste her again even though he wasn't touching her, and then she pressed her mouth to his. The fairy kiss hit him like a lightning bolt, stunning him so that he didn't kiss her back, *couldn't* kiss her back, couldn't even move.

She drew away, studying his face, suddenly uncertain, doubting, and it was this doubt that galvanized him. Strength surged through him, and with a groan, he threw his arms around her, crushing her to him as if he would draw her into himself, finding her mouth with eager lips and forcing his way inside to sweep the tender recesses with his avid tongue and drink her intoxicating essence.

She clung to him fiercely, knocking off his hat and burying her fingers in his hair. She even, at his urging, moved her tongue against his, tentatively at first, then more boldly until desire raged like wildfire and he had to stop or take her right here on the ground.

He pushed her away to arm's length, then held her there, almost afraid she might evaporate as she had so many nights in his dreams. But she stood there, real and warm and just as breathless as he. Questions swirled in his mind, so many things he wanted to know, *needed* to know, but when he opened his mouth, the most ridiculous one popped out.

"Did he kiss you?"

Her eyes widened in surprise. "What? Who?"

"Garland, the other day in his office. You came out looking so . . ."

"Oh!" she exclaimed in sudden amusement. "Is that why . . . ? No, he didn't . . . I mean, yes," she quickly amended and grew even more amused when she saw his outrage. "He kissed my hand."

She lifted it from his shoulder to show him which one, and Cal clasped it desperately and pressed his mouth into her palm, then turned it and covered the

181

back with kiss after kiss until he'd adored every inch of it.

If this was a dream, Leah wanted to savor every moment of it. "Or maybe it was this one," she mused, offering her other hand for Cal's attention when he'd finished with the first one. I must be crazy, she thought vaguely as Cal's mouth trailed across her other hand, which explains why I'm acting this way, silly and coy and flirtatious and not like myself at all.

When he'd finished with her other hand, his gaze met hers again, and for a long moment he simply stared into her eyes as if trying to read something there, something he hadn't expected to see or perhaps something he couldn't quite believe.

"Why didn't you marry him?" he demanded.

She blinked in confusion. "Mead?" she asked.

He nodded.

"Because I didn't have to."

"Didn't have to?" he echoed. He looked outraged. "You mean you thought you were . . . ?"

His voice trailed off ominously, and for a moment Leah didn't know what he meant. Realization brought the heat to her face. "Oh, no! I mean, I wanted to get married so I could leave my father's house. I wanted to get away from him, and I thought if I had my own home, I could even get Brad away, too, at least sometimes. But then he died, my father," she clarified, "and I didn't have to leave, so I broke my engagement."

"Didn't you love him?"

"I . . . no," she admitted. "Not really. I was fond of him," she added when she saw the satisfaction in Cal's eyes, not wanting to remove *every* reason for him to be jealous of Mead.

"And are you 'fond' of me, too?" he asked, challenge in his voice.

Could such a tame word describe her feelings when Cal Stevens kissed her? Hardly. "Not . . . exactly," she hedged, but that was enough for Cal.

With a groan, he took her in his arms and claimed her once more, sealing his possession with heated kisses and urgent hands that pressed her to him until there was no longer any separation between them.

Desire roared through her, swallowing reason and restraint, compelling her to get close and closer still, to hold him tight and tighter still, until even that was not enough. At last, when they were both gasping, he tore his mouth from hers again and simply held her, his arms like iron bands binding them together, his beard-roughened cheek pressed to hers, his breath rasping in her ear.

"I'm not a rich man, Leah. I can't offer you anything like you've been used to, but I've got some money saved," he was saying, each word a painful gasp. "I've been thinking for a long time I should get a place of my own, but I never had any reason to before. It won't be much, at least not at first, but — "

Good heavens! Hadn't it been just days ago she was explaining to Brad why she couldn't possibly consider marrying Cal Stevens? Reality hit her like a dash of cold water, and she pushed away until she could see his face. "Cal, you . . . we . . . can't . . . It's too soon!" And it was. Even if he could overcome all her previous objections, they hardly knew each other, and marriage was a big step, an *enormous* step, and Leah didn't even know if she wanted to marry, or if her reasons for doing so were right, or if Brad might need her or — "

"This isn't about Brad," he said urgently, as if reading her thoughts. "I'm not saying this because you're his sister."

Until this moment she hadn't even considered the possibility, and the thought brought her crashing back to earth from wherever his kisses had carried her. "I didn't think — "

"There's something between us, Leah. It was there the first time we met. You feel it, too. I know you do."

She did, of course, and even if she'd wanted to deny it, her behavior had proved otherwise. "But that isn't enough, Cal. Just look at Brad and Espy."

Slowly the fire in his eyes died, and he straightened to his full height, dropping his arms so he no longer touched her. Instantly she felt bereft, but she resisted the urge to reach for him again. She needed to think, and when she was in his arms, she couldn't think at all.

Feeling suddenly chilled, she realized she had dropped her shawl. Cal bent down and retrieved it for her, shaking off the dust before handing it back. While she wrapped it around her shoulders with unsteady hands, he scooped up his hat and slapped it against his leg a few times before settling it on his head again. The wool of the shawl provided none of the heat Cal's kisses had given her, and she fairly trembled when she remembered the power passion held. No wonder people did crazy things for love. If only Leah could believe this was really love.

"There are so many things to consider," she offered lamely.

"Yeah," he agreed gruffly. "You don't know much about me."

"And you don't know much about me."

184

He grinned mirthlessly. "I know everything I need to."

What did that mean? Leah couldn't bring herself to ask, probably because she suspected it had something to do with her less-than-circumspect response to his kisses. "And there's Brad to consider," she reminded him as primly as she could manage. "We don't know how he'll react when he finds out you're his father, and you don't seem in any hurry to tell him."

He stiffened at the implied criticism, but she lifted her chin in defiance, refusing to apologize.

"He's got a lot on his mind right now," Cal said.

"So he does, but the situation isn't going to change any time soon. How long were you planning to wait?"

His expression grew stony. "As long as I can. Like you said, we don't know how he'll take it. He might run me off."

"Oh!" Leah cried in dismay. Of course! Why hadn't she realized he'd been holding off for fear of rejection? No one could blame him for wanting to spend as much time with Brad as possible before breaking the news that might part them forever. "I'm sorry. I just didn't think!"

Forgetting her resolve, Leah reached out to him, and he grasped her hand as if she were a lifeline. "And what if he did run me off? What would you do?"

Leah had no idea, which was why she had to think, something she couldn't do with Cal Stevens's disturbing blue eyes watching her so closely. "We need some time to work all this out," she said, knowing the answer wouldn't satisfy him but unable to give him any other.

He dropped her hand and took a step back. "Sure. I can wait. I've got nothing better to do anyway."

He was angry, and she suspected he had a right to be, but before she could think of anything to placate him, they both heard the sound of a running horse.

"What the . . . ?" Cal muttered, stepping around the corner of the house to see what the trouble might be.

Leah followed, and they saw Brad on horseback, streaking away toward the setting sun.

"Doesn't that damn fool know not to start a horse at a dead run?" Cal demanded.

"Something must have happened," Leah told him over her shoulder as she fairly ran back toward the front of the house, a lump of dread forming in her stomach.

Cal murmured what might have been a curse as he hurried after her. The front door was still standing wide open, and inside they found Espy weeping hysterically while her father sat by looking grim and making no attempt to comfort her.

"What happened?" Leah asked, going to Espy's side and slipping an arm around her thin shoulders.

Espy replied by wailing even louder and burying her head in Leah's shoulder. Helplessly, Leah looked to Wilkes for an explanation.

"The younguns had themselves a little fuss, is all. Seems like the boy's been scaring Espy with talk of cutting her out of his will or some such."

This revived Espy, who jerked away from Leah as if she'd just discovered she'd been snuggling a grizzly bear. "It's true!" she screeched. "He told me. He's got that lawyer fixing everything up right now. He's gonna leave everything to *her*." She stabbed a finger contemptuously toward Leah. "It ain't natural for a man to love his sister more'n he loves his own wife!"

"That's not the reason —" Leah began but Wilkes shouted her down.

"It ain't natural at all," he agreed, "but I figure we know who rules the roost around here, don't we?"

"Mr. Wilkes," Cal said in a voice that sent chills up Leah's spine. "You better remember you're a guest in this house."

Wilkes snorted his disgust. "Maybe you think I'm afraid of you, Stevens, but you don't scare me, not when I'm standing up for what's right, and it ain't right for a man to leave his money to his sister and leave his wife to starve."

"Espy won't starve," Leah informed him, raising her voice to make herself heard. "And it's foolish to argue over what becomes of Brad's property when he dies when he's only seventeen and likely to outlive us all!"

She glared at Wilkes, silently daring him to hint that Brad might fall victim to an accident and confirm her worst suspicions of him.

He glared back for a long moment, but when he spoke, his voice was more reasonable. "It still ain't right, and nobody can tell me it is. I might just have me a talk with this lawyer myself and see about getting things changed back the way they should be."

"And it ain't too late!" Espy piped in triumph. "Brad ain't signed it yet, so there's still time to fix it!"

"Espy," Leah said, trying to be reasonable. "Brad should have explained to you that you and your children will be provided for. You'll always have a home here and —"

"— and I'll always have to ask you for every dime I spend and every piece of bread that goes into my mouth!" Espy shrilled. "No thanks! *Pa,* you got to do something!"

"Don't think I won't, neither! I'll have me a talk with that boy, first chance. Nobody treats my girl like trash and gets away with it!"

Leah was so angry, she could barely speak, but she managed to force the words past her clenched teeth. "I'm sure Brad would appreciate any advice you have to give him, Mr. Wilkes, but since he isn't here at the moment, perhaps you'll leave us now. Espy is upset. That can't be good for her, and your presence is only making things worse."

"Pa!" Espy wailed in protest.

Wilkes drew himself up straighter, stuck out his chin, and probably would have told Leah exactly what he thought of her invitation to leave, but Cal took a menacing step toward him, and he instantly deflated. His beady eyes darted to Leah, to Cal, and back to Leah again. "I know when I'm not welcome, but I'll be back. That boy needs some sense talked to him, and I aim to do it."

He stomped out in a huff, slamming the door behind him. The instant he was gone, Espy uttered a howl of outrage, bolted from the sofa, and raced away toward her bedroom. The sound of the bedroom door slamming shook the pictures on the wall.

Leah winced and looked at Cal. For a long moment they silently offered each other comfort. At last she said, "Cal? Brad shouldn't be —"

"I'll go after him."

In a moment he was gone, and Leah buried her face in her hands. Thank heaven he was here. What would she have done without him?

Cal saddled the first horse he could catch in the corral and, not wanting to duplicate Brad's mistake, started out slowly but no less determinedly than Brad had. Gradually he worked the horse up to a gallop, but he hadn't gone far when he saw the boy walking his horse up ahead.

Brad turned to watch his approach and stopped to wait for him. Cal slowed and reined up beside him. "You got something against that animal that you're trying to kill it?" he inquired sarcastically.

"He's all right," Brad said, patting the horse's neck. "I'm sorry, Cal. I didn't mean to act like a damn fool, but I had to get away. They were . . ."

"What were they doing?" Cal prompted, feeling the impotent rage he always felt when Brad was suffering and he could do nothing to prevent it.

"They were saying things about Leah. Espy thinks Leah hates her."

"Espy hasn't done much to make Leah *like* her, but all that aside, you oughta remind Espy it was Leah's doing that you two got married in the first place."

"I tried," Brad complained, "but you don't know Espy. She don't let a man get a word in edgeways."

"Then don't wait for her to let you," Cal advised. "You're the man. It's your job to tell her how things are going to be."

Brad frowned. "She wants Leah to move out. She says things'll be better between us once she's gone."

"Do you believe her?"

Brad shook his head. "And I can't put Leah out. It's her house, too, never mind what Pa's will said. And it's

189

my job to take care of her, at least until . . ." He looked hopefully at Cal.

Cal couldn't help grinning back. "Well, things between us *are* looking a little better than they were, but Leah's not going to marry *anybody* until she's sure you'll be all right. It's all up to you, boy. You've got to sit your wife down and tell her how things are going to be. Then, when Leah sees you've got her under control, she'll be free to think about leaving you on your own."

Brad sighed. "I never knew life could get so complicated."

Cal grinned sympathetically. "Just wait 'til you've got a son of your own."

The time passed slowly, but finally Leah heard the sound of horses in the yard. She looked out to see that Cal had found the boy and brought him home, but when Brad came in, he was alone. Leah realized Cal was being considerate, allowing her privacy with Brad to work out a family problem in which he had no right to interfere, and she was touched because she knew how very much he would want to help his son through this.

Brad looked like a naughty boy who'd been dragged home for punishment, and Leah could hardly resist the urge to hug him.

"I hated to send Cal after you, but I was afraid your horse might break a leg or something," she said gently.

He nodded forlornly. "Yeah, it was a damn fool thing to do. Cal already told me."

"Espy told me what you were arguing about."

Brad straightened defiantly. "You don't need to worry. I ain't gonna change my mind about the will."

She *had* been a little worried, but she was more concerned about Brad's relationship with his wife. If it didn't improve, Espy might yet wear him down to the point where he was willing to do anything to win her good will. "I think you should have a talk with Espy, and explain—"

"There's no talking to her," Brad insisted. He began to pace. "Every time I try, she just starts crying or screaming or both."

"Brad?" Espy screamed from the hallway. "Is that you?"

Brad muttered a curse, and for a moment Leah was afraid he might bolt again, but when Espy appeared in the hall doorway, he stood his ground.

"Well, look what blew in with the tumbleweeds," she remarked caustically.

"It's a sorry thing when a man gets drove out of his own house," Brad snapped right back.

"Nobody drove you anywheres. You just ain't man enough to face up to—"

"Ain't man enough!" he shouted. "I'll show you who ain't man enough!"

"Brad!" Leah cried, but he was already chasing Espy back down the hall. She started after them, but stopped when their bedroom door crashed shut, remembering how their last argument had ended. She certainly had no desire to go bursting in to find them thrashing around on the bed.

They were screaming now, but in a few minutes . . .

A cup of tea was what she needed, she thought, rubbing her throbbing temples. A cup of tea in the kitchen which was far enough from the bedrooms so she wouldn't be able to make out Brad and Espy's shouted imprecations.

If only she could think of some excuse to have Cal here with her.

Leah awoke with a start, groggy and disoriented and wondering what on earth she was doing in the kitchen. Then memories of last night returned in a rush. The argument that had gone on until the wee hours of the morning without abating until even the tea wouldn't keep Leah awake any longer and she had dozed off with her head on her arms on the kitchen table.

Juanita was bustling around, making breakfast and politely ignoring Leah, as if it were the most natural thing in the world to find her sleeping in the kitchen. Leah pushed her drooping hair out of her eyes and rubbed her stiff neck.

"Good morning," Juanita said blandly, and Leah smiled back sheepishly.

"That was a silly thing to do. I was waiting until Brad and Espy went to sleep, but I must have dozed off."

"They fight. All night."

The Hardings would never have any secrets from Juanita. "Did you hear what it was about?"

"Same thing. Always same thing."

Leah nodded dully and wished Cal Stevens were here. Not that he could have done anything, but Leah would have sold her soul for a strong shoulder and a pair of comforting arms just then.

But that's not enough, she reminded herself sternly, and she'd better stop thinking that it was. Resolutely, she pushed herself to her feet. Every muscle in her body protested, and a groan escaped her.

"You should go to bed," Juanita advised.

"Don't fix me any breakfast, and don't call me unless the house in on fire," Leah said as she shuffled wearily out of the kitchen. At least she could rest in peace all morning since Espy never rose before noon now that she was a lady of leisure.

No sooner had that consoling thought crossed her mind than Brad's bedroom door flew open and Espy stepped out. She was dressed in her wedding gown, a brand new bonnet perched jauntily on her head, and she was wrestling a sloppily tied bundle through the doorway.

At the sight of Leah, she hesitated for a moment, then continued, her expression defiant. Leah had to step out of the way so she could pass, since she obviously had no intention of stopping.

"Are you going someplace?" Leah asked, following her.

"Yeah, if it's any of your business. You'll be happy to know I'm leaving!"

"Leaving?" Leah echoed stupidly. She must still be asleep and having a nightmare.

"Yeah, *leaving*. Nobody wants me here, and I don't stay where I ain't wanted," she informed Leah over her shoulder as she trundled into the parlor.

Brad was there, waiting, his expression grim and furious.

"Brad, what's going on?"

"Espy's leaving me," he said tightly.

Was the whole world going crazy?

"Are you going back to your father?" she asked incredulously.

Espy sniffed her contempt for such an idea. "I don't have to go back there so he can treat me like a slave again! I got friends I can go to!"

With that, she stomped out the front door. Leah turned to Brad. "You can't just let her walk out! She's carrying your baby!"

Brad looked at her as if she were a none-too-bright child. "She's just trying to scare me, Leah. She thinks if she goes away for a day or two, I'll come crawling to her and beg her to come back. For Pete's sake, she's only going to Sally Beamish's house."

"Beamish?" Leah cast about frantically to place the name. "The blacksmith's family?"

"Yeah, they got a daughter went to school with Espy. Espy figures they'll take her in."

The idea was so bizarre, Leah could hardly credit it. "She actually thinks she can just move in with them? A married woman? Who's in a family way?"

"I told you, she ain't serious. If she was, she'd be going to her pa."

"Who'd likely send her right back here again. He knows she's not worth anything to him unless she's your wife."

"Just what I figured. She wants me to stew for a few days without her, so I figure I'll let her stew, too."

"Brad!" Espy screamed from the front yard. "I'm tired of waiting! I want to get shed of this place!"

Brad shrugged, gave Leah a wink, and hastened to do his wife's bidding.

Leah slumped down onto the sofa and sighed. Well, maybe she had misjudged her baby brother. Maybe he *could* deal with the harridan he'd married. Maybe she'd just spent a nearly sleepless night for nothing. And if he could, maybe Leah would, finally, be free to think about her own life for a change and the man who wanted a place in it.

"You'll be sorry, Brad Harding," Espy said for at least the tenth time since they'd left home. Brad was hauling her bundle from the back of the buggy while she waited at the end of the Beamish's front walk. "You'll miss me when I'm gone."

"I'm sure I will," Brad agreed solemnly, wondering whether the Beamishes would even let her in the door when they saw she was fixing to move in on them.

The Beamish's front door opened, and Sally Beamish stuck her head out. "Espy?" she called uncertainly.

Espy preened in her new finery. "It's me all right. I come to show you all my new duds."

Sally squealed with delight and ran down the porch steps to greet her visitors, her plump figure jiggling inside her calico dress. She obligingly oohed and aahed over Espy's wedding ring and her new dress and her even newer bonnet while Brad stood silently by.

When Sally paused for breath, Espy gave Brad a haughty look and snatched the bundle from his hands. "I'll take that. I'll see you later, Brad."

"Yeah, sure," Brad said, fighting a triumphant grin.

"What else've you got?" Sally was asking, her homely face alight with fascination as Brad climbed back into the buggy.

"Let's go inside, and I'll show you," Espy replied.

Brad didn't look back as he drove away. So he'd be sorry, would he? Not on the longest day he lived. If anybody'd be sorry, it was Espy, and he knew just how to make her that way. Brad turned the buggy onto Main

Street and pulled up in front of Mead Garland's office. He found his old friend in his office.

"Brad, good to see you," Mead exclaimed, jumping up from behind his desk and hurrying forward to shake his hand. "I was going to send you word tomorrow. I just finished drawing up the will."

Brad smiled broadly. "I can't tell you how glad I am to hear it, Mr. Garland. Reckon I could sign it right now?"

Garland chuckled in surprise. "I can't see why not. We'll need a witness, but that shouldn't be too hard. Is anyone with you? Leah can't be a witness, of course, since she's named in the will, but that Stevens would do since he isn't a beneficiary."

"No, nobody's with me except Espy, and I've left her at Sally Beamish's house for a visit. If it's all right, I'll go out right now and see if I can find somebody. I'm in sort of a hurry."

"Espy anxious to get home, is she?"

Brad smiled grimly. "She ain't going home with me. She's gonna spend a day or two with Sally."

Mead's eyebrows rose in surprise, but he was too well-bred to remark on the strangeness of this situation. Instead, he slapped Brad on the back and said, "Well, then, let's see who we can find. There's bound to be someone at the mercantile who wouldn't mind stepping in for a minute to help us out. You go there, and I'll check the saloon in case you don't find anyone."

"Oooh, you sure fell into it with Brad Harding," Sally exclaimed when the last of Espy's finery had been spread on her bed for examination. "How many dresses did you say Mrs. Otto is gonna make for you?"

"Three," Espy said with feigned boredom.

" 'Course, I woulda got more, but with the baby coming, Mrs. Otto said it was foolish to make dresses I couldn't wear later."

"Oh, Espy, then you'll get more new ones! It's so exciting! I don't envy you the baby, though. Ma, she carried on something awful when little Sammy was born. I don't reckon I'd care if I never had to go through it."

Espy shrugged. "My ma just dropped 'em like they was nothing. I figure I'm made like her, so I ain't too worried. What I don't like is taking care of 'em. I had about all I ever wanted of taking care of younguns at home."

"But you'll have a maid, won't you? Maybe Brad'll even get you a wet nurse. Then you wouldn't have to bother with the baby at all."

"Now that's an idea. *He* had a wet nurse. 'Course he was adopted, so his mother couldn't feed him herself, but I don't see why I have to. Then I wouldn't have to get up at night with the brat, neither!"

"Oh, Espy, being married must be such fun! Sit down and tell me all about it. How long can you stay? I know Ma'll invite you and Brad to supper if you want."

Espy began to gather up her finery and toss it into a pile so they could sit on the bed. "I figured I'd stay a few days. That way we can really visit."

Sally gaped at her. *"A few days?"*

"Sure," Espy informed her. "I'm a married woman now. I don't have to answer to nobody."

"But what about Brad? He won't like you to be away like that!"

"Who cares what Brad thinks? I've left him, anyways."

"Left him? What on earth are you talking about?"

"Well," Espy allowed, "I haven't really left him. I'm only letting him think I have. See, he treats me mean, and I figured if I showed him I didn't need him, he'd be all sorry and start treating me nicer."

"But you can't stay here!" Sally insisted. "What would Ma say?"

"She don't have to say anything. I've stayed here before, haven't I?"

"But you're married now! It ain't the same."

"I don't see how it's different."

"It is, though, and Ma'll know how and she'll tell us and tell us. She won't let you stay, I just know it. If you want to leave Brad, why don't you go back home?"

"Why'd I want to do a fool thing like that?" Espy asked angrily. "Pa wouldn't let me stay anyways. He'd say a wife's place is with her husband and all that. He likes having me living in that big house where he can visit and feel like he's important, too. And even if he did let me stay, he'd just want to . . . Well, I won't go there." She slapped the clothes she held back onto the sheet into which they had been bundled and began to tie them up again.

Unable to go back to sleep after learning of Espy's plans, Leah forced herself to eat some breakfast after all. She was just about to go in search of Cal so she could tell him what had happened before he left for the range when she heard Homer Wilkes's shouted greeting.

Not wanting to invite him into the house when Brad and Espy weren't there, Leah hurried out to the front porch. The men had spilled out of the cookhouse, and Pete Quincy and Cal Stevens were striding across the yard toward where Wilkes sat his horse at the foot of the porch steps.

"I come to talk to that boy," Wilkes announced. "Where is he?"

"I'm afraid he isn't home just now," Leah said coldly, realizing how much she felt the constraint of her woman's skirts. If she were a man, she could at the very least physically intimidate Wilkes. At the most, she could throw him bodily off the place.

"Not home?" Wilkes echoed incredulously. "You mean he never come back last night?"

"Of course he came back," Leah explained, raising her voice so Cal and Pete, who had just arrived, would be able to hear the explanation. "He and Espy were up most of the night . . . talking," she hedged. "I'm afraid Espy has decided she no longer wishes to live with Brad, and he's taken her into town. I believe she plans to stay with a friend there."

"The hell you say!" Wilkes shouted, swinging down from his horse. "I don't believe a word of it! Where is she? *Espy!*"

"She isn't here," Leah insisted, stepping in front of him when he climbed the steps and would have rushed past her into the house.

"Wilkes, stop right there," Cal ordered in the voice he apparently reserved exclusively for addressing Homer Wilkes.

Wilkes whirled and glared down at Cal who had moved up behind him. "You stay out of it, Stevens. This is family business."

"She ain't here," Cal told him. "They drove off early this morning. We all saw them." He gestured to indicate the rest of the men who nodded their affirmation.

Wilkes whirled accusingly back to Leah. "If she really left, she would've come home, to me, so where is she?"

"I believe she said something about visiting Sally Beamish."

Wilkes swore violently, making Leah flinch, but she clenched her hands together and refused to acknowledge how he had repulsed her. "Don't that girl have a brain in her head?" he asked of no one in particular. Then he turned his sly glance on Leah again. "But don't you worry, none, Miss Leah. I'll have her back here before you can say Jack Robinson."

Leah wasn't a bit worried. "Mr. Wilkes, I think it would be best if you didn't interfere, and let Brad and Espy work things out themselves."

"Oh, you'd like that, wouldn't you?" he scoffed. "If we leave it to them, he'll tell her good riddance, and she'll be having that baby out in the street!" Muttering imprecations against his headstrong daughter, Wilkes stomped down the steps and back over to his horse. In an instant he was mounted and riding away toward town.

Leah was silently muttering a few imprecations of her own. Well, at least if Brad fails, she consoled herself, Wilkes might succeed in getting her back. They would never let her have her baby on the street, of course, but the idea of her running around heaven-only-knew-where was frightening. Espy might think she was capable of taking care of herself, but Leah suspected differently, and the girl certainly wasn't capable of taking care of a child alone. Too late Leah realized she should have warned Wilkes not to beat the girl.

Cal and Pete had rushed to her. "What happened?"

Cal demanded, and Leah felt a sense of relief to have him by her side. "We saw them driving away this morning, but we thought — "

"They fought most of the night, and this morning Espy announced she was leaving Brad." Leah smiled wanly at their shock. "Brad believes she was only trying to frighten him into giving in to her. She plans to visit a girlfriend in town, although I can't imagine the girl's family will allow her to stay more than a day or two, especially when they understand the situation."

"Well, *I* don't understand the situation," Pete complained. "If she wanted to leave, why didn't she go home to her pa?"

"Because," Cal said, answering Leah's smile, "he would've sent her right back here. You saw the way he acted. He wants her here."

"And he's right," Pete said. "A woman's place is with her husband. Brad shouldn't've let her go in the first place."

"He felt it would be a good lesson for her to discover no one was willing to take her in," Leah explained to Pete, although she found her gaze returning again and again to Cal. How wonderful to have someone with whom to share the burden, someone who understood, someone whose eyes told her he was concerned about her as well.

"I'll take Miss Leah back inside," Cal told Pete, who nodded absently, still perplexed by the doings of the younger generation.

Leah's heart fluttered alarmingly in her chest as Cal came up the porch steps and took her arm to lead her back into the house. "Are you all right?" he asked gently. "You don't look like you got much sleep last night."

"I didn't," she admitted, feeling deliciously frail and feminine and wishing she were brazen enough to actually laid her head against his shoulder. "But I do think your son is showing signs of impending manhood. What did you say to him last night?"

"You mean after I pinned his ears back about running a cold horse like that and taking a chance of getting his neck broke?" Cal's smile was warm and conspiratorial, just as if they were parents discussing their wayward child. In a way, they were, only without the intimacy that should have developed over long years of a loving relationship between them. It could yet develop, though, she caught herself thinking. If she would let it.

"I'm not exactly an expert on marriage," Cal was saying as he seated her on the sofa and sank down beside her, "but I told him he'd better take a firmer hand with Espy or else she was going to drive him crazy."

"He seems to have taken the advice to heart. For the first time this morning, I actually believed he might be able to work things out with her. At least he was behaving like a man and not like a spoiled little boy."

"If he's spoiled, it's because you spoiled him," Cal reminded her.

"I did not!" she replied indignantly, then she saw the teasing gleam in his beautiful blue eyes. "Well, maybe I did a little, but he's a good boy, and he'll make a good man."

"I owe you for all you did for him."

Leah swallowed the lump of emotion forming in her

throat. "And I owe you, for giving him to me in the first place."

His mouth curved into a slow smile. "I could give you more like him, Leah. A whole houseful to keep you so busy you wouldn't even have time to worry about Brad and Espy anymore. We've still got time. There's a lot of years ahead, too many to spend alone."

Leah's heart throbbed with yearning, and her loins ached for the children he promised and the getting of those children. He was right, there was something between them, something she recognized now as desire and which held the promise of the lasting devotion she had craved for so long. The prospect was exciting and not a little frightening. She managed a thin smile.

"You should be careful what you offer, Mr. Stevens. I might take you up on it."

His smile broadened. "I'm counting on it."

Brad walked out of Mead Garland's office, grinning with satisfaction. The will was signed and witnessed and, according to Mead, completely official. Brad had accomplished a good day's work already, and it wasn't even ten o'clock yet.

Of course, he thought as he climbed back into the buggy, just doing it wasn't enough. Espy had to know he'd done it before it really counted. Still grinning, he turned the buggy around and headed back toward the Beamish's house. He might even find Espy sitting on the stoop, her clothes in a bundle at her feet, waiting contritely for him to return for her.

She wasn't on the porch, and he admitted he hadn't really expected her to be, but she appeared soon enough when he knocked on the door.

"Brad!" Sally Beamish exclaimed in an extra loud voice so Espy would be sure to hear. Sure enough, Espy came swishing up, looking not quite as cocksure of herself as she had when he'd left her a while ago.

Indeed, after a moment's consideration, she burst into tears and threw herself into his arms. "Oh, Brad, you came back for me! I knew you would! Didn't I tell you, Sally? I knew he wouldn't leave me!"

She sobbed uncontrollably into his shirtfront, and Brad stood awkwardly, patting her and trying not to feel like a damn fool. This isn't exactly what he'd expected, but it would do. Yes, it would do just fine.

"Sally, maybe you could get Espy's things," he suggested before Espy could say anything. "I reckon we'd better be going on home now."

Sally closed her gaping mouth with a snap and dashed off to do his bidding. Not wanting to waste any more time — or take any chances on Espy picking another fight before he could get her away — Brad started her out of the house and managed to get her into the buggy by the time Sally returned with the bundle of clothes.

"I told her she couldn't stay here," Sally whispered as she handed it to Brad, who nodded sagely and mouthed a silent "Thanks" as he placed the bundle in the back of the buggy.

Espy cried until they were out of town, then she pretended to pull herself together and wiped her face with one of her brand new hankies.

She drew a long, unsteady breath and let it out in a dramatic sigh. "I forgive you, Brad, but from now on you're going to have to treat me better. I can't stay up all night fussing and fighting. I need my rest, what with the baby and all. I've got the headache something fierce this morning."

Brad looked at her askance. "Wouldn't let you stay, would they?"

"I could've stayed if I wanted," she insisted, pouting prettily. "It's just that when I got there, I realized I'd made a terrible mistake. I love you, Brad, and I couldn't bear to be without you. And you must've missed me, too, or you wouldn't've come back."

She took his arm and laid her head against his shoulder.

Brad sighed with satisfaction and decided not to tell her about the will just yet. That could wait until later, until after she'd had a while to be grateful he'd taken her back without any fuss.

They drove for a few minutes in blissful silence while Brad savored the first milestone in what was undoubtedly going to be a rocky marriage. Then he saw something in the road ahead.

"What the . . . ?" he muttered, and Espy straightened to see what had disturbed him.

"What is it?"

"Looks like something blocking the road."

"There wasn't nothing here this morning," Espy complained.

"Well, there's something here now." He slowed the horse as they approached what appeared to be a large mesquite bush blocking the way. The thing was too big to have blown there by itself, but why would somebody have put it here on purpose?

He stopped the buggy, muttering his disgust.

"How'd it get there, anyways?" Espy wanted to know, personally insulted at being inconvenienced.

"How should I know? It'll be gone in a minute though." He patted her knee. "I'll be right back. Here, hold the reins."

He hopped nimbly out of the buggy and approached the bush, glancing around for some sign of how it had come to be there. The ground around it had been brushed clean, purposely, he noted.

He stood for a moment, puzzling over this, then something exploded in his chest, slamming him to the ground. The roar came then, an echo from faraway, and a woman's screams, screaming his name, but all he could see was the clear, blue sky, and the buggy jouncing toward him, horse's hooves flying.

Runaway, he thought with vague alarm in the second before everything went black.

Chapter Seven

Leah watched the shadows in the yard growing long and pulled her shawl more tightly around her against the late afternoon chill. She was silly to worry. She'd told herself that a hundred times since noon, but it didn't seem to help.

Thank heaven Cal had come in at noon today. Sensing her anxiety, he'd promised to work close to the house in the morning, and when Brad hadn't returned by dinnertime, he'd offered to go looking for him.

But what could be taking them so long?

It was probably nothing, she told herself again. Probably Cal had found Brad at the saloon, drowning his sorrows over Espy, and had decided to sober him up before bringing him home. That would be like Cal, not to want her to see the boy drunk. Yes, there was most certainly a reasonable explanation for the delay, one they'd all laugh at later. Not today, perhaps, but someday.

Meanwhile, Leah didn't feel a bit like laughing, and with each minute ticking by, her apprehension grew. Or was it foreboding? But why should she be so frightened? Brad had only driven to town, the same thing he'd done a thousand other times. Nothing had ever happened to him before. Why should she think something had now?

In spite of the biting wind, Leah was sitting on the porch when the first plume of dust appeared from the approaching wagon. She didn't recognize the vehicle when it finally came into sight, but she did recognize the accompanying rider, and her shoulders sagged with relief. Cal was back, and that must be Brad driving the wagon. He must have had trouble with the buggy, a loose wheel, perhaps, or a broken spring. She wondered why he'd chosen to rent a wagon from the livery instead of simply borrowing a horse from someone. How wasteful. She'd have to speak to him about it. A married man, soon to be a father, should have more sense of responsibility.

Cal kicked his horse into a run and easily outstripped the lumbering wagon. He was eager to get back to her, she thought with some gratification, and smiled to herself. In a day or two, they'd have Espy home where she belonged, and then Leah would be free to think about her own future and what place Cal Stevens might have in it.

She walked to the top of the porch steps to meet him and to hear his explanation, an expectant smile curving her lips. The smile died when Cal reined in before her and she saw his expression.

His face was ashen, his eyes bleak, and Leah's heart froze in her chest. Cal swung down from his horse, leaving it ground-hitched in the yard, and strode toward her, his hands closed into fists as if he wanted to beat something or someone but didn't know who or what.

Fear rose in her, black and terrifying, and every instinct told her to flee before she heard what Cal was going to tell her because she didn't want to hear it, didn't want to know what she already knew, the only thing horrible enough to cause Cal Stevens such despair.

"Brad?" she croaked through her fear-constricted throat.

Cal bounded up the steps and took her by the arms. "Leah," he said gently, so gently her heart died within her.

"No!" she cried, turning to look, certain she would see him driving the wagon, perched high on the seat, waving jauntily.

But the man driving the wagon wasn't Brad. It was Tom Jackson who worked as the town barber and who — Oh, God — doubled as the town's undertaker.

Horror stunned her, turning her arms and legs to lead. Only her eyes functioned, and they saw too much, far too much. It isn't true! her mind screamed. It *couldn't* be true!

"NO!" She fought Cal, knowing she had to get to the wagon so she could see for herself and then she would know he was wrong, *prove* he was wrong. Brad wasn't . . . he couldn't be . . . *No!*

But Cal wouldn't let her go. Iron hands gripped her, holding her as she struggled frantically. "Leah!" he shouted, shaking her until her head snapped and forcing her to look into his eyes, eyes so full of pain she couldn't bear it.

"Leah," he said more gently, his voice breaking just as her heart was breaking. "There was an accident."

She shook her head, fighting the tears welling in her

eyes. If she didn't acknowledge it, if she didn't cry, it wouldn't be true and Brad would be alive, riding over the hill . . .

But Cal's grip tightened, holding her to reality, making her understand what she didn't even want to know because if she knew it, she would die, too. The pain was already crushing her, squeezing her chest so she couldn't breathe and her heart couldn't beat, and she didn't even want to stop it because if Brad wasn't coming over the hill, she didn't *want* to be alive.

"They were on their way home," Cal was saying so carefully, as if each word were a piece of broken glass being dragged through this throat.

"They?" she asked stupidly, thinking he might say someone else, *anyone* else.

"Espy and . . . and Brad."

Tears scalded her eyes, blurring his image. She didn't want to see him or hear him or know what he was telling her, but that didn't stop him.

"They were on their way home," he repeated. "There was something in the road, a mesquite bush. Somebody'd put it there, and Brad stopped for it, to get it out of the way."

Leah easily pictured the scene in her mind and saw no hint of danger. No one could get hurt doing something so simple, so it wasn't true, and if she listened closely enough, she'd hear the mistake. There *must* be a mistake.

"Nobody knows what happened next, but we figured . . ." His voice broke again, and Leah thanked God she couldn't see him through her tears. Simply hearing his pain was almost more than she could stand, and she whimpered in despair.

"We figured," he forced himself to say, "that some-body was there, waiting to ambush him."

The wagon was lumbering into the yard, the noise as loud as thunder, echoing through her head, drowning out his words, except she could still hear them even though she couldn't stand to hear them because the horror grew with each one and the horror was already too great for anyone to bear.

"He . . . he didn't suffer," Cal said thickly, and the last shred of will holding her together snapped.

"Brad!" The cry was a wail of anguish torn from her very soul. Pain overwhelmed her, filled her, an agony too great for her body to contain, and it broke free on a wrenching sob.

Cal's arms closed around her, holding her to him, smothering her anguish against his chest. Vaguely, she realized he was trembling, too, but she couldn't think about his suffering now, not now, not yet. She could only sob while a thousand visions of Brad raced through her mind: the baby she had cherished, the toddler she had nurtured, the boy she had patiently trained, the near-man she had prized. Lost now, so terribly, tragically lost, before he ever had a chance to do anything with his life, and nothing left to show he'd ever been.

Except . . .

Dear God, how could she have forgotten? She pulled away so she could see Cal's face. "Espy! You said she was with him when it happened? Where is she? I must go to her! The shock . . . the baby . . . I . . ."

Her voice trailed off when Cal didn't respond, when all expression died from his eyes. What was wrong with him? Why wouldn't he tell her?

"Where is she?" Leah demanded, clutching his shirt,

on the edge of panic.

Cal's gaze drifted from hers, slowly, reluctantly, turning away. Even more reluctantly, she followed it until she saw the wagon that had stopped now, right in front of them. Tom Jackson sat slumped in the seat, discreetly studying his boots, not wanting to intrude on their grief, and Leah forced herself to look past him, to look at the back of the wagon, to see its awful burden.

And there—Oh, God, no!—she saw not one but *two* plain wooden boxes. No, no, *no!* her mind screamed, and the protest came out as an inarticulate wail of anguish that echoed through her head and through the empty recesses of her heart, the pain so great no mortal could survive it. Leah didn't want to survive it, and when the darkness teased at the edges of her mind, she surrendered willingly, gladly, to its blessed oblivion and slumped limply in Cal Stevens's arms.

She awoke from the faint to find herself lying on the couch. Juanita crouched beside her, waving the foul smelling salts beneath her nose.

A dream, she told herself. It had been a terrible nightmare, but when she saw the tears streaking Juanita's face, she knew it was only too true, the horror too real. Unable to witness Juanita's grief, she looked away and saw Cal standing over them, his face gray, his eyes still bleak. Instinctively, she reached for him, and he came close, taking her hand in both of his. He knelt beside Juanita, and the three of them huddled together for a moment.

The words were bitter in her mouth, but she had to ask, she had to know. "What happened? Tell me everything."

Unable to meet her eye, Cal looked down at her hand which he still held. "Like I said, Brad got out of the buggy to clear the road. Somebody was waiting for him. I found the place, but it had been swept clean of tracks." His voice grew steadier as he explained, as if reducing the tragedy to a list of facts made it somehow more bearable. "He took a shotgun blast full in the chest."

Leah cried out in anguish, covering her mouth with her free hand to hold back the sobs because if she started crying now, she would never stop.

"He never knew what hit him, Leah," he assured her urgently. "He didn't feel a thing."

She nodded, absurdly grateful for that small mercy. "And Espy?"

"The shot must've scared the horse or something. Anyway, it bolted, and the buggy flipped over. She . . . her neck was broke."

Somehow this made it worse, knowing Espy and the tiny life she carried had been unintended victims. The darkness beckoned again, but this time Leah resisted its sweet oblivion, clinging tightly to Cal's hand as if it held her to reality.

"Who did it, Cal?" she pleaded. "Who could have done such a thing? And *why?*"

"Nobody knows," he told her grimly. "Like I said, the place had been swept clean, and I couldn't find any tracks. They've sent for the county sheriff."

"He'll find whoever did this," she said, but even she could hear the doubt in her voice. If Cal hadn't been able to find a clue, how could the sheriff?

Cal squeezed her hand and said, "Some folks are

coming from town. The women said to wait until they got here. They'll take care of everything."

Leah nodded, feeling the tears coming and unable to stop them. They flooded her eyes and streamed down her cheeks. Beside her Juanita sobbed softly, and Leah wondered vaguely how men could keep from crying, how they could bear the pain without the tears. Poor Cal, he'd had Brad so briefly, and now he had nothing at all.

She squeezed his hand even more tightly as the first sob shook her, and then she was in his arms, weeping against his chest, finding the comfort he always offered and giving some in return. They clung to each other for a long time, until Leah was too weak to cry anymore and slumped against his shoulder, trying not to think but unable to stop.

A vision of the two stark boxes lying in the wagon bed swam before her mind's eye, and she shuddered. "We can't leave them out there," she said brokenly. She had to say it again before Cal understood what she meant. "Bring them inside, into the house," she pleaded, and Cal nodded his understanding.

Tenderly, he released her and laid her back against the cushion before rising to his feet. He moved slowly, as weary as she with grief and anguish, but he did go, and soon he and Tom Jackson had transferred their grievous burdens to Brad and Espy's bedroom.

By then, other wagons had begun to arrive, neighbors and people from town, all bringing food and kind words, words meant to solace what was inconsolable. Leah listened numbly, nodding at each person, acknowledging the kindness without feeling it, without letting herself feel anything because if she did, she

214

would disintegrate, and she couldn't indulge herself, at least not yet, not until Brad and his wife were taken care of.

Mead came, too, murmuring softly, taking her hand in his and pressing it gently. Too gently, she judged, wishing for hands less soft and tended, wishing for Cal's wordless comfort, but he had vanished into the evening, leaving her to her friends.

The ladies from town were as good as their word. They took the broken bodies from the coffins, washed and dressed them and laid them out on the bed that Espy had left unmade that morning in her haste to get away.

The sun had set by the time the ladies had finished their work. They summoned her hesitantly into the bedroom. Mead offered to go with her, to hold her hand, to support her through this, but she didn't want Mead, she wanted Cal who wasn't there. So she went alone, the ladies hovering solicitously, ready to console or revive, as occasion demanded.

Brad and Espy lay with eyes closed and hands folded, as if in stately sleep, and in the lamplight they didn't even look unnaturally pale. They might almost have been alive if one didn't stare long enough to notice they didn't move, didn't breathe . . .

Leah waited while the tears spilled down, drenching her cheeks and somehow, mysteriously, easing the grief until she could bear it again. Then she entered the room and approached the bed. Espy lay nearest the door.

She looked so young and innocent, all trace of petulance erased by the peace of death, like a porcelain doll, except for the small mound of her stomach beneath her

215

skirt. At the sight of it, Leah pressed her fist to her lips to hold back the cry of anguish for the third death that had occurred today, the death that ensured there would be no future for these two children.

"I put one of her new dresses on her," Nancy Otto was saying quietly. "I hope you don't mind, but it was almost finished and she seemed to like it so much when she was in the other day for a fitting."

Only then did Leah notice what the girl was wearing, a rust-colored wool suit that matched the copper of her hair. Leah remembered convincing her it was just the thing to make her look like a grownup married lady, and once again tears blurred her eyes.

Leah swayed, and Nancy's arm went quickly around her, but Leah fought the darkness once more. Fainting was a luxury she wouldn't allow herself, not yet, not yet. Gently pushing away from Nancy's grasp, Leah moved resolutely around the bed, determined to face what she knew would be the most difficult moment of her life.

Brad did not look as peaceful as Espy. They had closed his eyes and smoothed out his face, but knowing him as she did, Leah could see the last spasm of pain etched on his well-loved features. Pain and puzzlement at what was happening to him. Leah blinked furiously, not allowing the tears to blur her vision of him, drinking it in desperately so she could store it up for all the years when she must live without him.

With that expression on his face, he should have been pacing. He always paced or moved, was never still like this, as still as death.

Someone pressed a handkerchief into her hand, but she made no move to wipe the endless tears, not wanting to be distracted. They'd dressed him in his suit, she noticed, the one in which he had been married such a short time ago. She could easily see the padding they had put under his shirt to cover the wound in his chest. He hadn't suffered, Cal had said. Would that his survivors could fare as well.

Her tears fell on his pale, still face as she bent for the kiss he would have denied her in life. He was too old for such things, he would have said, and now he would never be any older. A spasm of pain shook her as her lips touched the marble of his cheek, so cold and unyielding. So dead.

Leah didn't remember leaving the room or how she came to be lying on her own bed. Someone gave her some brandy which made her choke but also warmed away some of the chill she thought might stay with her for the rest of her life. She lay, looking up at the ceiling, for hours, unable to sleep but unable to get up either, while the women moved around soundlessly, like ministering angels.

The preacher arrived around midnight, summoned from his circuit once again for an emergency at the Rocking Horse Ranch. Leah roused herself long enough to consult with him about the service. He seemed as shaken as she that this young couple whom he had married scant days ago now lay cold and still, and she found herself offering words of encouragement instead of receiving them.

Mead Garland had stayed, and he sat with her as they discussed appropriate scripture passages and hymns. Every now and then he patted her hand and offered a suggestion. After what seemed an interminable time, the arrangements were complete, and the minister took his leave to spend the night in the bunkhouse.

Although many other people were also spending the night, Leah found herself alone in the parlor with Mead. Tomorrow the two coffins would be placed here while the rest of her friends and neighbors came to pay their respects, graves were dug and filled, food eaten, and condolences offered.

"They still haven't found Homer Wilkes," Mead said in the same hushed voice everyone used now when they addressed her.

"Where could he be?" she wondered aloud, thinking of the children whom he had left alone.

"Probably got drunk and wandered off someplace to sleep it off, which I understand he often does. He'll show up, and when he does, someone will tell him."

"Did anyone think about the Wilkes children — ?"

"Oh, yes, Mrs. Beamish and her daughter went out there to stay with them. They'll bring them over in the morning, whether or not Wilkes shows up."

Leah nodded, wondering how she would get through the next day, how she would get through the rest of her life carrying the pain of this tragedy. "Who could have done such a thing?" she asked for the first time.

"A madman, Leah. There's no other explanation," he said softly, earnestly. "We suspect that robbery was the motive, which would explain the bush in the road to make them stop. The bandit must have panicked when he saw he'd killed an innocent woman, too. I'm afraid we might never know."

"We'll know," she said with certainty. "Do you think Cal Stevens will rest until he finds out who murdered his son?"

Mead seemed startled by the question. "I really hadn't given it much thought, Leah. Quite frankly, I don't know for certain if Stevens really was Brad's father, and neither do you, no matter what your soft heart might tell you. For your sake, I hope he's as faithful to his son's memory as you think he will be, but don't be too surprised if he drifts out of your life as suddenly as he drifted in now that there's no chance of getting any part of Brad's fortune."

Leah felt a spark of irritation at Mead's assumptions, but he had also reminded her of something about which she should have been concerned. "The ranch! What will happen to it now? Will Homer Wilkes have a claim since Brad died without a will?"

Mead smiled gently. "But he did have a will, Leah. He came by my office this morning and signed it while he was in town. It was the sheerest luck I happened to have it ready, but . . . At least you'll have no worries on that score. Everything is yours now, just as he wanted."

Except that she had no wife or child to care for in Brad's stead. She'd worked hard through the years to provide a good life for her brother and his children, but what good was the ranch without Brad? What good was anything without Brad?

She looked to Mead, but didn't even bother asking the question. He wouldn't understand, no one would understand except . . .

"Where's Cal?" she asked suddenly.

"Stevens?" Mead asked in amazement. "I'm sure I have no idea. I haven't seen him."

"He should see Brad before . . . before they put him in the coffin. He should have a chance to say a private good-bye."

Mead frowned in patent disapproval. "Leah, I don't think —"

"Go find him, please. Mead, for me," she added, shamelessly taking advantage of his feelings for her, something she would never have otherwise dreamed of doing.

He smiled sadly. "You know I can never refuse you anything. I think you're making a mistake, but I'll see if I can find him. Will you be all right here alone for a few minutes?"

"I'm hardly alone," she pointed out. "The place is crawling with visitors."

He nodded, patted her hand once more, and hurried out. Leah sat there in the dimly lit parlor for a long moment, trying not to feel the pain, trying not to wonder how people survived such unspeakable tragedies. Then she heard a noise in the hallway, the unmistakable sound of Brad's bedroom door closing.

She was on her feet in a moment, dashing down the hall to see who had disturbed them, who had dared . . .

A tall figure emerged from the shadows, creeping stealthily toward the back of the house. "Cal?" she called, recognizing him at once.

He stopped instantly and turned to face her. "Leah, what are you doing . . . ?"

He never finished his question because she was in his arms, clinging to his strength, burying her face in his shoulder.

"I was looking for you. I sent Mead to find you," she said against his shirt.

"Juanita let me in the back way after everyone else

220

left. I didn't want anyone to see me in there." His voice was ragged, as if with unshed tears.

"You shouldn't have to sneak around like that. He was your son!"

His arms tightened in silent gratitude for her acknowledgement, but he didn't confirm the statement. "It's better if nobody knows now. There'll be enough talk without that, too."

Leah wanted to argue with him, but she simply didn't have the strength. "How will we stand it?" she asked in despair.

He was silent for a long minute, then he said, "The same way everyone else does. Life goes on, even when we don't want it to. In a few days, you won't cry whenever you think of him. In a few months, a day will go by when you don't think of him. You'll survive."

"Whether I want to or not," she added grimly. They held each other for a few more moments, until Leah realized how it would look if anyone were to come down the hall. As Cal had said, there would be enough talk.

Gently, reluctantly, she disengaged herself from his arms. "How did they look?" she asked, gesturing to the bedroom door.

Although it was dark in the hall, she thought she saw a tremor shake him. "The women did a good job."

"Oh," she said in dismay. "I forgot, you'd seen them . . . before."

He nodded and drew an unsteady breath.

"Who . . . who found them?"

"I did."

"Oh, Cal!" she cried in anguish. "I'm so sorry! I didn't know! I didn't even think to ask."

"I'm glad it was me," he said, sounding anything but

glad. "I wouldn't've wanted a stranger to see them like that."

Leah wouldn't have wanted anyone else to find them, either, but before she could say so, her bedroom door opened, and one of the women stuck her head out.

"Leah?" she asked, then noticed Cal standing in the shadows. "Oh, I'm sorry to interrupt. I heard voices and—"

"That's all right," Cal said brusquely. "I was just leaving." He turned back to Leah. "You'd better try to get some sleep."

She nodded. "You, too."

"See you in the morning."

He disappeared into the shadows again, and one of the women came and led her back to her bedroom, undressed her, and put her to bed like a weary child.

Afterwards, when Leah remembered the day of the funeral, she recalled only isolated events.

Homer Wilkes, who finally showed up at midmorning, still raving drunk and nearly hysterical with grief. He'd thrown himself on Espy's open casket, embracing her lifeless body and fairly dragging it from its haven until Pete Quincy and some of the men were able to get him away.

The oldest surviving Wilkes girl lifted her younger sister up to the casket.

"Why don't she open her eyes?" the little one asked.

"Because she'd dead."

"Like Ma?"

"Yeah, like Ma."

Sally Beamish's homely face red and swollen from weeping. "I should've let her stay at my house. Then at least she'd be *alive!*"

The sheriff who arrived around noontime and expressed his condolences gravely. He'd be talking to people, he said, and he'd have some questions for her later, when she felt up to it.

Mead Garland's hands, patting and guiding and bringing her a plate of food she couldn't eat. And his voice, kind and soft, reminding her he was there to take care of her and always would be.

But mostly she remembered Cal Stevens's eyes — Brad's eyes — as blue as the sky and bleak with despair, staring at her across the open graves as they listened to the minister reading promises of eternal life to those who believe.

At the end of that long day, Leah sent the women who would have stayed with her home to their families, wanting nothing now except solitude. Mead Garland was among the last to go, and even then he left reluctantly.

"I can stay in the bunkhouse, Leah," he assured her. "I'd like to be close in case you need me."

"If you paid me that kind of attention, you'd start a lot of gossip," Leah pointed out, only half teasing.

He smiled warmly. "I wouldn't mind having my name linked with yours. I've been wanting just that for a long time."

"Please, Mead, I just can't . . ."

"Of course, I understand completely," he said quickly, reading her weariness. "Forgive me for pushing you, but perhaps you can excuse a desperate man for trying any advantage. At least let me come by tomorrow afternoon just to see how you're getting along. If you don't want me to stay, all you have to do is say so,

223

but I'll need to reassure myself that you're all right."

"Of course," she said, knowing she couldn't possibly refuse in light of the way he had supported her all day. She waved as he mounted his horse and rode away toward town. The setting sun was blood red on the horizon and cast an eerie glow over the yard and the ranch buildings. From the porch, Leah could just make out the neat picket fence surrounding the Harding family cemetery and the graves of her parents and her infant siblings and now the brother she had loved, his sad little bride, and their unborn child. She couldn't see the raw mounds of earth that marked these new graves, and she didn't want to see them, not again today.

Closing the heavy door, Leah leaned against it, savoring the silence. Juanita was in the kitchen, sorting through the leftovers from the funeral feast. The older woman hadn't said much, she never did, but Leah knew she felt Brad's death almost as keenly as Leah did. The house would be so empty without him. Their *lives* would be so empty without him.

Mechanically, Leah made her way to her bedroom and, with a sigh of relief, stripped off the black dress she had vowed never to wear again and slipped into her nightdress. She was so exhausted, surely sleep would come tonight, she told herself as she crawled into bed and pulled the covers up to her ears. The red glow from the setting sun filled the room, turning everything the color of blood. Leah closed her eyes against it and tried to block out the memories as well. For once her body obeyed her commands, and she sank into a fitful sleep.

She was riding in the buggy. The brilliant sunlight had bathed everything in a golden glow, so bright she almost didn't recognize Brad sitting on the seat beside her. She had to squint to make him out, but he smiled his carefree smile at her, and she smiled back. They were going someplace important, although she couldn't quite remember where. She only knew she had to get Brad there quickly, quickly before it was too late.

She slapped the reins on the horse's rump and he stepped up the pace, trotting briskly, but not fast enough. They had to hurry, hurry. She slapped the horse again, calling out. Sensing the urgency, the horse began to run and the buggy began to sway, side to side, faster and faster, tipping on one wheel and then the other.

"Help me!" Leah cried, but when she looked at Brad, his eyes were wide and staring and the front of his shirt was soaked with blood. "Brad, no!" she screamed, but he didn't hear, and his head flopped from side to side in the tilting buggy.

"Stop!" she screamed, sawing on the reins, but the horse didn't hear or couldn't hear and didn't stop and the buggy was spinning, spinning, and Brad flew out and disappeared, but there was a baby in his place, a tiny baby wrapped in a blanket, and Leah snatched it up in her arms, holding it tight against the spinning of the buggy. The baby screamed in terror, its cries filling her head, but she didn't let it go, would never let it go, because it was Brad's baby and she had to keep it safe.

The buggy stopped with a jolt, throwing Leah free, but she held onto the baby and when she stopped rolling, she opened the blanket but the baby was gone.

"No!" she wailed, looking frantically around. Where had it gone? She must find it. She had to find Brad's baby! But where could it be?

Then she knew, knew instinctively, and she scrambled to her feet and started running, running and running, up the hill, up to the picket fence. It was cold, so cold, and the wind whipped her skirts and her hair, trying to hold her back, but nothing would hold her back because she had to find Brad's baby, and she would find it, she *would!*

"Leah! My God! Leah!"

Cal's voice came to her as from a great distance, and she could hardly hear it above the howling of the wind, but she didn't stop, she had to keep going, keep running, but now something was holding her and she couldn't move. . . .

"Leah, can you hear me? Leah!"

She woke with a start and saw Cal Stevens scowling down at her in the moonlight. "Cal?"

"What in God's name are you doing out here?" he demanded, as near frantic as she had ever seen him.

She glanced around, suddenly aware she was no longer in her bed or even in her bedroom. Good God, she was outside! How in the world . . . ?

Cal was pulling off his sheepskin jacket and wrapping it around her, covering her nightdress. "My God, you're barefoot, too!" he exclaimed and lifted her into his arms.

"I have to go up there," she told him desperately, peering anxiously over his shoulder at the neatly bordered graveyard.

"You don't want to go there," he told her patiently, as if he were speaking to a child. "I was just there, and believe me, you don't want to go."

"But the baby . . ." she began, then realized it had all been a dream.

"What baby?" he asked.

226

"I . . . I was dreaming."

"I figured. You didn't answer me when I called you. At first I thought you were a ghost."

He wasn't teasing, and Leah felt the prickle of tears. She'd been so close to saving Brad's baby in the dream, it was hard to let it go, to accept the harshness of reality again. Wearily, she let her head fall onto Cal's shoulder as he carried her back to the house, up onto the porch and through the still-open front door.

He pushed the door shut behind them. "Should I call Juanita?"

"What time is it?"

"I don't know. After midnight, I guess. I couldn't sleep."

"Oh, no, don't wake her. I'll be fine."

But he didn't put her down as she had expected. Instead, he carried her down the hall and into her bedroom. The moonlight cast just enough light to see by, and he set her down in the stuffed chair she kept near the stove for reading. Quickly, efficiently, he lit a lamp and threw some kindling onto the smoldering coals in the stove while Leah shivered within the folds of his huge coat. In a few minutes he had a fire going, and Leah felt the warmth seeping back into her bones.

"You do that a lot?" he asked.

"What?" she answered in confusion.

"Sleepwalk."

"Oh, no, I've never . . . not ever before."

He nodded once, then looked down at her bare feet where he saw a trace of blood mixed with the dirt. "You've cut yourself," he said. "We'd better clean it out before it gets infected."

Without waiting for her consent, he took the pitcher

from her washstand and disappeared into the hall. Leah looked down at her feet and realized she couldn't even feel them. How long had she been wandering around outside in her nightdress? she wondered in dismay. Had anyone seen her? How humiliated she would have been if anyone but Cal had found her.

In a moment he returned, and in another moment, he'd poured the lukewarm water into the basin and set it at her feet. Before she could protest, he grasped her by the ankles and set her feet to soak in the water. Instantly sensation returned, and with it the pain of her cuts and the tingling of the cold.

With infinite care, he bathed away the dirt and blood with the soap and cloth he found on the washstand, cradling her feet in his hands and resting them against his thigh.

This was, part of her reminded her sternly, scandalously improper. He should never have encountered her in her nightdress or entered her bedroom, and he most certainly should never have even seen her ankles, much less held them in his naked hands.

"The cuts aren't bad," he remarked as he worked. "I don't think you even need a bandage. Just don't go walking around barefoot anyplace for a day or so."

He smiled at his joke, but the smile was sad, and Leah noticed his eyes were red-rimmed, as if he had been weeping in the dark as he stood beside his son's grave. Her heart ached for him, for his loss and for the fact that while she had been lavished with care, no one had offered him so much as a word of comfort.

When he had finished, he set the basin aside and toweled her feet dry, his touch as gentle as a mother's. "They're still like ice," he said with some concern, and swiftly unbuttoned first his shirt and then his under-shirt.

"What are you doing?" she asked, knowing she should feel alarmed but unable quite to work up the proper enthusiasm for it.

"I'm going to warm up those feet, and then I'm going to put you to bed where you belong."

To her astonishment, he tucked her feet inside his shirt, right up against his bare chest. The warmth was so exquisite, she gasped aloud, closing her eyes in bliss while his work-roughened hands massaged life back into her calves.

"We're being terribly wicked," she murmured, acutely aware of his hands caressing her legs. She opened her eyes a slit so she could see his face.

"Oh, yes," he agreed. "In some Indian tribes it's considered a sin to see a woman's feet before you're married to her."

"It certainly is in our tribe," she said, and he smiled a smile that didn't quite touch the sadness in his eyes.

The lamplight made odd shadows on his face, and Leah realized he should have looked sinister. Instead, she felt drawn to him in a way she'd never felt drawn to another man, drawn to his strength and his kindness and drawn to other things, too, things so vague, she didn't have a name for them.

In the darkness his hair was even blacker than black, and she noticed he had the same black hair curling on his chest. It tickled the soles of her feet now that the feeling had returned to them, and she wiggled her toes experimentally against his heated skin.

"Hey, none of that," he scolded in a semblance of

229

playfulness, and his fingers closed around her ankles in a silent warning.

"Sorry," she murmured with a small smile. "I didn't know you were ticklish."

"I'm not," he insisted, although his fingers tightened slightly around her ankles, cautioning her not to try to find out.

Her smile widened, and suddenly she was struck by the lightness of their mood. "I thought I'd never smile again," she said in wonder.

"I never had much to smile about at all until I came here. I didn't even know how lonely I'd been."

Leah hadn't known she was lonely, either, not until she'd met Cal Stevens. Since his arrival, her life had been filled with crises and problems, but he'd solved his share of them, too. Above all, he'd made her feel alive, a feeling she hadn't even known she missed.

The room was warm now, and Leah stirred within the cocoon of his jacket. The heavy fabric had absorbed his scent, and she inhaled it greedily even as she felt the rise and fall of his chest beneath her bare feet. The moment was shockingly intimate: they were alone in her bedroom, she was practically naked, and he was . . .

. . . looking at her like he wanted to devour her. The knowledge sent a frisson of awareness racing over her, and every nerve in her body leaped to attention. He wanted her. She'd known, of course, at least since two days ago when he'd kissed her behind the house and assured her he had the financial means to take a wife.

But not just any wife, *her,* Leah Harding, the woman whose life had been so boring just short weeks ago but which had been marked by more trauma in the days since than anyone should have to face in a lifetime. And she had shared every one of those traumas with Cal Stevens, just as she wanted to share her grief with him now and take the comfort she knew she could find in his arms.

She stared at him, seeing as if for the first time the breadth of his shoulders, the leanness of his hips, and the power of his thighs. Her need was great, but she had no words to tell him, nor did she know the coy artifices women used to lure men. The opening of his shirt and the tantalizing glimpse of chest it provided tempted her, and she could almost feel those crisp, dark hairs springing under her fingers.

The thought made her breathless, and this time she couldn't blame her breathlessness on her stays since she wasn't wearing any. She wasn't wearing much of anything at all, in fact, and her nakedness beneath her gown suddenly seemed deliciously sensual. Surely, Cal thought so. He *must*. Leah found herself wanting to feel his nakedness, too.

"Cal, my . . . my hands are cold, too," she tried, already imagining them slipping inside the warmth of his shirt to find the steady beating of his heart.

He went perfectly still, not even breathing as Leah was in a perfect position to know. "You want to warm them inside my shirt." He didn't ask, and his voice sounded wary.

"If . . . if you don't mind," she said, beginning to regret her impulsiveness. What if he didn't want her after all? What if he found her clumsy attempt at seduction silly? Not that she was really trying to seduce him, of course, she just wanted . . .

"I don't think that would be a good idea," he said, so carefully.

231

"Why not?" she heard herself ask and wanted to snatch the words back the instant they left her mouth.

"Because . . . What do you think would happen next?"

"I . . ." She wanted to look away, would have run away if he hadn't been holding her feet so tightly, but his gaze held hers just as tightly. "I wanted you to hold me."

"For comfort?"

And so much more. "Yes!" she lied.

"No," he replied and drew an unsteady breath. Then he took her feet from inside his shirt and set them on the floor, releasing her with notable reluctance, but releasing her nevertheless. "I'd better go," he said fumbling for his buttons.

"No, Cal, I . . . I don't want to be alone!" she cried, hating herself for her weakness but too weak to be any stronger.

He'd started to rise, but he stopped, and his gaze touched her like a burning brand. "If I stay, I'll be more than a comfort to you."

All the air left her lungs in a painful gasp. She hadn't meant . . . she didn't want *that!*

Or did she? Although her mind was rebelling in outrage, her body was reacting much differently. Beneath the thin fabric of her gown, her nipples hardened, and the ache she had felt before and called a longing for children of her own now took on a new meaning entirely. She wanted children, surely, but even more, she wanted life and the getting of life, she wanted passion and . . . and *love*. Cal Stevens could offer her all of that and more.

He waited now, still and watchful, alert for the

232

slightest hint of her decision. She managed a tremulous smile.

"Please stay."

In the next second he was on his feet, hauling her out of her chair and into his arms. She went willingly, eagerly, offering her lips, her mouth, her body, for his ravishing.

He plundered her mouth, sweeping it thoroughly with his tongue while his hands plundered her body, exploring her shoulders and back through the fragile covering, then swooping low to cup her bottom in both hands and pull her securely into the cradle of his thighs.

She, in turn, yanked open his shirt to expose the broad expanse of his chest, then spread her palms across it, wanting to touch everything at once. His breath caught as she trailed her fingers through the lush hair and found a flat, male nipple as erect as her own.

Then she slid her arms around to caress his back and pull him to her so the aching of her breasts might find solace against the hardness of his chest. Her heart thundered against his as she caressed the satin of his back, and when neither of them could breathe anymore, he broke the kiss, swept her into his arms and carried her to the bed.

She touched her lips to his cheek, delighting in the prickle of his beard and the musky maleness of his scent. Then he laid her down on the bed, pressing another kiss to her mouth before releasing her. The sheets were icy, and robbed of his warmth, she shivered, but he pulled the blankets over her and tucked them in around her.

"I'll only be a minute," he promised as he drew away

233

and stripped off his shirt in one swift movement. He sat on the bed to pull off his boots, and Leah slipped her arms around his waist, laying her cheek against his shoulder as he worked.

Hurry, she thought to herself. Hurry before my nerve fails me, before common sense rears its ugly head and robs us of this moment.

When he had finished with his boots, he ran his hands along her arms until he came to her fingers, then gently disengaged her grip on him so he could rise and peel off the jeans he wore.

The sight of a man in longjohns should not have startled her. She'd seen Brad in his longjohns plenty of times, but this was different, so very different, because Cal was so very different from every other man she'd ever known. Moving like a panther, sleek and lean, he went to blow out the lamp they'd left burning by the stove. Leah watched his every step, admiring how broad shoulders gave way to narrow hips, his body so blatantly masculine. She fairly burned with the need to hold him close and take his weight and open to him, offering what she'd never offered to any man.

He blew out the light, and darkness descended, but she heard the unmistakable padding of his bare feet as he returned and the faint rustle as he removed the last of his clothing. The tingling anticipation became flickering anxiety when she felt the bed sag with his weight and his body slid under the covers with hers. What was she doing? Was she *crazy?* Taking a man to her bed, a man she hardly knew, a man who . . .

He reached out and gathered her to him. Her hands grazed naked flesh, her feet touched naked shins, and she recoiled at so much masculinity.

"You're trembling," he whispered against her cheek.

"I've never . . . I don't know how . . ." she stammered, mortified and terrified all at once and wishing she knew how to send him away even though her body had already begun to melt at his touch.

"Shhh," he said softly. "I'll show you."

The assurance only raised new doubts. Where had he learned so much about it, and did she really want to know? Perhaps he'd made a career of seducing young women. Perhaps he'd left a trail of bastards halfway across Texas.

But before she could consider those possibilities, his hand settled on her hip, proprietary and profoundly disturbing. A small gasp of surprise escaped her, a gasp that gave way to a sigh when his hand began to move, fondling and caressing, tracing her curves through the nothingness of her gown until even she became impatient with the barrier, so she did not object when he slid his hand beneath it to touch her bare skin.

His work-roughened palm abraded deliciously against her sensitized flesh as he traced her thigh, brushing his thumb along the crease where her legs were pressed tightly together, up and up, until he touched the mound of curls at the apex of her thighs. She started, but he had already moved on, spreading his palm over her hip again while his long fingers stretched out to graze her belly and her waist and the smooth cheek of her bottom, around and around, circles ever wider until he covered her belly with his palm then traced the place where one smooth cheek met the other. His touch sent shivers racing up and over her, and into her, too, stirring sensations of which she'd never dreamed her body capable.

Her tension evaporated along with the very last of her reservations. If this were folly, then fools were wise, and Leah wanted the greatest wisdom of all. Her apprehension gave way to anticipation again, and when his mouth sought hers, she returned his kiss with abandon, pressing her breasts to his chest and burying her fingers in the raven softness of his hair.

But his explorations were only beginning, and Leah's straining tempted him to new frontiers. His questing fingers delved further beneath her gown until they found the swell of her breast and claimed it for his own, cupping it almost reverently, filling his palm with it so the tender tip rose and burrowed into the haven of his caress. Reaction streaked through her like chain lightning whose sparks settled deep in her belly and smoldered into an entirely new reaction.

Restless now, wanting without knowing what she wanted, Leah rubbed her leg against his, glorying in the abrasion of his hair-roughened flesh against her. When his knee nudged her legs apart, she opened willingly and wrapped her legs around it as he teased his thigh against her most sensitive spot and stoked the fires of wanting.

With a groan, he rolled her on her back and flipped her nightdress up to her neck so she was completely exposed. Grateful for the darkness that shielded at least a portion of her modesty, Leah had only a moment in which to register that protection before he launched his new assault.

His mouth left hers and trailed down until he captured one pebbled nipple between his lips. Leah cried out in surprise, but when his tongue began to lave, her protest became a sigh of ac-

236

quiescence. Desire churned and heaved within her, bubbling up like a simmering volcano struggling for release, but Leah had no idea how to release it.

Then he parted her thighs again and slipped his hand between them, stroking, caressing, ever so gently working his way upward and upward, until he cupped the mound of curls. Instinctively, she raised her hips, pressing the swollen nub into his palm while his fingers teased lower, coaxing the tears of need from deep inside until she was moist and ready for him.

No longer did she fear. No longer did she doubt. She wanted and desired with a fervency that would drive her insane if it was not satisfied. Tiny, pleading sounds escaped her, and she clung to him desperately, holding his mouth to her breast while her hips moved in glorious counterpoint to his caresses.

As if responding to some unspoken signal, Cal rose up and moved over her. She felt the weight of his desire burning against her belly, igniting a need to be filled, to be complete, and she grasped his flanks, entreating him for fulfillment. Then she felt the first tentative prodding, the seeking for welcome, and she opened to it, lifted to meet it, and took him into herself.

He entered her slowly, infinitely careful. She'd heard there would be pain, but she felt none, only a slight tightness which he eased past until they were one. She clung to him, savoring what she now knew of union, thinking this was all and how exquisite it was, and beautiful, too. He loomed over her in the darkness, his breath coming in ragged gasps as he touched his forehead to hers and whispered her name, over and over again, like an incantation to some mystical rite.

She reached up and touched his face, wishing she

could see it, wishing she could read his expression and know if he felt as wondrous as she did.

"You're mine now," he rasped, and her heart answered, "Yes!"

Then, before she could think, he was moving away, then back again, sending sensation swirling through her. Again and again he plunged, until in desperation she met his thrust, and desire exploded within her. Yes, oh, yes! her heart sang as her body answered ancient urges and discovered brand new ones.

She clasped him to her, reveling in his satin strength and the tensile power quivering beneath her fingers. Instinctively, she wrapped her legs around him, wanting to draw him close and closer still, until there was nothing between, nothing held back. Passion swelled into compulsion that drove her on and on, faster and faster, while desire surged molten, sizzling along her nerve ends until her whole body was one quivering mass of need, straining and yearning toward the ultimate, mysterious something that lay just out of reach, just beyond, just too far.

But she was close now, closer yet. She gripped his shoulders frantically, digging in her nails, arching her back, gasping his name, pleading for what he alone could give, and just when she thought she would go out of her mind, it came. Release in a shuddering spasm of ecstasy, wrenching through her in blazing tumult, again and again, over and over, as he filled her with the life she'd craved, until at last she lay spent and replete.

Cal, too, was spent, and his weight bore down on her, a glorious burden to which she clung while they both sobbed for breath. After a few moments, he stirred slightly, shifting the bulk of his weight from her so she could breathe more freely while still leaving their legs intimately entwined.

Leah burrowed into his embrace, her only haven from the world that lay beyond this bed and the pains of loss just waiting to consume her. If she held herself very still and didn't think, her wearied body would surrender to sleep and nothing else could hurt her this day.

"Don't leave me," she entreated.

"Never," was the promise she heard in the last second before sleep claimed her.

Night passed in a dreamless, peaceful void, but when she awoke the next morning, he was gone.

Chapter Eight

Leah sat bolt upright in bed, stiff muscles groaning in protest, and looked around frantically, but Cal was gone. So much for promises in the night, she thought in despair. The basin sat on the floor by the chair, just where he had left it, but every other trace of his presence here last night was gone.

Except, of course, for the traces he had left on her body, the soreness in unaccustomed places, the chafe of whisker burn on her cheeks, the sense of emptiness she felt at not having him here. How could she deal with Brad's loss without him?

Even as the tears welled in her eyes, she called herself a fool. What had she expected? A little pillow talk and a proposal of marriage? She'd sought comfort from him, and he'd given her passion to help heal the pain. No one had said anything about undying love or even commitment, and she certainly didn't need Cal Stevens or any other man to help her with anything. She'd faced death and grief before, and she could do it again. Even he had pointed out that life goes on, and as unbearable as the agony might seem today, time would ease it to the point of bearing until she was able to function again.

Angrily dashing the tears from her eyes, she threw back the covers and swung her legs to the floor, grateful for the crisp morning air that raised gooseflesh and shocked her blood into circulation again. She had enough anguish with which to deal without agonizing over Cal Stevens or imagining a romance where there had been only mutual need or berating herself for taking what she'd wanted from him.

She didn't love Cal Stevens, and she didn't care whether he loved her, either. By the time she had bathed and dressed, she had almost convinced herself of it, too.

Juanita was working in the kitchen, kneading fragrant bread dough, when Leah wandered in a few minutes later in search of breakfast. The carefully wrapped leftovers from the funeral cluttered virtually every flat space, but Leah couldn't bring herself to go rummaging through them. Ignoring Juanita's questioning look, she sliced herself a piece of bread from a loaf in the breadbox and forced herself to take a bite.

Wordlessly, Juanita left her dough and, after wiping her hands on her apron, poured Leah a cup of coffee from the pot on the stove. Leah sipped gratefully at the strong black brew, washing the dry bread down her even dryer throat. Only then did she risk a glance at Juanita. Did the Mexican woman know Cal had been with her last night? Did she know what had happened between them?

Juanita gave no sign of knowing anything and went back to her methodical kneading while Leah finished her bread and coffee. She had just set the empty cup into the sink when she heard booted feet on the stoop outside the back door. Then the door flew open and Cal Stevens was there.

"Is she up yet?" he asked Juanita before he saw Leah. He stiffened in reaction, which wasn't surprising because Leah felt a strong reaction herself, much like a blow to her stomach that forced all the air from her lungs.

"He has been here three times this morning," Juanita reported with mild disapproval. "You have sleep very late."

Leah couldn't think of a single thing to say in response, so she just stared speechlessly at Cal who looked alarmingly grim. Or perhaps he just looked determined. Leah felt too shattered to decide.

"We need to talk," he said after a minute of uncomfortable silence during which Juanita went on kneading her bread.

"Yes," Leah replied stupidly. *Three times?* Had Juanita said he'd been here three times already this morning? It wasn't *that* late, either, probably not past nine o'clock. But he'd already come looking for her *three times.* "Let's go into . . . my office," she decided, choosing the most private place she could think of short of her bedroom.

He nodded and followed her as she made her way through the house to the small room off the parlor from which she conducted the business of the ranch. He closed the door behind him with a decisive click and leaned against it.

Turning to face him, Leah felt suddenly claustrophobic, as if all the air in the room had evaporated, as if Cal

Stevens's imposing presence had squeezed it out. He *was* imposing, too, dressed — she suddenly realized — in his suit, the one he'd bought for the wedding. Squelching the painful memories the association caused, she found her voice.

"What did you want to talk about?"

Stupid question, she berated herself, and she felt even stupider when he said, "Last night."

Laying a hand over her churning stomach, she said, "All right."

He drew a deep breath. "You were upset last night."

She was upset this morning, too, but she just nodded once to acknowledge his statement. Maybe she should tell him outright that she didn't hold him responsible for what had happened, didn't expect anything from him, had learned long ago not to place her trust in men. . . .

"You were upset," he repeated, "which explains why you . . . forgot yourself." Leah winced, but he went doggedly on. "I know you'd never do something like that otherwise, and I admit I took advantage, but I want you to know that I did it because I've wanted you since the first time I saw you. I told you before, there's something between us, and now you know what it is. We should've married first — I asked you once, but you weren't ready then — but since we didn't, I think we ought to marry now."

Leah's head was spinning, and she groped for her desk chair and sank down into it. *He wanted to marry her,* and this wasn't the first time he'd asked. Of course it wasn't. He'd asked her the night before Brad . . . which was why she hadn't remembered, not even this morning when she thought he'd left her.

"Are you all right?" he asked solicitously, hurrying to her side.

She wasn't sure. "You . . . you weren't there when I woke up this morning."

"I had to be in the bunkhouse when the men woke up."

Of course. He couldn't let the men know he'd spent the night in her bed. She should have thought of that.

He took her hands in his, and she realized her fingers were cold with shock. "Leah, listen to me. You put me off before because of Brad, but now . . ."

His voice grew hoarse, and he stopped as pain swirled in her as well. "We . . . I'm in mourning now," she said, looking at the worn black dress she'd put on this morning. A woman in mourning couldn't marry. Society forbade it.

"Are you saying you want to wait a year?" he demanded impatiently.

"Not *want* to, but—"

"But nothing, Leah." He sounded almost angry, and his tanned skin had taken on a ruddy tinge. "Maybe you haven't had time to think about it yet, but after last night, maybe we *have* to get married."

She gasped. She most certainly hadn't had time to think about it, but he was absolutely right.

"I already lost one son, and I've lost him twice," he was saying. "That's more than enough for one lifetime, and I don't mean to let it happen again."

Vaguely she recalled her suspicion that he had left a string of bastards across Texas and knew how wrong she had been. But . . . "We can't just get married. People will talk."

"People will talk no matter what, and I'll tell you

something, Leah, I'm not going to wait a year before I make love to you again. I'm not even going to wait a few days. I'm going to sleep with you tonight and every night from now on, so if you're worried about what people will say, you'd better make it legal before the sun goes down again."

An inner voice whispered a warning. She hated being ordered around. She hated men who tried to run her life. But her body was remembering his touch, remembering the sweet oblivion of passion that could make even the unbearable bearable. An aching need formed like a fist in her belly, an emptiness for which she now knew the cure. The life she'd planned for so carefully had been destroyed by a single shotgun blast, but Cal was promising her a new one, giving her hope when she thought all her hope lay buried behind a white picket fence.

Still holding her hands, he pulled her to her feet and into his arms. His kiss was gentle at first, but she didn't want gentleness anymore. Slipping her arms around his neck, she clung to him in desperation, knowing she had finally found the love she hadn't even known she'd been missing.

Because she did love him, madly and passionately and desperately, the way she'd never allowed herself to love anyone, the way a woman can only love the man to whom she gives herself, body and soul. She'd dreaded the years of loneliness ahead, but now she needn't fear them anymore. She would have Cal beside her.

Reluctantly, she pulled her mouth from his and said, "Yes! Yes, I'll marry you!"

A triumphant smile lit his face and his arms tightened possessively around her. "We shouldn't wait."

No, not another day, she thought, and said, "The preacher . . . ?"

"He left at first light this morning," Cal admitted a little ruefully. "I couldn't very well ask him to stay until I talked to you."

"And of course I overslept. Can we catch him?"

Cal nodded. "I made sure I knew which way he was headed."

"I guess we should leave right away." Her head was spinning again. This was her *wedding day*.

"Soon as you're ready," he agreed.

Ready? Good heavens, she couldn't be married in this horrible old dress. Mourning or not, she wouldn't wear black to her wedding. "Just give me a few minutes to change."

"I'll get a wagon hitched."

He kissed her once more, hard and fast, then he was gone. Leah took a moment to catch her breath and to let the reality of what she had just done sink in. She must be mad to even contemplate running off to elope with a man she hardly knew, but for some reason it seemed like a completely sane and rational thing to do. In fact, given the senseless tragedy she had endured for the past few days, it was the sanest and most rational decision she could make for herself. If she were only to commit one impulsive act in her entire life, this would be it. Without allowing herself to consider it further, she hurried off to her bedroom to change.

Leah had just finished putting on her new lavender gown—the one she'd worn for Brad's wedding—and was doing up her hair again when Juanita came in.

"You are going somewhere?" the older woman asked.

"Yes, uh, Mr. Stevens and I have some business."

Juanita's dark eyes stared blankly, but Leah had the uncomfortable feeling she knew exactly what that business was and why it was so urgent. "You will be back tonight?"

"Yes, of course, why wouldn't we be?" she asked, feeling flustered and wondering if Juanita could tell why.

Juanita just shrugged and went on about her business. To Leah's relief, she was nowhere around when Leah slipped out the front door to find Cal waiting with the wagon in the yard.

Smiling his approval at her appearance, he helped her up onto the seat, then climbed up beside her. From up here Leah could see the picket fence around the cemetery, and a lump formed in her throat. Could it have been just days ago she'd planned Brad and Espy's wedding? So much had happened, it seemed like a lifetime ago; two lifetimes in fact, Brad's and Espy's.

Cal's hand covered hers which were clenched in her lap. "Don't cry," he said, making her aware that she was.

Hastily, she dug her hankie from her purse and dabbed the tears away. Then she gave him a tremulous smile. "I'll be all right as soon as we can't see the graves anymore."

He replied by slapping the team into motion. Leah forced herself to look straight ahead and not to think until they were out of sight of the ranch. Only then did she allow herself to relax and enjoy the beauty of the day in which she was to be married. The night chill had dissipated in the brilliant sunlight that shone from a cloudless sky which was exactly the color of Cal's eyes . . . Brad's eyes, too, but she didn't let herself linger on the thought. Instead she concentrated on the man who was soon to become her husband, with whom she would spend the rest of her life, with whom (God willing) she would have a family.

What little she knew about him seemed to indicate he was a good choice. He'd been patient and kind, and he'd never tried to bully her, but there was much she simply did not know. He had proved himself an able father for Brad, but how would he cope with a baby? And what was he like when he was angry? Or discouraged? Would they be able to laugh together once enough time had passed that they felt like laughing again? And would their loving always be as exciting as the first time?

So many questions, so many things to learn. Did all brides feel this uncertainty about the man to whom they were entrusting their entire future? Probably not, she reasoned, since few brides eloped with men they hardly knew.

Absently, she watched two hawks in the distance. At first she thought they were searching for prey, but she soon noticed their swooping was too aimless, too . . . too *playful* to be serious business. They seemed almost to be teasing each other, soaring through the air, parting only to come together again, then to part once more, but never for long.

"They're mates," Cal said after a while. "They're playing."

"Playing!" she exclaimed in surprise.

"Sure, animals play, too," he informed her with just a hint of smugness. "Just like people." His eyes glowed with an expression she recognized now as desire, and her body quickened instinctively in response, although she tried not to let him see her instantaneous reaction. Surely if she loved him, surely if he could make her feel as if a fire had started in her belly simply by looking at her, surely everything else would fall into place. "Hawks mate for life," he added, and her heart melted.

"Just like people," she replied, slipping her arm through his as he drove the wagon. Yes, she thought, surely everything else would be all right.

The sun was directly overhead by the time they caught up to the Reverend Mr. Underwood. He'd stopped for his nooning at a ranch house along the way and fortunately had decided to linger after the meal.

Leah knew the rancher and his wife, had known them for years, and after they had expressed their condolences on the loss of her brother, they stood with ill-concealed curiosity, waiting for an explanation for her presence on their doorstep.

Cal saved her from having to make one. "Leah and I would like to get married," he informed the flabbergasted minister.

Reverend Underwood opened his mouth to protest at the unseemliness of their request, but something in Cal's expression stopped him cold. His overly large Adam's apple bobbed as he swallowed loudly. "Why, certainly," he said at last.

The rancher and his wife, their eyes wide with amazement, ushered them inside where Reverend Underwood performed the ceremony with nervous haste. The absence of a ring shortened the already brief ceremony even more, and before she knew it, Leah was accepting the chastest of kisses from her groom and heard herself addressed as "Mrs. Stevens" for the first time.

The lady of the house insisted they eat before heading back home which was, after all, a trip of several hours, and since they'd had nothing to eat since morning, Cal and Leah agreed. The others had already eaten, but they sat with the newlyweds while they did so, making Leah feel as if she were on display in a museum. Fortunately, Cal seemed even less inclined than she to linger, and soon they were on their way again.

Less than an hour had passed since they had pulled up to the ranch, and Leah mused that the entire episode had about it a strange air of unreality, as if it hadn't happened at all. Indeed, except for a piece of paper, she had nothing to proclaim her Cal's wife, no ring, no gathering of friends and family, no blessing from the community. . . .

"It wasn't much of a wedding," Cal remarked, as if reading her thoughts.

"We couldn't have had much of one anyway, under the . . . circumstances," she said, remembering the expressions of shock on the faces of the rancher and his wife. It was an expression she would be seeing a lot in the future when people found out she'd eloped the morning after her brother's funeral.

Of course, it was nothing to the looks she would have gotten if she had proved to be with child and had no husband.

"At least I should've remembered a ring," Cal murmured in disgust. "You should've had a ring."

"I forgot, too," she reminded him. "We can get one later."

His frown told her he knew it wouldn't be the same,

and of course it wouldn't. Nothing about this wedding would be special or memorable, just as nothing that had happened the past few days was anything Leah cared to recall either. The tragedy was too closely bound up with what should have been a joyous occasion, and Leah realized she would never henceforth be able to celebrate her anniversary without also reliving the pain of her brother's death. The prospect did not bode well for a marriage already on shaky ground before it even began.

Neither of them spoke much during the ride home, and the sun had set by the time their wagon rumbled into the ranch yard. The evening shadows hid the graveyard, much to Leah's relief. Pete Quincy wandered out to meet them, his eyes questioning above the tangle of his grizzled beard, and Leah managed a smile and she allowed him to help her down from the high seat.

"I'm sure you're wondering where we've been all day."

"The thought did occur to me," he admitted, eyeing Cal suspiciously. "I was afraid this hombre'd run off with you."

"You're absolutely right, I'm afraid," Leah said, praying that her foreman and old friend would accept the news she had to give him. "Cal and I were married this afternoon."

He needed a second to comprehend, and when he did, his eyes grew just as wide as she had expected.

"Married!" he exclaimed, his gimlet gaze darting between them. Cal had climbed down from the wagon and stood beside her. Now he put a hand possessively on her shoulder.

"That's right," he said, a silent challenge in his voice daring Pete's disapproval.

Pete didn't hear it, however. He was still too busy being surprised. "I'll be damned! Oh, I'm sorry, Miss Leah!" he added quickly. "I just can't hardly believe it! Stevens, I don't know how you managed it, but I'd like to shake your hand. Can't tell you how relieved I am to know she's gonna be took care of from now on."

Now it was Cal who looked surprised as Pete pumped his hand, and Leah who was experiencing a form of mild outrage. "Pete! I don't need anyone to take care of me, and that certainly isn't the reason I married Cal!"

Pete grinned. "I don't reckon it is. You're prob'ly in love and all that, but when you get to be my age, you realize love ain't the most important thing."

Leah felt her face burning at the mention of love, and beside her Cal stiffened slightly, as if the word made him uncomfortable, too. Small wonder. He hadn't mentioned the subject to her and probably hadn't even considered it. He'd wanted her, he'd said, wanted her for more than just one night, wanted her enough to take her to wife so he could have her. She'd been willing to settle for that, and she wouldn't begin to regret her choice now.

"And what makes you such an expert on marriage?" Leah chided Pete.

"Never having been married myownself," Pete replied cheerfully. Indeed, Leah's marriage had put him in a singularly good mood. "Which is why I know it ain't all that romance that keeps two folks together. It's what they give each other, and this fella here, he can give you just what you need."

Leah was entirely too mortified to inquire as to what that might be, although Pete's smug grin dared her to ask. When she glanced at Cal, she caught him grinning, too, a conspiratorial, masculine grin as if he and Pete shared a secret.

"Well," she said sharply, anxious to escape Pete's knowing gaze, "I'd better get up to the house."

"You go on with her, Cal," Pete said, addressing Cal by his first name for the first time, a sure signal of his acceptance. "I'll take care of the horse and wagon."

Cal's hand still rested on her shoulder, and he slipped it around her as they walked. Leah didn't think she liked the familiarity, especially when she wasn't sure whether she should be angry with him or not.

"What was all that about?" she demanded, peering up at him through the evening shadows.

"All what?" he asked in surprise.

"All that with Pete. What does he think you have to give me?" Although her cheeks burned, she refused to drop her gaze.

Cal's grin returned. "You heard him, he just thinks I can take care of you."

"And *you* heard *me,* I don't need anyone to take care of me."

He considered this as they walked up the porch steps, and the provocative glitter in his eyes made Leah's heart flutter in her chest. "Then I guess we'll just have to think of something else for me to do for you, won't we?"

Before she could think of a suitable response to this outrageous question, they'd reached the top step, and Cal was bending to pick her up.

"What on earth . . ." she exclaimed as he lifted her high against his chest.

"You may not have had a ring or much of a wedding

either, but at least you're going to get carried across the threshold."

For self-preservation, Leah had to throw her arms around his neck, bringing her face excitingly near to his. He was still grinning at her from beneath his broad-brimmed Stetson, and he swooped in to take a nibble from the sensitive skin beneath her ear. The impulsive move startled a squeak from Leah who had never squeaked in her life.

Provoked by the superior smile he was giving her when he drew away, she returned the favor, ducking under his hat brim to playfully sink her teeth into his earlobe.

"Hey!" he cried, a shudder of reaction rippling through him as he strode across the porch. "Keep that up, and I won't even wait until I get you inside, Mrs. Stevens."

"Wait for what?" she asked innocently as he bent to work the doorknob while trying to keep his grip on her.

"Maybe I ought to just show you," he growled with a mocking leer, kicking the door wide and maneuvering her through it.

"*Show* me?" she exclaimed in feigned disappointment. "I thought you'd do more than that!"

"*Leah!*"

They both looked up in surprise to see Mead Garland standing in the middle of the parlor, an expression of abject horror on his handsome face. "What is the meaning of this?" he demanded.

Leah's playful mood dissolved into dismay, and she didn't need to see Cal's face to know he was furious. His whole body had gone rigid with it. Without waiting to be asked, Cal let her feet slide to the floor but he kept his other arm draped around her shoulders as he held her firmly to his side.

"Mead," she managed breathlessly. "I didn't expect you."

"I told you I would come by this afternoon to see how you were doing," he reminded her, every bit as furious as Cal.

Oh, yes, she did remember, but only vaguely. "I . . . we were out."

Mead's glance darted to Cal, then quickly back to her again. Obviously, he couldn't decide whether to risk offending a known gunfighter. "Yes, Juanita told me you'd been gone most of the day," he said, choosing tact.

"We were," Cal said before she could reply. "We got married this afternoon."

Mead's horror at seeing Cal carrying her into the house was nothing compared to his reaction to this. He turned literally white and his chest began to heave so that Leah began to fear for his well-being. *"Married?"* he spat out, as if the word were vile. "You can't! He's lying! Leah, whatever he forced you to do . . ."

He took a step toward them, and Cal's hand tightened possessively on her shoulder, but before Mead could come any closer, Leah said, "He didn't force me to do anything! We . . . we'd been discussing marriage for some time," she said, thinking it was only a small lie. "I wanted to wait until Brad . . ." Her voice caught on the shards of memory, but she forced herself to go on. ". . . until Brad was settled, but now . . . now it seemed foolish to wait any longer."

"Foolish?" Mead scoffed, perfectly livid and barely able to control his rage. "Your brother isn't even cold in

255

his grave! Have you thought about what people will say?"

"I don't think this is any of your business, Garland," Cal said, the ring of steel beneath his words, but Mead was too angry to recognize the danger he was courting.

"None of my business?" he snarled. "Leah and I were engaged!"

"A long time ago," Cal reminded him.

"No, not a long time ago! *Now!* We talked about getting married just the other day, apparently at the same time she was talking to you about it!"

Leah felt Cal's shock, but she was too angry to do more than lash out at Mead. "That's not true!" she cried. *"You* talked about it, but I never gave you any encouragement!"

"You told me I could call on you this very afternoon!"

He was right, of course, and Leah could only stare at him in despair. How could this have happened?

"I think you'd better leave, Garland," Cal said through clenched teeth.

Mead made a visible effort to regain his dignity. "Not until I've said one more thing. Leah, it's not too late. We can have the marriage annulled. I mean, if you haven't . . . Well, there's hardly been time!"

The color was coming back to his face, and Leah felt it rising in hers as well, but she dared not look at Cal for fear of what her expression might reveal. "Mead, like Cal said, this is none of your business. I don't want an annulment, and I don't need your help."

"Leah!" he cried, almost pleading. "Don't you know what you've done?"

"I think I do," she replied stiffly, but he was shaking

256

his head and glaring at Cal, apparently having decided he would risk offending him and offending him thoroughly.

"Leah, we still don't have any idea who killed Brad, but it stands to reason it would be someone who had something to gain from it."

Cal's hand tightened on her shoulder, and she instinctively stepped in front of him as if she could physically protect him from the accusation she knew was coming. "Cal had nothing to gain from Brad's death!"

"Didn't he?" Mead scoffed. "Think about it. Even if he could prove he was Brad's natural father, he wasn't likely to get anything from the boy. But with the boy dead, he could have the whole ranch!"

"But Cal didn't inherit the ranch," Leah reminded him scornfully. "I did!"

Mead smiled sadly, tolerantly. "Yes, and according to law, the instant he married you, everything you own became his property."

The shock went through her like a lightning bolt. She'd known, of course. Everyone knew husbands owned their wives' property. She just hadn't thought . . .

"You're pretty free with your accusations, Garland," Cal said in a deceptively mild voice.

"Just pointing out facts," Garland countered.

"Then you've forgot some. What about Homer Wilkes? He stood to gain a lot more than I did."

Mead glared at him contemptuously. "How? The will left everything to Leah."

"But he didn't know Brad had signed the will. If Brad died before he signed, Espy would've inherited everything."

"Then why did he kill Espy, too?"

"He didn't know she'd be along. Nobody did. We all thought she'd be staying in town."

"Which was why it would have been the perfect time to ambush Brad because he'd be alone. Or maybe you saw them coming back to the ranch together," Mead speculated, "and thought this would be your chance to take care of them both so you'd have Leah and the ranch all to yourself!"

Cal made a growling noise in his throat and would have lunged for Mead if Leah hadn't turned and grabbed him by the arms. "Don't! Please, Cal! He's only trying to provoke you!"

Cal's blazing gaze turned down to her, and he studied her face closely. "Do you believe him?"

"Of course not!"

"Why?" Mead challenged. "Because he's your husband? Ask him where he was that morning. Did anyone see him?"

But she knew no one had seen him. He'd worked alone that morning, having promised to stay close to the ranch so he could check in with her at noon to see if Brad had returned.

"It was the perfect plan, Leah," Mead insisted. "Kill them both, and it wouldn't matter if Brad had left a will or not."

Leah whirled to face him. "But Espy wasn't murdered! Her death was an accident."

"A convenient accident. How do we know the killer didn't plan to shoot her, too, but the runaway saved him the trouble?"

Leah felt the tremor of rage shaking Cal, and she looked into his eyes, entreating. "Please, don't! For

258

me?" she whispered. Then, knowing she couldn't restrain him much longer, she said to Mead, "You'd better leave now."

"Leah . . ." he entreated, but she would have none of it.

"*Now,* Mead. I don't want you here, and I certainly don't want to hear your wild accusations."

Mead straightened indignantly, pulling his waistcoat with a jerk. "I'm just afraid they aren't as wild as you'd like to think, but of course I have no proof or I would be sending for the county sheriff tonight. When I do, believe me, I will, and until then, I want you to know that I am at your disposal, Leah, for whatever services I can perform for you . . . legal or otherwise."

"Mead!" Leah cried in warning when Cal tried to push her out of the way so he could get at him.

Mead needed no further inducement, and he scrambled away, toward the still-opened door, and was bolting across the yard toward his horse before Cal could even move to stop him.

"Son of a bitch," Cal muttered and drove his fist into his other palm with a smack that made Leah jump. Then he turned the force of his fury on her. "Did you tell him you'd marry him?"

"Of course not!" she cried, outraged.

"But you were talking to him about it," he accused.

"No! *He* was talking about it, or at least he was saying a lot of silly things about how he never stopped loving me all these years and now that Brad was married maybe we could start seeing each other again. I didn't even realize what he had in mind! I just thought he wanted to be friends."

"Friends?" Cal snarled contemptuously. "A man and

a woman can never be *friends,* especially not when they've already been lovers."

Leah gaped at him. *Lovers?* Where had he gotten an idea like that? She already told him she'd never loved Mead.

She was still speechless when Juanita asked, "He is gone, yes?"

They both jumped and turned to find her standing in the hall doorway.

"He has wait for hours," she explained blandly. "He keep asking when you be back. I do not tell him you marry. I tell him nothing."

Leah finally found her tongue. "How did you know we were married?"

Juanita shrugged. "I know. I fix the bedroom for you, the big room where the *patrón* sleep. And I fix supper, too. You eat?"

Although eating was the last thing on her mind, Leah nodded, thinking food might help the headache forming behind her eyes.

"Come then." She disappeared in a swish of skirts, leaving them staring at the empty doorway.

Cautiously, Leah turned to Cal. His expression was blank, as if he'd wiped it clean, and she could see only a trace of the smoldering fury in his clear eyes.

"I don't want to fight about Mead Garland on my wedding night," she said.

"Do you even want a wedding night?" he countered coldly. "Maybe you want to think over Garland's offer."

Frustration roiled within her. "You heard what I told him."

"Yeah, and it's a little late for an annulment anyways. You couldn't claim to be a virgin, especially when . . ."

"When what?" she snapped, mortification scalding her.

"Nothing," he said just as shortly. "Let's go eat."

She turned on her heel and stalked off toward the dining room, not even looking back to see if he was following or not. Well, she'd wondered what he would be like when he was angry, and now she knew: stubborn as a mule and twice as thickheaded. She would gladly have strangled Mead Garland for causing all this.

Juanita had set the table lavishly, using the tablecloth they usually saved for Christmas and the silver Leah hadn't seen in years. Candles burned in the centerpiece Juanita had moved down to illuminate the far end of the table where they were to sit. A thoroughly romantic setting which was totally wasted.

Cal entered the room behind her and followed her down to where the two places had been laid. Leah was just about to take her usual seat at the head of the table when Juanita appeared from the kitchen and saw her. She shook her head firmly and nodded to the other chair.

At first Leah couldn't imagine why Juanita wanted her to move, then she realized that the master of the house should sit at the head of the table. For seven years, Leah had filled that role, and the thought of giving it up brought a lump to her throat. On the other hand, she wasn't really the master here any longer, legally or any other way, as Mead had already pointed out. By marrying Cal, she'd ceded that position to him.

As boorishly as he was behaving, he certainly didn't deserve any special favors, but then, how could she blame him for being jealous at discovering her former lover in the parlor as he carried his bride over the threshold? Things weren't going to get any better until one of them made a concession, and this was such a small thing to do.

Lifting her chin determinedly, Leah moved on to the chair to the right of the head and seated herself without a word. As she spread the fine damask napkin in her lap, she felt Cal's gaze upon her. Looking up, she caught him studying her as if trying to fathom her motives in changing seats.

She smiled slightly. "Aren't you going to sit down?"

Her question broke his reverie, and he pulled the chair out and sat, although he still kept glancing at her as if afraid she might do something untoward. Or perhaps because he thought she already had.

Juanita served them silently, fried chicken and gravy over fluffy mashed potatoes, corn fritters and stewed apples and chocolate cake. Although Leah hadn't felt particularly hungry when she sat down, the delicious aromas reminded her stomach of how little it had taken in today, and she ate ravenously.

Cal, too, seemed to enjoy the meal, although he didn't say a word. Leah couldn't think of anything to say either, and by the time they finished their cake and coffee, the silence weighed heavily on her.

She was almost glad when Cal said, "I reckon I'll go down to the bunkhouse and get my things."

"All right," Leah agreed with relief, rising to help Juanita clear the table.

Cal rose from the table and left without a backward glance. He didn't really trust himself to look back for fear he might do something to make things even worse between them. Damn it to hell, they hadn't been married a day and already he'd messed up. What in God's name had made him think he was a fit match for a woman like Leah Harding? What had made him think he had the slightest idea of how to treat her or talk to her or make her happy?

No answers came to him as he hurried from the house and across the ranch yard to the glow of lights shining from the bunkhouse windows. That was where he belonged, with men as crude as himself where he didn't have to weigh every word and never had to worry about hurting anyone's feelings. Damn it to hell. What had he gotten himself into?

The men all looked up from their various activities when he entered, and he could see the sudden caution in their eyes. This morning he'd been one of them, but now he was the boss. For a long moment, no one moved, then Pete Quincy cleared his throat and said, "This here fellow just married himself the best woman in Texas. Ain't anybody gonna congratulate him?"

At that, the men jumped to their feet, and one by one moved up to pump Cal's hand and wish him luck. A few bolder ones even managed a joke about being leg-shackled now. When they had finished, Cal *knew* he'd made a mistake. How was he ever going to live up to their expectations? And if they ever found out that he'd already made Leah despise him . . .

But he didn't have to worry, he thought bitterly, no ordinary cowboy would ever dream of berating the infamous Cal Stevens, not if he valued his life. Pushing that vile thought from his mind, he moved over to what had been his bunk and began to gather his meager possessions. All too soon he had them tied in a bundle, a bundle he'd carried how many times from place to place, moving, always moving on when the job was done. This was the first time in his life he'd ever packed up because he was going to *stay* someplace.

Aware the men were watching and not wishing to appear reluctant to join his bride, he hefted the bundle and headed for the door, giving the men what he hoped was a jaunty wave. They were too in awe of him and Leah to make the lewd remarks one might expect at a time like this, but he knew the same thought lurked behind every pair of eyes watching him leave: tonight he would know Leah Harding.

If only such a thing were possible. If only a man really could know a woman simply by possessing her body. Cal had a sinking feeling he might never really know Leah Harding.

He paused on the bunkhouse porch, set his bundle down and rolled himself a smoke. Anything to delay his return to that house, he thought. As he worked with the paper and tobacco, Pete Quincy came out onto the porch, too.

Feeling he had to explain why he hadn't gone rushing back to his bride, Cal said, "She don't like smoke in the house."

Pete nodded sagely and puffed on his pipe. When Cal had got his own cigarette lit, Pete said, "Not many folks understand Miss Leah."

Cal tried to conceal his surprise. "Are you one who does?"

"I understand some things, like why she is the way she is. It was her old man's doing. He always wanted her to be a boy."

"She told me," Cal remarked encouragingly.

"He couldn't stand it that she wasn't, particularly when it got to be real clear she would've been a hell of boy. Smart as a whip, and wasn't nothing she couldn't do in the old days, ride and rope and even shoot. She even learned to skin a deer to please him. 'Course, she never could please him, no matter what she did."

"She said trying only made him madder."

Pete nodded again. "Yep. I reckon he couldn't help thinking what a man she'd've been if she'd had the sense to be born male. She finally gave up trying to be a boy, but she never stopped trying to please him, not even after he died. I've been watching her these last seven years, and I can see it just as plain as day. She's run this place better'n any ten men could've, just like she was trying to show him or something. You know what I mean?"

"I think so," Cal mused, thinking Pete *did* understand things about Leah he didn't.

"She was trying to be ma and pa both to the boy, and she was so busy doing it, she never had no life of her own. I don't reckon she was very happy, but she never had time to notice and wouldn't've cared even if she had. Brad was the only thing she cared about in this world, and I reckon losing him like that might've killed her if you hadn't been here."

Cal gaped at him. He'd never considered himself Leah Harding's savior. If anything, he'd thought she was his.

"Yep," Pete confirmed, "now she's got something else to think about and somebody to look after her for a change. It ain't right for a woman to do it all alone like she done all these years. I expect you'll take on some of the load for her, though."

Cal took a deep drag on his cigarette. "Mead Garland thinks I just married her to get the ranch."

Pete swore eloquently. "I seen him come running out of the house like his tail was on fire. I sure am sorry I forgot to tell you he was here this afternoon, but when you said that about getting married, it went plumb out of my head. That son of a bitch. I wouldn't pay no attention to anything he says."

"Maybe you wouldn't, and neither would I, but I'm not so sure about Leah. He also told her I was the one with the best reason for killing Brad."

"The hell you say! Don't he know the boy was your son?"

"Oh, yes, he knows all right. He figures that once I realized I'd never get anything from the boy, I fixed it so Leah would inherit the ranch, then killed him and married her."

Pete swore again, even more impressively. "That's the kind of plan a lawyer'd figure out all right."

"Don't tell me you never thought of it," Cal said.

"No, in fact, I didn't, but then, I seen you together with Miss Leah and the boy. Ain't no doubt in my mind how you felt about both of 'em."

Once again Pete had amazed him, and Cal could think of no reply.

After a minute, Pete said, "Onliest thing I can't figure out is how you got Miss Leah to marry you so quick."

Cal had no intention of explaining. Instead he said, "I promised I'd give her another boy to take Brad's place."

"Well, now, that's a project worth taking on," Pete said, grinning broadly. "And here I am, holding you up when you're wanting to get started."

Cal grinned back perfunctorily, glad Pete couldn't know how much Cal was dreading going to bed with what he suspected would be a very reluctant bride. Left with no other choice, however, he tossed down his cigarette, ground it out with his heel, and hefted his bundle again.

"You treat her good now, or you'll have to answer to me," Pete warned cheerfully.

"Sure thing," Cal replied in the same spirit and headed off toward the house. He'd only gone a few steps, however, when he sensed something amiss. This sixth sense had saved his life more than once, and he glanced furtively around, trying to find the source of what had disturbed him.

Naturally, his gaze touched the white picket fence on the hill, still visible even in the pale moonlight, and there he saw a shadowy figure lurking.

"Who's up there?" he asked Pete who hadn't moved.

Pete sighed gustily. "Homer Wilkes. He's been hanging around all day, bawling like a baby over them graves. I reckon he's feeling guilty for treating that poor girl so bad all her life. You want me to run him off?"

Cal considered. He didn't particularly want Homer Wilkes anywhere near Leah, but he also knew what it was like to be a father and stand by the grave of your dead child. "No, leave him be. Just don't let him bother Leah."

"Don't worry none about that," Pete assured him.

Juanita hadn't tolerated Leah's help for long and had sent her off to her new bedroom. Leah hadn't been in

267

this room since they'd done their annual cleaning last spring, and entering it now seemed more than strange. Juanita had removed all the dustcovers and polished the massive mahogany furniture until it gleamed. The four-poster pineapple bed — with pineapples carved on all four posts — was made up with the tester and spread Leah's mother had crocheted for her trousseau when she'd married Leah's father so long ago.

The stove had heated the room to a warm coziness, and a lamp on the dresser cast an inviting glow, perfect for a romantic wedding night. Leah only wished her own mood matched that of the room. Instead she was still angry and disturbed by the scene with Mead and her argument with Cal afterwards. The only way she'd kept her sanity for the past two days was by not letting herself think about Brad's death. Consequently, she also hadn't thought about who might have killed him. They'd told her there had been no clues, and since she was the only one to profit from his death, she'd managed to convince herself his killer must have been a crazed stranger intent on robbery. No one who knew Brad could have taken his life, or so she'd told herself.

Now Mead had caused her to doubt. Not that she believed any of his nonsense about Cal being responsible, but the stranger theory was equally absurd. Who would stage such an elaborate scene just to stop someone who may or may not have been carrying anything worth stealing? Hardly anyone she knew carried more than a few dollars in cash with them, and if someone had simply wanted the horse and buggy, he didn't have to *kill* for them. And of course Brad and Espy hadn't been robbed at all.

Could Mead have been right? Could someone have

deliberately murdered Brad? But who? Who would have profited?

Leah didn't want to think about the answer to that question, not now, not on her wedding night. And remembering this was her wedding night brought all kinds of new anxieties, for which she called herself a fool. After all, she wasn't a trembling virgin, as Cal had so pointedly reminded her just a little while ago. She'd actually had her wedding night last night, so she had nothing to be frightened of now.

Unfortunately, she did feel anxious. Not fearful exactly, but awkward and strained, aware of how real everything seemed tonight, not at all like last night during which everything had been veiled by the mists of passion.

It was still early for bed, but she just couldn't bear the thought of sitting up with Cal for another hour while they stared at each other across the parlor and waited for this moment while Leah grew more and more uneasy. Swiftly she undressed and washed and slipped on her nightdress and robe. At least that part would be over, and she wouldn't have to worry about whether or not he was in the room while she performed these rituals.

Feeling slightly less nervous, she sat down at the dresser, finding her toiletries already moved over and laid out for her, and began to unpin her hair. She was halfway through her ritual hundred strokes when she heard Cal's footsteps in the hallway.

Instantly her heart began to pound, and her hand stilled as she waited. But to her surprise, he knocked. The courtesy eased her apprehension somewhat, and managing a smile at her own foolishness, she said, "Come in."

She turned on the stool to face him, and he caught her eye the instant he walked into the room. Pausing just for a second, he took her in with one swift glance, then looked away, as if he'd been caught doing something improper. He examined the room then, taking in the opulence of the furnishings and the lace curtains on the windows.

"This where your parents slept?" he asked gruffly, his tone making her wonder what he thought of the place.

"Yes," she said. "It's been empty for a long time." She tried to read his expression, but whatever his true thoughts, they didn't show on his face. Was he impressed by the lavishness or offended by it? Was he honored to sleep in her father's room or insulted? "If you'd rather, we can use my room," she ventured.

"No, this is fine," he said, although he didn't sound as if it were. "Where should I put my things?"

Leah had discovered the drawers Juanita had left empty for him, and she pointed to them. "Over there. There's room in the wardrobe for anything you want to hang up, too."

He nodded stiffly and went to the chest, carrying his bundle. As he unpacked, Leah went back to brushing her hair, watching him in the mirror and wishing she could think of something to say to break the tension between them. She wanted to reassure him that she didn't really believe he'd murdered Brad, but bringing up the subject of Brad was fraught with dangers, not the least of which was the distinct possibility that Leah might dissolve in the tears she'd been fighting ever since yesterday.

And mentioning Mead Garland seemed unwise in

the extreme. She would never forgive him for what he'd done today, not only for making their homecoming so unpleasant but for accusing Cal of only marrying her to get the Rocking Horse. Not exactly the sentiment a new bride wishes to hear, she thought angrily as she laid down her brush and began to braid the length of her hair.

Her fingers worked swiftly at the familiar task, leaving her mind free to mull over Mead's other wild accusations. Too many of them had had the ring of truth or at least the strength of logic. Fortunately, she couldn't believe Cal had just married her for her property, not after last night, not after the passion they'd shared.

Of course, if they hadn't shared that passion last night, they wouldn't have married today. Leah never would have considered such a wild impulse otherwise. At least Mead didn't know about that. He probably would have accused Cal of seducing her in order to ensure that she would marry him no matter what.

The thought stunned her, and instinctively, her gaze sought Cal in the mirror. She found him finished with his task and watching her. He frowned when he caught her eye.

"Something wrong?"

"No," she hastily assured him, wishing it were true. Dropping her gaze, she quickly finished braiding her hair and tied it off, not daring to meet his eye again lest he read her doubts.

It wasn't true. It couldn't be true. Cal would never . . . But how could she be sure? What did she know about him, after all? He'd *seemed* genuinely concerned about Brad, seemed even to love the boy, but such sentiments might have been calculated simply to win them over.

But he'd wanted to marry her even when Brad was still alive! she told herself frantically. Then she could almost hear Mead's voice arguing, Yes, he'd proposed the night before Brad died, when he'd probably already made his plans. And seducing her had been so easy, she'd *made* it so easy. He couldn't have known she would cooperate so well, but he must have suspected how vulnerable she would be, how desperately lonely.

And he'd never said he loved her, never even hinted.

"Leah?"

She started at the word and glanced up to find his frown had deepened. Dear God, please don't let him guess what she'd been thinking. She tried to smile. "Yes?"

"Are you going to bed now?"

Her mouth went dry, and she tried to swallow. No, she wanted to say, not yet, not until I've been able to convince myself you're the man I thought you were and not the murderer Mead accused you of being. "It is a little early . . ."

"But it's been a long day, and you look about done in."

She felt done in, too. She nodded numbly, wondering if he could see her fears, wondering if he would care if he did.

He'd started to unbutton his shirt, although he was still watching her, a faintly puzzled frown still creasing his rugged face. If he did sense her fears, he wasn't letting them keep him from his purpose. Dropping her gaze in what she hoped he would take for modesty, she rose from her stool and went to the bed. Pulling off her robe, she laid it across the foot and, with unsteady fin-

272

gers, pulled the coverlet back to reveal crisp white sheets. Without looking up, she slid between them and pulled the covers up to her chin.

Lying stiffly and staring intently at the crocheted tester above her head, she heard the sounds of his undressing. Would he come to bed naked again, as he had last night? She found the prospect both exciting and terrifying. He's your husband, she told herself, and you love him. You loved him enough to defy every convention you've ever held sacred so you could marry him. You loved him enough to lie with him even before that. Are you going to let a few angry words from a jealous man destroy all that?

Cal blew out the lamp and the room went dark. Once again she waited while he padded to the bed and came to her. Naked, yes, naked, she thought as she surrendered to his embrace and clasped his bare shoulders. His lips felt alien on hers, his tongue intrusive as he probed her mouth.

Everything was the same as before, the questing hands, the avid kisses, yet everything was different, too. She tried to respond, forced herself to return his kisses, to mimic his caresses, but she couldn't force the passion, couldn't conjure the desire that had driven her last night.

When he touched her down there, she jumped, not ready, not willing, but when he would have pulled away, her mind screamed No! She wanted him, she did, and she pulled him to her, taking his weight, opening in silent invitation, urging him with hands and lips until she overcame his resistance. His hardness filled her, and she clung to him frantically, desperately wanting but feeling nothing.

273

He said her name, but it was a question. What was wrong?

But he mustn't suspect her doubts, mustn't know. She loved him. She wanted him. Yes, that's what she must think about, and she tried, she really did.

He hadn't moved, so she did, churning her hips until he had no more questions, until he moved with her, breathless and gasping, his skin damp, his muscles straining against the inevitable, overwhelming force until he could resist no longer.

"I can't . . ." he cried hoarsely, and of course she didn't want him to and wouldn't let him. When he shuddered with release, she cradled him to her, weeping silently and telling herself that even now they might be making the child that he'd promised. Surely he would love her if she carried his child. Then they would be all right. Then she could forget everything Mead had said.

He lay still for a few moments, sobbing for breath, but this time his weight was unwelcome, crushing down on her. Fighting to breathe, she pushed at his shoulders until he rolled away. Instantly self-conscious, she snatched her nightgown down again, unable to stand even the possibility that her naked flesh might touch his again. She was too sensitive, too vulnerable, and she was still crying. Before he could see, she turned away, putting her back to him, pulling the covers to her mouth so no betraying sound would escape.

Cal flopped over onto his back and drew a deep breath. He released it on a long sigh that didn't sound like a sigh of satisfaction. He threw his arm over his eyes, and for a long time they simply lay there, each of them pretending to be asleep and knowing the other wasn't.

Leah stared into the darkness, soundless tears seeping from her eyes and dropping to the pillow while she listened to the sound of Cal's irregular breathing and prayed he wouldn't ask her what was wrong. After what seemed like hours, she finally drifted off to sleep, but she knew he was awake long afterwards. She knew because his anger haunted all her dreams.

Chapter Nine

Out of long habit, Cal awoke at dawn, his bod[y]
from holding himself away from Leah even in slee[p]
glanced over to find her still turned from him, he[r]
hunched as if defensively, and he stifled a groan [of de]
spair.

Flinging back the covers, he eased out of bed[, careful]
not to wake her and swiftly found a pair of jean[s and]
slipped them on. As quietly as possible, he gather[ed his]
clothes. He would wash in the kitchen so he wo[uldn't]
disturb her — and wouldn't encounter her haunted eyes.
Hurrying to the door, he paused just before opening it
and looked back one last time.

She seemed so small and defenseless huddled beneath the covers, his heart ached. From here he could
just see the top of her head and the honey-colored braid
he'd watched her make last night. He'd wanted to ask
her to leave her hair loose for him, so he could run his
fingers through it and luxuriate in it as he'd fantasized,
but after seeing her wariness of him, he hadn't been
able to find the words to ask.

All he'd wanted to do was make her happy. What a

gold-plated fool he'd been to even imagine he was capable of it. Not only had she realized she'd made a mistake in marrying him but she was beginning to think he might be a murderer in the bargain.

She'd never come to love him now. He'd known it last night when she'd tried so futilely to pretend she wanted him when all the time she could barely tolerate his touch. Which only proved how desperately she wanted a child, so desperately she was willing to endure his lust to get it.

And now she'd *never* do more than endure him.

Fury and despair roiled within him, bitter as gall. He pulled open the door and rushed out, remembering to close the door softly behind him.

Leah awoke reluctantly hours later, knowing instinctively, even before she could consciously think, that she did not want to face this day. With awareness came the crushing agony of all the things she'd been able to escape in sleep, and she groaned aloud at the rush of memories.

Brad and Espy, the graves on the hillside, Cal's seduction, their hasty marriage, Mead's accusations.

And last night. Leah would never have suspected one could feel so separate from someone during the very act of love. Or so alone when lying just a heartbeat away from one's husband.

What was she going to do? Instinct told her she must confront Cal and tell him of her fears, but common sense forbade it. How did a woman explain to a man that she needed him to reassure her he hadn't killed her brother or seduced her because he wanted to possess

277

her ranch? Simply knowing she had those suspicions might destroy any chance of happiness between them or even drive him away completely.

And she couldn't lose him now, not when she had no one and nothing else left, not when she needed him so desperately, not when she loved him.

She rolled over, compelled to touch him, to hold him, but his place was empty and cold, and she was as alone as she would ever be. Only the indentation on the pillow beside hers showed he had ever been here, and she pulled it to her instinctively, burying her face in it to inhale his lingering scent and clutching it to her aching heart.

So great was the pain in her heart, she did not at first notice the more familiar pain below. Only when she felt the warm blood did she realize what it signified.

No! her mind cried as she pressed her palms to the menstrual cramping in her abdomen. This was more than she could bear, more than anyone should have to bear. She and Cal had not made a baby together, and there had been no reason for their hasty, scandalous marriage. No baby and no hope that the child would draw them together. No hope at all.

She buried her face in the pillow where he had lain and wept.

Later that morning, Leah was sitting in the parlor knitting — Christmas was coming and she always gave the men socks for Christmas — when she heard a wagon pulling up in the yard. A visitor, just what she needed, she thought in dismay, and just in time for dinner. She would have to invite whoever it was to partake of their

278

noon meal. And explain she was married now. And explain she wasn't exactly sure where her husband was this morning because he hadn't even spoken to her before he left their marriage bed. She didn't even know whether he was coming back or not.

Resignedly, she stuffed her knitting back into the bag on the floor beside her chair and pushed herself to her feet, stretching to ease the ache in her back. At least the cramps were better, although she knew she looked pale and wan as she always did this time of month, and not at all like a glowing new bride.

Before she could go to open the door, she heard the clatter of familiar footsteps on the porch and the door flew open. Cal paused a moment, having seen her standing there, and in that moment her heart lurched painfully in her chest. How handsome he was and how very much she loved him, but the automatic joy evaporated when she saw how his expression grew guarded the instant he saw her.

Slowly, much more slowly than he had opened it, she closed the front door, then he pulled off his Stetson and ran a hand through his hair. Carefully, never taking his eyes off her, he hung the hat on a peg by the door and came a few steps closer, studying her as if he'd never seen her before.

Leah tried to smile, acutely aware of how strained her expression must be, and he frowned in response. "What's the matter?" he demanded. "Are you sick?"

Then she realized he must have noticed how peaked she looked. "No, not really. I just . . . I got my monthly this morning."

Leah had never said such a thing to a man before, and for one awful moment, seeing Cal's puzzled expression, she thought she was going to have to explain. Then understanding dawned, and he nodded once, stiffly. But he had no other reaction, and Leah was afraid he did not understand the full implication.

"That means I'm not . . . with child," she forced herself to add.

Reaction flickered across his face, but was gone too quickly for her to identify the emotion he had felt. Disappointment? Relief? Suddenly, she *had* to know what he felt.

"There wasn't any reason for us to get married after all," she goaded him.

His eyes narrowed to indigo slits. "Are you sorry we did?"

"I didn't say that!" she protested.

"You didn't have to."

"What does that mean?"

"Nothing."

The stubborn set of his jaw told her he had no intention of going on with this discussion. Ordinarily, she wouldn't have stood for that, would have pushed and prodded until he answered her, but something nagged at her, something she'd almost forgotten. Oh, yes, the wagon she'd heard in the yard. If they had company, they couldn't stand here arguing. . . .

"I heard a wagon. Is someone here?"

"No, I . . . that was me."

Driving a wagon? Whatever for?

"I went to town this morning," he said, answering her unspoken question.

"Why?" Trips to town were usually reserved for weekends and special business.

He rubbed his palms on his pant legs in an uncharac-

280

teristically nervous gesture, then closed them into determined fists. "I got you a present."

Something flickered inside her, something that felt like hope struggling to life again. "You did?" she asked stupidly.

Encouraged slightly, he came a few steps closer, until she could smell the scent of wind and sunshine clinging to his clothes, until she could see he had shaved that morning. The men never shaved before going to work the cattle because their sweat would make the newly scraped skin burn painfully. If they shaved at all, they waited until evening, but Cal had shaved for her today, so he could go to town to get her a present. She smiled.

He reached into his vest pocket and pulled out a tiny drawstring bag. His eyes were still guarded, as if he were unsure of her reaction, and he offered the bag, dropping it into the hand she held up for it.

She hadn't expected anything so small. He'd taken a wagon, after all. With her heart pounding in her chest and her fingers clumsy with excitement, she struggled with the fine strings until the bag opened and the gleaming gold circlet spilled out into her palm.

A tiny cry of joy escaped her, and she looked up to catch uncertainty in his eyes. He covered it quickly, but not before she saw how worried he was about her reaction. "You should've had a ring before," he said gruffly. "I figured the sooner the better."

She nodded, not quite able to speak around the lump in her throat. Oh, please, God, let it fit. She swallowed the lump and held the ring out to him. "Would you put it on for me?"

He blinked in surprise, but then his broad shoulders relaxed ever so slightly, as if the tension that had been holding him suddenly eased. "Sure," he said and took the ring from her.

She held out her bare left hand, no longer embarrassed for him to see it shook slightly because he held it steady as he slipped the ring on her finger.

"It fits," she murmured in surprise, unable to take her eyes off the shining gold that proved, finally, she was Cal's wife.

"I told the lady in the store it had to be small."

She nodded again, truly unable to speak now because the lump was back and tears were welling in her eyes, tears of relief and happiness and hope because she knew he cared for her, he really did. Before she could stop them, the tears began to roll down her cheeks.

"Don't you like it?" he asked in alarm.

"Oh, yes, I do!" she sobbed, hugging her ringed hand to her breast.

"But you're *crying*," he protested "Look, if you don't like it, we can . . ."

"But I *do* like it!" she insisted. "I *love* it!" And I love you, too, Cal Stevens, and now I know there's a chance you might love me back or at least might come to love me back. "I'm crying because I'm happy!"

Plainly this was a new concept to Cal, one he didn't entirely believe, so she threw her arms around him and hugged him just as tightly as she could. After a moment, he hugged her back, still not sure but more than willing to hold her.

"Thank you," she whispered, touching her lips to his smoothly shaven jaw. "You've made me very happy."

He smelled wonderful and felt wonderful, so strong and solid and virile, and when his mouth closed over hers, she surrendered completely to his kiss. Clinging to him, she reveled in the solid feel of his shoulders beneath her hands and the silken texture of his raven hair when she buried her fingers in it to hold his mouth to hers, never wanting the kiss to end.

But he was stronger than she, and after a while, he broke it, pulling slightly away so he could see her face. "There's more," he assured her raggedly.

"More?"

"I got you another present. It's outside." Oh, yes, the one he'd needed a wagon for. Plainly he thought that if she was this pleased over a little ring, she'd be ecstatic over the larger gift, and he couldn't wait to see her reaction.

Leah couldn't wait either. "Show me," she said, taking his hand and pulling him toward the door.

He was smiling. He looked so much like Brad when he smiled, Leah didn't know how she could stand it, but she also couldn't stop looking at him because she loved him so very much and because she was suddenly so happy.

She threw open the front door and drew him out behind her, almost laughing in her joy, but when she spun around to see what he might have brought her, she saw the buggy.

The sight of it was like a blow, stunning her and jarring a cry of anguish from her lips. Cal's arm was around her in an instant.

"It's not the same one," he told her urgently, holding her tightly, as if he were afraid she was going to fall. "It's not the same one."

He said it a few more times before she finally registered that it really *wasn't* the same buggy in which Brad and Espy had died. Of course it wasn't, it couldn't have been. That one had been wrecked.

"It's a new one," he assured her gently when he sensed she had finally understood him. "Well, not brand new exactly. I got it from the livery. Pete said you'd miss the . . . the old one because you used it all the time to drive yourself back and forth to town. I thought . . ."

He'd thought she'd appreciate a replacement and the independence it represented. He'd been thinking of her, trying to make her happy. Although the pain still throbbed in her heart, she couldn't help feeling cherished, too. In spite of the unpleasant associations, Cal couldn't have given her a more practical — and thoughtful — gift. She blinked away the tears and gave him the smile he deserved.

"I know. It's a wonderful present."

"Would you like to try it out? Just a little turn around the yard to get the feel of it?"

She didn't, of course. The memories of Brad and Espy setting off on their last journey were too vivid. But she would have to drive it, sooner or later, and better that the first time be with Cal beside her. "Just let me get a shawl," she said, hurrying inside to fetch the one hanging just inside the door.

When she emerged from the house, Cal was waiting to hand her into the buggy. Now she could see it more clearly, more rationally, and she realized it wasn't at all like the old one. All buggies were black with hoods over the seat, but this one was smaller than the old one, and lighter. A little higher, too, she noticed as Cal lifted her to the seat.

"You drive," he said, taking his place beside her. "See how you like her."

He untied the reins and handed them to her. For an instant she remembered her dream, the one where she'd been riding in a buggy with Brad dead beside her, but she forced the vision from her mind. She wasn't going to let the past destroy what little happiness she had left. She *couldn't*.

The buggy drove like a dream, and by the time they had completed their turn around the yard, Leah was smiling again. When Cal lifted her down, his hands lingered at her waist, squeezing slightly and sending a bolt of desire through her.

Soon, she thought, looking up into his eyes and seeing an answering desire glowing there. In a few more days they could be together again, and then nothing would prevent them from being completely happy.

While she stood on the porch and waited for Cal to unhitch the buggy and take it into the barn, Leah at last allowed herself to think of the future that lay ahead for them. She'd be more careful this time and not expect too much at first. She and Cal still didn't know each other very well, and they would have a lot of adjustments to make. But he *was* the man she'd thought him, and they *could* be happy. It would just take some time.

Enormously cheered by the thought, she took Cal's arm when he returned and led him into the house for the noon meal which they ate in companionable silence. Leah was acutely aware of the weight of her new ring all through the meal and couldn't help admiring it from time to time. Cal seemed to be admiring it, too, although he didn't look as if he trusted her mood. She admitted she'd given him little reason for confidence and vowed to try to be more consistent in the future.

From now on, she'd do her mourning in private and let Cal see only her happiness.

When they had finished their meal, she went with him out to the front porch where he enjoyed his after-dinner smoke.

"I reckon I'd better start earning my keep around here," he said between drags on his cigarette. "I told Pete I'd work with the men this afternoon."

She opened her mouth to protest — after all, he was her husband and didn't need to turn his hand — but she remembered with a pang that she wasn't the boss around here anymore. If Cal wanted to work, it was *his* decision, not hers. Instead she said, "I'll miss you."

"Sure," he said wryly, only half believing her. "Get some rest this afternoon," he added as he headed for the corral.

Self-consciously, she touched her cheek and wondered if she still looked as wan as she had earlier. Surely not. Surely her newfound happiness showed on her face.

That afternoon Leah felt well enough, and yes, strong enough, to take some flowers up to the graves. It was a job she'd been avoiding, not wanting to come face-to-face with her pain again until she felt more able to deal with it. Now, with Cal's ring on her finger and her hysterical fears allayed, she made her way up the hill toward the picket fence without the terrible sense of dread that had haunted her ever since the accident.

Her hands full of wildflowers, she walked slowly, welcoming the tears this time for the cleansing she knew they would bring. By the time she pushed open the gate and entered the enclosure, she could hardly see for crying. Kneeling between the two small mounds

286

that marked Brad and Espy's resting places, she cleared away the withered remains of the funeral tokens and carefully spread the fresh offerings in their place. Then she pulled a handkerchief from her pocket and began to dab at the tears coursing down her cheeks.

The plain wooden markers wouldn't last long, she thought, thinking how stark they looked against the raw earth. She'd have to order a marble headstone. Now would be a good time, since they'd just sold cattle in the fall and had money to spare. . . .

The thought of money made her suddenly wonder how Cal had paid for the buggy. Her credit was good in town, she knew, and she could certainly afford it. And Cal was her husband now and owner of all she possessed. It was really *his* money he had spent, she reminded herself and tried not to feel annoyed.

But dammit, it *was* her money. He could have at least consulted her.

"Now ain't that sweet?" Homer Wilkes inquired sarcastically, making her jump.

Heart pounding in reaction, Leah scrambled to her feet and blinked away the last of her tears to see him standing just outside the fence. "What are you doing here?" she demanded.

"I come to see my girl, or do you have some objection?"

He was bleary-eyed and slightly unsteady on his feet. Drunk, she decided, just as he had been at the funeral. Perhaps even ever since the funeral.

"No, of course I have no objection. It's just that you frightened me. I didn't hear you come up."

"I didn't come up," he informed her. "I been here most of the day. I even seen you with your new buggy,

287

riding around like the Queen of Sheba. I just been keeping outta sight in case you took it in mind to run me off."

"Why would I do that?" she asked, reminding herself she should temper her natural disgust for the man with pity for his loss, which was just as great as hers. "You're welcome to come whenever you like."

He glared at her, wavering slightly. "Real generous of you," he sneered. "But then I reckon folks like you can afford to be generous. And what do you care, now that you've got a man of your own to take up your time? Didn't let no grass grow under your feet, neither, did you?"

This was not a subject Leah cared to discuss with Homer Wilkes. She brushed off her hands and slipped out the gate, latching it behind her.

But Wilkes wasn't about to be ignored. "You're the talk of the county, did you know? Everybody wants to know how come you run off with that stranger when your brother wasn't even cold in the ground yet." Leah turned away, determined not to dignify his gossip with a response, but she wasn't fast enough for him. "Now me, I figure you done it 'cause he asked you, and the reason he asked you was because with Brad gone, you was rich. No man ever wanted you until then, but as soon as the boy was in the ground—"

"Mr. Wilkes!" Leah cried furiously, whirling back to face him. "That is quite enough! If you want to be allowed to visit your daughter's grave, you'll have to keep a civil tongue in your head. If you can't . . ." She let her voice trail off on a silent warning.

"What'll you do?" he blustered, undaunted by her

rage. "Have that fancy gunnie of yours kill me like he killed my girl?"

Leah gasped in outrage, and Wilkes cackled in delight.

"What's the matter, missy?" he taunted. "Didn't think I knew? Or maybe you didn't know yourself. Yeah, I reckon that's it," he concluded, grinning fiendishly. "You didn't know, but it only stands to reason. He must've figured you just right, a spinster so desperate for a man that she'd jump in bed with the first one that wanted her!"

He shouted the last because Leah was halfway down the hill, running to get away from him and his filthy lies. His laughter echoed after her as she raced into the house and slammed the door behind her, falling limply against it while she gasped for breath. She covered her face with both hands, and only when she felt the moisture on her cheeks did she realize she was crying again, sobbing this time with impotent rage. If only she were a man, she'd . . .

But she wasn't a man and never would be. And if she were, surely no one would ever have said such things to her. No one ever would again, though, because Cal would run him off and tell him never to return and . . .

Except she couldn't tell Cal to run him off because she couldn't tell Cal what he had said, not if she wanted to maintain the fragile truce they had established today. She couldn't even ask Cal to send Wilkes away because drunk as he was, Wilkes wouldn't hesitate to make the same accusations to Cal's face. No, she'd have to handle this herself. And she'd have to keep Wilkes's accusations a secret.

At least she'd keep them a secret for as long as she

could, but that might not be very long. If Homer Wilkes was saying these things, others might be, too. She knew Mead Garland thought them and wouldn't hesitate to agree if others voiced the same concerns.

With a groan, Leah staggered over to the sofa and sank down onto it. What was she going to do? Cal couldn't be guilty of such a heinous crime, not against his own son.

But of course, except for Mead and Pete, she was the only one who knew Brad had been Cal's son. If others knew, it would silence these rumors instantly. On the other hand, the truth would be even more sensational, which was why Cal had wanted her to keep his secret in the first place. What *was* she going to do?

She didn't know, but she did know she was going to do *something*. Cal was her husband now, and she would protect him. All she had to do was figure out a plan.

She was still trying to figure one out the next morning as she dusted the parlor furniture. A night spent in Cal's arms—he'd held her tenderly even though they couldn't make love—had made her even more determined.

Giving the mantle a last swipe, she was just turning to the table when she heard an approaching rider. Feeling a surge of anticipation, she rushed to the window, half expecting to see Cal returning early for dinner. He'd promised to come in today, even though the rest of the men would take their noon meal out on the range. Her heart sank when she recognized the county sheriff sitting his horse in her yard.

Quickly, she removed her apron and tucked up the stray strands of hair that had come loose during her morning's work. The sheriff's shouted greeting came clearly through the closed door, and Leah pulled it open, not letting her reluctance show. How she'd been dreading this interview and the terrible memories it would stir up.

"Sheriff Klinger, won't you come in?"

The sheriff touched the brim of his hat in acknowledgement and swung his barrel-shaped body down from his horse. After tying the animal at the hitching post by the porch and taking a long, thoughtful look around the ranch yard, he slowly mounted the steps to join her on the porch. She led the way into the house, closing the front door against the stiff autumn wind.

"Juanita! Bring some coffee for the sheriff," she called down the hallway after inviting the sheriff to take a seat.

He waited politely until Leah had seated herself in one of the wingbacked chairs, then took the other one. He was a solidly built man approaching middle age. His dark hair was touched with gray, and his face heavily lined, more from sun and weather than from time. His dark eyes seemed to have seen too much of the world, but they also appeared to overlook very little. If anyone could find Brad's killer, surely this was the man.

Clasping her hands in her lap, Leah tried to smile but failed miserably. "I don't suppose you've come to tell me you've caught the killer."

He shook his head solemnly. "Not yet. These things take time. I'm sorry I have to bother you at all, but I won't keep you long. I've pretty much got the whole story from everybody else, so there's just a few more

291

things I need to ask. Exactly who knew that Cal Stevens was the boy's father?"

Leah's jaw dropped. "How . . . ? Who . . . ?"

"Stevens told me himself," the sheriff explained gently. "He said he wanted me to understand how he fit into all this. He said your foreman, Pete Quincy, knew and your attorney, Mr. Garland. Who else?"

"I . . . Juanita knows."

"Juanita?"

"Our housekeeper. She was Brad's wet nurse." Leah blinked against the sting of tears.

As if on cue, Juanita appeared carrying a tray with two cups of coffee. The sheriff took one and gulped down the steaming brew. Leah set her cup on the table beside her chair.

When Juanita had gone, the sheriff asked, "Who else knew about Stevens and Brad?"

"No one."

"You're sure the boy didn't know?"

Leah's throat tightened. How foolish they had been to deny Brad this knowledge. But then, who could have guessed he wouldn't be here to tell? "No, we . . . That is, Mr. Stevens wanted to wait until . . . until things settled down a bit. Brad had just . . . gotten married, you see and . . ." She had to stop and press her fingers to her lips to stop their trembling.

"Yes, I know all about it. Mr. Wilkes explained everything in great detail."

She could imagine. "He doesn't know about Brad and Mr. Stevens."

"So I gathered, and I haven't been telling anybody who didn't already know, ma'am."

"Thank you," she said in a near whisper. "I appreciate that."

"No trouble. You folks have got enough trouble." He shifted in his chair, and drained his coffee cup. "So, you didn't know Cal Stevens until he showed up on your doorstep a few weeks ago."

Leah winced, seeing the next question lurking in his eyes. "No, we had never met. I'm sure you've heard the story of how we'd met before and he'd come here to court me, but we . . . I made that up to explain Mr. Stevens's presence here to Brad until . . ."

"Until what?" he prompted.

"Until I could verify Mr. Stevens's story." How long ago it all seemed now, as if a lifetime had passed.

"And did you verify it?"

"Oh, yes. I sent Pete Quincy out, and he spoke to Mr. Stevens's family. Also, I noticed a marked physical resemblance between Brad and Mr. Stevens."

The sheriff's bushy eyebrows rose. "You did?"

"Yes," she said, a little annoyed. Was she the only person to have seen it? "Expressions, mannerisms, things like that."

"I see," the sheriff murmured, as if he saw something else entirely. "And did Mr. Stevens stand to gain anything by Brad's death?"

"Certainly not! As I'm sure you know, Brad left everything to me."

Sheriff Klinger nodded. "Yeah, I know. It does seem kind of funny for a boy his age to think of making a will, though."

"It was Mr. Stevens's idea," she explained. "Mr. Wilkes had made some remarks that led us to believe he might do Brad some harm so Espy would inherit the ranch and Wilkes could move in here. We thought if Wilkes knew Espy wasn't the heir, Brad would be safe."

"Looks like your plan didn't work."

Leah pressed her fingers to her lips again, determined not to weep. After a moment, she was able to say, "Then you think Wilkes killed Brad."

"I haven't made up my mind yet. Do *you* think Wilkes did it?"

Did she? Mead Garland's wild accusations against Cal echoed in her head, but she dismissed them. Mead was simply jealous. And Cal had pointed out that Wilkes certainly had the best motive. "As I said, I did think, perhaps, that Homer Wilkes might have been considering it."

"Then why'd he kill the girl, too?"

"But she wasn't supposed to be with Brad," she reminded the sheriff. "And besides, her death was an accident."

Plainly, this was not a new theory to Sheriff Klinger. "Only one problem with that, ma'am. You see, Homer Wilkes is a drunk and a sloppy drunk at that. Even sober, I doubt he could plan out anything as careful as this murder was planned out. There wasn't one clue left. Not so much as a hoofprint. This job was done by somebody who'd done it before."

Leah grasped at this straw. "Then you think it was a stranger, someone intent on robbing whoever came by?"

"No, ma'am. I think your brother was the intended victim all right."

But this didn't make sense. Leah frowned in confusion. "But who . . . ?"

"Do you know your husband has himself quite a

reputation as a hired gun?"

Leah was on her feet instantly. "That's ridiculous! Cal loved Brad. He was his *father,* for heaven's sake!"

Or so he said, a voice echoed in her head. In any case, he was a father who'd never seen his son before a few weeks ago. Such a tie couldn't be so very strong.

"And what did he have to gain from Brad's death?" she challenged, speaking as much to herself as to the sheriff.

Sheriff Klinger looked up at her blandly. "Looks like he gained the whole ranch."

Leah opened her mouth to protest, but before she could speak she heard the sound of another rider approaching. "That sounds like my husband now," she told the sheriff. "Perhaps you'd like to make these accusations to his face."

She wished he would, because she wanted to hear Cal's replies, *needed* to hear him refute the sheriff's insinuations.

Sheriff Klinger rose slowly, apparently unconcerned about facing Cal. "It's kind of unusual to get married as quick as you did, isn't it? I mean, the day after your brother's funeral and all and to a man you've only known a few weeks. Folks are sure to gossip."

Leah cast about frantically for a suitable reply, but couldn't think of a single thing she could tell the sheriff to explain her scandalous behavior. With relief she heard Cal's familiar step on the porch, and in the next moment, the front door opened and he stepped inside.

He nodded to the sheriff, pulling off his hat and hanging it up. "Have you found anything yet?"

"Afraid not," the sheriff told him calmly, as if he hadn't practically accused Cal of murder just minutes ago. "I've just been tying up a few loose ends here with your wife. She's been very helpful."

Leah stiffened in irritation. She hadn't been the least bit helpful, at least not in confirming his theory that Cal was the killer. "How much longer are you going to let a murderer run around loose, Sheriff?" she challenged.

He seemed unperturbed by her annoyance. "I can't arrest him until I know who he is, ma'am, and I sure don't want to make a mistake."

"I should hope not," she replied sharply.

His smile told her he understood her pique. He glanced at Cal. "You two'll let me know if you think of anything that might help, won't you?"

"Sure," said Cal, so casually Leah wondered if he had any idea he was the sheriff's main suspect. "I'll walk you out."

While Cal and the sheriff exchanged a few words out in the yard, Leah fumed impatiently. Then she had to wait while Cal took care of his own horse. Finally, he made his way back to the house. The wind had tousled his hair, giving him a rakish air. Leah resisted the urge to run to him and smooth the raven locks even though she longed to feel his arms around her. She had more important things to accomplish first.

"He thinks you killed Brad," she informed Cal the instant he had closed the front door behind him.

Cal seemed only mildly concerned. "Does he?"

"He must have been listening to Mead Garland. He said exactly what Mead said the other day, about how you could have killed Brad to get the Rocking Horse."

"Is that what you think?"

"No!" she cried, surrendering at last to the urge to

touch him. She ran to him, and he caught her to his heart. "Oh, Cal, it's like a nightmare that won't end," she said, clutching his shirt with both hands. "First Brad and Espy, and now people thinking you're responsible. We have to tell people you're his father! Then they'll know you couldn't possibly have done it!"

"But Garland and the sheriff already know I was his father," Cal reminded her grimly. "That hasn't stopped them from thinking I did it."

Leah gazed up at him in despair. "Then we have to find out who really did it!"

Cal's eyes were indigo, clouded and troubled. "I doubt the sheriff would take too kindly to us poking into his business," he said after a moment.

Leah couldn't believe her ears. How could he be refusing to find his own son's murderer? Hadn't she bragged to Mead on the day of Brad's death that Cal would never let the murder go unavenged, that he wouldn't rest until the person responsible was punished? Yet, she suddenly realized, Cal had made no effort whatsoever in that direction. True, their marriage had delayed him, but since then he'd just been working here at the ranch as if he had nothing better to do. "Aren't you even going to try to find out?"

"I already told you. There was no sign, no way to track the killer. The only thing to do is figure out who had a reason. The sheriff is already doing that."

Leah felt a chill, a sense that something was very wrong, and she no longer wanted to be in Cal's arms. She pulled away, and he did not try to hold her. "I . . . Dinner is probably ready," she said lamely. "You'll want to wash up."

He studied her face for a moment, as if looking for

some sign there. Then, without another word, he strode off toward the kitchen.

No, she told herself as she watched him go, he isn't a killer. He's the man you love. He *can't* be a killer.

And somehow she must find a way to prove it, if only to convince herself.

The next morning, the plan came to her. Really, she supposed she'd known what she would have to do all along. She just hadn't wanted to do it because doing it would require her to leave the haven of her home.

As long as she stayed within the confines of the ranch, Leah could nurse her pain and shield herself from speaking of Brad and the tragedy of his loss. Here no one asked her who could have done such a thing or looked at her askance because she'd eloped with a stranger the morning after the funeral.

But the time had come to face people and answer their questions, both spoken and unspoken. Leah had never cared what people thought of her before. When her father had died, she'd taken over the ranch and run it like a man, never giving a thought to whether other people thought she was behaving inappropriately. She'd faced down disapproval before. Surely she could do so again.

And she must if she was to get the information she needed to find out who had really killed her brother.

With that in mind, Leah waited until Cal had left for the day. Then she dressed carefully in one of her black dresses, put on one of her black bonnets, and informed Juanita she was going to town.

"Alone?" the Mexican woman asked with a worried frown.

298

"Yes. Mr. Stevens got me a new buggy so I could come and go as I please, and this morning I please to go to town."

"What you do there?" Juanita asked skeptically.

"I'm going to order some new dresses. I . . . If I'm going to be in mourning for another year . . ." She gestured helplessly at the sad-looking dress she wore, and finally Juanita nodded her sullen approval.

"You will be back when he comes for dinner?" Once again Cal had told her he would come home for the noon meal.

"I'm sure I will, but if I'm delayed for some reason, don't wait for me. Mr. Stevens will want to get back to work."

This time when Leah climbed into the new buggy, she didn't allow herself to think about the past at all. This time, she was intent on the future as she slapped the little bay gelding into motion and watched him start out at a lively clip, as anxious to get on with things as she was.

Leah passed no one on her way to town, and when she arrived, she found the main street fairly deserted since few people made the trip during the week. Pulling up at the livery, she told the stable boy she would be in town for a few hours. Then she set out for her first stop: Nancy Otto's house.

The dressmaker was plainly surprised to see her but recognizing a potential customer, welcomed her profusely. "We all heard about your marriage, Leah. You must tell me all about it," she insisted as she escorted Leah inside.

"There really isn't much to tell," Leah hedged, wondering if Nancy's interest was merely friendly concern or a desire to be the one woman in town with the freshest source of gossip.

"But it's all so wildly romantic. Everyone's been wondering who Mr. Stevens was and why he'd come here, and now we find out he was courting you all along, for months and months. How long have you known him?"

Oh, what a tangled web we weave, Leah lamented silently, but managed a coy smile. "Long enough to know he was the man I wanted to marry."

"Well, people were absolutely scandalized to hear you'd eloped right after the funeral, or at least they pretended they were. Just between us, I think the women were jealous. Not many of them would've had the courage to do something like that, but then, you've never worried about convention. I envy you, Leah."

"Do you?" Leah asked in genuine surprise as Nancy seated her on the sofa.

"Can you doubt it? All the old biddies are whispering about you, saying such things were never done in *their* day, but I'll bet any one of them would've done the same thing if they'd had the chance. They're just mad because no man ever swept them off their feet. Come to think of it, I'm mad, too!"

Nancy's warm smile belied her words, and Leah found herself smiling back. "You could elope with any one of a dozen men if you said the word."

Nancy shook her head. "None as exciting as Cal Stevens, and until I find one, I like being a widow and making my own way. Which reminds me, you didn't by any chance come in to order a trousseau, did you?"

Leah's smile faded. "Not exactly. I do need some new clothes, but I'm afraid they'll have to be black."

Nancy sobered, too. "Of course. I'm sorry. I should have thought . . ."

"It's all right." Leah forced herself to smile again. "You were the one who told me I needed some new clothes, and you were right. How quickly do you think you could make me up some dresses?"

In short order, she and Nancy had decided on a pattern and fabric for two new gowns, one of which would be ready in a few days. Since Nancy had so recently taken her measurements, the only thing left to do was decide on a time for Leah to come back for a fitting.

As she was preparing to leave, Leah asked as an apparent afterthought the question she had mainly come to ask. "What are people saying about . . . about Brad's death?"

Instantly Nancy's face softened in sympathy. "Everyone thinks it was a terrible tragedy. He was so young, and that poor girl—"

"No, I mean, who do people think did it?"

Nancy's fair face reddened as Leah waited implacably for a reply. "I . . . Why, nobody knows," she stammered uncomfortably. "It must have been a robbery, somebody who didn't know who'd be coming along. Isn't that what you think?"

Leah wished she did. "I don't know. I'm just praying they can catch whoever did it."

"We all are," Nancy assured her. "I don't think anyone will feel safe until they do."

Leah sighed as she made her way down the street after bidding Nancy farewell. The dressmaker hadn't wanted to tell her, but Leah was now sure that other people shared Mead Garland's opinion of Cal. She wanted to deny the rumor to people's faces, but she had a feeling everyone would be just as loath as Nancy to repeat it to her, and denying it without having heard it seemed a clear case of protesting too much.

Lost in thought, she wandered into the mercantile.

"Why, Leah Harding!" the storekeeper's wife exclaimed from behind the counter. "Or should I say Mrs. Stevens. I hope you're not here to tell me your ring didn't fit."

Leah put on her best smile. "No, I'm not, Mrs. Tomkins. It fits perfectly." She held out her hand to show her.

"I'll be. It sure enough does. That Mr. Stevens, he was something coming in here the other day. I tried to get him to buy a bigger size, but he wouldn't hear of it. Said it had to be real small because you had such dainty hands. I let him have his way, but I was sure he was wrong. Just goes to show, doesn't it?"

"Yes, it does," Leah said, ignoring the expectant expression on the other woman's face. Plainly, she was desperate to ask Leah all about her elopement but good manners forbade it.

When Leah offered nothing else, the woman said, "What can I show you today?"

Suddenly Leah realized she had no idea. "I think I'll look around a bit, if you don't mind."

"Don't mind a bit. Take your time."

Leah strolled away, trying to look purposeful. She'd also have to think of a way to bring up the subject of the murder before leaving the store and without revealing that had been her sole purpose for coming in here in the first place.

The aisle she had chosen happened to contain men's ready-made clothing, and Leah stopped before a display of shirts. She could buy something for Cal, she thought, if only she knew what he might need. Size, too, might be a problem, although she could probably make an educated guess.

As she examined the various choices, she was vaguely aware of a man who had been at the rear of the store but who was now moving down the aisle toward her. When he got close, she glanced up, expecting to see a familiar face. Her half-smile of greeting faded when she saw a stranger instead.

"Mrs. Stevens?" he asked to her surprise.

"Why, yes," she replied, instantly suspicious. Instinctively, she drew back a step.

"I'm sorry. I didn't mean to alarm you," he said with an ingratiating smile. Unfortunately, it did nothing to reassure her because smiling or not, the man was quite simply frightening.

He stood almost as tall as Cal, but he was strikingly thin beneath his black broadcloth suit. Hollow-chested and hollow-cheeked, he looked down at her with eyes so pale gray as to be almost colorless and which were sunken in his face. Her first thought was that he must be consumptive, a dying man who looked to be at death's very door, but aside from his gauntness, he gave no other indications of illness. In fact, when she had studied him for a moment, she realized he exuded an aura of strength and competence not very much different from Cal Stevens's.

"How did you know my name?" she asked, not bothering to hide her annoyance.

"I heard Mrs. Tomkins speak to you when you came in. Please forgive me for taking the liberty of approaching you when we haven't been introduced, but I believe your husband is an old friend of mine."

"Cal?" Leah didn't think she wanted this man to be a friend of Cal's.

"Calhoun Stevens, yes," he confirmed. His voice had a silky quality about it that was meant to soothe but which Leah found grating. "We've known each other for a long time."

"Is that why you're in town? To see him?"

"Oh, no. I had some . . . some business here, and imagine my surprise when I discovered Cal had settled in the area."

"I'll be happy to tell him I saw you today, Mr. . . . ?"

"Oh, I'm sorry once more. It's been a long time since I've conversed with a lady, and I've forgotten my manners," he said, his smile showing crooked teeth. "Jakes is my name. John Jakes."

"Pleased to meet you, Mr. Jakes," Leah lied, growing more uneasy by the moment because she had finally realized what had disturbed her about this man even before she'd heard his name. He was a gunfighter, a man whose reputation exceeded even Cal Stevens's. And if the blankness of his eyes was any indication, he'd earned every bit of that reputation. "I'll tell my husband I saw you."

"You do that, Mrs. Stevens, and please also convey my congratulations on his marriage. He's a very lucky man."

Although he seemed perfectly sincere, Leah had the nagging feeling he was mocking her. "If you and my husband are such old friends, perhaps you'll want to tell him yourself," she suggested, hoping to see chagrin.

Instead Jakes smiled again. "I may do that."

Something in his tone made her skin crawl, and Leah

unconsciously backed up another step. "I . . . I'm afraid I must be going," she said, disgusted with herself for being so cowardly but knowing she had to get away from him. The last thing she saw was his sardonic grin as she fled the store, ignoring Mrs. Tomkins's offer to help her find whatever she wanted.

Out in the street, Leah took several deep breaths of fresh air, surprised to find herself trembling. What on earth was the matter with her? The man hadn't done or said a single thing to justify such a reaction. On the other hand, he was naturally so menacing, she supposed he never actually had to *say* anything to frighten people.

She had started walking, not noticing where exactly, only aware that she needed to put some distance between herself and Mr. Jakes. She was so lost in thought that she only vaguely heard someone calling her name. Only when Mead overtook her and grabbed her elbow, did she finally notice him.

"Leah, what in heaven's name is wrong? I called you three times and you didn't even look up. Are you all right?"

His handsome face was creased into a concerned frown, and that concern touched her. He was dead wrong about Cal, of course, but at least he genuinely cared about her. "I . . . I'm fine, really. I just met the strangest man in the store. He . . ." She shuddered.

"You're pale, Leah. Maybe you ought to come into my office and sit down for a moment."

She looked around and realized they were directly across from his office, and, truth to tell, she did need to sit down for a moment. Nodding her agreement, she allowed him to lead her across the dusty street and into the building, through to his private office where he seated her in one of his client chairs.

"Can I get you a glass of water?"

She nodded, and he poured her one from a carafe on his desk. Sipping it gratefully, she at last looked up and found him frowning down at her. His anxiety made her feel a complete fool.

"I'm sorry I alarmed you, Mead. I'm fine, really." She forced herself to smile.

"You certainly didn't look fine. What happened? You said you met some man. Who was it?"

"He said his name was Jakes."

"Oh, my God! That devil had the nerve to speak to you?"

"You know him?"

"I know *of* him," Mead said. "He's been hanging around town for the past few days, and people have been talking. What did he say to you?"

"Nothing offensive," she assured him, somewhat gratified by his outrage. "He just said he knew Cal."

"I'm not surprised. The man's a hired killer, just like Stevens."

"Mead!" Leah exclaimed furiously.

"Everyone knows it," he insisted. "You can choose not to see the truth if you like, but you can't change it."

Leah thrust the water glass into his hand and jumped to her feet. "I won't stay here and listen to you insult my husband."

"Leah, someone has to talk some sense to you!" Mead said to her back as she stalked out of his office. "Your brother is dead, and someone has to warn you before you meet the same fate!"

Leah whirled on him. "Are you insinuating I'm in

some kind of danger?" she demanded.

Somewhat taken aback, Mead swallowed. "Well, it's certainly a possibility. I mean, he killed once to get the Rocking Horse, and now that he has it, he has no more use for you."

Leah had an overwhelming urge to slap his insolent face, and if she stayed in his presence another second, she would give in to it. Without another word, she turned and stormed out, leaving Mead gaping in her wake.

Nearly blind with fury, she strode down the street until she reached the livery where she ordered the stable boy to hitch up her buggy. She'd been in town less than an hour, and the boy looked as if he were going to remind her of that until he saw the expression on her face. Then he hastened off to do her bidding.

Still seething, Leah jumped into the buggy the moment the boy brought it out of the stable and slapped the horse smartly. The little bay set off at a lively pace, and as soon as Leah judged he'd warmed up enough, she urged him into a trot.

This whole trip had been a terrible mistake, she told herself, and the mistake had been in not bringing Cal along. Yes, that was it, she decided. She should have faced the town with Cal beside her so they would know she didn't believe a word of Mead Garland's lies. Cal wasn't a murderer. He couldn't have killed his own son.

No, the sheriff said Brad had been killed by someone who'd killed before, someone experienced at such things, someone capable of a cold-blooded ambush. Someone, she suddenly realized, like John Jakes.

And Jakes was an old friend of Cal's.

The thought stunned her, but before she could do

more than think it, she heard a loud *crack,* like the sound of a shot, and the buggy was tilting, just like in her dream, and the horse let out a scream and began to run.

Leah clung frantically to the reins, but the whole world had gone mad, and she was jouncing out of her seat, and the buggy was flying through the air and so was she.

Chapter Ten

Cal rode at a gallop, scanning the road ahead and trying to convince himself he was on a fool's errand. Leah was fine. She'd probably got to visiting with somebody and forgotten the time. Women were like that. She'd laugh when she heard how he'd come charging out after her the instant Juanita told him she wasn't back from town yet. At least he prayed she'd laugh.

He just wished he could shake this sickening sense of foreboding and the overwhelming certainty that he'd once again encounter a wrecked buggy and a broken body. . . .

The screaming came to him faintly above the pounding of his horse's hooves, a plaintive wail like the cry of a lost soul, and his heart turned to stone. *No!* he shouted silently and rode like a fury toward the sound, closer and closer, until the shape of the buggy materialized in the distance.

NO! The screaming swelled, filling the air, filling his head, louder and louder, the sound of an animal in agony, and at last he saw the horse still harnessed to the overturned wagon, twitching helplessly with its two front legs snapped like twigs, dangling and useless.

He sawed on the reins, bringing his horse to a sliding halt as he looked about desperately for what he most feared to see.

"Leah!" he shouted and heard no answer but the wailing of the dying beast.

The buggy lay smashed like egg beside the road, the horse still tangled in the traces, but he saw no sign of Leah, none at all. He jumped from his saddle before his horse had even stopped and raced for the wreck. At his panicked approach, the injured bay screamed louder and began to thrash, trying desperately to rise on his broken legs. Its eyes rolled wildly in fear and torment, silently begging Cal to help him as men had always helped him.

Instinctively, Cal drew his pistol as he ran, and the instant he reached the horse, he took careful aim and fired. The animal shuddered and went still, its death scream dying on a wheeze. Into the silence he yelled, "Leah!" and this time he heard an answering cry, but so faint he couldn't place it.

"Leah!" he shouted again, and the reply came more plainly.

"Here! I'm down here, under the buggy!"

Dear God! He dodged around the dead horse, and then he saw her or at least part of her. Her head and one arm were all that was visible. The rest of her lay trapped beneath the overturned buggy.

"My God, are you . . . ?" He didn't even know what to ask as he dropped to his knees beside her, and when he lifted his hand to touch her, he saw her eyes widen in terror.

Only then did he realize he still held his smoking pistol, and he stuffed it hastily back into its holster.

"Are you hurt?" he asked, reaching for her again but stopping short of actually touching lest he injure her more.

Leah stared up at him, speechless in the aftermath of the terror that had claimed her when she'd seen him raising the pistol toward her head. For that one second, she'd thought, "It's true!" but she'd been wrong, so very wrong! Now she could see his face was ashen with terror for her, and the hand hovering over her face trembled visibly.

"No, I . . . I'm not hurt," she managed after a moment. "At least I don't think I am, but I'm caught somehow. I think my dress is tangled . . ."

Before she could even finish the sentence, Cal was lifting the buggy, tipping it upright so effortlessly Leah could only marvel when she remembered her own fruitless struggles to move it even one inch. Sure enough, her skirt and petticoats were caught in a spring, and when the fabric refused to pull loose, Cal produced a wicked looking knife from his boot and sliced it free with one swipe. The knife then disappeared as quickly as it had appeared, and Cal heaved the buggy over the rest of the way. It fell into the road with a crash and a cloud of dust.

Leah had only succeeded in pushing herself up on one elbow before Cal was at her side again. "Don't move," he commanded her. "Let me check for broken bones first."

His hands moved over her quickly, impersonally, finding every bruised and battered place but locating nothing actually broken. "Can you move your legs?" he asked, lifting the weight of her skirts and petticoats to watch her do it.

"Yes," she said, demonstrating. "I told you, I'm not seriously hurt, although I expect I'll be black and blue all over tomorrow and . . ."

Her voice trailed off when her gaze met his and she saw the emotions roiling in his blue eyes. In the next second she was in his arms being crushed to his chest while his eager hands moved over her back as if he couldn't quite believe she was real and had to verify the matter by touching every part of her.

Her battered body wanted to moan in protest, but not one sound escaped her lips as she clung to his solid strength. For hours she had lain beneath the buggy, listening to the horse's anguished screams and struggling fruitlessly to free herself. Now she was safe, in her husband's arms, and only now could she give way to the terror she had suppressed for so long. Release came on a wave of tears, and she buried her face against his chest and sobbed.

He held her, rocking her slightly and stroking the tangle of her hair as she wept while he murmured incoherent phrases of comfort.

"You're safe now. It's all right." The words registered after a while, and Leah was able to relax in his arms and choke back her sobs until at last she was calm again.

When she was, he let her pull away and wipe the moisture from her cheeks with her sleeve. But he still held her in the circle of his arms, as if loath to let her go, and when she was finished, he asked, "What happened?"

Remembering, she shuddered. "I was driving home, and I was going pretty fast, I suppose, but not terribly fast. Anyway, I heard this noise, a cracking sound—"

"A gunshot?" he asked sharply.

"No," she assured him. "That was what I thought at first, but then the buggy started wobbling like crazy, and I realized it was the axle or something underneath the buggy. Anyway, something broke. The wheels started to fall off, and the horse bolted, just like . . ." She didn't have to remind him it had been just like when Espy was killed. His grim expression told her he remembered only too well. "I suppose I'm lucky the horse broke his legs, poor thing." Otherwise, he might have dragged the buggy farther and she might have been . . . She shuddered again. "He was in such pain, and there was nothing I could do."

Cal gathered her to him again and held her for a long moment while she pushed the horrible memories away. "It's all my fault," he murmured. How could it be his fault? she wondered, but she felt too weary to argue. After a few moments, he eased her head from his shoulder and said, "I'd better get you home."

She could only nod and allow him to lay her back on the ground again while he went to fetch his horse which had wandered off somewhere. Every bone in her body ached, and Leah lay staring up at the clear blue sky and whispered a silent prayer of thanks that Cal had come so quickly. Thank God he was the kind of man to ignore her message not to be concerned if she was late. She closed her eyes and let the tears slip silently down into her hair.

After what seemed only minutes, Cal returned, leading his horse. The animal was reluctant, smelling the blood of the dead horse, but Cal brooked no argument, and soon he had Leah seated in front of him in the saddle, headed for home. Leah rested her head against Cal's chest and, comforted by the steady beating of his heart, she was finally able to believe she had been rescued.

"Damn that Rhodes," Cal was muttering, referring to the man who owned the livery stable. "He sold me a faulty buggy."

"I'm sure he didn't have any idea . . ." Leah objected.

"He better not have," Cal replied. The coldness in his voice made her shiver, and she clung more tightly to him.

At last they reached the ranch, and Cal lifted Leah gently from the saddle and started to carry her into the house. "I can walk," she insisted, although her protest sounded pathetically feeble even to her own ears. Cal simply ignored it.

"Juanita!" he shouted the instant they stepped through the front door. The Mexican woman came scurrying into the room and cried, *"Madre de Dios!"* when she saw Leah's bedraggled appearance.

"I'm not hurt," Leah told her, feeling absurdly guilty for causing Juanita such distress.

"What happen?" she demanded.

"The buggy wrecked," Cal said, and Juanita gasped and crossed herself.

"It was an accident," Leah insisted, but no one paid much attention to her.

"She doesn't seem to have any broken bones," Cal reported, "but she was pretty banged up. We probably ought to put her in the tub to soak for a while."

"*Sí*, take her into the bedroom."

Leah knew she should be annoyed at the way they were talking about her as if she weren't present, but she simply didn't have the energy to protest. After having felt so alone and abandoned lying there beneath the wrecked buggy for so long, she was rather enjoying being fussed over. Consequently, she didn't object when Cal carried her into the bedroom and deposited her in a chair, then began to remove her shoes.

He'd just finished when Juanita came in with two buckets of steaming water. "You will get the tub, no?" she asked, and Cal was gone in an instant, leaving Leah vaguely disappointed because she had been wondering how much more of her clothing he planned to remove.

As it turned out, he removed none of it. When the tub had been filled to Juanita's satisfaction, he discreetly withdrew, leaving Juanita to the job of undressing her.

"What happen?" Juanita inquired again when she saw the hunk cut out of Leah's skirts.

"It . . . it was caught and Cal cut it," Leah explained, remembering the knife and the mysterious way it had appeared and disappeared. How many other things did she not know about this man she had married?

Juanita began to make clucking sounds as she peeled away Leah's ruined clothing and found the evidences of her ordeal stamped into her flesh. Leah moaned aloud when she realized that tomorrow, when the bruises had had a chance to form, she would really be a sight.

Then Juanita removed Leah's drawers and encoun-

315

tered yet another barrier. "You cannot bathe," the Mexican woman exclaimed. "Not when you have the curse!"

"It's over now," Leah said wearily, removing this last reminder, "or just about. Close enough that I doubt I'll get sick if I get into the water anyway."

Satisfied, Juanita helped her into the tub, and Leah lowered herself gingerly, painfully aware of each scratch and scrape as the hot water touched them. Still clucking, Juanita gently soaped a washrag and began to bathe Leah as she hadn't been bathed since she was a child. Ignoring Leah's feeble protests, she carefully cleansed every inch of her body, then proceeded to shampoo her hair.

Leah surrendered to her ministrations, reveling in the soothing comfort of the warm water and Juanita's gentle hands. She sighed with bliss as Juanita's fingers massaged her scalp and scrubbed away the last of the debris from her ordeal.

When Juanita had finishing rinsing the soap from her, she wrapped a towel around her dripping locks and said, "Need more towels."

As she bustled from the room, Leah forced her weary arms up out of the water and began to dry her hair. When she'd rubbed most of the moisture from her sodden locks, she ducked her head and began to wrap the towel around her head, turban style, but she found the top of the turban kept wanting to dip into the bath water.

Frustrated, she pushed herself up out of the water, cursing her weakness and the sudden chill on her wet body as she struggled with the weight of her hair in the saturated towel. Hearing the door open, she reached blindly out for a replacement, and one was pressed into her hand. Discarding the wet towel, she quickly wrapped the dry one around her head and looked up, straight into Cal's eyes.

She froze, mortified at her nakedness yet somehow unable to make any move to cover it. As if his very presence had mesmerized her, she stood transfixed while his gaze drifted over her, touching her breasts with their cold-puckered nipples, her belly, her thighs, and the cluster of curls that marked the place which was suddenly strangely warm in spite of the chill.

The heat spread inexorably, sweeping up and over her. She might have named it embarrassment if she had felt the slightest bit embarrassed, but inexplicably, she did not. Instead she felt a kind of pride when his gaze met hers once more and she saw his expression. Blatant admiration mingled with fierce possessiveness, and she felt the heat of his gaze like a hand upon her quivering flesh.

Slowly, as if moving in a dream, he set the stack of towels he held onto the stool on which Juanita had been sitting. A tin of salve slipped out and clunked to the floor, but neither of them paid any attention. Cal pulled a towel from the top of the stack and ever so carefully shook it free and spread it on the floor beside the tub. Then he offered his hand to help her out.

Leah's heart pounded in her chest, and her breath came in shallow gasps as she placed her fingers in his and stepped from the tub. She never would have believed that simply watching him watching her could be so exciting, but she fairly trembled with

317

it while he reached for another towel.

Tenderly, he patted the fine linen against her face, then her throat where a pulse beat wildly, sending the blood pounding to her ears. Moving on, he blotted her shoulders, the edge of the towel teasing against her breasts until her nipples puckered painfully, aching to be touched. But he didn't touch them yet. Instead, he dried her arms, taking first one wrist between his strong fingers and holding the arm up until he had toweled its length, then ministering to the other.

Now, she thought as he lingered over her underarm, perilously close, but he fooled her again. Turning her slightly, he started on her back, rubbing more briskly, stirring her blood and sending delicious shivers racing over her. Down and down he moved, into the curve of her waist, and she held her breath as he hesitated there, closing her eyes against the anticipation and sighing when his hand caressed one smooth cheek through the damp thinness of the towel.

The heat from his hand seemed to radiate through her, settling deep in her belly which clenched with need as his fingers kneaded, lower and lower, close, so close, nearly touching her secret place on the pretext of drying the backs of her thighs which she'd pressed so tightly together.

Then he was in front of her again and hesitating no longer. With both hands he spread the towel across her chest, cupping her breasts, taking their weight into his palms. His gaze locked with hers, his eyes blazing, and she could see every detail of his face with supernatural clarity. The thick, straight brows. The sooty lashes curling up. The wedge of his nose. The jet pinpoints of beard dotting his jaw. The fine curve of his lips.

His nostrils flared, as if he were taking her scent, and his fingers found the nubs of her nipples through the cloth. Her breath caught as he coaxed the pebbled buttons tighter and tighter still, the sensation as sharp as pain but infinitely sweet, until she thought they might actually pierce the fabric to reach his flesh. Just when she was ready to tear the towel away herself, he moved on, sliding down her rib cage, dipping into her waist, both hands moving over her, anxious not to miss an inch.

Down her belly, his palm scorching through the damp linen, then just grazing her curls and onto her thighs, petting, caressing as he knelt before her. Chills again, darting up into secret places no matter how tightly she squeezed her legs together.

He patted her knees, before and behind, tickling the sensitive bend, then forcing it upward, lifting until she could no longer resist and her foot left the floor. Cool air rushed in, touching the burning places while he gently toweled first one calf and one foot, then the other. When he set the second one down, she tried to close her knees again to hold the fire inside, but he'd foiled her, leaving his hand between. He worked the towel upward, sliding on while she tightened against him, holding him in now while she pretended to resist.

Her gaze locked on the ebony swirl of his hair, and she could see the tremulous rise and fall of her breasts as she fought for breath. Up and up, closer and closer he came, his strength easily overcoming hers, especially since her goal was the same as his. Like living flames licking her flesh, nearer and nearer to the fire within, his hand slid onward until at last he cupped her womanhood.

She bit back a cry, sinking her teeth into her lip as he gently chafed the towel back and forth, his fingers like brands burning through the damp cloth to her aching flesh. Dear God, did he know what he was doing to her?

Then Cal lifted his head, and she saw his face. He knew, all right, and the knowledge glittered in answering desire. Her knees dissolved and in another instant she was going to disintegrate completely if he didn't . . .

"Cal," she said brokenly, pleading.

He started as if awakening from a dream, and instantly his desire changed to chagrin. Muttering what might have been a curse, he jerked his hand from between her thighs and tossed the towel away as if it had burned him. Forcing himself not to look at her again, he snatched up yet another dry towel, clumsily unfolding it, and thrust it at her. "You'd better get in bed before you get chill," he murmured, turning away before she could protest and hurrying to turn down the bedclothes.

Confused and belatedly embarrassed, Leah wrapped the towel modestly around her, although it was barely large enough to afford much modesty at all. What had happened? What had broken the mood? She'd been so certain Cal was as aroused as she. . . .

And when he'd finished at the bed and turned to face her again, she realized he was. There could be no mistaking the bulge straining against the front of his jeans. But he still wasn't looking at her, not directly at least, and suddenly Leah knew he didn't dare, not without tempting himself beyond bearing.

Now she was more confused than ever. What was wrong with him?

"Can you walk or should I carry you?" he asked hoarsely, gesturing to the bed.

Could he possibly think she wasn't capable of walking that short distance? she wondered incredulously, and then the truth dawned on her in a blaze of understanding. Of course he did! Hadn't he carried her into the house and into this very room? She'd been through a terrible ordeal, so terrible that he believed she might collapse if forced to walk across her bedroom. No wonder he couldn't believe she'd want to make love!

Biting back a smile of triumph, she started for the bed, clutching the towel around her but no longer taking pains to hold it too very securely. With every step her mind raced with possible solutions to her dilemma. She could simply tell him of her desire, of course, but somehow that seemed too easy, particularly in light of the torment through which he had just put her.

She still hadn't quite decided on a course of action when she reached the bed, but the instant she put her knee onto the mattress, a plan fell into place of its own accord.

"Ouch," she cried when the raw skin of her knee rubbed against the sheet. Drawing back instinctively, she examined the wound and suddenly remembered how many more she had just like it.

Cal muttered another curse. "Juanita gave me some salve to put on those."

While he was looking for it, Leah sat down on the

edge of the bed and arranged her towel for maximum effect. After a bit of searching, Cal located the tin on the floor and retrieved it. Turning quickly, he apparently was caught off guard by the sight of her sitting there so demurely and so nearly naked. He literally lurched to a stop, but Leah smiled encouragingly.

His approach could only be termed cautious, and he doggedly refused to look at where she'd left the towel gaping to expose her bare hip. When he held the tin out to her, she shook her head, silently refusing to take it. "Maybe you'd better put it on. I don't think I can reach all the places."

The sight of Cal Stevens so unnerved delighted her, but she kept her expression innocent as once again he knelt before her. After prying off the lid, he scooped up some salve with one finger and began to dab it gingerly on first one knee and then the other. Interestingly, his breath seemed labored, as if he were performing a difficult task, but he pressed on, treating the scrape down one of her shins with brisk efficiency.

When he had finished, she held out an elbow for him. Her towel slipped a bit, exposing most of one breast before she was able to catch it, and although his expression remained stony, she could tell from the way his neck reddened that he'd noticed. By the time he'd treated both elbows, he was fairly panting from exertion.

"You've got some scratches on your back," he informed her in a strangled voice. She pretended not to notice his distress and obediently began to turn until inspiration struck and she proceeded to lay herself facedown on the bed. Loosening the towel, she eased it down to her hips, even though she knew perfectly well the scratches were up near her shoulder blade.

Cal stood and would have leaned over, but she slid over to make room for him to sit. She turned her face away so he wouldn't see her smile when the bed sank under his weight. Lightly, almost reverently, he dabbed the salve on her wounded shoulder, then found a spot on the back of her thigh that needed attention. His warm breath stirred the tiny hairs on her legs and raised gooseflesh that wasn't from a chill.

The towel lay across her hips, silently inviting him to remove it, but he didn't so much as touch it. "All finished," he informed her gruffly, making Leah frown with frustration. What did she have to do to get seduced, anyway?

With a sigh, she played her last card and, ignoring the protest of sore muscles, flipped over without making the slightest attempt to take the towel with her.

Cal's strangled gasp was reward enough for her boldness, but he said, "I'd better get your nightdress."

He would have, too, except that Leah caught his arm and held him fast. "Cal, aren't you even going to kiss me?" she demanded.

He swallowed loudly, and Leah couldn't help noticing his breath was still labored. "I don't think that would be a good idea."

"Don't you want to?" she cried in desperation.

His gaze drifted down her naked body, but only got as far as her breasts before he snapped it back to her face again. "I wouldn't be able to stop at a kiss."

She smiled beatifically. "Good."

She was reaching for him, but he grabbed her arms,

his expression almost as desperate as she felt. "Leah, you . . . I don't want to *hurt* you."

"I don't think you could," she replied.

This time he didn't stop her when she slipped her arms around his neck and pulled his mouth down to hers. The kiss was wet and hungry but all too brief because before Leah even had a chance to become out of breath, he was pulling away.

She started to protest until she realized he had already begun to pull off his boots. Relaxing back against her pillow, she allowed herself a smile of triumph as she watched him stripping out of his clothes with an eagerness that made her laugh in delight until at last he stood naked before her, naked and completely aroused.

At the sight of him, the laughter died in her throat. "Oh, my," she said weakly.

"Change your mind?" he asked, making no move to join her on the bed.

"No, but . . ." Dear heaven, she shouldn't be staring at him so shamelessly, but she'd never dreamed . . . "You're so beautiful."

He laughed derisively, but it was true, nevertheless. He looked like some fine piece of sculpture come to life, with the corded muscles of his arms and shoulders and the broad expanse of chest blanketed by the thick curling hair she had noticed before. What she hadn't known before was the way that hair arrowed down to his belly to the most magnificent part of all. How on earth had he managed to . . . ? But of course he had, so there could be no question it was possible, no matter how unlikely it might seem. No wonder it felt so marvelous to have him inside her!

The emptiness within her throbbed. She wanted him then, needed him as she had needed nothing else in her life. Lifting her arms to him, she called his name, and he came instantly, lowering himself carefully and holding her so tenderly she wanted to scream.

But now she knew the power of touch and what one lover could do to another. She didn't want gentleness or kindness, she wanted lust and she knew how to get it. Opening her mouth, she teased his lips with her tongue until he groaned. Then she plunged her tongue inside to find its mate for a moist, sensual duel which she gladly lost.

Finding his hand, she guided it to her breast while her other hand played along his flank, coaxing and teasing. His manhood lay against her thigh, hot and heavy and provocative, and she moved sinuously against it until with another groan, he clamped his hands on her hips to still them.

"Not yet, you little witch," he whispered, shifting his own hips to cover hers and hold them in place. Now she felt his desire against her belly, tantalizingly close, but when she tried to open her legs in invitation, he clamped his strongly muscled thighs around hers and held her helpless.

For a moment she squirmed in resistance until his mouth closed over hers again for a kiss that went on and on, demanding everything, giving everything, drawing and draining until resistance was impossible. When she was limp and mindless, he dragged his lips from hers and trailed them down her throat.

Oh, yes! she thought, arching toward him, offering

herself to the ecstasy of his mouth, and this time his assault was wanton. Capturing one pouting nipple in his mouth, he suckled greedily, wrenching a startled cry from her lips as desire exploded in her. When both nipples were wet and rosy and alert, he tormented them with his teeth, nipping the sensitive flesh to the edge of pain, then soothing it with the rough comfort of his tongue until Leah gasped for breath and clung to him desperately.

Each pounding heartbeat throbbed within the echoing emptiness of her loins until need became compulsion, but still he ignored her wordless pleas for release. Instead, he moved on, trailing biting kisses over her ribs and down to her stomach, teasing her navel with his tongue, then moving to the flat plane of her belly.

At last her legs were free, and instinctively she spread them, inviting, beseeching, but instead of coming back up to take her, he kept moving down, closer and closer. . . .

She uttered a yelp of protest which died on a moan of pleasure as his tongue found the sensitive nub. The throbbing convulsed into ecstasy as he held her helpless and completely vulnerable and performed the most exquisite torture upon her.

Incoherent now, she writhed beneath him, wanting, needing, yet holding back because she wanted him inside her when it happened.

"Cal, please," she begged. *"Please!"*

At last he heard her and rose up, looming over her, working his way over her without touching her until his lips brushed hers. She threw her arms around him and tried to pull him close, but he resisted, holding himself aloof so that her breasts just grazed the furred wall of his chest and the weight of his desire just teased against hers.

"Touch me, Leah," he entreated, his voice thick. "Put me inside you."

She gasped, more from amazement than from shock. She'd wanted to touch him all along, wanted him to be as lost as she. She just hadn't known how.

Tentatively but eagerly, she reached between them and took the smooth shaft in her hands, marveling at his heat, his strength. This time, *he* gasped, and Leah knew a swift sense of feminine power. Wanting him, *all* of him, she guided him to her and took him into herself.

He moaned her name as he slid into her welcoming depths, filling the yawning emptiness with the promise of ecstasy. Slowly, he lowered himself, touching his belly to hers, then stomach to stomach, then chest to breast, until she'd taken his entire weight.

"Are you . . . all right?" he gasped against her mouth.

She was far better than all right. "Yes," she breathed, dismissing the faint protests of bruised and battered portions of her anatomy. What did a little pain matter in the face of such bliss? She slid her arms around him, reveling in the satin smoothness of his skin beneath her palms and the tensile strength she sensed.

Leah lifted her chin until her lips touched his. Their breaths mingled, warm and sweet, in the instant before he claimed her mouth fully, sweeping it with his tongue to capture every bit of her essence. Leah's body seemed swollen with desire, straining at breasts and hips, too full of need to retain it all.

Yet still he made no effort to proceed, holding himself motionless until she could bear the tension no longer. Driven, she sought to drive him, too. Lifting her hips, she pressed her pulsing desire against him, squeezing until he gasped as the threads of his control snapped.

And then they were riding, striving, plunging together in a frenzy of desire. The world dissolved, leaving just the two of them joined together, united in the struggle. Arms and legs, hands and lips, questing and caressing, clinging and fondling, while they swirled in the vortex, around and around, faster and faster, until the heat of their passion roared into a white-hot inferno, melding them into one blazing entity.

For a long time afterwards, they clung to each other, trembling with the aftershocks. Leah held him inside of her for as long as she could, loath to admit it was over and that they must, ultimately, part again. But it *was* over, and his strength finally drained. She could hold him no longer, and he, reluctantly at least, rolled off of her.

Robbed of his warmth, she shivered, and he moved hastily to pull the bedclothes over them. In the cocoon of covers, they snuggled together, their bodies still slicked with passion, their hands still hungry to touch. A dreamy weariness settled over her, weighing her bones and beckoning her to sleep, but she fought the temptation. This moment was too precious to miss.

With her head resting on his shoulder, Leah inhaled his musky maleness and the fragrance of their passion that had mingled into the sweetest of scents. She draped her thigh over his, rubbing to accentuate the difference between her smooth skin and his hair-roughed flesh. And, of course, she was seeking knowledge, too, and at last she found it with her leg, the mound of his manhood. No longer brave and strong but tamed and sated and quietly resting. Until next time, she thought with a triumphant smile.

Cal drew a deep breath and released it on a long, contented sigh. "I was afraid . . ." he murmured and stopped himself.

"Afraid of what?" she prompted, lifting her head so she could see his face.

He smiled and shook his head, but she wasn't going to be put off. "Afraid of what?" she insisted, tugging ruthlessly on a lock of his chest hair.

"Ouch!" he complained, slapping her hand away. "Stop that!"

"Only if you tell me what you were going to say," she warned.

He sighed again, this time in defeat. "I was afraid it would never be like that again between us."

"Why?" she asked in surprise.

"Because . . . Well, after our wedding night . . ."

Leah winced. "I . . . I was tired that night. And upset."

"And wondering why I'd married you."

"No!" she cried. "I didn't believe him!"

"Didn't you?" he challenged.

Well, perhaps she had, just a bit, but she certainly wasn't going to admit it. Instead, she chose to make light of the matter, knowing exactly how to distract him. "No," she said with a provocative smile, "because I already knew exactly why you'd married me." She moved her knee again, nudging it against the sleeping mound while her hand caressed his waist in wider and wider circles until she was touching the black curls that crowned his manhood.

He submitted only for a moment before grabbing her hand and stilling it. He tried to look stern, but his finely molded lips twitched suspiciously. "And is that why *you* married *me?*" he taunted, lacing his fingers through hers.

"Well," she teased back, "it was certainly an incentive."

His mouth settled into a complacent smile, but his eyes still held questions. "We're good together, aren't we?"

Good? Leah didn't think that even began to cover it. "Quite satisfactory," she agreed coyly.

"Better than . . ." he began but stopped, clamping his lips together. The teasing light in his eyes vanished.

"Better than what?" she insisted, but he looked away, silently refusing to reply. "Cal," she warned, pinching a lock of hair and giving it a tug.

"Better than Garland," he said tightly, still not looking at her. "Or whoever was your first lover."

"What?" she cried in astonishment, pushing herself up onto one elbow in spite of her protesting muscles. "What are you talking about? *You're* my first lover!"

He wouldn't budge. "You weren't a virgin, Leah."

"I most certainly was! Couldn't you tell?"

"There wasn't any blood."

Blood? What did blood have to do with anything? she wondered in outrage, then remembered the vague hints she'd heard in whispered conversations, the warn-

330

ings of pain she hadn't felt. But pain or no, she'd been innocent, although how one went about proving such a thing, she had no idea. "I don't have the slightest idea what you're talking about, nor do I have the slightest idea how to soothe what is obviously your wounded male pride, but rest assured, you are the first and only lover I have taken or intend to take. If my word isn't good enough for you, then to hell with you." Furious, she pushed out of his arms and gave him her back.

Of all the stupid, pigheaded, ignorant . . . She blinked frantically against the sting of tears. Everything had been so beautiful, and now . . .

"Leah?"

She refused to answer him. Stupid, pigheaded . . .

He lay a hand on her shoulder, and she went rigid in response.

He cleared his throat. "You never . . . ?"

"No!" She tried to shake his hand off but it wouldn't move.

He cleared his throat again. "I reckon I should've warned you before you married me. Sometimes I can be a damn fool."

Warily, she looked at him over her shoulder, then cautiously rolled onto her back so she could see him clearly. Now he was propped up on his elbow, looking down at her. "Is that an apology?"

His eyes were bleak. "I'm not used to apologizing. I'm not even sure I know how."

"You just say, 'I'm sorry, Leah.' "

Plainly, he *wasn't* used to it. "I'm sorry, Leah," he said grimly.

"Are you?" she demanded.

"Yes. I . . . I don't know what made me think you'd . . ."

"No blood, that's what you said," she reminded him sternly.

"Yeah, well, I guess there could be other reasons for that."

"There must be." She was still mad enough to spit, but the apology was helping some. Adjusting the covers modestly over her breasts, she crossed her arms in silent challenge.

He considered her thoughtfully for a long moment, then suddenly his eyes widened in amazement. "Oh, my God!"

"What?" she cried when he flung himself over on his back and covered his face with both hands.

He shook his head, but his chest was heaving, and Leah grabbed his arm to pull a hand away. He fought her, but whatever emotion had gripped him had also weakened him, and after a few moments, she dragged one hand from his face and discovered he was *laughing!*

"What's so damn funny?" she demanded.

The question sent him into paroxysms, and although he didn't actually allow himself to laugh aloud, he was convulsed with it. Leah waited, helpless and fuming until he regained control over himself. At last, he was able to cast a sly glance in her direction. "I thought ladies weren't allowed to swear."

"I'll do more than swear at you if you don't tell me why you're laughing."

"It's just . . ." He had to take a breath. "I happened to think, I guess it's true what they say . . . Why they warn young girls about . . . Why

332

women aren't supposed to *ride astride.*"

Leah gaped at him. "You mean it . . . ? That's why . . . ?"

He nodded smugly. "Didn't anyone ever warn you?"

"Not about losing my virginity! I thought they were just upset because it wasn't done, it violated tradition, that sort of thing."

He grinned. "Looks like it violated something else."

Leah humphed and would have given him her back again, but he clamped a hand on her shoulder and held her flat to the bed. "Why're you still mad?" he inquired, genuinely puzzled.

Leah asked herself the same question, and the answer came with unpleasant swiftness. "You're a fine one to accuse me of not being a virgin! You know I didn't know the first thing about it, but *you're* practically an expert!"

It was true. From the things he'd done to her, she was certain that his indiscretion with Brad's mother had been only the first of many such experiences.

She waited in vain for a denial, knowing she would hate him if he lied, yet wanting him to all the same. When at last she hazarded a glance at him, his expression was somber.

"I can't deny it, Leah, and I can't make any excuses. The only thing I can tell you is that of all the women I've ever known, you're the only one I ever wanted to marry."

Leah stared at him dumbfounded. He'd chosen her above all others, and if that wasn't exactly a declaration of love, it was pretty darn close. "Oh, Cal!" she cried, melting in response.

"You aren't going to cry, are you?" he asked in alarm.

She forced back the impending tears and managed to smile. "Of course not, even though I'm incredibly happy."

He still seemed a little wary, but he settled down more comfortably, still propped on his elbow, and just looked at her for a long time. Even though the bedclothes covered her, his scrutiny made her self-conscious. What did he see? A plain woman, already past her youth, who now had been banged up in a carriage accident. And her hair! Good heavens, she'd completely forgotten it lay in a damp tangle. She must look a sight!

"Leah," he said after a while.

"What?"

"Oh, nothing," he replied with a smile. "I just like to say your name. Leah. It's from the Bible, isn't it?"

"Oh, yes," Leah said, the old bitterness welling up. "Leah was the girl nobody wanted."

"What?" Cal asked in amazement.

"You remember the story," she said. "It's from the Old Testament. Jacob fell in love with his cousin Rachel, and he worked seven years to earn her hand, but when the seven years were up, her father tricked him. He gave Jacob Rachel's older sister Leah instead. Presumably, the bride was veiled, and Jacob didn't notice the substitution until morning, but he didn't want Leah because Rachel was so much more beautiful. So he worked another seven years for the woman he really loved. Naming me Leah was my father's idea of a joke, you see, because he didn't want me, either."

The memory still hurt, no matter how many times

Leah told herself it didn't matter, and she looked up in surprise when Cal's fingers stroked her face. "He was a fool then. He should have named you Rachel. Either that, or ol' Jacob picked the wrong sister."

Leah could actually feel her heart swelling with happiness, driving out the pain and bitterness of the past. No wonder she loved him so much! "Oh, Cal!" she cried again, and this time she flung her arms around him and pressed her mouth to his.

Heaven only knows what might have happened next, but Leah's stomach took that opportunity to growl loudly and determinedly. She had to stop kissing Cal because he was chuckling. "Oh, dear," she murmured, mortified.

"Getting hungry?" he asked, and suddenly she realized she was.

"I'm starved!"

"So am I," he admitted, grinning. "We both missed our dinner today. Of course, if you've got other ideas . . ." he added, running a hand provocatively over her naked hip.

It was a difficult decision, since Leah could already feel her body responding to his touch, but her stomach growled again and made the decision for her. "Maybe we ought to eat first."

"First?" he echoed, pleased. "I'll hold you to that promise." Giving her hip a final squeeze, he rolled away, threw back the covers and rose from the bed.

Leah took a moment to admire his broad back and firm buttocks, then started to get up, too.

"Oh, no, you don't," Cal informed her when he saw her intention. "You're staying right where you are.

I'll get Juanita to bring your supper on a tray."

"I don't want to eat alone," she complained.

"Then we'll both eat on trays, but you're not leaving that bed."

She batted her eyes innocently. "If you're afraid I won't keep my promise . . ."

He'd been putting on his jeans, and now he paused in the process of buttoning them to cast her a lascivious glance. "I'm not afraid of anything. I just want you to rest after what happened."

Oh, yes, she thought, remembering what had brought her to this bed in the first place. He was right, of course. She could already feel her muscles tightening and bruises forming. In a few hours, even rolling over would be an ordeal, and by tomorrow, she probably wouldn't be able to move at all. "Yes, sir," she said with mock meekness.

His eyebrows arched skeptically, but he didn't question her sincerity. As he pulled on his shirt, he said, "Maybe we'd better find your nightdress, too, before Juanita comes back. We don't want to shock her."

Leah doubted they could. Surely, she knew what they'd been doing for the past hour, but Leah didn't argue when Cal fetched her nightdress and helped her slip it on, nor did she object when he fluffed the pillows and helped her sit up in bed so she could brush out the mess her hair had become. Having him fuss over her was gratifying enough to allow her to forget her independence for the moment.

Remembering why she had gone to town in the first place this morning, Leah couldn't help smiling. If only Mead Garland could see them now, he'd know just how foolish his suspicions about her husband were. She'd been exactly right to decide that her next foray into town should include Cal so all the world could see their relationship.

Unfortunately, such a trip would have to wait a few days. By the time Leah had eaten her reheated dinner, the soreness she had been expecting had hit in force. She even had to beg off her promise to Cal. He was sweetly understanding and endearingly disappointed, but he promised to collect double at the first opportunity and tucked her into bed after giving her a stiff dose of whiskey to ease the pain. Her last glimpse of him was as he pressed a light kiss to her mouth as her heavy eyelids drooped.

Seeing she was asleep, Cal tiptoed out, but he paused at the door for a moment, because he wanted one last glimpse of Leah. She was, he thought for the thousandth time, the most beautiful woman alive. He hadn't even suspected *how* beautiful until he'd seen her this afternoon in all her glory as she emerged from her bath. God, he'd thought his heart would burst at the sight of her. He'd never wanted a woman so much in his life, and miracle of miracles, she'd wanted him, too. Another miracle was the way passion flared between them, like nothing he'd ever experienced before. Even with all his previous knowledge, he'd never dreamed it could be like that between a man and a woman. And to think, he'd almost lost her today.

The memory fired anew the fury he had felt earlier. Dammit, Rhodes had sold him a faulty buggy, and that buggy had almost killed Leah. The man would be sorry he'd ever met up with Cal Stevens.

* * *

"Better let me do this, Cal," Pete Quincy was urging, not for the first time as they waited in the sunshine the next morning for the spring wagon to be hitched up. Cal had left Leah in bed this morning fairly covered with bruises and barely able to move. He closed his hands into fists when he thought of the man responsible.

"I want to tell Rhodes to his face what I think of a man who'd—"

"Now you don't know he done it on purpose," Pete said. "Fact is, I've never knowed Rhodes to cheat anybody, least of all one of the Hardings, and you can't think he'd take a chance with a known gunfighter."

Part of Cal knew he was right, but he didn't want to be calmed down. He was furious and wanted to take that fury out on someone.

"Look," Pete argued, "that girl means a lot to me, too, and I ain't about to stand by and let something like this happen to her without doing something about it. Why don't you let me and the boys pick up what's left of the buggy and take it in to him. We'll tell him what happened and give him a chance to see if he can figure out what went wrong. You wait an hour or so, then follow. If he don't have a good story by then, I'll *help* you beat his brains out."

Cal looked down at the older man and reminded himself he wasn't the only one who cared about Leah. Swallowing his rage with difficulty, he said, "All right. But I'm only waiting an hour. I don't want to give him time to leave town or anything."

Pete grinned. "No chance of that. We'll hog-tie him if we have to. Oh, and Cal?"

"Yeah?"

"At least listen to what he has to say first, will you?"

Cal grinned back. "I reckon you'll hog-tie *me* if I don't, won't you?"

"In a minute," Pete promised.

Seeing the wagon was ready to go, Pete mounted up and, after giving Cal a silent salute, started out.

Exactly an hour later, Cal followed, and by the time he reached the livery stable in town, he was in a towering rage. Fortunately, Pete was waiting for him in the doorway.

Cal could see the wagon with the smashed remains of the buggy sitting inside the building, and the sight of it enraged him anew. "Where's Rhodes?" he demanded.

"Now just a minute, Cal. This wasn't his fault," Pete said, holding up both hands to stop him from entering.

"He can tell me that himself, can't he?" Cal snarled, ready to take the livery apart board by board if he had to in order to confront the man he held responsible for Leah's accident.

But he didn't have to. Oscar Rhodes stepped forward from the shadowy interior of the livery. He looked unnaturally pale and he was sweating profusely, but only an innocent man could face Cal so boldly.

"Mr. Stevens," he said in a voice that only wavered slightly, "I'm real sorry about what happened to Miss Leah, and if you insist, I'll give you your money back for the buggy, but what happened wasn't my doing."

"Maybe you can prove that?" Cal challenged.

"I can. Come right this way."

He led Cal into the livery, to the wagon with its unfortunate burden. Lying on the tailgate were the remains of the broken axle. Rhodes lifted one piece and held it out. "Look at this."

Cal held the edge of the broken shaft to the light and instantly he saw what Rhodes meant. Half of the edge was splintered, the way wood would look if it had broken naturally, from some weakness, but the other half was perfectly smooth. "Looks like somebody cut it."

"Just what I suspect," Rhodes confirmed. "Sawed it about halfway through and then . . ." He offered Cal the other piece of the shaft. "You can see it better on this piece. See the dried mud?"

Cal nodded as his fury evolved into naked horror.

"I figure whoever did it packed the mud over the cut place so it wouldn't show," Rhodes said.

"You know what this means, don't you?" Pete asked. "Somebody tried to kill Leah."

Cal had already come to the same conclusion, and his heart had turned to stone in his chest. His fingers tightened around the axle, squeezing it as if he could crush the wood with his bare hands.

"We're gonna have to tell her," Pete was saying. "She has to know."

"No," Cal said, laying the axle back in the wagon with deliberate care. "We aren't going to tell her a thing. She's already upset enough over all that's happened."

"But —"

"But nothing," Cal insisted. "She won't be in any danger because I'm not going to let her out of the house until I find out who did this."

"You got an idea, then?" Pete inquired.

Did he? Cal considered all the possibilities and discarded every one. Nobody stood to gain anything from Leah's death.

Nobody, that is, except Cal Stevens.

Chapter Eleven

Leah stared up at the intricate pattern of the crocheted tester over her head, a pattern she had committed to memory during the three days and nights she'd spent lying in this bed, afraid to move for fear of disturbing one of her many injuries. Cal had even started sleeping in another bedroom for fear of bumping her in the night. She should have been grateful he was so considerate, but she hated sleeping alone now that she'd known the comfort of his arms. She also hated having him see her like this, weak and helpless and horribly disfigured with swellings and bruises that ranged from black to scarlet. Some of them were even green.

And Cal *had* seen her, too, because no matter how she'd protested, he'd insisted on rubbing her down with the foul-smelling liniment himself. Twice a day he applied it; but only after dosing her with huge quantities of whiskey that left her woozy and reeling and barely aware of the pain his ministrations caused. At least he let Juanita handle the baths she also took twice a day in an effort to ease the soreness.

The problem, Leah decided as she examined the intricately entwined threads above her head, was that her body had simply slept too much and now refused to do so anymore. She glanced over at the bedside table where a half-empty bottle of whiskey stood. It would bring oblivion, sweet peace in which she felt no pain and didn't even have to remember the tragedies that had recently marred her life, but Leah was sick of oblivion. She was sick of being helpless, and she was sick of this bed.

A good sign, she told herself with a smile. She must be getting better. Gingerly, she tried bending her arms and found she could do so without crying out. Next she tried her legs, and although her muscles protested more vigorously, she decided the pain was bearable.

"Juanita!" she called, easing herself into a sitting position. The door opened, and Juanita stuck her head inside. "I'm ready for my bath now, and will you look in my trunk and see if you can find a dress I can wear without a corset? I'm going to get up today."

For a second, Leah was afraid Juanita would protest the decision, and Leah didn't think she had the energy to argue with Juanita *and* get out of bed on the same day. Fortunately, the Mexican woman smiled approvingly and bustled off to do her bidding without another word.

An hour later, Leah sat in one of the wing chairs in the parlor, her feet resting on a stool, a pillow cushioning the back of her head. She wore a brown calico wrapper that Juanita had found in the bottom of her trunk and which hung loosely from her shoulders over a minimum of underwear. So long as she didn't move too much or too suddenly, Leah could almost convince herself she was almost back to normal.

Smiling at the thought, she heard a horse riding up to

343

the house. When no one shouted a greeting, her heart leaped at the thought it must be Cal coming to pay her a surprise midafternoon visit, and when the visitor opened the door without bothering to knock, she was certain of it.

Her welcoming smile faded when she saw Mead Garland in the doorway, however.

"Leah!" he exclaimed happily when he saw her sitting there. He quickly closed the door behind him against the autumn chill. He pulled off his hat, hung it on a peg by the door, and hurried over to her. "How are you feeling?"

"Better," she said, frowning up at him. "And by all means, make yourself at home, Mead," she added sarcastically.

His handsome face showed surprise, then chagrin. "Oh, I'm terribly sorry for just walking in like that, but Juanita was so put out with me for knocking and shouting the first time I came to see you, that I've just started coming in unannounced."

"What do you mean, the first time?" Leah asked, wondering if all the whiskey she had drunk the past few days had muddled her brain.

Mead was smiling again, as charming as ever, and without waiting to be asked, he took the chair opposite hers. "I've been to see you every day since the accident."

Now Leah really was concerned. "I don't remember you being here."

"Of course you don't," he said cheerfully. "Juanita wouldn't let me see you. She always said you were sleeping."

"I probably was."

Mead nodded sagely. "How are you feeling now? Obviously, you must be better since you're up."

When Leah weighed the agony she'd caused herself by moving from the bedroom out here, she was no longer certain if she felt improved or not, but she was too well-mannered to complain to a guest. "I'm doing surprisingly well."

"It's a miracle you weren't . . . seriously injured." Although he'd caught himself, Leah knew he'd been about to say "killed," a thought she had also entertained a time or two during her sojourn in bed.

"Yes, it is a miracle," she agreed. Then she remembered what he'd said earlier. "You've been here every day since the accident?"

He nodded. "Didn't anyone tell you?" Although Mead was also well-mannered, he let just a bit of his pique show.

"I . . . I haven't really been awake much."

They both jumped at the loud "humph" from the hall doorway. Juanita stood there, arms akimbo, glaring at Mead. "I tell you, *no visit,*" she reminded him.

He stiffened, obviously annoyed at being reprimanded by a servant, and Leah was annoyed, too. "Juanita, is that any way to speak to a guest?" she chided. "And Mr. Garland tells me he's been to see me every day. Why didn't you tell me?"

"Man should not visit you. You married."

The argument was certainly logical. Leah had to bite back a smile. "I'm still allowed to have *friends,* Juanita, and Mr. Garland is one of my oldest friends. You should have told me he'd been here."

"You drunk."

This was probably also true, and Leah coughed to cover her chagrin.

"Really, Leah, I don't know why you put up with her," Mead whispered angrily. More loudly, he said, "Did Stevens order you not to tell her?"

Juanita glared even more fiercely and crossed her arms over her ample bosom in a gesture of defiance, but she didn't say a word.

Before Mead could take offense at her refusal to answer his question, Leah said, "Juanita, would you get Mr. Garland a cup of coffee?"

Juanita turned on her heel and disappeared into the hallway. Mead sighed explosively. "Honestly, Leah —"

"She means well, Mead. She probably thought it would upset me to know you were visiting and I wasn't able to see you."

His frown said he didn't believe that for a minute, but he said, "I'm sure she was acting on Stevens's orders. I can't help thinking he doesn't want us to see each other."

"Whyever not?" Leah asked in genuine surprise.

Mead gave her a self-mocking grin. "Because he knows how I feel about you, Leah. No man wants a besotted suitor calling on his bride."

Of course! Hadn't Cal been livid when he'd thought she and Mead had once been lovers? For a delicious moment Leah savored the idea that Cal might still be jealous of Mead. The very idea was ridiculous, of course, since he had nothing whatsoever to be jealous about. Still, she found the thought gratifying. She might even ask Cal about it later when he came home.

They could hear Juanita's clumping footsteps long

before she reappeared. Leah rolled her eyes at the childish display of temper, but when Juanita finally stomped into the parlor and grudgingly presented Mead with his coffee, Leah refused to acknowledge that she had even noticed the disapproval. "Thank you, Juanita. You may go now."

"You go back to bed soon," Juanita said. "The señor not like if you make yourself tired."

"Thank you for your concern, but I'm perfectly capable of judging when I'm ready to return to bed. You may go now," Leah added with more force.

Left with no choice, Juanita clomped away again. When her echoing footsteps had died away, Leah smiled apologetically. "She's always been very protective."

"I don't suppose she told you I brought flowers the first time I came, either," Mead said.

"No, she didn't," Leah replied, thinking she would have a nice, long talk with Juanita at the first opportunity. "I really appreciate your attention, Mead. I can't excuse Juanita's rudeness, but I hope you'll forget it."

"Of course. I just wish I could forget what happened to you."

Leah started to shrug and caught herself just as the first twinge of pain shot up her neck. Consciously relaxing her shoulders, she smiled, just about the only movement she could make without incurring distress. "Accidents happen, Mead. At least there's no permanent damage and—"

"You don't have to pretend with me, Leah," he interrupted. "I know everything. I saw the axle with my own eyes. That's why I've been trying so desperately to see

347

you. Leah, don't you know there's only one person who had a reason to do it?"

Leah gaped at him. "Do what? I don't have the slightest idea what you're talking about."

He gaped back at her. "My God, you don't, do you? Thank heaven I came when I did." He set his coffee down on the floor and leaned forward earnestly, bracing his elbows on his knees. "Leah, your accident wasn't an accident at all."

"What do you mean?" she asked, feeling the warning prickles of foreboding.

"I mean someone sawed the axle of your buggy nearly in half. It was only a matter of time until—"

"Who told you this?" Leah cried, horrified. "We have to tell Cal!"

"Cal?" he scoffed. "He already knows."

"That's impossible!" she insisted. "He would have told me."

"Exactly what *I* would have thought. Certainly what I would have *done* if you were *my* wife. This was an obvious attempt on your life since you're the only one intended to drive that buggy, the buggy he bought especially for you."

"Mead!" Leah cried in horror. "That's quite enough."

"Is it?" he replied, his cheeks mottled with rage. "Listen to me, Leah. The man buys you a buggy so you can drive yourself any place you want to go, and the first time you take it out, it wrecks, nearly killing you, and all because someone took a saw and cut the axle nearly in two."

"Stop it! I won't listen to any more of this ridiculous—"

"It's not ridiculous!" Mead insisted desperately, dropping to his knees in front of her. "Leah, I love you. You know that's true. I'd never say or do anything to hurt you." He took her hands in his and wouldn't let her pull away. "If he didn't do it, who did?"

"I can't imagine, but I know *he* didn't!" Leah exclaimed, wishing she were strong enough to free her hands from his feverish grip.

"How can you be sure?" he prodded. "What do you know about him besides the fact that he's a killer?"

"I know he loves me!" she informed him.

"Love?" Mead sneered, squeezing her hands until they ached. "What does a man like that know of love?"

Leah could have told him, of course, but delicacy forbade speaking of such intimacies. "He . . . he knows . . ." she stammered, but Mead just shook his head.

"I suppose he's professed his undying devotion to you, whispered flowery phrases, or maybe snippets of poetry, to you in the dark of night."

Leah felt the betraying heat in her face, and when Mead's expression grew smug, she knew he'd seen her blush. "I didn't think so. Leah, don't let sentiment blind you to the truth. You're in danger. Someone deliberately tried to murder you, and there's only one person who might have a reason to want you dead."

"That's ridiculous!" she insisted. "As you yourself pointed out to me, Cal already owns everything I have. He'd gain nothing from my death!"

"Nothing except his freedom!" Mead's eyes were wild, revealing the depth of his concern for her. "Without you around, he could dispose of the Rocking Horse however he wished and be on his merry way. A man like that would stop at nothing!"

They both jumped as the front door flew open and crashed into the wall. Cal stood in the doorway, his face contorted in rage. "Now ain't this sweet," he said with menacing calmness.

Leah realized how the scene must appear to Cal, Mead kneeling before her holding her hands. Once again, she tried to jerk her hands free, and this time Mead released them and scrambled to his feet.

"Stevens," he said uncertainly, plainly afraid.

Cal came into the room, moving slowly as if he were stalking prey. Cursing the weakness that prevented her from rising to stand in front of Mead, she said, "Cal, it's not what you think."

"It better not be," he replied coldly, and Leah saw his gun hand flex.

"No!" she cried in panic, launching herself to her feet. Every muscle in her body screamed in protest, and the scream clawed its way out of her throat as an anguished cry. Before she realized her legs would refuse to hold her, she was falling forward.

Strong arms caught her, sending new agonies pulsing through her, and as if from a distance, she heard Cal shouting, "Keep your hands off her!"

Then Cal was there, lifting her into his arms. Through the red haze of pain, she saw his face contorted in fury and knew she had to protect Mead. "Don't hurt him!" she begged. As misguided as he was, Mead had only been trying to help her.

A muscle twitched in Cal's jaw, and his eyes went

350

cold. He jerked his head toward Mead. "Get out, Garland, and I don't ever want to see your face around here again, understand?"

To his credit, Mead hesitated, as if he were just as afraid of leaving her with Cal as he was for his own life. "Go on, Mead," she urged. "I'll be fine."

A tremor went through Cal, as if her words had touched a nerve, and before she could see what Mead's reaction was, Cal was carrying her down the hall to the bedroom. The jarring of each angry footstep sent pain exploding through her, but she gritted her teeth against it, refusing to cry out, until at last he reached her bed and laid her gently down upon it.

The blessed stillness slowly brought relief as her outraged body quieted and the agony faded to a dull ache. Then she opened her eyes and found Cal staring down at her. His expression was guarded, and try as she would, she couldn't tell what emotions he might be feeling. Instinctively, however, she knew she must reassure him about her meeting with Mead. "He . . . It wasn't anything romantic," she tried.

His dark brows lifted in skepticism. "Then why was he holding your hands?"

Leah wanted to groan with frustration, but she steeled herself. "Because he's very worried about me. He told me the axle on the buggy had been deliberately cut."

The muscle in his jaw flexed again, but he did not reply.

Leah stared up at him in disbelief. She'd been amazed he hadn't told her before, but she could think of a dozen reasons why he might have decided to wait —

her physical condition being the main one. But now there was no longer any reason to protect her from the knowledge. Or was there?

"Cal, is it true?" she asked in rising panic. "Did someone really try to kill me?"

"Damn him," Cal muttered. "Damn him to hell. I should've wrung his stinking neck."

"Who?" she cried. Did he know who'd done it?

"Garland, who else? For telling you instead of minding his own damned business. What else did he say? There must've been more."

There had been, of course, but she didn't dare tell Cal about Mead's accusations. Instead she said, "Why didn't *you* tell me? If someone really did try to kill me, I'm in danger!"

"Not so long as you stay in this house. I didn't see any reason to scare you for no reason. You're perfectly safe here, and I'm not going to let you out of my sight until I find out who did it."

She felt some measure of relief. At least he'd been thinking about her safety, and maybe he was right about not worrying her. Heaven knew she'd had more than enough unpleasant things to contemplate lying here day after day. But . . . "Who could have done it, though? And *why?*"

"I figure it was the same person who killed Brad and Espy."

She knew who he thought guilty of that crime. "But Homer Wilkes won't gain anything from my death!"

"I didn't say anything about Homer Wilkes," he reminded her coldly.

"Then who? I don't have an enemy in the world!"

352

"Don't you?" he asked, his eyebrows high again. "I figured for sure Garland had pointed out at least one person who might have a reason for wanting you out of the way."

He had, of course, and Leah was too weak to pretend otherwise. Seeing the truth on her face, Cal frowned bleakly. "I'll send Juanita in," he said, turned on his heel and left.

She called his name, but he didn't stop, didn't even hesitate, and she moaned in despair. Cal *couldn't* have tried to kill her any more than he could have killed Brad and Espy.

But who *could* have? Only a heartless, cold-blooded murderer who . . . The face of John Jakes came to her, followed by the memories of their meeting in the store the day of the accident. She'd completely forgotten about the man and hadn't even thought of mentioning their meeting to Cal. Could Jakes have . . .? But why? And for whom?

Like an echo, she could hear Mead's voice warning her that Cal was the only one who would benefit from her death. And John Jakes was an old friend of Cal Stevens's.

Cal found Juanita in the parlor. The Mexican woman was frowning in disgust. "I tell him no visit," she informed him.

He nodded. "Take care of Leah. I've got some business."

"You kill him?" she asked with surprising mildness.

Cal almost smiled in spite of his fury. "No," he assured her. "He's not worth the trouble, but I know

353

somebody who is, *if* I can find him."

"You will be back for supper?" she asked.

"Don't plan on it," he said over his shoulder as he strode toward the front door.

Outside, the wind had picked up and was sending dust devils dancing in the yard. He checked the sky with a practiced eye and judged the weather would hold at least as long as the daylight. If he was lucky, he'd be back long before the threatening storm hit.

The pounding of his horse's hooves and the biting wind in his face helped calm him somewhat, which would help if he accidentally overtook Mead Garland on his way back to town, Cal thought with grim amusement. Never in his life had Cal killed a man who hadn't been threatening to kill him first, but he'd come awfully close to doing just that this afternoon when he'd found Garland on his knees at Leah's feet. Good God, it looked as if the bastard had been proposing to her, but just the fact that he'd had his hands on her at all had been enough to make Cal want to tear him limb from limb.

She'd known it, too, and her first instinct had been to protect Garland. The memory of her pleading for him was as bitter as gall, almost as bitter as the memory of the suspicion clouding her honey-colored eyes. Garland had made her doubt him again, and now the only way he could erase that doubt was to find the real killer.

The buildings of town finally loomed into sight, and Cal slowed his horse as he approached the outskirts, scanning the buildings instinctively for signs of an ambush. Everything was as quiet as he might have expected, considering it was nearing suppertime and most everyone would have headed toward home for the evening meal.

A few horses still stood outside the saloon, and Cal pulled up there and tied his beside them. Automatically, he hitched his gunbelt back to its proper position so that the grip of his pistol just brushed the fingers of his right hand when it hung by his side. Then he loosened the gun a bit so it would slide more easily from its holster if necessary. Satisfied, he strode across the warped wooden sidewalk and stepped through the batwing doors.

Sweeping the room with his practiced gaze, he instantly found the man he was looking for. John Jakes sat alone at a table in the corner, his back to the wall, a game of solitaire spread out before him, and a half-empty bottle of whiskey at his elbow.

Cal knew the instant Jakes recognized him. The gunfighter laid his cards down with deliberate care, spread his hands on the tabletop, and smiled. "Stevens," he said with no apparent surprise. "It's been a long time."

"Not long enough," Cal said approaching the table with the same care he would use approaching a rattlesnake. He didn't think Jakes would go for his gun in here. Cal had too much of an advantage, but he wasn't going to let down his guard. "Drinking alone?" he remarked when he had reached the table.

"Not anymore," Jakes replied cheerfully. "Bartender, a glass for my companion, if you please." He nodded toward the chair opposite his. "Have a seat."

Cal toed the chair out and lowered himself into it, keeping his own hands in plain sight so Jakes wouldn't get too nervous. The man looked exactly the same as he had the last time Cal had seen him more than five years ago: like a corpse that had walked away from its own funeral. Anybody would think Jakes was dying, but he'd always looked that way, or at least as long as Cal had known him.

The bartender brought over a glass and set it in front of Cal, then left as quickly as he had come, as if he sensed the tension between the two men and didn't want to be anywhere near if trouble started. Using his left hand, Jakes picked up the bottle and poured Cal a shot before refilling his own glass. Neither man made any move to drink.

After a moment Cal said, "What brings you to town, Jakes?"

"Business," he replied.

"Business must be bad then. I never knew you to kill women before."

Something flickered in those colorless eyes and was just as quickly gone. "I *don't* kill women."

"No," Cal agreed. "You just let them die accidental."

This time the flicker flared into a blaze of fury. "And maybe you'd tell me what women you're talking about."

"Espy Harding, for one. My wife, for another."

"I never heard of Espy Harding," he said, although Cal knew it was a lie. "And I can't imagine anyone wanting to harm your charming wife. Did she tell you? We met the other day in the store. A lovely woman. Allow me to congratulate you on your good fortune."

Cal went cold. Leah hadn't said a word about meeting Jakes, and Cal couldn't imagine why not. Unfortunately, he couldn't take the time to wonder about it

356

now. "Thanks," Cal said sarcastically. "I've got something to show you." He reached into his vest pocket, slowly so Jakes would know he wasn't going for a hideout gun. Fishing the items from the pocket, he laid them on the tabletop: two pieces of twig and several small stones. Pushing them casually with his fingertips, he arranged them in what might have been an arbitrary design. When he had finished, he said, "I found this at the spot where Brad and Espy Harding were killed."

"Did you now?" Jakes replied with apparent unconcern.

Probably, he *wasn't* too very concerned, even though they both knew that hired killers often left their own particular arrangement of sticks and stones at the scene of the crime so whoever had hired them would know they'd done the job. They both also knew the arrangement on the table was the one John Jakes used.

"You knew, of course, that the boy was my son," Cal said.

"I'd heard," Jakes said.

Cal went cold inside. Whoever had told him was probably also the person who had hired him. "And where'd you hear it?"

Jakes smiled ferally, easily reading Cal's thoughts. "From some two-bit lawyer here in town. Sometimes he drinks too much, and when he does, he forgets to keep secrets."

Cal should have guessed as much. Unfortunately, the clue was worthless. He knew Mead Garland wasn't the one who had hired Jakes. Even if Cal could find a reason the lawyer might have wanted Brad dead, Garland certainly wouldn't want to hurt Leah. "And naturally, you're willing to buy this lawyer drinks so you can get him to talk."

"I do so hate to drink alone." Jakes's cold eyes gave nothing away, but after a few seconds, he added, "I also heard the girl's death was an accident."

This was Jakes's way of telling Cal he hadn't meant for Espy to die without actually admitting he'd killed Brad. Even though Cal had already known, hearing Jakes admit it brought the rage welling up. He swallowed it down with difficulty and nodded his acknowledgement. "I just don't want my wife having any 'accidents' either."

"I told you before, Stevens, I'm not a woman killer."

"Then why're you still in town?"

"I like it here. I might even decide to stay permanent," he said with a grin.

"Oh, you will," Cal assured him, grinning back, "whether you want to or not."

Still grinning, Cal rose to this feet and stared down at Jakes until the other man's pale face blotched with red. Then he turned and strode sedately from the saloon. Although turning his back on Jakes went against the grain, he knew Jakes wouldn't shoot him in the back, at least not in front of witnesses.

No, Jakes would try to ambush him the way he'd ambushed Brad. The safest thing to do was to kill Jakes here and now and get it over with, but Cal couldn't do that until he'd learned who had hired Jakes and why. As soon as he did, though, Brad's killer *would* be staying on permanently, six feet under.

Leah tried to stay awake until Cal returned home, but her body betrayed her, and when she awoke the next morning, he was already gone. Somehow she knew he wouldn't be paying her any more midday visits, either, and Juanita even took over the task of rubbing her down with the liniment after her morning soak.

When she'd finished, Leah got dressed, determined not to linger in bed another day. She spent the morning in the kitchen, sitting at the table and helping Juanita knead the dough for bread.

"Where did he go last night?" Leah asked Juanita for the third time when she'd finally set the dough aside to rise. After her days in bed, the activity had exhausted her, and Leah slumped in her chair, hoping this time Juanita would choose to reply. Juanita only answered the questions she chose to.

This time she glanced at Leah and frowned. "I tell him he should kill Señor Garland, but he say no."

"Juanita!" Leah cried in outrage, but the Mexican woman was unmoved.

"He no good. He just want your money."

"Cal?" Leah asked in horror.

Juanita snorted in disgust. "No, Señor Garland. He no want *you*. He has no blood."

Leah rolled her eyes. She should have known better than to get into a conversation with Juanita when she was so tired. "Everyone has blood, Juanita," she explained patiently.

Juanita snorted again. "He not a man. He never kiss you. Señor Stevens, he has blood. He take you to his bed and make love to you —"

359

"Juanita! " Leah exclaimed, mortified.

Juanita shrugged her rounded shoulders. "You like it, too."

She did, of course, which only mortified her more. "This is not a subject I wish to discuss."

"I not discuss. I tell you. Garland no good. You see."

Juanita certainly had some strange notions, Leah mused, and it never did any good to argue with her either. Leah was much too tired to make the effort, anyway. She had just decided she would retire to her bed for a short rest before the noon meal when she heard booted feet clumping down the hall.

"Juanita, where is she?" Cal demanded as he burst into the kitchen.

He saw Leah at once, and she instinctively rose to her feet, her heart fluttering absurdly at the sight of him. She'd been so certain he was too angry with her to take the trouble to visit her at noon, but here he was and . . .

Except he still looked angry. His blue eyes blazed like the center of a flame, and his gaze swept over her from head to toe. He didn't seem pleased at what he saw, and Leah instantly regretted not having spent more time on her appearance.

But oddly enough, he asked, "Why're you all dressed up? Expecting another visit from Garland?"

"No!" she exclaimed in outrage. "I don't imagine the poor man will ever show his face here again, thanks to you."

"My pleasure," he replied stonily, then glanced at Juanita, taking note of the fact that she was listening intently to their every word. "Leah, I need to talk to you."

Since Leah needed to talk to him, too, she said, "Certainly." Lifting her chin, she made her way to the doorway in which he still stood. Frowning down at her, he looked formidable, but she refused to be intimidated. Just as she began to think he wouldn't step out of her way, he did, and she breezed past him, into the hallway. For just a second she debated where to go for this meeting and quickly decided the privacy of their bedroom was the ideal spot since it was the one place Juanita wouldn't dare enter without permission.

If Cal objected he didn't say so, and instead followed her in silence and closed the door behind them. Leah went directly to the bed and sat down on it, remembering her earlier resolve to rest. Cal, on the other hand, still stood by the door, as if he were reluctant to enter any further. She looked at him expectantly.

"What're you doing up and dressed?" he demanded.

"I happen to be feeling better, and I'm tired of being an invalid. I was up and dressed yesterday, too, if you recall."

"I thought that was just because Garland was here."

"I didn't even know he was coming! Which reminds me, he said he's been here every day since the accident. Why didn't anyone tell me?"

Cal pressed his lips together until they turned white, then he said, "Because I didn't know it was so important to you."

Leah felt a headache starting behind her eyes. "It wasn't *important* to me," she insisted with dogged patience. "I told you, there was nothing romantic about his visit. I would just like to be treated with common courtesy in my own house."

361

"Don't worry, Leah. I haven't forgotten it's *your* house."

Leah wanted to scream in frustration. What on earth was wrong with the man? He absolutely refused to be placated. "Cal, please, I don't want to argue with you, especially when there's nothing to argue about." She tried a smile, although it felt awfully weak. "What did you want to talk to me about?"

If anything, his expression hardened even more. "Why didn't you tell me you'd met John Jakes?"

Her jaw dropped in surprise. "Because I'd forgotten it myself! He spoke to me in the store when I was in town, just before the accident. After that, I didn't think of him again until yesterday, and this is the first I've seen you since!"

He glared at her, obviously not certain whether to believe her. At this point, she couldn't have cared less whether he did or not. "He said he was an old friend of yours. Is that true?"

For the first time since he'd walked in the house, his expression changed from furious to something else, although Leah couldn't quite say what. "Not exactly."

"Then what, exactly?" she prodded.

"I know him. We had a . . . a run-in, a long time ago. And we aren't *friends*."

"What do you mean? What kind of run-in?"

"It was a range war, down in south Texas. We were on opposite sides. Because of Jakes, my side lost."

"What did he do?" Leah asked, although she had a pretty good idea it was nothing she wanted to hear about.

"He killed the man I was working for."

362

Leah's jaw dropped again. "Then why is he . . .? I mean, why didn't you hang him?"

"Like I said, our side lost, and the law wasn't about to cross his boss. Besides, nobody saw it happen."

"Then how do you know Jakes did it?"

"He left his sign beside the body. Then he disappeared. I haven't seen him since, until today."

"Why is he here? Did he come to see you?"

Cal shook his head. "I told you, we aren't friends. My guess is he was hired to kill somebody."

"But who . . . ?" she started to ask when the truth hit her. *"Me?"*

"He says he doesn't kill women, and I've never known him to, but Espy's dead, isn't she?"

"Espy?" she asked, then realization dawned again. "Oh, God! Did he . . . ? *Brad?*"

Cal nodded, his face as rigid as if it had been carved from stone. Leah's eyes flooded with tears, and she covered her mouth with both hands to hold back the sob lodged in her throat. A thousand questions whirled in her brain, but before she could ask a single one, Cal said, "I don't want you to leave this house, Leah. Do you understand?"

She nodded dumbly.

"I don't think he'll bother you here, but I'll get one of the men to stand guard just in case."

At last she forced the words past the constriction in her throat. "But why? Who would . . . ?"

"I don't know," he told her baldly. "But I aim to find out."

Cal rode at a gallop, hoping to catch the men at their nooning. He had a pretty good idea where they'd be, and he'd have them all together so he could tell everyone at once that Leah's life was in danger.

Hellfire and damnation, if only he knew *why,* maybe he'd have some chance of figuring this whole thing out. The trouble was, none of it made any sense. The only person with any kind of grudge at all against Leah was Homer Wilkes, and God knew, Wilkes could never afford to hire a man like John Jakes. Wilkes might've promised payment in the future, maybe against some imagined inheritance from Leah's estate because of their relation by marriage, but Jakes would never accept a deal like that. He always demanded half his money up front.

No, Jakes was working for somebody with money, but who? The only other person involved in all this was Mead Garland, and Cal had already eliminated him. Although Garland could certainly afford Jakes, he'd be the last person in the world to want any harm to come to Leah, or Brad either, for that matter. If Garland wanted anyone dead, it would probably be Cal.

At that thought, the hairs on the back of Cal's neck prickled, a warning he'd felt before, a warning he'd learned to heed. Instinctively, he jerked his horse's reins, swerving to the right just as the rifle shot echoed across the prairie.

Cal had told her not to leave the house, but Leah didn't think his warning meant she couldn't walk out on her own front porch. As the setting sun painted streaks of gold across the sky, Leah stood at the top of the porch steps, pulled her shawl more tightly around her and gazed out at the horizon. Cal had also told her he would send one of the men to guard the house, and although he hadn't specifically said so, she'd been certain he was going to do so immediately. Yet no one had come, and Cal hadn't returned, either.

There was probably a perfectly reasonable explanation, Leah told herself for the hundredth time, but even still, she couldn't quite shake the feeling of foreboding she'd had all afternoon. Nor could she shake the sense that she'd done this before, waited for someone she loved to return only to learn he never would.

Shuddering at the thought, Leah caught some movement from the corner of her eye, and when she turned to look, she saw Homer Wilkes's bedraggled figure standing in the yard only a few feet from the end of the porch.

"Mr. Wilkes, you startled me," Leah said uneasily. Indeed, he would have startled anyone. He looked as if he hadn't shaved in days, or eaten either, for that matter. His eyes were sunken and red-rimmed, and his clothes even more disheveled than usual, as if he'd slept in them more than a few nights.

He started toward her, shambling and unsteady, his sunken eyes glittering with an unnatural light. Later she would wonder why she had stood and waited for his approach, but at the time, he seemed to pose no threat. Indeed, he looked far more pathetic than dangerous.

"You took her," he said when had reached the porch steps. "You took her away from me, you an' your brother. She was all I had."

As repulsed as she was, Leah's heart ached in response to his obvious pain, a pain she shared. "But you've got your other children. You have to pull yourself together, Mr. Wilkes. Think of them." Leah knew he'd come to the graves every day since the funeral, and sometimes he even slept on the ground beside the picket fence. Although she hadn't actually seen him since her accident, from the looks of him, he hadn't changed his habits in the past few days.

"I don't care nothing about them other younguns. It was Espy I wanted. I loved that gal, and she never needed herself no other man until your brother came along, tempting her with fancy clothes and a fancy house. It's all your fault, too. If you'd've kept your nose out of it, she would've stayed with me!"

He looked doubly pathetic, making his assertions while he swayed unsteadily on his feet, as if a strong gust of wind would knock him over.

Leah smiled kindly. "You're forgetting the baby, Mr. Wilkes. I wouldn't have even considered letting them marry except for the baby, and you must've known that was best, too, under the circumstances."

"You don't know a damn thing about the circumstances!" he cried, furious. His face mottled, and he lurched toward the steps, grabbing the rail to hold himself erect. "You think that baby was your brother's, don't you? Well, that's what she wanted you to think, but it wasn't! Espy didn't need no snot-nosed kid! She had herself a real man, the man who put that baby in her belly!"

He pulled himself up to his full height in a bizarre gesture of pride while Leah stared at him in abject horror, frozen with revulsion while her mind screamed denials of the unspeakable.

As if from a distance, she heard an approaching horse and someone calling her name. Someone, not Cal, was all she registered until Mead Garland vaulted from his saddle and stepped in between her and Wilkes.

"Leah, what's going on here?"

Leah blinked and shivered, forcing herself to see something besides Wilkes's disgusting pride, to hear something beside the awful words he'd spoken. Lies, she told herself over and over again. No one could . . .

Mead was shouting at Wilkes who cringed under his wrath and began to slink away. Then Mead bounded up the steps and slipped his arm around her waist. "Are you all right? You're white as a sheet. What were you thinking of, coming out of the house in your condition? You should be in bed!"

As he spoke, he led her back into the house and closed the front door firmly behind him. When he had seated her on the sofa, he went to the cabinet that held the liquor and poured her a snifter of brandy. Cradling it in the palm of his hand, he carried it to her and forced her to take a swallow.

She choked on the burning liquid, but welcomed its answering warmth. For some reason she felt chilled to the bone, as if all the blood in her body had turned to ice. It wasn't true, she told herself over and over, and blinked at the sting of tears.

"What on earth was he saying to you out there?"

Leah wasn't about to explain. She shook her head and shivered again. "He's a horrible man. He . . . he blames me for Espy's death."

"He's crazy," Mead declared. "Someone should lock him up. You should certainly not allow him to hang around the ranch the way you do. I've heard he actually sleeps by the graves. That's not normal, Leah. Normal people do their grieving at home."

He was right, of course, but as Leah now knew, Homer Wilkes was far from normal. She took the snifter from Mead's hand and drank down the rest of the brandy. Only when its warmth had seeped into her bones was she able to think of anything else.

"Mead, what are you doing here?" she asked, suddenly realizing his visit might not be such a good idea.

He smiled his most winning smile. "I came to see how you're doing. I came in the evening so I would be sure your husband was here and so he couldn't accuse me of . . . well, of whatever it was he thought I was doing when I was here before."

Leah felt the heat in her cheeks and tried to blame it on the brandy. "Cal didn't . . ." she began, then realized the futility of lying. "Cal is a little jealous, I'm afraid."

"And he has every right to be. I would be, too, in his place. Nobody wants a man his wife once loved calling on his bride."

"Or holding her hands," Leah added, deciding not to bother telling him she had never really loved him. There was no sense in hurting him now, so long as he knew she certainly didn't love him anymore.

He smiled sheepishly. "I'm afraid my feelings for you got the best of my good judgment. I hope you'll forgive me, and believe me when I say it will never happen again."

"I certainly will, but I'm not the one you have to convince," Leah reminded him.

His smile faded. "Which is why I chose to come here tonight. I don't want your . . . your husband to have any reason to suspect my intentions. I only want what's best for you, Leah. I've been thinking about what you said, and although you'll understand if I don't have the same confidence in him that you do, I'm willing to admit I might have been wrong about him. If *you* care for him, he can't be all bad."

Leah couldn't help smiling. "You're very generous, Mead."

He smiled back. "I know," he said slyly. "Now where is the lucky gentleman so I can tell him to his face."

Leah's smile died. "I . . . He hasn't come home yet. But I expect him any minute," she added hastily.

"Then I'll wait, if you don't mind. I don't want him to accuse me of sneaking around behind his back to see you."

"Of course you can wait. And if you haven't had your supper, you're certainly welcome to join us," Leah offered rashly. For all she knew, Cal would throw Mead out on his ear, but surely if Mead apologized, Cal would have no objections to his staying.

Apparently, Mead shared her uncertainties about Cal's reaction. He shook his head. "I'll wait until your husband invites me before giving you my answer. Now, would you like to tell me what Homer Wilkes was saying to you when I rode up?"

Leah had almost forgotten the horrible encounter with Wilkes, and of course she couldn't possibly tell Mead what Wilkes had said. In fact, she didn't think

369

she could tell *anyone,* not even her own husband. Fortunately, she heard the sound of horses in the yard.

"I hear the men, now," she said with false brightness. "Cal will be with them." Without waiting for a reply, she set the brandy snifter aside and stood up, pleased to note her legs felt steady beneath her.

Mead followed her outside, and sure enough, her men had arrived home after their day of work. She didn't see Cal at first, but she did see his horse, which stood surrounded by the rest of the men who had left their mounts unattended in the yard instead of proceeding to unsaddle them as they usually did.

Leah scanned the group again, and once more she failed to find Cal among them. He must have gone into the barn, she told herself. After all, his horse is here and
. . .

Just then, Pete caught sight of her and came loping over. "Where's Cal?" he asked as soon as he was within speaking distance.

Leah's heart constricted. "I thought he was with you. He left here around noon to find you."

Pete stopped at the bottom of the porch steps, his expression grave. "We ain't seen him since this morning."

That wasn't possible. "But that's his horse, isn't it?" Leah insisted, fighting panic.

"Sure is. He was waiting for us out by the corral when we rode up just now. Looks like he come home all on his own."

No, that *wasn't* possible. Cal would never . . .

"And, Miss Leah?" Pete was saying. "There's something looks like a bullet track on the saddle."

Chapter Twelve

Thank heaven Mead was here, Leah mused as she stared out the window at the darkness and willed Cal to appear. Thinking about her husband, about how little time they'd had together and how she'd never even told him she loved him, Leah knew she would be going crazy right now if Mead hadn't been here to comfort her.

"I wish you'd eat something, Leah," Mead said from the sofa. "Or at least try to get some rest. You haven't been out of bed long, you know."

"Where could they be?" she asked, oblivious of any personal discomforts. "What could be taking so long?"

"They had a lot of ground to cover, and it's dark, remember? He could be anyplace."

The instant the men had determined that the gash in the cantle of Cal's saddle had indeed been caused by a bullet, they had set out to look for him. Unfortunately, with less than an hour of daylight left, their chances of finding him had been slim at best, especially if he was lying somewhere wounded or . . .

"He'll probably turn up here on his own in the morning, footsore and fit to be tied," Mead continued reasonably, but Leah knew he was only trying to reassure her.

"Not if he's hurt," she argued. The night wasn't terribly cold, but if Cal had been shot . . .

"There wasn't any blood on the saddle," he reminded her. With a sigh, he rose from his seat on the sofa and came over to where she still stood by the window. Gently but firmly, he turned her away from it and led her back to the sofa. "Even if that *was* a bullet mark on the saddle — and we don't know that it was, regardless of what your men may think — Cal might well have just jumped off his horse to take cover."

"Then why isn't he home yet?" she demanded as she allowed him to seat her on the sofa. "He left here at noon, and now it's close to nine o'clock. Even if he had to walk all the way back, he would have been here by now!"

"Leah, there could be a thousand explanations," Mead said patiently, sitting down beside her. "He hasn't lived around here very long. Perhaps he just walked off in the wrong direction."

Only a city man could have suggested such a thing, and Leah smiled in spite of herself. "I don't believe a word of it, Mead, but please keep talking. You're the only thing keeping me sane."

He smiled back and took her hand in both of his. "I'm trying, and you mustn't give up hope. Everything will be fine, I promise you."

Leah just wished he had the power to keep that promise. "If only this wasn't so much like the time I was waiting for Brad and . . ." Her voice broke on the tears she'd been fighting for so long, and Mead slipped his arms around her and pulled her head to his shoulder.

372

"Don't cry, Leah," he begged as she did just that. "You aren't alone. I'm here, and I'll be here for as long as you need me."

Leah wept for a while and allowed Mead to comfort her. Then, her tears spent, she remained in his arms, absurdly grateful for the human contact. How long they sat like that, she never knew, but after what seemed hours, she heard the sound of riders outside, then Pete Quincy was calling her name.

Instantly Leah broke from Mead's embrace and, ignoring her own lingering aches and pains, ran to the door and out to the porch.

"We found him, Miss Leah!" Pete was shouting, but Leah didn't allow herself to believe it until she saw Cal with her own eyes, lowering himself from where he'd ridden behind Pete's saddle.

Picking up her skirt with both hands, she bolted down the stairs and across the yard, straight into Cal's arms. The strength with which he held her told her more than words could that he was really and truly all right. She clung to him for as long as it took to convince herself he was actually there, then pushed away and looked up into his face.

"What happened? Where have you been? Are you hurt?"

She looked him over from head to toe but could see no visible damage in the poor light filtering out the open front door into the yard.

"I'm fine," he said, sounding as if he was.

"He's a little lame," Pete contradicted slyly. "He'd been walking a ways when we finally found him. Best get him inside so he can soak his feet."

"And so he can tell me where he's been all this time,"

Leah added with wifely outrage. "You scared me to death! All I could think was . . ." But she caught herself. There was no use in going into all that now. Cal was home, and nothing else really mattered. She looked up at Pete and the other men. "Thank you for finding him. Thank all of you."

The men were grinning back at her, proud of their accomplishment, and Leah had an urge to kiss every one of them. Of course, she couldn't surrender to such an impulse because the men would be mortified at the very thought.

"Yeah, thanks," Cal was saying. "You fellows saved me from wearing out a perfectly good pair of boots."

They chuckled in response and turned their horses, heading for the barn. Leah slipped her arm around Cal's middle and let him lean on her shoulder as they headed for the house. She was staring up at his face, drinking in the sight of him, so she saw the reaction before she felt his body stiffen in response. What on earth? she wondered in the second before she glanced up to see Mead standing on the porch waiting for them.

"Mead came out to apologize to you," Leah explained hastily. "And when you didn't come home, he kept me company while I waited. He was very kind, Cal."

Cal didn't even glance at her. "I'll bet," he said through gritted teeth.

Mead gave them his best professional smile as he sauntered down the steps and across the yard to meet them. "I'm glad you're all right, Stevens. Leah was terribly worried about you."

"If you expect me to thank you for keeping her company, you're going to be disappointed," Cal said coldly.

Leah wanted to shake him. "Cal, Mead came here to *apologize* to you. He came here to see *you,* not me."

"Yeah, sure," Cal said. "Well, now you've seen me, so you can go."

"Cal!" Leah cried in exasperation. "Is that any way to speak to a guest?"

"It's all right, Leah," Mead assured her good-naturedly. "This is obviously not the best time to work out our differences. I'm just glad I was here when you needed me, and I'm glad you don't need me anymore. Please, let me know if there is anything else I can do for you. Good night to you both."

She saw that he'd already retrieved his hat, and as she murmured her thanks, he strode away to fetch his horse.

Cal watched him go, making no move to continue on into the house until Mead had disappeared into the barn.

"Cal?" Leah said, drawing his attention back to her.

She felt him sigh, and then he allowed her to lead him up the porch steps and into the house. Juanita hovered just inside the door, ready to take his hat and murmuring incomprehensibly in Spanish.

When Cal had slumped wearily down onto the sofa, she said, "You will eat, no?"

"I will eat, yes," Cal replied, "and don't bother to heat it up. I could eat a whole steer raw. Just put something on a plate."

"Sí," Juanita said over her shoulder as she hurried from the room.

Leah perched on the sofa beside him, alarmed at how tired he looked in the lamplight. "Are you really all right? What happened? Tell me everything."

He drew a deep breath and released it on a long sigh. "Pete said you found my horse."

"Yes, and we saw the bullet mark on the saddle, or at least we thought it was a bullet mark. Was it?"

He nodded, and Leah's heart constricted. "Somebody took a potshot at me — actually a couple of potshots — while I was on my way to find the men. Luckily, none of them hit me, but I had to get out of the saddle quick so I wouldn't make such a good target, and the horse got away from me."

Leah laid a hand over the pulse beating furiously at her throat. "Did you see who it was?"

His finely molded lips thinned. "No, but I've got a pretty good idea."

Remembering the coldness of John Jakes's eyes, Leah did, too. "But why would he want to . . . to kill you?" She could hardly make herself say the word.

"Maybe because he figures it'll be easier to get to you if I'm out of the way. Maybe he just doesn't like me. Or maybe just for old time's sake. Who knows? The important thing is he didn't succeed."

Unable to speak, Leah could only nod. She wanted to throw her arms around him again and hold him close, but something in his expression forbade any show of affection just yet. She could hardly believe he was still jealous of Mead, but apparently he was. Swallowing the tears clogging her throat, she said, "So you lost your horse and had to walk back, but where have you been all this time?"

"I didn't start walking right away. I figured he might wait around until he could catch me on foot, so I holed up until dark. The men found me a little while ago."

"Oh, Cal, I was so scared!"

"Were you?" he asked as if he didn't believe it for a minute, then he bent over and began to pull off his dusty boots.

"Of course I was! I thought you'd been shot and were lying bleeding somewhere with no one to help you."

As if he hadn't even been listening, he sighed with relief once the boots were off and started to massage his feet through his socks.

"Let me . . ." she started to say, but Juanita called from the hall doorway to tell him his food was ready.

Without even looking at Leah, he rose from the sofa and started toward the kitchen. Not knowing what else to do, Leah followed, noticing he limped slightly and wondering if she really shouldn't fix a basin so he could soak his feet. Walking in high-heeled cowboy boots must have been a painful ordeal.

Not as painful as actually getting shot, though, she reminded herself.

Cal murmured his thanks to Juanita as he lowered himself into a chair at the kitchen table and dug into the pile of beans she had set out for him. Between bites, he gulped the steaming coffee or devoured the cold biscuits sitting on a plate nearby, apparently oblivious to his wife who sat silently across from him.

And try as she might, Leah couldn't think of a single thing to say to break that silence. She'd been so frightened at the thought of losing Cal, she'd thought she might go crazy, but now he was back, safe and sound, and she was beginning to wonder if she hadn't lost him already. For a few minutes outside just now when he'd held her, she'd thought he was every bit as happy to see her as she was to see him, but now . . .

Cal wiped up the last of the beans with the last biscuit, popped the biscuit into his mouth, then drank down the last of the coffee. "Thanks, Juanita," he said again as he rose from his chair and dumped his dirty dishes into the sink. He was already heading out the door before Leah was out of her chair.

"Cal, wait!" she called, and caught up to him when he stopped in the hallway. "Where are you going?"

His face was stony, and only his eyes betrayed any expression at all. They glittered down at her, but for the life of her, she couldn't begin to guess what he was feeling. "It's late and I've had a rough day. I'm going to bed."

"All right," she agreed readily. At least in the privacy of their bed, she could hold him close and . . .

"You ought to go to bed, too," he added. "I'll see you in the morning."

This time she didn't call him back. This time she simply stared after him, mortified, because this time she knew he didn't want her. Didn't want to see her or talk to her or sleep with her. Totally humiliated, she waited until he'd closed the door to his room, the room that had once been hers. Then she hurried to their room and shut herself safely away before finally surrendering to the tears of anger and frustration and despair.

The next morning Leah came awake slowly, reluctant to face the day and whatever new pain it might bring. At least she had decided one thing when she'd been tossing and turning in the wee hours of the night. Today she was going to have it out with Cal once and for all. Today she would tell him how she felt about him, and today she would find out how he felt about her, too. As devasating as the knowledge might be, she simply had to know so she could put an end to all this uncertainty. With someone trying to murder them both, they might not have another chance.

Since she was still too sore for a corset, Leah dressed carefully in the wrapper she had been wearing the day before and took great pains with her hair, knowing instinctively that Cal was still in the house. She wasn't certain how she knew, but she knew, nevertheless. Too nervous to even think about breakfast, she set out immediately to look for him.

She found him in the office, bent over the desk, so absorbed in what he was doing that he didn't appear to notice her.

"Good morning," she said.

He didn't react, which told her he'd known she was there all the time. Slowly, deliberately, he continued with his task for a few more seconds, then lay it aside and looked up, half turning to face her. "Good morning."

When he turned she saw what he was doing. It seemed an odd task for first thing in the morning. "Why are you cleaning your gun?" she asked in alarm, instantly forgetting what she had come here to discuss.

"Because I always clean it when I'm going to use it."

Alarm turned to terror. "But why? Why would you have to use it?"

His eyes were as bleak as she had ever seen them. "Because I have to face down John Jakes."

"No!" she cried, horrified. "That's crazy! Why would you do a thing like that?"

"Because," he said, picking up a clean cloth and methodically wiping his hands on it, "he tried to kill me.

379

That's the way things work out here, Leah. I figured you already knew that."

She did, of course, but she had never approved of the situation. Now that her own husband was in danger, she approved even less. "But you don't have to kill him yourself. We can send for the sheriff or even the Rangers. They'll come. They're the law, Cal. It's their job to take care of this."

Slowly, as if he were considering her proposal very carefully, he lay aside the rag, then looked up at her. "He killed my son, Leah, and my son's wife and child. He tried to kill you, and he'll try again, if I let him. This is *my* job, and I can't turn it over to anyone else."

"Well, if you're so all fired anxious to protect me, what'll happen to me if you fail? If he kills you instead? Tell me that!"

Cal's mouth was set in a grim line. "He may get me, but I'll take him with me. You'll be safe, no matter what."

"Safe!" she fairly screamed. "What good is *safe* if you're dead? I don't want to spend the rest of my life alone, Cal!"

"I'm sure Garland will make sure you aren't alone," he said bitterly.

This time Leah really did want to scream. "I don't want *Mead,* I want *you!* I . . ." This wasn't exactly the way she'd intended to tell him, but it would have to do. "I love you, Cal! That's why I married you, and that's why I want to spend the rest of my life with you instead of letting some two-bit gunslinger shoot you down in the street!"

His astonishment was almost comic. "What did you say?"

"I said I love you," she snapped. "And if you don't come over here and kiss me right now, I'll—"

She didn't need to finish the threat because Cal was out of his seat and across the room in the blink of an eye. His arms came around her, crushing her to his chest, and his mouth found hers unerringly. His kiss was hot and wet and demanding, and she opened to it hungrily, wrapping her arms around his neck and never wanting to let him go.

His scent enveloped her, and she inhaled it greedily while she buried her fingers in the raven softness of his hair. Only then did she realize exactly how much she'd missed his touch and how desolate she would be without it.

Even when they couldn't kiss any longer and had to break for air, they still clung to each other, panting and gasping. Cal rested his forehead against hers while his hands moved lovingly over her back and shoulders. "I didn't think it was possible," he murmured.

She ran her fingers over his face, tracing the beloved curves and angles, reveling in the warmth of his flesh. "You didn't think what was possible?"

"That you could love me."

She pulled away so she could see for sure if he was serious. Apparently he was. "Why on earth do you think I married you?" she asked in astonishment.

"Because you had to, or thought you did. Because I seduced you."

Leah was so delighted she almost laughed aloud. "If I remember correctly, *I* was the one who asked you to stay that night."

"Because you were lonely and upset and—"

"Oh, for heaven's sake!" Leah exclaimed in exaspera-

381

tion. *"Not* because of that! Because I *loved* you, and I wanted you. I knew you were just . . . That you only wanted . . ." She broke off, too embarrassed to explain any further.

His lips twitched slightly, as if he were holding back a smile. "That I only what?" he prodded.

Leah would have refused to answer, but his arms tightened around her, silently warning her he wasn't about to let her go until she did. "I know you didn't *love* me," she forced herself to say. "That . . . that you were only taking what I offered, but I hoped . . ."

Her face was burning with humiliation, and damn him if he wasn't smiling at her embarrassment. "And what did you hope, little wife?" he inquired archly.

Little wife? Where on earth had that come from? She had no idea, but it gave her the courage to say, "I hoped that someday you'd love me, too."

His grin widened, and he started shaking his head, but before Leah could give way to despair, he said, "Too late for that. I've loved you since . . . God, I don't even know exactly when. Maybe since that first night when I sat down at the table with you and wondered what it would be like if I belonged here and you were my woman and . . . What's so funny?" he demanded.

Leah was so happy she couldn't contain it. *"We* are," she said, still laughing joyously. "All this time I've been wondering if you'd ever come to love me when you already did, and you were worrying about me when . . . But if you love me, why wouldn't you sleep with me last night?"

He frowned down at her, totally perplexed. "I didn't sleep with you last night because I haven't slept with you for a week. You were hurt, remember?"

"But I wanted you to sleep with me last night! I'm practically well now, and I'd been so scared when I thought you might be lying dead somewhere on the prairie and I needed to hold you and—"

"Then why didn't you say so?" he demanded.

"How could I when you wouldn't even look at me?" she countered.

"What do you mean, I wouldn't even look at you? I looked at you!"

"You did not! And you stomped around here like somebody'd done something to hurt your feelings and—"

"How was I supposed to act when I come home and find you with Mead Garland?"

Leah gaped at him. "Were you *jealous?*"

Now his frown was disgruntled. "Of course not."

But Leah wasn't fooled. "You *were,* admit it!"

His arms were still around her, but Leah could feel him withdrawing emotionally. "Garland is the kind of man you should've married, Leah. I can understand if you're having second thoughts . . ."

"Second thoughts!" Leah exclaimed in exasperation. "I've hardly had time to have *first* thoughts, but all of them have been about how I could get my husband to love me as much as I love him. I never think about Mead Garland at all!"

He still looked skeptical. Leah cradled his rugged face with her hands. "Cal, listen to me. I love you. You're my husband. I married you because I wanted to be with you, and I want to be with you now. What can I do to prove that to you?"

His expression softened, and something mischievous

twinkled in his eyes. "Do you want to be with me *right* now?"

It took Leah a minute to comprehend him, and even then, she wasn't quite sure. "You mean . . . ?"

"I mean, you look like you should be in bed, little wife."

She pursed her lips to hold back a smile. "I don't want to go alone."

The twinkle flickered into a flame. "You don't have to."

Desire surged through her, and she pulled away, catching his hand and drawing him with her. "Well, in that case," she began as she backed toward the door.

She didn't need to say more. Cal came willingly, eagerly, and by the time they reached their bedroom, they were fairly running. Cal slammed the door behind him with one hand and caught Leah to him with the other. Their kiss was long and passionate as hands explored, relearning remembered delights, until the restriction of clothes became too much.

By silent consent, they pulled apart and began to fumble with buttons and fastenings. Within seconds, Cal had dropped his empty gunbelt to the floor and stripped out of his shirt. He rushed to help Leah lift the wrapper over her head and discard it in a heap. In her chemise, Leah allowed Cal to lead her to the bed where he sat to remove his boots while Leah stepped out of her shoes and waited, uncertain how much undressing was actually necessary.

When his boots and socks were off, Cal rose to his feet and began to unbutton his pants. "You haven't stopped, have you?" he inquired archly as he peeled the jeans over his hips and stepped out of them, leaving him in his long underwear.

"I didn't . . . that is, I'm still awfully bruised and . . ."

He'd already unbuttoned his long underwear to the waist, but he stopped instantly, his expression sobering. "God, I'm sorry! I thought you wanted . . . I don't want to hurt you . . ."

"Oh, I'm not worried about getting hurt!" she assured him just as instantly. "I just . . . I don't want you to see me like this."

His eyes widened in surprise. "I saw you before," he reminded her.

"Yes, but we weren't . . . I mean . . ." Oh, dear! Would she ever be able to discuss such things with him without blushing as furiously as her burning cheeks told her she was?

"We weren't going to make love?" he suggested slyly, entirely too amused by her chagrin. "Well, now, I'm not sure we're going to this time, either. I'd better see if you're well enough first, which means I'll have to examine you."

Before Leah could even think of a protest to this outrageous proposal, Cal had grabbed the hem of her chemise and was lifting it over her head, leaving her in nothing but her pantalettes and stockings. Instinctively, she made a grab to cover her naked breasts, but Cal was faster and caught her hands.

"You weren't this modest the other day," he chided, reminding her of her wantonness the day he'd helped her out of her bath. The memory sent her blush speeding downward, over her breasts and underneath her pantalettes to warm her most secret places.

"Cal," she pleaded, but he was shaking his head.

385

"Now are you going to take those things off, or do I have to do it for you?" he inquired with mock sternness, nodding toward what was left of her garments.

Leah had just finished gauging how quickly she could skim out of her clothes and scramble under the bedcovers when she felt Cal's fingers at her waist. The tie gave way, and the pantalettes slithered to her ankles.

The cool air swirled around, touching the places that burned from both embarrassment and desire. The bed beckoned with both its comfort and its offer of concealment. "Cal, shouldn't we . . .?" she began feebly, but he was too distracted by the sight of her naked body to pay much attention.

He caught her hands again and held her arms out so he could see every inch of her except what her stockings covered from the knees down. The passion in his eyes changed instantly to concern. "Good God," he murmured, seeing the many-hued remnants of her accident marring the whiteness of her skin.

"It's a lot better than it was," she assured him. "And I don't hurt nearly so much."

He dropped her hands as if her skin had burned him and stepped back quickly. "I don't know what I was thinking. You shouldn't . . . It's too soon. God, I must be crazy . . ."

He was going to leave her, she knew he was, but she wasn't going to let him.

"You *are* crazy if you think you can come in here and undress me and make a lot of promises, and then not go through with them!" she informed him, planting her hands on her naked hips.

He stared at her in amazement, or at least he tried to, although Leah could tell his gaze kept dropping from

386

her face to her breasts. He'd jerk it back again, but he couldn't keep it on her face for more than a few seconds.

After a minute or so, his struggle became amusing, and Leah could hardly suppress a smile. "I'd like something to look at, too," she said with mock sternness. "Are you going to take off that union suit, or do I have to do it for you?" she demanded, echoing his earlier question.

He glanced down in surprise, as if he'd forgotten he was still wearing it, and when he looked back at her, he grinned. "I think I'd like you to do it."

Excitement sparked across her nerve endings. Surely she was behaving shamelessly, but that only seemed to add to the excitement. Slowly, she stepped closer to him, acutely aware of his musky masculine scent and the breadth of his shoulders looming over her own nakedness. Carefully, she reached up and parted the garment where he had already unbuttoned it, revealing the darkly furred wall of his chest.

At her touch, his breath caught and held, and his body stilled expectantly. Emboldened by his response, she pushed the fabric over his shoulders and down, revealing the muscled flesh of his arms. Like an obedient child, he pulled his arms free and waited for her to continue.

The garment hung about his waist, still buttoned the rest of the way. With fingers unsteady from excitement, Leah began to work the buttons loose while she tried not to think of how wicked it must be for a woman to stand naked before a man and remove the most intimate of his clothing.

As each button slipped free, the garment slid a bit

lower, revealing more and more of his hips and belly until Leah became aware of the throbbing swell of his manhood just beneath her fingers. Uncertain whether she should stop or continue, she pulled her finger away for a second, and the garment slid free, completely exposing his arousal.

Leah cried out in surprise even as her body melted in response, dewing the insides of her thighs and turning her bones to jelly as she faced the blatant evidence of his desire.

"You wanted something to look at," he reminded her hoarsely.

She nodded, unable to look away, drawn inexorably by his power. "I'd forgotten," she murmured, remembering all too vividly the way she'd boldly taken him in her hand and guided him to her.

She was trembling when he clasped her hand and drew her to the bed. Her nipples had hardened into aching nubs, and her belly throbbed with emptiness as he lowered himself to the mattress and pulled her down on top of him.

"You'll tell me if I hurt you," he whispered against her heated skin, and she nodded, unable to speak. Her body touched his everywhere, and sensation exploded inside her.

His hardness pressed against her belly, his chest teased her swollen breasts, his hair-roughened thighs chafed against her smooth ones. Only her calves, still encased in their silk stockings, were protected from the onslaught, but Cal wasn't so protected. When she rubbed her calf against his, he groaned.

"Oh, God, that feels good," he murmured.

Leah could have returned the compliment had she

388

been capable of speech, because Cal's hands were working a similar sort of magic by stroking up the backs of her naked thighs and over the curve of her bottom and back again, his callused palms teasing and tormenting her delicate skin and sending delicious shivers racing over her.

Instinctively, Leah settled into the cradle of his hips, pressing her need against the evidence of his and rocking in an imitation of the union she craved. He responded by capturing one pursed nipple in the heat of his mouth and suckling until she moaned with pleasure, then capturing the other and treating it to the same torment. Tiny streaks of lightning raced from her breasts to her loins and struck a fire that blazed into an inferno of desire.

Her hips churned against his, silently pleading, but Cal was momentarily too busy to respond. His fingers were frantically pulling the pins from her hair and tossing them to the floor until the weight of it pulled the mass loose and it came tumbling over her shoulders.

Cal buried his hands in it and pulled her face to his for a kiss that demanded everything and gave all in return. When it was over, Leah thought she would die from wanting him, but when she tried to roll them over, he stopped her.

"No, like this," he breathed, and lifted her hips, positioning her until his hardness met her softness and she took him into herself with a sigh of ecstasy.

Bracing herself on his shoulders, she gazed down into his eyes and saw her own wonder reflected back at her. Adoration radiated from him, and he touched her reverently, her face, her breasts, her hips, her thighs, as if he were paying homage to a goddess who had bestowed upon him life's greatest gift. In that moment, they were truly one, and Leah felt as if her soul had actually joined to his.

The moment stretched, trembling between them like a golden thread that quivered with the tension, tighter and tighter, until at last it snapped and they surrendered to the blaze of passion. Cal taught her the rhythms with gentle hands, guiding her into this new realm with urgent patience. Leah rode him with abandon, glorying in her power as she watched his beloved face twisted in the agony of ecstasy.

Her hair spilled around them, imprisoning them in a honey-colored cave where only pleasure dwelt and where they were willing captives. With each thrust, Leah's own pleasure increased, surging unbearably, building moment by moment, like the pressure of a volcano preparing to erupt. But Leah fought it, resisting the compulsion for release to savor the torment of need as she rode her stallion higher and higher, harder and harder. Their bodies slickened and their breaths came in ragged gasps, but still they rode, united, joined, toward the ultimate, final goal that sent them soaring together into paroxysms of bliss.

Leah threw her head back and cried out in release, then collapsed on Cal's chest to be cradled there and held through the earth-shattering aftershocks.

When the cataclysm ended, she lay there, limp and spent, filled with a pleasure deeper than any she had ever experienced because she knew that Cal loved her, too. And because she knew he would no longer dream of facing John Jakes and risk losing what they had only just found together.

Release and the exhaustion of a nearly sleepless night

began to take their toll, and Leah felt herself slipping away into the oblivion of sleep as Cal's hands stroked her hair and his warm breath stirred against her cheek. It would always be like this between them, she thought just before sleep claimed her. He would never leave her now.

But when she awoke several hours later, he was gone.

Chapter Thirteen

Leah bolted from the bed, heedless of her protesting muscles, and snatched her robe from where it hung on a peg on the wall. Throwing it on, she raced from the room, calling Cal's name.

He must be here somewhere, she told herself frantically, and she was an idiot to imagine anything else. She'd been so worried about his crazy plan to meet Jakes that she was just being irrational at simply not finding him still in their bed.

It was, she realized vaguely, nearly noon. Surely, if Cal was gone, he'd merely gone out to work with the other men, considerately leaving her to get some much-needed rest.

Unfortunately, the explanation was too logical, and Leah couldn't even force herself to believe it.

At the sounds of Leah's shouts, Juanita came from the kitchen, wiping her hands on her apron and shaking her head in disapproval at the ruckus.

"Where is he?" Leah demanded as Juanita came down the hall toward her.

"He go to town," Juanita said calmly.

Terror clutched at Leah's heart. "Are you sure? Did he tell you that?"

"*Sí*, he go to kill somebody," Juanita reported calmly.

Leah cried out in anguish, and Juanita hurried to her side. "He say he must," Juanita assured her, as if that would comfort her.

"I know," Leah murmured in defeat. What a fool she'd been to think mere love could influence a man like Cal Stevens. But maybe it wasn't too late. Maybe she could still stop him. "I've got to get to town. Did Cal leave any of the men here?"

Before Juanita could reply, they both heard the sound of booted feet running through the house. Pete Quincy appeared in the hallway and lumbered toward them. "What's wrong?" he demanded breathlessly.

As he came closer, he noticed Leah wore only a robe, and he stopped abruptly, obviously embarrassed. " 'Scuse me Miss Leah. I didn't know—"

"Where's Cal gone? Do you know?" she snapped, having no time for such luxuries as modesty.

Plainly, Pete was loath to tell her. "He had some business . . ." he hedged.

"Did he go to face John Jakes? Tell me!"

"Yes, ma'am," he said reluctantly. "But you don't have to worry none. Cal knows how to take care of hisself—"

"Hitch up a wagon, Pete. I'm going to town."

"Now, Miss Leah, Cal said for me to keep you here—"

"I don't give a damn what he said! I'm going if I have to saddle a horse myself! And I'm going with or without you!"

"Cal said I wasn't to leave you alone," Pete insisted.

"Then you'd better hitch a wagon, hadn't you?" Leah said over her shoulder as she hurried off to her bedroom to dress.

Her clothes were still scattered just where she and Cal had dropped them a few hours earlier, and as she scooped them up, Leah didn't allow herself to recall the beauty of what might have been her last time with her husband.

Juanita followed her into the bedroom, practically radiating disapproval, but Leah ignored her as she threw off her robe and began to pull on her clothes.

"You should not go," Juanita said sternly. "He no want you to go."

"He might get himself killed, Juanita!" Leah exclaimed. "Do you expect me to sit here twiddling my thumbs?"

"You should eat," the Mexican woman observed.

"I'm not hungry," Leah replied as she jerked her dress on over her head. Although she'd had nothing to eat all morning, the very idea of food revolted her, as did the thought of calmly consuming a meal while her husband might be lying dead in the street somewhere.

"You be sick," Juanita predicted, making Leah want to scream.

Leah chose not to respond to this ridiculous remark, and hurried over to her dressing table where she began to ruthlessly brush the tangles out of her long hair and twist it back up into some semblance of order. Remembering how Cal had tossed the pins on the floor, she made no attempt to find those, but instead dug into the glass dish of extras lying on the dressing table. Within minutes she judged herself to be presentable, planted a bonnet on her head, and raced out with Juanita at her heels.

In the parlor, she grabbed a shawl without even missing a stride, then barreled through the front door to find Pete just bringing the spring wagon from the barn.

"You should eat," Juanita called after her as she fairly ran to the wagon.

Without waiting for Pete's assistance, Leah jumped up onto the seat and said, "Let's go!"

After casting her one last, disapproving glance, Pete clucked the team into motion while Leah grabbed the seat to keep from falling off.

"Ain't no call for you to go running off like this," Pete said after a few minutes. "Cal ain't no boy you've got to look after all the time, like . . ."

"Like Brad, you mean, don't you?" she challenged when he hesitated.

"Cal ain't no boy," Pete reiterated stubbornly.

"I know he isn't, but he can get killed just like Brad did, all the same! Am I the only one who realizes that?"

"No, ma'am, but he explained it to me. See, there's two kinds of gunfighters. There's the kind that just shoots it out over a poker table in a saloon, and for that, you gotta be lightning fast 'cause when you're standing so close, it don't matter if you aim or not. It's just who gets off the first shot. Then there's the kind that faces off in the street. In the street, it don't really matter who's faster, only who's got more nerve and can shoot straighter. Jakes, he's the first kind, and Cal, he's the second kind. Jakes don't stand a chance in a fair fight. Cal'll get him for sure!"

"But what if he gets Cal, too!" Leah cried in exasperation. "Why won't anybody admit there's a good chance Cal will at least be wounded?"

Pete frowned, apparently unwilling to confirm her worst fears. Still, they both knew that even if Jakes only succeeded in getting a bullet in Cal, it could be a death sentence nevertheless. Even a nonfatal wound might become infected or induce pneumonia or a thousand other ailments. At the very least, Cal could be crippled for life, and for what? Oh, why were men so stubborn? Why couldn't he just have called the Rangers, like she had asked?

Leah shivered and pulled her shawl more closely around her. "Can't you hurry?" she snapped in annoyance, certain they were traveling at a snail's pace.

As if her impatience had at last infected Pete, he snapped the reins and urged the team to a faster clip. Although Pete didn't say another word, he continued to watch her warily from the corner of his eye, as if afraid she might do something untoward. For her part, Leah needed all the restraint she could muster just to refrain from jumping down off the wagon and running toward town, so certain was she that the wagon would never reach its destination.

Cal felt the unnatural calm and heightened awareness that always overcame him at times like this. As he walked down the side of the street, he saw every detail of every building, every particle of dust floating in the air, every light and shadow, and every crevice that might conceal a manhunter. Each sound was magnified, until the creak of a board rumbled like a thunderbolt, and the beat of his own heart pounded like a sledge.

Jakes knew he was coming. He'd sent word with one

of the men even before Leah had found him this morning. That was why he couldn't back down. That, and the fact that he couldn't allow Leah to remain in danger for another day. Maybe he was selfish, but he didn't want to live in a world without her. He had to keep her safe, even if it meant he wouldn't be here to see it.

But of course he had no intention of dying, not today or for a long time to come, and especially not when he knew Leah loved him and was waiting for him. He'd promised her a child, a child they could raise together, and he had every intention of keeping that promise.

The street was oddly still, even for a weekday, so Cal knew word was out. Everyone would be hiding behind closed doors, afraid of catching a stray bullet and waiting for the trouble to be over so they could resume their normal lives.

Jakes would be hiding, too. He wouldn't take the chance of meeting Cal in the street, not if he thought he could ambush him instead. All Cal had to do was figure out *where* he was hiding and flush him out, but so far he hadn't had much luck. As he came up to the livery, he realized he'd walked the length of town, all the way from Mead Garland's office to here, without incident. Either Jakes had left town, or he was playing with Cal, trying to break his nerve or make him panic.

Cal paused, his back to the wall of the livery while he considered the situation. He'd only been there a moment when he heard the tiny sound that raised the hairs on the back of his neck and caused him to whirl just in time to see John Jakes step from the livery stable doorway into the sunlight, gun raised.

The silent afternoon exploded.

* * *

At long last the buildings of town came into view, and Leah leaned forward on the seat, as if she could somehow force the horses to get there faster. "Please, please, please," she prayed over and over, afraid even to voice her request for Cal's safety lest the fates hear and mock her by taking his life.

Then, over the rumble of the wagon, Leah heard the muffled burst of a volley of gunshots.

She cried out in protest as terror froze her blood. "Did you hear it?" she demanded of Pete who nodded grimly.

"Could be anything," he said, but without much conviction.

"Hurry!" she shouted, wanting to leap from the seat.

Pete whipped the horses into a run, and they came careening into town in a cloud of dust. In her panic, Leah had expected to come upon a scene of carnage in the main street, but oddly enough, the street was completely deserted. Twisting on her seat to see in all directions, Leah could find not one living soul anywhere as Pete brought the wagon to a halt at the end of town.

The instant the wagon stopped, Leah jumped up, standing to see better, but finding nothing to see. They were practically in front of Mead Garland's office, and just as she was about to shout Cal's name, the office door burst open and Mead came running out.

"Leah, what on earth are you doing here?" he cried as he dashed over to the wagon.

"Did you hear the shots?" she demanded as she climbed down from the wagon with Mead's assistance. "What happened?"

"Leah, I . . ." Mead's handsome face crumpled in dismay.

"What?" she screamed in panic, grabbing his lapels. "Tell me!"

Mead's hand clasped her arms as if he were afraid she might fall. "I'm afraid . . . it's all over."

Terror clutched at her throat, stopping her breath, and her heart lurched to a halt. "Cal?" she cried in anguish.

"He's dead," Mead said gently.

Leah felt the blood rushing from her head, and she saw Mead's lips moving, but she heard nothing more as the darkness closed over her and she slumped into Mead's arms.

Leah fought consciousness, squeezing her eyes shut, sensing the anguish that loomed, ready to pounce the instant she emerged from the dark oblivion.

But although she resisted, someone was calling her name, urging her back and waving something foul-smelling beneath her nose that cleared away the haze and brought reality crashing in again.

She looked up into Mead's face, and there she read again the tragedy that had destroyed what was left of her life. "No!" she protested feebly. She wouldn't believe it until she saw Cal's body with her own eyes!

But Mead was shaking his head. "I'm terribly sorry, Leah. I know it was a shock. I shouldn't have . . . I should have broken it to you more gently, but it was a shock to me, too. I couldn't believe it when I heard what Cal intended to do, but there was nothing I could do to stop it. I did send for the sheriff, but of course he won't be here until tomorrow and—"

"What happened?" Leah insisted, pushing herself

upright. She was lying on a bed, and when she looked around, she realized Mead must have taken her to his own room above his office.

"You fainted," Mead explained. "I carried you up here and—"

"No, I mean, what happened to Cal?" she snapped impatiently. "Don't spare my feelings, Mead. I have to know."

Mead shook his head. He was sitting on the bed beside her, which would be highly improper under normal circumstances. Unfortunately, Leah couldn't even imagine normal circumstances anymore. "As I understand it, he challenged that gunfighter, Jakes, to a duel," Mead explained gently. "I don't approve of such things, of course, and would have tried to talk Cal out of it if I'd thought for a moment he would listen to me—"

"I know, I know!" Leah cried. "What happened when they fought?"

"I can't give you a description, since I was behind closed doors when it happened, as were all the responsible citizens of this town. All I know is they shot each other."

"If you didn't see it, then how do you know?" Leah demanded, eager to grasp at any straw.

"Because I do," he said, infinitely patient. He took her hand. "Leah, you've had a shock, and it's not the first one you've had in the past few weeks, but as terrible as all this is, I want you to know you aren't alone. I'll do everything I can to help you through this, and although it's certainly much too soon to speak of such things, please remember I love you and I'll do anything—"

"If you'll do anything, then take me to Cal!" Leah exclaimed, certain her husband wasn't dead, certain she would know if he was. She forced him to move while she scrambled off the bed. "Where's Pete?" she asked, remembering her foreman had accompanied her.

"He went to claim the body. Really, Leah, you shouldn't exert yourself like this. The shock —"

"I only fainted because I haven't had anything to eat all day," Leah said, recalling Juanita's warning. "I won't faint again, I promise. Now take me to Cal."

As she strode across the room, she heard the sound of running feet taking the outside steps two at a time. That would be Pete coming back to tell her about Cal, and she froze, afraid to hope, afraid to know, afraid for the door to open and . . .

The door flew open, and there stood Cal, well and whole and alive. For a second, Leah didn't trust her own eyes, then she heard Mead's muttered curse and knew he was real.

Joy sluiced through her, but before she could take so much as a step toward him, Mead's arm clamped around her waist.

"Don't move or I'll kill her."

Leah couldn't believe this was happening. It must all be some nightmare she was having, but then she felt the cold metal of the gun barrel pressed against her cheek, and she knew it wasn't a dream.

"Mead, what . . . ?" she began, but his arm tightened warningly around her.

"Shut up!" he commanded, and she could hear the edge of panic in his voice. What on earth was going on? She looked to Cal frantically, but he seemed remarkably unconcerned about her situation.

"You're not going to kill her, Garland, and we both know it," Cal said calmly. "Now put the gun down."

"What makes you so sure?" Mead asked, the crack in his voice negating the swagger of his challenge.

"Because Jakes told me everything."

"He was supposed to kill you! He assured me that he would!" Mead cried, and suddenly everything came clear to Leah, too.

"*You* were the one who hired Jakes?" she demanded.

A big mistake, she realized instantly, as Mead's arm tightened even more, sending spasms of agony through her bruised ribs. "I told you to shut up!" He jammed the gun barrel into her cheek, making her cry out.

Cal instinctively took a step toward them, but Mead's shout of warning stopped him cold. "I told you not to move, and now I'm telling you to get out of the way and let me pass. If you ever want to see her alive again, you'll let me leave here with her. I'll let her go when I've gotten a good headstart."

"Give it up, Garland. If you kidnap a woman, every man in Texas will be on your trail."

"I'll take my chances," Mead said, and Leah could hear that his initial panic was fading. He was more in control now, thinking and planning. "Now take your gun out with two fingers and lay it on the floor, nice and easy so I don't get startled and accidentally pull this trigger."

No! Leah wanted to shout, but she didn't dare utter a word for fear of startling Mead. *Don't give up your gun!* she silently pleaded with Cal, but in spite of her warning, he did just as Mead had commanded and lay his pistol on the floor.

When he had finished, Mead said, "Now move away

from the door. Over to the window, real slow."

What was Cal thinking? she wondered frantically. Did he have a plan? Would she ruin everything if she tried something herself or was Cal depending on her to create a distraction?

As Cal edged over to the window, Mead dragged Leah along in the other direction, toward the door and escape.

Cal watched with seeming unconcern, and after a moment, he said, "You know, Garland, if you kill her, you'll be doing me a favor."

She felt the shock go through Mead, and he stopped where he was. "I knew it," he said triumphantly. "You were the one who fixed the buggy, weren't you?"

"Of course," Cal said with a nonchalance that chilled Leah's blood. It wasn't true! She knew it wasn't! Yet he smiled at her horror. "You were right all along, Garland. I only married her to get the Rocking Horse. After you killed the boy, what other choice did I have?"

"I didn't kill anyone!" Mead exclaimed furiously.

"Oh, sorry," Cal said, not sounding sorry at all. "I meant after Jakes killed the boy for you. You must've been awfully sure Leah would marry you to go to all that trouble."

"She would have, too, if it hadn't been for you. I should've known she'd mess things up somehow, just like she did before."

Before? Before what? Leah's mind was reeling, and she couldn't take it all in, not with a gun pressed to her face and Mead's grip on her ribs making every breath a searing agony. But if Mead had loved her enough to hire a man to kill her husband, perhaps . . . "Mead," she choked. "You're hurting me."

"Good," he replied, dashing her hopes. "It's no more than you deserve. If you'd done things right and married me the first time, none of this would've happened. The boy would even still be alive. It's all your fault, Leah, and it's time you took the blame."

The blame for what? Leah wondered, but Cal was speaking.

"She's no use to you now, Garland. You'll get away faster without her, and then you won't have all the men in Texas after you. Leave her here, and nobody'll follow you. I promise."

Leah held her breath while Mead considered the offer, all the time staring at Cal's face and trying to read the motive behind his offer. Cal was trying to get Mead to let her go, telling him anything, making any wild promise that came into his head.

Yet he'd admitted trying to kill her himself. None of this made any sense at all.

At last Mead made a strange sound. It took Leah a second to realize it was a chuckle of derision. "She was right about you, Stevens. She said you cared about her, and I guess you do. A minute ago, you were trying to tell me I'd be doing you a favor by killing her, and now you want me to let her go. Which is it?"

Cal hesitated a moment before he said, "Whichever suits your fancy, Garland," but the hesitation had given him away, both to Leah and to Mead.

"Well, now, maybe we can work something out after all," Mead said slyly. "If you're so worried about keeping Leah alive, maybe you're willing to do just about anything to keep her that way."

"What do you mean?" Cal snapped, no longer even pretending to be conciliatory.

"I mean, I want the ranch. I've waited seven years and had three people killed to get it, and I figure I've earned it. I've got Leah, and you've got the ranch. Maybe we can work out some sort of trade."

Cal's expression had hardened to stone, and he glared murderously at Mead who chuckled again at his dilemma. "You're a lawyer," Cal pointed out. "Maybe you should draw up some papers."

"Good idea," Mead said just as someone else started bounding up Mead's outside steps.

Pete! Leah thought, getting ready to break away the instant Mead was distracted, but it was Homer Wilkes who barged into the room instead. Leah was more astonished than Mead, and by the time she recovered enough to think of escape, he had recovered, too, and held her even more tightly.

"Good," Wilkes said with obvious satisfaction when he had taken in the scene. "You've got her."

"What are you doing here?" Mead demanded, obviously as puzzled as Leah.

"I been looking for her since she left the house, waiting for my chance. She killed my girl, you know. Took her away and put her in the ground. I never wanted Espy to leave, but Leah Harding always gets her way, don't she?"

Leah had never seen Wilkes look so wild, and he was even more unkempt than usual. And he didn't seem the least bit surprised to find Mead holding a gun to her head. "Mr. Wilkes, Mead is threatening to kill me," Leah tried, hoping to shock him into going for help.

Instead, he grinned. "He ain't gonna get the chance," he said. "The buggy accident didn't work, and I'm tired of waiting for a second try." He raised his hand, and in

405

it he held a pistol which he pointed straight at Leah.

Everyone shouted at once, and the pistol belched fire. The roar filled the room, and Leah slammed to the floor, certain she was dead as pain exploded through her battered body.

Above her, two men struggled frantically, and another gunshot roared, splintering the ceiling. Smoke fogged the room, stinging her eyes. Someone kicked her, and she rolled away instinctively, coming to her knees, ready to flee, except that by the time she looked up, everyone in the room had gone still.

Mead Garland lay on the floor, his face ashen, both hands pressed to the red stain spreading across his chest. Cal stood over him, holding Mead's gun in his hand, but looking at Homer Wilkes who lay on the other side of the room, unmoving.

At first Leah couldn't imagine what had happened to him or where all the blood had come from, and then she saw the knife protruding from his throat, the same knife she'd seen Cal draw from his boot the day of her accident.

Only Cal seemed unscathed, although he hadn't moved a muscle, and for the first time Leah realized she, too, had not been hurt in the melee. The pain she'd felt had just been her abused body's protest at being thrown to the floor, which is, she recalled, exactly what had happened.

Mead had thrown her down to protect her from Wilkes's shot and . . . She looked back at Mead and realized he must have taken that shot himself. Leah blinked, hoping the scene would change or vanish, but everything remained exactly the same, and at last she called out to the one person who could make everything

406

ight again.

"Cal?"

He started, and his gaze snapped to her, his pistol coming up as if he were ready to do battle once again. Then he saw her and lowered the gun instantly. "Leah, are you hurt?" he asked, stepping over Mead as if he'd been a piece of fallen furniture and hurrying to her side.

The fog of gunsmoke still stung her eyes but that wasn't why she was crying when Cal took her in his arms. "No, I'm fine," she sobbed against his shirt front as he held her.

After a moment, she realized he was trembling, too, and his heart pounded against her ear. He clutched her to him in a grip that bordered on painful, but she didn't protest. They clung together for several seconds until they heard Mead calling her.

"Leah, Leah, where are you?"

Cal jerked to attention and turned to face him, pistol ready, but Mead obviously no longer posed a threat.

"Leah, I saved your life," he said weakly. "Please, you have to forgive me!"

Cal rose to his feet and helped Leah up. Together they approached the fallen man and stood over him. Leah had considered him a friend for so long that she had trouble even now feeling any animosity toward him.

"Leah, please!" he begged.

"Afraid to meet your Maker, are you, Garland?" Cal said coldly. "It's too bad Brad and Espy aren't here to ask, too. Then you could go with a clear conscience."

"I didn't mean for Espy to die," Mead insisted, his handsome face gray and twisted with pain. "She wasn't supposed to be there."

"But Brad was, wasn't he?" Cal said. "Everything worked out perfectly. He'd just signed the will, and you were the only one who knew it, so you sent your hired killer after him."

"She wasn't supposed to be with him," Mead insisted. "I don't kill women. I wouldn't have harmed you just now, Leah. I was only trying to scare Stevens."

Leah felt numb as she stared down at the man who had caused her so much anguish. Then she remembered something else he'd said. "Mead, you said you'd had *three* people killed. Who was the third?"

His lips formed a twisted smile. "Your father, of course. I made it look like an accident, so no one ever suspected! He told me that if I married you, he'd cut you off without a cent. I had to get rid of him before he could change his will, but the joke was on me, because he'd never intended to leave you the ranch in the first place."

"So you never wanted me at all," she realized, glad to note the knowledge hurt only her pride. No wonder he'd released her from their engagement so easily when he'd discovered Brad was the only heir. Unfortunately she herself had renewed his plans by having Brad draw up a will naming Leah as his heir. And because of that she herself was responsible for Brad's death.

Tears filled her eyes, blurring the vision of Mead lying on the floor. Cal's arm came around her, supporting her, and she clung to him.

As if from a distance, she heard Mead pleading, "I got rid of your father for you, Leah. You should thank me for that, at least. Leah, please . . ."

Outside, she could hear men approaching, probably

drawn by the sound of gunfire. Pete was calling her name, then someone ran up the outside steps and burst into the room.

"What the hell?" Pete demanded, just before the room filled with men. Someone started to tend to Mead's wounds, and another man declared Homer Wilkes dead.

Too shocked to sob, Leah lay her head against Cal's chest and let the tears over which she had no control flow unchecked down her face. She could hear the rumble of Cal's voice as he explained to the others what had happened, but she made no attempt to comprehend. She'd heard and seen too much already this afternoon to absorb any more.

After a few minutes, Cal led her out into the sunlight and down the steps and lifted her into the wagon in which she'd ridden to town what seemed a lifetime ago.

They didn't speak on the long drive home, and when they arrived, Cal carried her to bed. Juanita fussed and made her drink some tea that tasted terrible and that made her sleep. When she opened her eyes again, the sky was dark, a lamp burned low on the bedside table, and she was alone.

She lay there for a long time, piecing together everything she'd learned and remembering all Mead Garland's protestations of love and promises to always take care of her. Just when she felt she'd gotten it all straight, the bedroom door opened, and Cal stuck his head in.

"You're awake," he observed, closing the door softly behind him and coming over to the bed. "How do you feel?"

She smiled wanly. "Like I've been on a three-day drunk. What was in that tea Juanita gave me, anyway?"

Cal smiled back and sat down on the edge of the bed beside her and took the hand she held out to him. "A little laudanum. We figured you needed some sleep more than anything. You had a bad shock."

"So did you," she reminded him.

"Yeah, but I've been through it before."

"What happened with Jakes? I never did hear."

Cal's smile disappeared. "Nothing much. He was waiting for me at the livery, hiding out until I came by. I figure he was going to ambush me and try to shoot me in the front so it at least looked like a fair fight."

"But you got him first."

"I was lucky."

Leah closed her eyes and whispered a silent prayer of thanks for such "luck." When she opened them again, she said, "Is he dead?"

"I expect so, by now. He wasn't the last time I saw him, though. Like Garland, he wanted to clear his conscience before he cashed in. I guessed it was Garland who hired him, and he told me I was right, but he wanted me to know Espy's death was an accident, and that he wasn't the one who'd caused your accident. Even a man like Jakes has a code of honor, and Jakes prided himself on never hurting a woman."

"So it was Homer Wilkes who cut the axle," she said, shuddering at the memory of his wild face in the instant before he'd pulled the trigger, intent on his final revenge.

"Yeah, and he'd been hanging around the ranch so much, he had the perfect opportunity, too. I don't know why I didn't think of that. I kept thinking one person had done everything, and that's what had me confused, I guess. I'd picked Garland right away for

410

wanting me out of the way, but I couldn't figure why he'd want you dead. If he wanted the ranch, he could only get it if you were a live widow."

"Homer didn't want anything except revenge," Leah explained. "He blamed me for taking Espy away from him."

Cal shook his head. "Kind of strange for a father, wasn't it? I mean, most men expect their daughters to get married and leave home sooner or later. I guess it was her dying that set him off."

Leah shuddered again, knowing she could never tell him the truth about the horrible things Wilkes had told her. It was, she decided, far better if no one else knew. At least then poor Espy could rest in peace.

"I'm not exactly clear on what happened in Mead's room this afternoon," she said, anxious to change the subject, even to something almost as unpleasant. "I know you threw your knife at Wilkes, and then you struggled with Mead for his gun, but did Mead really save my life?"

Cal's frown told her this was a sore subject with him. "He pushed you out of the way because you were still his only chance to get his hands on the Rocking Horse."

She'd understood that, of course, and she couldn't help smiling when she realized Cal was still uncertain enough about her feelings for Mead to want to denigrate him.

"I know he never loved me," she said. "And I know that you do. You proved it this afternoon, although I'll admit you gave me a few bad moments today."

"When?" he demanded.

"When I woke up and found out you'd gone off to face Jakes even after I asked you not to."

411

"I had to do that, Leah."

She sighed. "I know. And then you told Mead you'd only married me to get the ranch and that he'd be doing you a favor if he killed me."

"I was just trying—"

"I know exactly what you were trying to do," she assured him. "It's just that you wounded my pride, and I could use a little reassurance about just how much you do love me."

He gave her a skeptical look. "And how do you want me to reassure you?"

Leah considered. "Well, for a start, you could lay down here with me and hold me for a while."

In a flash, Cal had his boots off and was lying beside her, cradling her head on his shoulder. Leah held him for a long time, savoring the feel of him and the comforting sound of his breathing against her ear and the feel of his heartbeat against her palm.

"Cal?" she said at last.

"Hmmm?"

"I want you to make me a promise."

"What?" he asked cautiously, and she had to love him just for that. Most men would have recklessly promised her anything, but Cal wanted to be sure he could keep this one.

"I want you to promise me that you'll put your gun away and that you'll never get into another gunfight again."

"All right."

Leah looked up at him in surprise. "Just 'all right'?" she demanded. "Aren't you even going to give me an argument?"

"No," he said reasonably. "I'd pretty much decided I

412

had too much to live for now to take any more stupid chances like that, anyway."

Leah scowled at him, suspicious of such an easy victory. "I shouldn't trust you, you know, especially when you haven't kept the *first* promise you made me yet."

"And what was the first promise?"

"You promised to give me a child, and here we've been married practically four *weeks* now and you've hardly even *tried,* much less succeeded."

"I've *tried,*" he reminded her wryly, "but you've been unavailable most of the time."

"I'm available now," she pointed out.

His astonishment told her just how outlandish her request must seem in light of what she'd been through that day, but, "Please, Cal! I need you so much! And not just for the baby, either, although that would be wonderful because it would make losing Brad at least *bearable,* but because I love you so much and I need to feel your love right now and know it's real."

He touched her face with his fingertips. "It's real, all right. Don't ever doubt it, Leah."

"Then show me, Cal. Please!"

Unable to resist, he took her in his arms, and at the end of a day filled with destruction, Cal Stevens gave his wife the gift of life.

Author's Note

I hope you enjoyed reading Blazing Texas Nights as much as I enjoyed writing it. I promise you that Leah and Cal were much happier for the remainder of their lives than they were in this book and that they had lots of beautiful children.

My next project will be a series of four books about the Tate family that will trace the history of Texas from 1836 to 1900 through three generations of one family. Many of my fans have asked me to write about Indians, and now they will get their wish. The heroine of the first book is taken captive by the Comanche and rescued by a Comanchero. Her half-breed son is the hero of the second book, and his two children will each have their own book. I hope you'll watch for the Tates of Texas series.

And be sure to let me know how you liked this book. I love to hear from my readers, and I always try to answer every letter. For a newsletter and a bookmark, send a long SASE to

Victoria Thompson
c/o Zebra Books
475 Park Ave. So.
New York, NY 10016